ANGELA CLARKE

On My Life

**MULHOLLAND
BOOKS**

HODDER

First published in Great Britain in 2019 by Mulholland Books
An imprint of Hodder & Stoughton
An Hachette UK company

This paperback edition first published in 2019

1

A CIP catalogue record for this title is available from the British Library

Paperback ISBN 978 1 473 68152 1
eBook ISBN 978 1 473 68153 8

Typeset in Plantin Light by Hewer Text UK Ltd, Edinburgh
Printed and bound in Great Britain by Clays Ltd, Elcograf S.p.A.

Hodder & Stoughton policy is to use papers that are natural, renewable
and recyclable products and made from wood grown in sustainable
forests. The logging and manufacturing processes are expected to
conform to the environmental regulations of the country of origin.

Hodder & Stoughton Ltd
Carmelite House
50 Victoria Embankment
London EC4Y 0DZ

www.hodder.co.uk

You did anything to bury me, but you forgot that I was a seed.

Dinos Christianopoulos

The Start

I am covered in her blood. Her hair is caught between my fingers. Her blood is in my hair. I can smell her. Coconut shampoo, vanilla body spray, wet metal.

Robert is missing. I don't know where he is.

I don't know what happened.

I only know one thing.

I didn't do this.

Now

The crowd outside sound crazed. The noise rushes toward us as I'm pulled away from the courtroom. Mr Peterson, my solicitor, is running alongside me. His face furrowed, concerned. I can barely make out his words over my panicked breaths.

'Put your jacket over your head. Shield your face!' he shouts. 'There must be a way to take her out back?'

The officer ignores him, and pulls harder on the handcuffs that bind us together. The metal scrapes against my wrist. I can't speak.

'Cover your face!' Mr Peterson yells.

The officer is in his late twenties, the same age as me. Tattooed Sanskrit symbols burst out the top of his shirt and climb his neck. He doesn't look at me. His one barked instruction told me he speaks like I used to. He's from London. South. We might have gone to the same school, passed each other on the street. Did he move to Gloucestershire to escape the past too? His tattoos a roadmap to his new self. The dolphin on my bikini line is one of the only things left from my time on the Orchard Park estate. Always a stupid name for an ugly growth of concrete tower blocks. I erased everything else. Rewrote myself. But the faded blue ink remains. A childish mistake. Mistakes Emily won't get to make. A sob catches in my throat: I won't cry here.

Mr Peterson yells again, but his voice is lost under the roar of the screams outside. I grab at my Burberry mac with my free hand, try to swing it up and over my head. The fabric lands at a strange angle and I'm plunged into darkness. The shouts get muffled into indistinct anger. The officer pulls at me and I trip. It must be the steps.

'Jennifer! Jennifer!' voices yell.

How do they know my name? What do they want? The fabric of my coat is sucked into my mouth. I'm choking. Must pull it away. Must keep my face hidden. Must get air. I'm suffocating.

I can see feet, a swarm of legs against the barrier. The edges of camera flashes.

'Why did you do it, Jennifer?'

'Murdering bitch!'

'Burn in hell!'

Their vitriol sears chunks out of me. Has Sally at the office heard? Is she out there? I can't imagine anyone I know doing this. Slinging bile at strangers. At me.

'Hang her! Hang her! Hang her!' The chant is gathering pace. It's animalistic. Raw. I want to tell them I feel their pain too. But even if I could find the words, they'd never hear over this roar. The belt of my mac whips round and lashes at my back, as if carried by their hate. Can they get to me? Could they hurt me? I try to move toward the officer. The trainers they gave me, still laced for display in the shop, catch on the ground. The steps are the yellow Cotswold stone I normally love. It looks diseased now. My ankle twists. I trip forward. My arm is jerked up like a puppet's by the man I'm hand-cuffed to. Pain tears into my shoulder. The coat is caught and flicks back and away. I'm exposed.

A volley of camera flashes. There are a hundred screaming faces. I must get my coat. The tattooed officer pulls me on. Must cover my face. I try to use my hand but it's hopeless. Arms reach for me. The police are trying to hold them back. Flashbulbs explode. Everything's white. Bright.

I'm in our kitchen. The glass panel in the door is shattered. Flashes of red slice across the white walls. Emily's birthday cake falls from my hands. It smashes onto the floor, an eruption of icing and sponge. I can't look down. Won't look down.

'Jenna!' The voice rips through the chaos.

Ness! I can't see her. 'Ness!' I scream. Where is she? I try to stop; the crowd surges forward. A hand snaps out like a snake's tongue and claws at my arm.

'Keep moving!' the tattooed officer bellows.

'She's my sister.' Where is she? He pulls me on. There are barriers and a van. Oh god. A prison van.

'Jenna!' Ness's voice again.

I turn. I need her. I need to speak to her. Where's she been? Where's Mum? A flash of red hair. There!

'Get off me, you prick!' Ness shouts, barging aside a screaming man in a cagoule.

'Easy, love,' shouts a meaty policeman.

We're almost at the van now. 'I need to speak to her. Please.'

The hatred in the tattooed officer's eyes winds me.

'Jenna!' Ness is at the front now, hanging over the barrier.

'Is Robert with you?' It's my only hope. That the police have made a mistake. That for some reason he's there.

She shakes her head. No. The police said they found Robert's blood in the kitchen. He's missing. Gone.

Agony twists through my gut. The stone melts under my feet. I reach for Ness. For comfort. For support.

The officer jerks me back. The rabble seem closer. Ness is being buffeted from the side. 'Is Mum all right?' I shout.

She nods, tears in her eyes. 'We didn't know. The electric's been down – the phone's been out.'

My heart lurches. When did they find out? Now? Is that why they weren't here before? I was arrested two nights ago, charged yesterday. Mr Peterson said he couldn't get hold of them. I'd feared he was lying, that they might have believed this, refused to come.

Ahead, a female prison officer is unlocking the van. Sweat patches bloom under her white shirtsleeves. I can't do this. I need to speak to Ness. To Mum. To Robert. *Where is Robert?* My heart contracts. The floor threatens to suck me down. I twist back. Yell. 'My lawyer is called Mr Peterson. He's inside.'

'Bring back the death penalty!' shrieks a puce blur.

Mr Peterson must know where they're sending me, mustn't he? I can't get everything straight in my head. Can't make it all make sense. 'Mr Peterson will find out where I'm going.'

The mob bulges. The meaty policeman stumbles, falls backwards. A crack. The barrier holding back the howling mass tips. There's a rush forward.

'Jenna!' Ness screams as she's swallowed by heaving bodies. A multi-headed monster swells closer.

I could step toward them. Let them rip me limb from limb. Make this all stop. But I've got to stay alive for Robert. He must be out there. He needs me.

The officers either side of me shout. A hand grips my arm and pushes me up into the van's narrow corridor. I feel like I'm underwater, their voices muted bubbles. The step grazes my shin. I stumble. Try to put my hands out. The handcuffs lurch me back up. The guy chained to me undoes his cuff and I fall to the floor. He turns back and squares up to the advancing crowd. Behind him the police are fighting to keep them from the vehicle. From me. A photographer jumps over the barrier's legs and, camera up, starts snapping. I shield my face. Too little, too late. I see Ness through my fingers, behind the crowd, stooping to pick something up. My trampled mac. Mascara streaks her face. I haven't seen my sister cry since we were kids. It breaks my heart afresh.

The female officer jumps in and pulls the door closed behind her. Her foot catches the edge of my shin and I feel the skin pinch. The air shifts. It smells like a piss-stained alley. Stale, acrid, suffocating. Don't panic. It's just me and her as she towers above. She's in her fifties, her hair dyed straw yellow over wiry white. Her eyebrows dark and pencilled on. A sickly smile on her lips.

'Welcome to the sweatbox, Princess.'

Then

My mobile jolts to life on my desk. *Sally calling.* Sally calls my mobile when she wants to speak directly to me. She's that kind of boss: too efficient to be placed on hold. I pick it up. The other two girls who make up the S. Parr Recruitment Service are busy talking into their phones.

'They're all on calls, you would've got me anyway, Sal.' I press send on the email to the Cotswold Blue Cheese Company. 'I've just sent the cheese contract, by the way.' Another new client.

'Oh my darling girl, thank god.' Sally's voice is even higher than usual.

'You okay?'

I can hear echoing in the background. Is that a toilet flushing? 'Dear god, no. I must've eaten something that disagreed with me,' she hisses.

Ah. She's in the loo. This is awkward, even by her standards. 'Where are you? Do you need help?'

'Urgh. There's no way I can come back to the office, darling, you'll have to take my meeting this afternoon,' she says. It must be bad if she's missing a meeting.

I have her diary synced with my iPhone. 'The three thirty with Milcombe?' I took Mum for a Mother's Day treat to Field House spa, one of the Milcombe Estate hotels, last year. It was heavenly. Ranger & Co have run Milcombe's recruitment for years; if we at S. Parr can nab them it'd be a huge deal. 'Sure you don't want me to rearrange?'

'No, no, darling, muck their manager around and they'll be sticking with mangy Ranger. They've got a new build under-way. Renovating some stables. It's targeting the corporate away-day market, and all that. You can handle it.'

'Are you sure?' I've been here six years, and Sally treats me like her right-hand woman, but I still suffer from imposter syndrome. The fear that I'll be uncovered as a fraud picks at my seams. It's ridiculous really. I've told Sally I grew up on a sink estate and she says she doesn't care. I think that's because she has no idea what it really means.

Sally exhales forcefully. 'Oooof. No time to argue, they'll love you like I do. Kisses.' And she rings off.

Luckily, I know her system well. Sally's placed the files for today's clients on her desk, and within half an hour I'm up to speed. The plan is to offer them a cohesive package for their new venture. Top-dollar sourcing, shortlisting, and training. I can see that Sally's aiming to win them over with this project in the hope of getting introductions to the wider estate.

At three thirty I'm all set up in the meeting room. It's good to look busy when the client arrives. Becky is teed up and I hear her laughter and offers of tea or coffee as she and the client approach. A quick check of our glossy brochures and I'm ready. I stand up, smooth my white shirt down over my cigarette pants and smile as she opens the door. I almost forget to extend my hand when the man walks in.

Taller than me, with messy blond hair, he's wearing a green Milcombe Estate polo shirt, shorts, and, most incongruously, wellies. He greets me with a confident grin.

'Sorry for the attire, I've come straight from calving.' He holds out a hand and a piece of straw drops from his watch.

Surprise must have shown on my face, because he looks bashful. *Way to make him feel comfortable.* 'No problem. I'm Jenna.' His hand is soft for a farmer. I stop staring at his forearms. 'Sally's been unexpectedly detained, I'm afraid, so I'll be talking to you today.' *Let go of his hand. He's going to think you're mad.* I drop it.

'She's not expecting as well, is she?' he asks, concerned.

As well? He can't think that I'm pregnant, can he? I need to lay off the carbs. Sally's fifty-five and has no children, I'm not sure what to say. 'I . . . she . . . well . . . I think it's unlikely.'

His face creases with a smile and his eyes sparkle. 'I meant the herd. I heard she bought Bridge Farm last year.'

What's wrong with me? 'Oh, of course! I see!' He doesn't think I look fat. 'No, she rents the land out. Sally can barely keep a cactus alive.' My laugh comes out all squeaky. 'She definitely doesn't have livestock. God no.' I'm babbling.

He bends to retrieve the piece of straw from the floor. 'I'm making a mess again.' His voice is friendly. I catch basil and cedarwood as he reaches past me to the bin.

Behind him through the glass door, I can see Becky fanning herself and mouthing *he's hot!*

Ignore her. Stay focused. 'I'm so sorry, the calving comment threw me a bit. I wasn't expecting it.' I was expecting a corporate hotel manager. A less hands-on one.

'Have I put my foot in it again?' he beams. 'Bit of a bad habit. Size elevens, you see. Bloody great big things.'

I feel the urge to giggle. 'No, no, not at all.' I remember my manners. 'I'm so sorry, I didn't get your name?' Get a grip, Jenna. You're behaving like a schoolgirl.

'Let's start again, shall we?' He holds out his hand. 'No calves this time. I'm Robert. Lovely to meet you, Jenna.'

I smile and shake his hand again, strong, warm. My face flushes. Behind him I can see Becky crack up. I'm not used to men having this effect on me. A little too late, I remember to let go of his hand. For the second time.

We stand for a moment, looking at each other. And then it comes back to me: I'm at work, this is a meeting. 'Shall we?' I gesture at the table, trying hard not to meet his gaze, to keep my voice upbeat.

'Let's,' he says. A dimple forms on the left side of his face as he smiles.

I'm hyper-aware of all my limbs as Robert pulls the chair out for me, as if my body might throw me into him of its own free will. It knows before I do that I want him.

The meeting passes in a blur. I have no idea what's coming out of my mouth, or if I've completely screwed up our pitch. All I know is that when Robert tentatively asks, blond hair falling over his anxious eyes, if I would consider going for a drink with him, my heart sings. I'm going to see him again. I'm going to see him again!

Now

There's a thud against the side of the van. And another. They're kicking it.

'My sister's out there!' What if they turn on her? 'They might hurt her!'

'Should've thought of that before.' The prison officer smiles. She looks delighted.

My stomach drops.

Another thud against the van. There are shouts from outside. I know what they're saying. Saliva pools in my mouth. I need to use the bathroom.

The officer unlocks a door to her left. The van is lined with tiny metal cells.

'In,' she commands.

Panic is hauling itself up my throat. 'I get car-sick,' I say, as she pulls me toward the cell.

'You'll have something in common with our last guest then,' she says.

The smell hits me immediately. Rancid vomit. My whole body contracts. 'It's not clean!'

'It's been hosed down,' she grins. 'But they might have missed a bit.'

She pushes me toward the tiny, metal-lined cell. It's like a coffin on its end. There's a small metal bench. A tiny side window. No seatbelt.

'Please.' I can't go in there. 'I won't run, I promise. Please.' The smell catches in my throat. I'm going to gag.

She pushes me in. Hysteria scratches at me. She slams the door. I hear it lock. I swivel back. There's no other way out. One of the photographers outside has pressed a camera against the small window. The flash detonates, making dots in front of my eyes. I've seen photographers do this on the news. Hold cameras up over their heads to get the shot of the guilty party. But I'm not guilty. I didn't do this. There's been a mistake.

The noise outside increases. The prison officer is yelling something. There's the blast of a siren. And then the van lurches. I slam into the side of the cell and sit down with a bump. The smell is overpowering. I close my eyes and try to stay calm. We rumble over a pothole. Eyes wide open. It's all still here. This is happening. This is real.

'I didn't do anything!' I cry. 'I'm innocent!'

My words crunch under the wheels of the van. No one replies. No one is listening. I imagine I'm holding Emily in my arms, stroking her hair. I can't stop the tears any more.

Now

You're supposed to be innocent until proven guilty. I pleaded not guilty. Told the Magistrates' judge I didn't do this. But he locked me up anyway. On remand until the hearing. How long did the solicitor say it would be? Shock has mangled my brain. I blink grit. When did I last sleep? The custody cell had a board of a bed, a grey blanket. I remember holding it like I cradled Emily's body . . . I cried when they took my clothes and shoes for evidence. I'd hugged Emily in those clothes. They smelled of her. The T-shirt and jogging bottoms they gave me smell of plastic.

When they explained I was going to court I thought Mum or Ness would bring me new clothes. Now I know why they didn't. The prosecution said they'd found Robert's blood in the house. The police accused me of killing him. I couldn't. I wouldn't. I love him. They haven't found a body. That means he could still be alive. He could still be out there. My stomach tilts as the van turns. They're not looking for him because they think I killed him.

I slam my fist against the door.

'Let me out! Please!'

There's no response.

I rest my head against the metal and close my eyes. Each bump jolts the van and me, but there's something comforting in the pain. It's rooting me here. *If there's anyone out there who can hear this, please protect Robert. Please let him be okay.*

Does he know about Emily? My heart feels as if it's being squeezed. What happened? I replay it in my mind, but I always stop at the kitchen door. At the shattered glass.

The feeling of nausea rises again. This time I'm not going to win. 'Hey! Please! Stop! I'm going to be sick!'

I tip forwards. Oh god, there's no bag, nothing. My throat clenches and punches up. Liquid sprays out and onto the metal wall, the floor, splashing back onto my feet and legs. There's nowhere to escape it. I retch again. Someone must come now. They must stop the van. Acid burns my throat. My eyes are watering, my nose dripping. The bile makes me cough.

No one comes.

The van turns another corner and I slide toward the mess. There's nothing to clean myself with. It's disgusting, but it gives me a task to focus on. I take off one of the trainers they gave me and remove a sock. I wipe my face first, then my arms, then my legs and my shoes, before dropping the sock on the floor and trying to contain the situation there. It's better than nothing.

It feels like we're slowing down. Reversing. We must be parking. Through the small window to the side I can see a brick wall. Thank god, we're here. Then I remember where *here* is. Prison. I am going to prison.

I hear the driver's door slam. Then there's the sound of shouting. Who's shouting? They sound angry. Is it the driver? Maybe they're arguing with the prison officer? No, there are other voices too.

I can hear bolts grinding: the door into the van is being opened. They're going to let me out. Thank god.

'Get your hands off me!' shouts a man. *A man*. My heart starts to hammer. Surely they don't use the van for male prisoners too? 'Where you taking me! I got rights! My baby-mumma's coming with the kids tomorrow.'

I step back from the door.

'Shut it!' roars the female guard. There are multiple foot-steps. A struggle.

'I want my lawyer! You're bent, you fuckers! Get off!'

Shoes squeak on the floor. We're not *there*. We're picking up another prisoner. A male prisoner. They don't keep the men and the women together, do they? They're murderers, rapists. No, that's madness. You're letting your thoughts run away with you, Jenna. A small voice inside me whispers, *they think you're a killer.*

The guy is struggling. Rocking the whole van. Between spat words I can hear slivers about his kids. I think of Emily again and close my eyes. I could never hurt her.

The guards ignore him. They don't even shout back. The door slams shut.

If I don't speak now I'll miss my chance.

There are new voices outside. I wish I could see more than the wall. They're bringing another person in. I press my face fully against the crack of the door to see if I can hear who it is.

Another cell door opens. I can't remember how many there were – eight, maybe? I should've paid more attention. Will they fill them all? When will they drop me off? Are we even going in the same direction? This is a twisted bus service for prisoners. Is this one a man as well, or a woman?

I can hear the door being closed, movement in the corridor. This is my chance to get them to move me. To give me some water. I need the bathroom.

'Hello?' I say. *Too quiet.* 'Excuse me – could I get some water and some tissue? I've been . . .' I can't bring myself to say I've been sick, it's too embarrassing. 'I've had an incident.'

The female guard gives a barked laugh. '*An incident*? You break a nail, Princess?'

Keep calm. 'Could I use the bathroom?'

'No breaks!' Her hand slams against the door and I jolt back. No breaks? Is that legal?

'Is that a girl?' the guy to the left of me shouts. Goosebumps run over my forearms.

'Oh yeah!' the guard yells. 'Just your type, Boyd. Blonde and stuck-up!' She slaps her hand against the door again and it shakes. 'Something for your wank bank, that'll keep you quiet!' Then there's silence as the door is bolted.

I can barely breathe.

'I like blondes,' the guy to the left says. Can he see me? 'Guess what I'm going to do to you when I get out of here?'

'Shut up, man,' says another voice. The other prisoner. They're both men. It's me and two men. I back into the corner as much as I can and hug my arms round my body.

I shouldn't be here. I didn't do anything wrong.

'I can smell your pussy,' the guy on the left says.

Revulsion crawls over me. I screw my eyes shut. Put my fingers in my ears. Under my breath I start to count elephants – one elephant, two elephant – like I do between lightning and the roll of thunder to reassure Emily the storm is far away. But it's not far away. It's right here, and I'm caught in the eye of it.

Then

'Please tell me you are joking?' Becky's purple-lipsticked mouth is agog as I lace up my walking boots.

'He suggested I wear sturdy footwear.' Robert texted me directions to our date tonight; I'm to park up in Batsford-on-the-Hill and walk from there.

'Where's he taking you – a barn dance?'

I don't actually know where we're going. It's intriguing. And for a moment I imagine we're about to go on a true adventure. A hot-air balloon trip, rally driving! 'I'm sure it's just a pub.' One of the ones only locals know about.

'I still can't believe you said yes to Farmer Giles! Can you, Sally?' Becky has clearly had enough of sifting through applicants for the Snapdragon Bakery. Especially when it's so much more fun to make me squirm. She knows I hate discussing my love life. Or the lack of it.

Sally looks up and over her glasses, fountain pen still poised over her paperwork. 'Said yes to what?'

'Jenna is going on a date with the Milcombe Hotel manager.' Becky claps her hands together, revelling in her own gossip. I'm not a keen dater. I haven't been out with anyone since a friend set me up with a guy who made me meet him at a pizzeria at 5 p.m. so he could claim the Early Bird deal. He then spent an hour telling me about his pension plan while he dropped spaghetti sauce all over the table. And he wouldn't let me leave a tip, even though I'd paid for my half of the bill. He kept picking the note back up and thrusting it at me while talking about market value. I was so embarrassed that I went back the next day to give the waitress her due. That was eight months ago. Maybe I shouldn't have said yes to tonight?

Sally is obviously thinking the same thing. 'I thought you were off men?'

I'm not off men as such, it's just that I'm happy with my life. With me. I'm busy with work, and . . . oh god . . . 'It's not inappropriate, is it? Me seeing the client?' I can't believe I didn't think of this before. 'I'm so sorry, Sally. I didn't think it through. I don't know why I said yes really . . .'

'Because he's hot!' Becky cackles.

'No. I mean, yes, he is . . .' My cheeks flush. Why did I say yes? It's not like I don't get my fair share of offers. The barman at the Kilkenny has made it clear with his 'let me message you, baby'. And he's fit. Why on earth did I say yes to a client? 'Do you want me to cancel?' It was something in his eyes. The way he said it. I didn't get the sense he'd asked anyone for a long time, either. *Please don't make me cancel.* I'm surprised to realise how much I do want to see him.

Sally peers at me for a second too long. I always have the feeling she knows exactly what I'm thinking. Then a smile breaks over her lips. 'I met my second husband when I recruited the staff for his new restaurant. Just don't break his heart before you get the signature on the contract, my girl.'

Becky and I crack up. Typical Sally! Nothing phases her.

I park on the high street in Batsford-on-the-Hill. An American couple, in matching T-shirts, are pushing two huge cases into the Batsford Hotel. I follow the directions Robert sent me, turning off the high street and resisting the familiar earthy vanilla smell of a second-hand bookshop. Past the Golden Fleece pub, and down Bell Street. The road tapers off into a country lane, the markings sporadic like drips of ice cream, until they're gone completely. The late April sun turns the few houses I can see over the wildflower hedgerows honey gold. As instructed, I use them to navigate. Where am I going? One cottage on the left, two on the right, and sure enough, there is a sign for a footpath. I should be anxious meeting in such a deserted spot, but I feel nothing but excitement. Besides, Robert asked me out in front of Becky, hardly the move of someone who wished me harm.

Hedges press up against the path, casting me into cool shadow. The ground underneath is dry churned mud, sloping upwards. I turn and the hedges dwindle, and I'm on the top of a stunning vista. The fields and hills roll away like waves of watercolour paint. It feels like I have the whole world to myself.

'Not a bad view.' His voice comes from behind me, making me jump.

His blond hair is lit by the sunshine, his cream shirt and jeans rendered golden in the light. I whip my hand up to my face, trying to shield the flush I feel betraying me.

'Oh god, I meant the landscape,' he says, jumping up off the stile he's sitting on. 'That sounded unintentionally creepy. Not that you aren't incredible to look at too. Oh god.' He looks so stricken I can't help but laugh.

'Thanks, I think.' He said I was incredible to look at. *Incredible.*

He smiles. He really has the most amazingly long eyelashes. 'I'm not making a very good impression, am I?' he says. 'I'm a bit out of practice at all this.'

Does that mean I was right: he hasn't been out with anyone in a while? Jump in. Be honest. 'My last serious boyfriend was over a year ago.'

A shadow passes over his face. 'We lost Erica when Emily was one.' He swallows. 'She was a wonderful woman. The best mother and wife you could wish for, till she got sick.'

Oh god. 'I'm so very sorry.' My heart aches for him.

He smiles. 'It's okay. It was a long time ago.'

I want to reach for his hand, but it feels too forward. 'How old is your daughter now?'

'Thirteen, going on twenty-three,' he laughs.

'I bet she's a handful,' I say.

His eyes are so warm and full of feeling. 'I wouldn't have it any other way. She loves it up here.'

I turn back to look at the hills, aware of his heat next to me. 'It's beautiful.'

'It is,' he says. Out the corner of my eye I can see he's not looking ahead, but at me. I get that tingly feeling in my stomach. The one Becky calls 'the butterflies'. This is daft. I met the guy two days ago. I've only spoken to him twice.

'Right.' He seems to gather himself. 'I thought we could enjoy the view with a snack – how does champagne and strawberries sound?'

'Delicious!' What a sweet thing to do. Far better than sitting in the pub.

He bounds back to where he was sitting, and picks up a bottle and two glasses, which were leaning against the side of the stile. Holding them up as if in victory. His energy is contagious. 'You came prepared – but what about the strawberries?'

'Ah – hold this.' He hands me the bottle and the glasses. They're chilled, the glasses slippy against my fingers, like they've been kept on ice all day. He didn't just pick this up from Tesco. He's made an effort.

Out of his back pocket he pulls a square of brown paper. Unfolds it. It's a bag. 'How do you feel about pick-your-own?'

'Ha! But from where?' There're no fruit fields up here.

'We're going foraging,' he says. Then pauses. 'If you're okay with that? I mean we can always . . .'

'Amazing!' I clap my hands together. 'But where do we start?' All I can see are hedges. They all look the same – hedgy.

'Wild strawberries love dappled shade. So somewhere with quite a lot of shade, but that would get a bit of sun to ripen them.' He takes the glasses from me.

I shield my eyes. 'How about over there?' The hedge is thicker, higher.

'Good call. Wild ones are smaller than the ones you get in Waitrose,' he says, leading me toward the hedge. I'm keeping my eyes peeled. 'And they're less pointy-ish.'

'Is pointy-ish a word?'

'Genuine farming terminology,' he says.

'Like that?' I point to a spear of green upon which fruit hangs like red earrings.

'A bumper crop! You're a natural!' he says.

I gently tug on one of the berries and it comes away in my fingers. A waft of the familiar caramel musk hits me. Do they need washing? 'Can we eat them?'

'Absolutely.' He plucks one and pops it into his mouth.

I do the same. The berry is intense, as if the flavour of a handful of strawberries has been condensed into this one popping sweet. 'So good!'

We reach for the same berry at the same time, and our hands brush. The butterflies dance in my stomach.

Now

Bang! There's a metallic thud in front of me. Bang! The male prisoner is punching the wall. No, kicking it. Bang! Bang! Bang!

The guards must hear that – why is no one coming? I scrabble backwards but there's nowhere to go. The walls vibrate. Each clang reverberates through my head. My heart, my lungs, my brain are shaking. Bang! Bang! Bang! I cover my ears. My elbows slam into the sides of my cell as we round a corner. Bang! Bang! Bang!

How can they ignore this? Why is no one intervening? This is wrong. I feel my bladder contract. I need to pee. Bang! Bang! Bang!

'Stop it, man!' the other voice yells. 'Hey! Hey! Someone get back here!' He's banging on the wall too. I should help. I should try to do something. What if this guy is going to hurt himself?

'Hello!' I shout. 'Hello! Can anyone hear us?'

There's no reply. The bangs crescendo. The guy must be hurling himself against the walls now. Against his door.

The banging ceases. I exhale.

Then I hear him crying. He's trying to muffle it, but he's sniffing. Tears prick my eyes. I'm not scared any more. I stroke the cell wall in front of me. *You'll be all right, mate. We'll both be all right. Please. Just hang in there.*

We were on the motorway, but we've turned off. We're slowing properly now. I jump up. Black stone and barbed wire wash past the side window. It's too small to show anything apart from what it faces. I need the van to turn. Are we here? Is this it?

I try to wipe the sweat from my arms as we stop. I can hear the jangle of keys. We're reversing. Someone slaps the outside of the van. Not more paparazzi? No. It's a signal to stop. This is it. Suddenly I don't want to leave my hothouse cupboard. I know how it works here. I know nothing about out there.

The external door is unlocked. The floor rocks as someone steps up. I hear a bolt being pulled across. But my door doesn't move. I push at it. It doesn't budge.

'Come on, then,' the female guard says. There's a grunt, a movement. It's the guy. Another bolt. Both the guys. What about me?

I push my face against the tiny window and strain to see round the back of the van. They're in handcuffs. The female guard is there, and two other men in uniform. Which prisoner was crying? One's in his late forties, grizzled stubble on his face and a shaved head. His shoulders are broad, his arms the size of my thighs. The other guy is younger. He has short dreads. Both are scowling. You'd never know one of them was weeping minutes ago. It's about show, posturing. I need to remember that. Don't show fear.

The engine starts again. I'm going somewhere else? A different prison? No one explained. The road and fields outside blur behind my tears.

It's growing dark by the time the van slows and I hear the ominous tick, tick, tick of the indicator. My bladder is screaming.

We pass through a perimeter brick wall, old, Victorian maybe, curling up like a clawed hand, with barbed wire jagged fingernails along the top. And cameras. It reminds me of a black-and-white still of a concentration camp, or the Berlin

Wall. I haven't got any contemporary references. I've never been to a prison before.

We're on a driveway. The March frost covers the surrounding scrubland, rendering everything an eerie grey. The van turns on the winding approach and I gasp. My tiny window momentarily frames the prison.

It looms out of the ground, dominating the landscape. HMP Fallenbrook is notorious. I've seen it in the papers. A mountainous chunk of black bricks that the Victorians barely tamed to instil fear into people. The building itself, with its gothic spiked roof and small slatted windows, was supposed to act as a deterrent. I can see strangled, writhing gargoyles around the top, burning, stretched, and repenting in a perpetual hell of pain. I can't be locked up here. There must be a mistake. This place is for criminals. Psychopaths.

The van swings on along the drive and the ever-darkening sky fills my view.

The sound of the van's wheels on the road reverberates through me, a rat-a-tat-tat warning to run.

The engine cuts. Don't show fear. The back door is unlocked. There's the familiar lilt as someone boards. I try to square myself, ready. Kick the sock aside. Ignore the shameful flush I can feel creeping over my skin. My teeth are furred, my mouth raw. I must reek. Doesn't matter. Can't do anything about it now.

Heavy steps approach my cell door. It's her, I can tell. One of her boots squeaks as it slides along the floor.

The bolt is pulled across. The door opens. I force myself to keep my eyes locked on her face.

Her nose wrinkles as the smell of the cell – of me – hits her. She looks amused. 'Ready, Princess?'

Not at all. But I'm not showing her that. What would the girl who walked through the Orchard Park estate like she owned it do? I lean forwards and smile. 'Bring it.'

Shock flickers on her face for a second. This Cotswold 'princess' isn't quite who she thought. 'Move it,' she snarls.

Shapes form in the brittle light. Stone statues of beasts, one missing its head, flank the imposing double-height doorway. A greying carved buttress snakes round the entrance making it look hooded. Inside glows with the same sickly blue light of an NHS hospital.

'Welcome to your new home,' the female guard hisses behind me. 'It'll be a long time till you see the outside world again. If ever.'

I didn't do it. I look up to see a bird disappearing over the high building. Panic closes her fingers over my throat. Why didn't I spend longer looking out the window, drinking in the normality, when I had the chance?

I didn't do it. Either side of the stone statues, like fleshy knock-offs, stand two male officers in navy and blue uniforms. Both with blank faces. Fat fingers tucked into their key belts. I didn't know female prisons had male guards. I don't know anything about this. I like being prepared. When I was a teen I'd watch other people, people not like us, and see what they did. How they acted. That's how I became me. That's how I assimilated. I've only seen those two male prisoners. I haven't seen enough. I haven't learnt enough.

The female guard pushes my shoulder and I stumble inside. The reception reminds me of the police station. I'd never been in one before two days ago. It's a small, shabby waiting room, with a high desk. The chairs along the wall are screwed down. A chunk is missing from one of the plastic seats, as if an animal has taken a bite from it.

Behind the desk is another male guard, straight up and down, except for his pot belly, which rests on the desk like a balanced bag of shopping. Are there any female staff here? I feel exposed in my flimsy T-shirt. It doesn't radiate control, or strength, or any of the things I desperately need to project.

The male guard is looking at something on the desk. 'No
need to ask your name,' he says. 'Our celebrity guest.'

Huh? 'Sorry?'

'*Sorry*,' mimics the female guard in a high-pitched whine.
'Don't let this one give you any gyp, Kev.'

Are they trying to unnerve me? 'My name is Jennifer Burns.'

The guard called Kev emits a gruff guffaw. My stomach
twists. 'I know who you are,' he says.

I see it as he lifts the newspaper on his desk. The photo on
the front page. Me at a barbecue with Robert last summer. It
was on my friend's Facebook. It was hot, I'd been in the
kitchen. My cotton dress was thin, slightly too tight, too low. I
never wore it again. With the photo blown up this size you can
see the faint outline of a nipple.

'Nice titties.' He grins.

In the photo I have my hand looped casually round Robert's
waist. If I close my eyes I can smell him, feel him. He looks
tanned and gorgeous, in a simple blue T-shirt and khaki shorts.
He's looking at me with adoration as I smile at the camera. It
makes me seem uninterested in him. It is the perfect photo for
what they want to achieve. I feel the floor undulate under my
feet. Splashed across the top of the front page is:

*Lethal Attraction: Blonde slayer accused of killing 14-year-old
stepdaughter. Fiancé still missing.*

Then

'A second date already?' Becky squeals. She drops the pile of papers she's carrying onto her desk, and jumps up to sit on the edge of mine, like a gossipy pixie.

'It's just dinner.' I'm trying to play it cool, but the ridiculous grin on my face is probably giving me away.

'At his!' She claps excitedly.

I let the joy I've been feeling bubble out of me. 'Yes! He's going to cook!' I've never really had a man cook for me before. I lived with a guy for a year after uni, but we mostly ate cereal while we carved out our careers. We were too broke to buy anything more.

'I should think so too, after he made you eat in a field on your first date.' Becky's freckled face scrunches in distaste. She measures her prospective partners' worth on how many stars the restaurant they suggest taking her to has. But I'm not interested in all that. I mean, I can do the fine-dining thing if I have to, for work, but I've never really been comfortable there.

'It was romantic, different,' I say, remembering how Robert and I had sat on the grass, sipping champagne and eating our hedgerow fcast as the sun turned the sky from gold to orange to pink to red. As it finally dipped into the twilight blue of night, I shivered. Robert placed his coat round my shoulders and we kissed. Did I make the first move or did he? It was somewhere in the middle. Natural.

'You mean it was cheap!' Becky cackles.

'Money isn't everything,' Sally chides from her desk. 'Eddie is quite broke,' she adds, of her latest beau.

'Yeah,' says Becky. 'And quite twenty-five years younger than you.'

Sally smiles like the cat that got the cream. 'Like I said, money isn't everything.'

'You going straight there?' Becky says as she trudges back to her desk.

'He's coming to collect me after work.' My stomach buzzes at the thought. Those damn butterflies have taken up the Macarena.

'There, Sally, you'll get a look at him after all,' Becky says.

'As long as he's treating my Jenna how she deserves, he's fine with me,' Sally says, without looking up.

I know Sally's playing it cool herself; she won't be able to resist having a nosey. I've told Robert to stay in the car and I'll come out. He's passed the decision about which recruitment company they'll use over to the Milcombe board. I should probably feel more conflicted than I do, but I just feel excited. I know I'm being daft, it's only been one date, but it was the way we talked about everything. The state of American politics. The state of ours here. What we wanted to do in the future. All the places we'd love to see. Where we went to uni. He studied agriculture, which was no surprise given the baby cows. I did business studies, mostly because I didn't know what I wanted to do at that age. I told him I'd never even heard of a recruitment consultant till I graduated. And I stayed away from any conversations about childhood. I'm well practised at leaving out all the messy details. You can find common ground without all of that anyway. And Robert made it easy. He loved Danger Mouse as a kid and I loved Penfold. It turns out we've been to loads of the same exhibitions at The Wilson in Cheltenham, and we both love the Sherborne sculpture walk. It's a wonder we haven't bumped into each other before. Maybe we almost did. Maybe our meeting was fated.

I look at the clock. Three hours, seventeen minutes and eleven seconds till Robert is picking me up. I can't stop the smile from colonising my face.

5.31 p.m. and my phone bleeps. I'm up in seconds. I've already got my jacket on.

'Oh!' Sally looks at the clock. 'Is he not coming in?'

Becky pulls a comic shocked face. 'You minx!'

But I'm already at the door. 'See you tomorrow, ladies!'

I skip down the stone steps of the office. A car horn toots and I spy Robert in a battered Range Rover that looks like it's a relic from the last war. I wave and dash to the passenger's side. Behind me the blinds of the office twitch and two faces appear at the window.

Robert leans over to open the door. The car smells of dogs and warm baked bread.

'Hiya.' I suddenly feel shy.

'I see we've got an audience.' He nods toward Sally and Becky.

Becky is making kissy faces. They're so embarrassing! 'They're just cross I didn't invite you in.'

He grins. 'Do I need to keep them on side?'

'Absolutely. Otherwise I'm afraid they will kill you. Sally has a lot of land to hide the body on,' I say, deadpan, clambering in.

'The Cotswolds Mafia. I've been warned.' He gives them a wave. Becky immediately ducks back out of sight, but Sally doesn't move. There's something in her look that I can't quite place as Robert pulls away. My phone beeps in my hand: a message from Sally. My stomach shifts.

'So, did you have a good day?' Robert is talking to me.

Why would Sally message me? I blink. I get car-sick so quickly I can't look at the message now. Don't want to. Whatever Sally has to say can wait. I drop my phone into my

bag. 'Yeah, great. You? Oh. I almost forgot . . .' I pull out a
bottle of champagne. 'I brought a bottle. My turn this time.'

'That will go perfectly with supper,' he grins.

We're on the road out of town. 'You haven't actually told
me where you live.' I probably should have asked that before
getting into the car with him. But I don't feel threatened. I feel
comfortable. I ignore the strange look I've just seen on Sally's
face.

'In Broadpass. It's about twenty minutes away.'

That's near the Milcombe Estate. He could have a flat on
site. Is that what hotel staff do?

You mean it was cheap. Becky's words pop into my head.

He glances at me. Oh god, I didn't respond. 'Is that okay?'
He sounds unsure.

'Of course!' I don't care if he does live on site. It's nothing
to be ashamed of.

He signals and we pull out onto the A44. 'You're in
Middleway, yes?'

'That's right. It's just a two-bed flat, but I love it.' What if his
place is smaller than that? What if it's a room and I've made
him feel bad? But Robert doesn't look anything other than
thrilled to have me here and I soon relax, watching the fields
open around us like flower petals.

Just before the turning for the Milcombe Estate he signals. I
knew it. He does live on site. I hope he doesn't share a flat.
That's a terrible thing to think, but I can't cope with meeting
a flatmate now. He would have told me if there was going to
be someone else there, wouldn't he?

Trees kiss overhead and we bump across the cattle grid that
separates the estate from the road. 'How many properties
have they got now?' I know this from my work research before
our initial meeting, but I feel it'd be rude not to ask.

'Well there's Field House . . .'

'I've been there for a spa day with my mum and sister,' I say.

'Did you like it?' he asks. Again, doubt has crept into his voice.

'Are you kidding? It was stunning. I would love to stay someday.' Though it's a bit out of my price range.

'I can probably help with that,' he says with a laugh.

I clap my hand over my mouth. I can't believe I said that. He'll think I'm fishing for a discount. 'I didn't mean to sound like I was . . .' Or maybe he'll think I'm after a night in the hotel with him. I blush. I imagine lying on a big soft bed, Robert's lips moving down my neck, over my chest, down my stomach . . . I feel heat between my legs. My blush deepens.

He laughs. 'I'm glad you liked it.'

Now I can't stop thinking about me and Robert in a hotel room. Ahead the road turns into the Field House car park, the top of the house visible between the trees. But he drives past. Still climbing up the hill. Maybe there's separate staff accommodation? Or perhaps he's based at the new conference hotel? 'It's going to be called The Heron, isn't it? The one you're recruiting for?' I hope he can't tell from my voice what I've just been imagining. I cough. *Subtle.*

'Yup. And we've already got The Barns, which is a conference complex. This is like an extension.'

'Cool,' I say.

He laughs. 'You don't really want to hear about work, do you?'

'No,' I admit. 'I would like to know how the baby cows are, though.' I think about it. 'Wait, are they for the restaurant?' I hadn't thought of that. 'Please tell me they're for team-building exercises or something?'

'You're not vegetarian, are you?' His eyes widen.

'No.' I just hadn't made the possible connection between them and dinner. *You live in the middle of the countryside, Jenna.*

You're surrounded by farms. You sound like an idiot. I imagine what Robert looks like topless working in a field. Like a blond Poldark. I open the window.

'We were about to have an issue with dinner if you were,' he says. 'The calves are for dairy.'

We only kissed on our first date, and held hands. It was charming at the time, but maybe Robert doesn't fancy me that much? I can't stop fantasising about him. I see The Barns sail past. The Range Rover bumps as it climbs.

'That's the Heron site,' he points as we pass the new hotel.

As we crest the top of the hill, the whole of the valley opens up alongside us, providing the hotels with amazing views. We're also reaching the edge of the estate. The hedge that borders it snakes up toward us, meeting at a carved stone entrance that must be a relic from when it was built. It's gated now. Robert stops the car in front of it.

'Sorry, I just need to get the thingy.' He reaches over me to the glove compartment.

I greedily inhale his scent of basil and cedarwood. His arm touches my bare knee.

'Sorry.' He smiles at me sheepishly.

I can't answer. Can't trust myself to sound normal. I want him to kiss me. To touch me. *He's going to think you're an idiot. Speak!* I giggle.

He points something at the gate. It's a fob. The metal bars roll to the side. Where are we? He puts the Range Rover in gear and drives forwards, the gate rolls closed behind us. This is a lot of security for staff.

The road curves round in front of us and all I can think of are the opening credits of *Downton Abbey*. A huge country house appears to the left, much bigger than Field House. It looks like a National Trust property. I had no idea this was here.

He sees me staring. 'That's my parents' house,' he says.

I inhale sharply. He's joking, right? The driveway branches off, and we turn away from the mansion.

Through the trees, I catch glimpses of another house, Georgian, I would guess from the six large rectangular windows. It's as big as the hotel at the bottom of the hill. Robert stops the car. This can't be his place? My hands are shaking. He's a hotel manager. He likes cows. He drives a battered car. He watched *Danger Mouse*.

He pops his belt, opens the door and climbs down.

I grew up in a one-bed council flat on the Orchard Park estate. I'm not supposed to be here.

'Ready?' He gives me a warm smile. 'I promise not to give you food poisoning.'

'Sure,' I manage. 'Just need to . . .' I pull my phone out of my bag and wave it at him. This has to be a mistake.

As he walks round to open the door on my side, I shakily open the message from Sally. It says: *That's Robert Milcombe – his family own the whole estate!*

Now

Horror and anger flood through me and I want to rip the paper from his hands. How dare they print that! They don't know me. They don't know Robert. 'I love Robert. And Emily . . . I could never hurt them.' My voice wavers.

'Save it for court, Princess,' the female guard says.

I'm on the front page. I'm recognisable. Do they have newspapers in here? Everyone will think I'm the Blonde Slayer. A child killer. 'Will I be given protection?'

He raises an eyebrow. 'We don't have budget for bodyguards.'

Fear drips down my spine. 'There must be a procedure?'

'*Procedure*? Sure. We'll give you a new crime, a cover story if you like. Drugs, usually. You can tell people you were a party girl,' he laughs.

'But that's my photo – the other prisoners will know!' I know what they do to child killers. I saw it on the news when Ian Huntley's throat was slashed.

'If you don't calm down, I'll have to restrain you.' The female guard digs her bony fingers into my shoulder so it hurts. 'My granddaughter is the same age as that poor girl,' she hisses into my ear.

'Ow!' Kev must see what she's doing.

But he's drumming the fingers of one hand on the newspaper. Bored. He doesn't care.

They don't believe me. The poisonous reality spreads spores through my body. No one is going to protect me.

'Ready?' Kev cocks an eyebrow.

I feel like I'm back at school. I force myself to nod. 'Yes.'

'Ring, please.' Kev points at my hand.

My fingers close over the solitaire Robert gave me. 'It's my engagement ring.' It's the only thing from him I have. The only part of the old me.

'You can keep a plain wedding band only,' he says. On his own finger he wears a worn gold one.

'We're not married yet.' The words sting.

'You can apply to send it out or give it to a visitor. Or we will keep it till your release . . .'

The female guard snorts.

He takes a plastic bag from his desk drawer. I want to kiss the ring, it feels like I'm cutting a tether to Robert, but I daren't weaken myself more in front of them. I slide it off my finger and place it on the desk.

Kev picks it up, turning the platinum band over, watching the diamond twinkle in the light. I didn't want to take it when Robert gave it to me. I worried it was too much too soon. He laughed and said he'd never been more sure of anything in his life. Tears prick at my eyes. *I'm sorry, Robert.*

'Fancy,' Kev says, dropping it into the plastic bag. With a pen he writes on the outside of the bag. 'Fallenbrook is not responsible for any items that are lost or damaged. Unless you can prove a member of staff did it.'

And how would I do that? Injustice feeds my growing internal voice. 'What are you writing on it?'

'Your assigned prisoner number is A170788F. You will need this for all application forms . . .'

What will I be applying for?

'. . . incoming and outgoing post, and such. Don't forget it.'

'A170788F,' I repeat back. I've been reduced to a number. Another layer of me peeled away.

'Okay.' Kev nods at the female guard.

A smile spreads across her lips. Dread pools in my stomach. 'This way, Princess.'

I glance at Kev, but he's studiously focusing on the forms in front of him. He doesn't want to bear witness.

'In you go.' She shoves me toward a closed blue door.

The door opens into a small room. Grey walls. No windows. It smells of fear. A tatty blue medical curtain clings onto a pole by two remaining rings, it doesn't cover the bulky plastic moulded chair behind. I swallow. It looks like a cross between a toilet (with no pan) and a very poor copy of the designer chairs in Robert's parents' house.

The female guard pulls the door to after us. It's just the two of us. No cameras in here. She has a horrible look on her face.

'Strip,' she says.

I stare at her. 'You've got to be kidding.'

'Strip,' she repeats.

'This isn't fair . . .'

'Standard practice. No special treatment for you,' she snaps.

I can't believe this is happening.

'Hurry up. Unless you want me to do it for you?' She takes a step toward me.

I shake my head. I don't want her to touch me. My shoulder feels tender from her horrid probing fingers. Hurriedly I pull my T-shirt off. My skin prickles. Even the air feels dirty. She's staring. I tug my trainers off, wincing as they scrape past my heel. There's blood on my one remaining sock. Pull my jogging bottoms down. The police even took my underwear. I'm in the misshapen blue pants and bra they gave me.

'And the rest,' she adds, with a cold smile. I suddenly have a flashback of Ness doing this when we were little. I'd got wet, I can't remember how. Playing football in the pouring rain? And she made me take everything off so she could wash it.

I try to remember all the details of back then. Ness plaiting my hair. Walking me to school, my little hand in hers. I try not to think about what's happening now. I unhook my bra and slide my pants down.

'Turn around,' the guard commands.

How some days we'd get chips for tea. How Ness would tuck two wooden forks under her lip and pretend to be a vampire rabbit, like the one in the books I loved.

'Squat,' the female guard says, with a laugh.

I shouldn't be here. I do as instructed.

'Cough,' she orders.

I didn't do anything wrong. I force myself to cough. Shame burns across my body.

'Up.'

It's like a twisted game of Simon Says. I turn to face her, try to cover myself with my arms.

'Sit.' She points at the moulded chair.

Dread infects me. Why? What is it?

'Are you hiding something?' She claps both hands down onto my shoulders. Her boot squashes some of my toes. I can feel her stale breath on my face. On my flesh. Her jacket zip is cold against my breast.

'No.' I try to shake her off. Her fingers plunge into my muscle. She knows exactly where to press.

'Do you have any concealed weapons or phones?' She pushes me toward the chair.

Concealed weapons? A phone? Where would I hide something? She forces me down toward the chair. 'What's it going to do?' I brace for an electric shock.

'It's magnetic,' she says.

My legs make contact with the seat. Nothing happens. I imagine a phone or a knife ripping out of me.

The guard looks disappointed. 'Get dressed.' She kicks my stuff toward me. My naked buttocks peel off the plastic. I feel sick. Dizzy. Pathetically I scrabble for my clothes and put them on.

My skin feels raw. Kev is still filling in paperwork. I hug myself, feeling like I'm holding myself together. I never want to go through that again.

Outside, I can see another white prison van approaching. Another unfortunate inmate. Is she innocent too? The two male guards are still outside as it reverses, beeping, slowly obscuring the last of the light. Exhaust fumes seep into the room.

The radios of the guards outside crackle into life. '*Charlie, foxtrot, Oscar eleven. Prepare for arrival.*'

Kev looks up from his forms, alarm tracing across his forehead. 'Here we go,' he whispers under his breath. He removes the paperwork, and the pen pot from the desk.

What's happening? The female guard and I both look.

'Ready?' the bigger guard asks the other. They're both huge, I realise. Brick-wall men, swaggering like bouncers.

'As I'll ever be,' the second one grunts.

All the saliva in my mouth evaporates. Who is in the van?

Now

'Fresh meat?' the female guard asks Kev.

'Rotten, more like.' Kev is keeping his eyes fixed on the door of the van.

Should I be here? It doesn't feel like a good idea. The female guard takes hold of my arm.

'Can't be worse than this *thing*,' she says.

Thing? She made me squat naked and cough. She laughed at me. Shame fizzes into anger. I turn to glare at her. Like I faced down the guys who were bullying our Ness on the Orchard Park estate. 'What did you call me?'

She looks surprised, before contorting her face into a grimace. 'Show some respect. Call me ma'am,' she says.

Not likely.

She digs her nails into my arm. I feel the surface give, and blood sting its way out of my flesh.

I grit my teeth. I will not cry.

'Call. Me. Ma'am.' I can smell cigarettes and Marmite on her breath.

I ignore the jagged nails clawing into my skin, the empty feeling inside me, and cling to the anger. 'No.'

Behind me the van door slams. She lets go. It's as if we're in an aeroplane and the cabin pressure has dropped. My ears pop. All eyes are staring toward the new arrival.

She's flanked by the two guards. They have hold of her, the dark grey arms of her oversized hoodie so scrunched they look like elephant legs. Her hair is gelled flat to the top of her head. Her eyes are red-ringed burn holes in the dirty freckled concrete of her face. There's something familiar in its hardness.

'Jesus,' the female guard mutters beside me.

'Charlie Gould,' Kev whispers almost in awe.

Charlie Gould? Each of the fine hairs on my arms stands to attention. Charlie Gould the crazed killer? It can't be. I've seen her on the news. Her husband was head of some gang. And they thought he'd killed off all his rivals. He went down for it. Then new evidence came to light – she was torturing this guy. She cut off two of his fingers, broke his legs, but he escaped, and that's when the truth came out. The press are saying she did it. That she killed all her husband's rivals. She's a sadist. Surely they have different prisons for people like that?

I'm staring. We all are.

'What you looking at?' Charlie Gould's voice is smooth, not what I was expecting.

I blink. Oh shit. She's talking to me. Glaring at me. I look at the floor. I don't want trouble.

'Keep moving, Gould,' one of the male guards barks. Gould walks with a purposeful bouncing gait, as if she's spring-loaded. Moving to a beat we can't hear. Her trainers, bright, white, big, with complex laces, squeak against the floor.

I try to step back, but the female officer is behind me.

'And here's me thinking you was only getting one famous guest today,' she says.

I feel my face drop. *No*.

Gould looks at her as if she's rubbish, then back to me. 'Who the fuck is this?' She spits. The globule lands next to my foot. The male guards tense.

I turn my head, to stare at the woman officer. Plead with my eyes. *Don't do this*.

But she's not looking at me. 'You mean you don't recognise the Blonde Slayer?' She takes a step away from me, and makes a flourish with her hands, as if I'm a washing machine on QVC.

It feels like everyone is holding their breath. Except me. Mine's coming thick and fast. Gould looks me up and down like I'm a child, shrugs. Makes to move away, not bothered.

She doesn't know. It doesn't mean anything to her. I've got away with it.

The female guard is level with Gould now, circumventing the men either side of her, leaning in, delivering her hit of nicotine and sandwich spread into the face of the most feared woman in the UK. 'She killed her bloke's little kiddie.'

Emily's face flashes into my mind. A blink of her blue eyes. A flick of hair. *I didn't. I couldn't.*

'Scum!' Gould screams. Her elbows jut out. One guard falls backwards, the other staggers to the side.

My hands fly up. Must get away. Before I can get clear her elbow smashes into my nose. Pain explodes into black fireworks across my eyes. Her knee thumps into my chest. My back slams into the desk, propelling me forward.

'Get off!' The guards drag her away.

I smack into the floor.

'Gerroff!'

'Fucking paedo scum!' Gould is screaming. 'I'll kill you! I'll do what you did to that kiddie!'

An alarm sounds. High-pitched punches of noise assault my ears. Running feet. Gould is pinned to the ground. I can taste blood.

My eyes close on the smirking female guard.

In my mind I see Emily. The faint smell of chlorine from the pool mixed with coconut shampoo, her fine hair flies about her face as she dances past. I reach for her, but it's too late. She's gone. Everything goes black.

Now

'You're lucky I was in today.' The doctor, a puffy man with dark hair and a sloping face, pulls his plastic gloves off and throws them in the bin.

I don't feel lucky.

'Try not to get into any more fights.' He's studiously avoiding eye contact.

I didn't try to get into a fight this time. 'I wasn't—'

'You ladies need to learn some self-respect,' he says, interrupting me to point at the blood that's drying down my T-shirt. My words sound nasal. How bad is the damage? Will they give me fresh clothes? 'You need to learn how to peacefully co-exist.'

Fury rises in me. 'I shouldn't even be here. I haven't done anything wrong.'

'That's what they all say.' He shakes his head, already picking up the file for the next patient. 'What did you say your name was?'

'Jennifer Burns. Jenna.' I choke back the anger. Does he not know who I am? Charlie Gould does. She could be telling everyone these horrendous lies. She said she was going to kill me.

'And you're new today?' he says.

I nod.

'You're on my Induction list, we may as well get it done now.' He checks his watch.

'What does that mean?' It sounds official.

He pulls a fresh pair of gloves out of the box and the waft of latex makes me feel momentarily sick. He won't even touch me without gloves.

'General health checks, we'll take some blood samples, test for drugs—'

'I don't take drugs,' I snap.

His thick hairy caterpillar of an eyebrow twitches.

I don't.

'We'll check for lice, fleas . . .' he says. 'See if you need to apply for any prescriptions.'

Lice? Fleas? Do they think I'm an animal? What kind of people do they have in here? 'I'm not . . .' I want to say dirty. 'I'm not . . . infested.'

'Standard practice, Jennifer,' he says. He's using my name when he hasn't even told me his. 'Many of the inmates live rough, or in less salubrious settings, before arrival.'

I lived in a beautiful house, almost a mansion. I had my hair blow-dried on special occasions. Past-me comes kicking and screaming to the fore. I lived in a squalid flat, where my older sister fed me Pot Noodle when our mum was on benders. Is this the universe correcting itself? Should I always have ended up here? Robert and Emily and happiness were a mistake in the natural order. I'm being punished for trying to create a new, better life. I feel faint.

'You can leave your clothes in a pile on the bed,' the doctor says.

'What?' I don't want to strip again. I don't want to be naked in front of another stranger. We're alone. I can't clearly remember how many doors we passed through to get here. I was dizzy. Shouldn't there be a chaperone? If I cried out, would anyone hear me? Do the others think I'm just a flea-infested junkie? I think of Mum. Even if I was . . . that's no excuse to be mistreated. *Calm down. He's a doctor. You've got to trust he's a professional.*

He's pulling on his gloves. Still not really looking at me. There's no connection, it's like he's about to prepare meat for cooking. 'Clothes on the bed. Please.' It's an order.

There's no curtain I can pull across. No cover. I start to unlace my trainers. A little spot of blood is on the toe. I blink away the images of Emily. I don't have enough energy to fight any more. I pull my T-shirt off, and step out of the jogging bottoms.

The floor is cold, and though I can see the room is clean, it has that shabby, grubby feel. Not as bad as the room with the metal-detecting chair, but not much better. Damp discolours the wall and ceiling in one corner. The plasticised floor is peeling away like a half-eaten sandwich left on the side.

He's still looking at his notes, adding to them.

'No signs of burns, bruising or scars,' he mutters. 'Apart from fresh tissue damage to the right arm and nose.' He checks my elbows, and between my toes. 'No signs of track marks. Good girl,' he says, as if talking to a pet. 'Put your clothes on and we'll take some bloods.'

'Can I use the toilet?' My bladder is screaming. I'm surprised I didn't piss myself when that woman attacked me. I can feel the curling edges of a UTI. I've always been prone to them. Robert would tease me about my obsession with staying hydrated. The thought of swigging from a bottle of water is almost torturous now.

'When you're done here, ask the guard to take you,' the doctor says. 'Get dressed.'

It's like being a child again. Following instructions. This is what loss of liberty means. My life is now in the hands of others. But unlike family, these people don't care for me.

I hurry back into the T-shirt and joggies. I barely feel the needle go in.

There's a knock at the door. The doctor pulls the needle out, presses down with a small ball of cotton wool and says, 'Yes.'

A female guard, in the same uniform as Kev, pokes her head round the door. Cornrows twist across her head and end in a bun. 'Ms Burns got visitors.'

Visitors? Ness? Mum? I start pulling my trainers on. Maybe it's Mr Peterson. Maybe they've finally come to their senses. Realised this is all a mistake.

'We're done,' says the doctor, glancing at the guard and taking off his gloves.

'Good,' she says. 'Because it's the police.'

I freeze with one foot halfway in my shoe. The walls seem to pinch and close toward me.

Why are the police here to see me?

Now

They've found Robert. The thought plays over and over in my mind. Alive or dead? Alive or dead? The words bounce through me with each step. I'm following the guard's broad hips as we walk briskly back through the corridor. I want to run. Alive or dead? Her hips swing like a pendulum. Like a hanging body. Alive or dead?

'Do you know what this is about?' I say.

'No.' The guard shakes her head. She's wearing mismatched studs in her ears: gold in one, baby pink in the other. A small act of non-conformity in her uniform. It makes me warm to her.

My body is alert. I feel the cuts, the fingernails, the smashed cartilage. I need to pee. Now. My bladder contracts. I can't hold it any longer.

'Can I use the toilet?' I look around at doors we pass. Hurry. Alive or dead? Signs denote whom the rooms belong to. Education Officer. Welfare Department. The walls are covered in posters:

Suspect it? Report it.

It is a crime to bring onto prison grounds alcohol, tobacco, drugs, weapons, explosives, tear gas …

Suspect it? Report it. Alive or dead? The squeaks of my steps echo like small cries of pain up into the high ceiling. We turn into another corridor. More doors stretch away from us. Alive or dead? Hurry. I can't remember when we last saw a window. I feel like we've turned back on ourselves multiple times, as if we've been walking in a circle, tighter and tighter, and yet never reaching the centre.

The guard pauses to unlock a dark-brown wooden door with one of her many keys. 'Be quick.'

Robert could be waiting for me. 'I will.' Alive or dead? My bladder, sensing release, contracts.

I know very little about prison, but I know about prison toilets and showers. They're the thing of nightmarish jokes. Mercifully, I have the single cubicle to myself. The strong smell of bleach is not masking the stench of urine. I pull down my trousers, my knickers, and squat. Relief floods through me.

There's a cracked sink, with a bottle of antibacterial soap. I catch sight of my reflection in the warped mirror. The padding over my nose obscures much of my face. My eyes are red-rimmed, the bruising underneath already blooming into a deep claret purple. Robert could be waiting for me. I don't want him to see me like this. I whip off my T-shirt and wash my hands, my arms, under my arms, my face with the water. The hot tap doesn't give, so I have to make do with cold. The soap has a clinical smell, but least it's clean.

A bald towel hangs stiffly on the back of the door. It doesn't look like it's been washed in a long time. I opt instead for quickly blotting myself dry with wads of toilet roll. As I throw the tissue into the loo, my eyes seek out the small window high up the wall. It would have got dark around five thirty. Though the sky is now veiled by dappled frosted glass, I can still sense the glint of the moon. The winking stars. I know they're there. A primeval sense inside calls for uninterrupted sky.

The door opens behind me. I clutch my hand to my chest, as though caught in the act.

'Hurry up.' The guard signals with a jerk of her head. 'This is the staff loo.' She looks over her shoulder as if checking no one else has seen.

'Thank you.' *Thank you.*

By the time we reach reception we're virtually running. My desperation has infected her, powered us on.

In the foyer stands DI Langton, her black suit jacket folded over her arm, and DS Salinsky in the same navy suit he was wearing when they arrested me two nights ago. This is it. Alive or dead?

Then

I straighten my dress one more time. I opted for something floral. I usually wear this to work with a jacket. But the jacket would be too much. Or maybe not. I look up and Robert is watching me. His blue eyes are flashing in the sunlight that streams into his bedroom.

'Don't laugh at me.' I feel silly for being caught studying my reflection. I wasn't enjoying my appearance, more like critiquing it.

'I'm not laughing.' He comes over and sweeps my hair off my shoulder to kiss the base of my neck. Tiny pleasurable shocks pirouette across my skin, but we haven't got time. We have to leave in fifteen minutes.

'Try not to look so scared. It's only my parents,' he says.

I brush his hands away. Head downstairs. I will not be late. 'This is a big deal for me.'

Robert follows behind me, pausing only at Emily's door. 'Almost ready, darling,' he calls.

The geometric tiled hallway gapes expectantly at me. I need to keep busy. I'll clear up from lunch. The kitchen is my favourite room in Robert's house. The off-white walls and scrubbed wooden surfaces, made from richly dark-grained slices of an oak tree that fell on their land, give it a kind of high-end tree-house feel. Something magical, like a full-size Hobbit house, carved from the land around. It's a far cry from the dank, cramped sticky seventies kitchen in the flat where I grew up.

I wipe up the crumbs of cheese and bread from Emily's sandwich, and enjoy the way the surface undulates under my hand. Things were fine while Robert's parents were away. I could pretend they weren't really real. The people who live in the huge mansion, who were on a nine-month round-the-world cruise were an abstract. I mean they don't sound real, do they? The poshest person I've ever known is Sally, and even she has only been on a two-week cruise round the Caribbean. But Robert's parents are now a very pressing reality. They're going to think I'm a gold-digger. That I've tricked him in some way.

A Robert-shaped shadow appears, twisted slightly by the glass in the door to the lounge.

'You don't have to do that,' he says, as I pick up the knife we used to slice cheese.

I open the dishwasher. 'You have told them that I'm younger than you, haven't you?' There's ten years between me and Robert, and he's already been married once. And he has Emily. He's a single father. A widower. A proper adult, and I feel like I've been pretending. That I've wandered into some-one else's story.

'My mother is a good fifteen years younger than my father, younger still if you believe the age she says she is.' He winks at me.

My mother was fifteen when she had Ness. I swallow.

'Try not to worry, darling.' He takes the knife back out of the dishwasher, and starts running the tap.

'What are you doing?' I stare at him.

'Ah,' he says. 'These are Japanese – machine-washing damages the blade.'

There are so many rules to Robert's world that I don't understand. All these little things that another woman – a more suitable one – would get. 'I'm sure you put them in there the first night you cooked for me.' I remember watching his strong beautiful hands as he tidied up.

He gives me a cheeky grin, wiping the knife on a tea towel and returning it to the block next to the range. 'Don't tell the chef at Milcombe Hotel I mistreat them when I've had a drink, he made me invest several hundred in them.'

Several hundred pounds? On things you use to chop carrots! Yet another thing I have to get my head round. I cover my shock with a laugh.

Robert hangs the tea towel on the enamel hook and comes over, wrapping his arms around me. I relax into him.

'I thought you might be feeling a bit nervous,' he says, quietly.

Understatement.

'So I got you something.' He smiles.

'You didn't have to get me anything,' I say. Though I'm excited anyway. Last week he brought me the prettiest succulent for my desk at work. Emily and I christened him Harry, after Harry Styles, the singer she has a crush on.

'I know.' He reaches for his back pocket and pulls out a key.

'What is it?' I say.

'It's a key for here. This house.' His voice is suddenly serious. Anxious.

I try to say something.

'We're already spending most nights together, and I've discussed it with Emily.' He pauses, coughs. I touch his arm. He coughs again, louder. Is he getting sick? '*I said*, I've already discussed it with Emily.'

Nothing happens.

'Hang on,' he says.

He opens the door and yells, '*I said*, I've already discussed it with Emily!'

I stifle a giggle as Emily slopes into the kitchen, her headphones round her neck. 'Are you sure you're okay with this?' I say.

'Will you still take me shopping?' she says.

'Emily!' Robert says.

'Any time.' I grin at her.

Emily rolls her eyes at her dad. 'You and granny always want me to dress like some little girlie girl.'

I laugh.

'Well, how could you turn down such a fine proposal?' Robert grins.

It's only been six months since we met, but it already feels like forever. It feels perfect. I was worried Emily would reject me, but she never really knew her mother, and Robert hasn't dated anyone else. We like the same Netflix shows, and I get the feeling the rest of the family still babies her. I don't have to think about it. 'I'd love to move in,' I say. 'But only if your dad promises not to leave his dirty pants on the floor.'

'Urgh, disgusting, Dad!' she shrieks.

'Hey! I never do that!' He puts up his hands in mock surrender.

Emily grabs the key from him and hands it to me. 'The sooner you're in, the better.'

I finger the black fob that it hangs from. 'What's this?'

Robert's lips thin. 'It's a panic alarm.'

A what?

'It's so stupid,' Emily says. 'Granny makes us all have them.'

'She's very security conscious.' Robert shrugs, as if it's the most natural thing in the world. 'They're linked straight to the police: press the button and they come straight away.'

I take my finger away from the button.

'Like, overreaction or what?' Emily gesticulates with her hands. And suddenly I can see her as an adult sitting round a table waving a glass of wine, entertaining her friends with shrewd observations and take-offs of people she knows.

'Everyone in the family has one,' Robert says. 'And you're one of the family now.' He pulls both Emily and me into him. 'Come here, my favourite girls.'

'Urgh, Dad!' Emily says into his jumper, but doesn't pull away.

Family. I feel myself soften. 'What will your parents say?' I whisper. They're going to return from their holiday to find a stranger has moved in with their son and their granddaughter. I'm not sure how that's going to look.

'They're going to love you as much as we do,' Robert says.

Emily shrugs us both off and rolls her eyes again, before looking in the mirror to smooth her parting.

And I want so very much to believe him.

Now

DI Langton is frowning at the bandage on my face.

DS Salinsky's patent brogues creak as he carries a plastic cup of tea to Langton, and places one in front of me with precision. Ex-military, I'd guess. This is it. Alive or dead? I grip the cup, using the burn on my fingers to stop me from screaming.

'Have you found Robert?' They've driven up to talk to me. It can only be one thing.

Salinsky scratches at his crewcut. 'Cut the crap and tell us where the body is, Jenna.'

They haven't found him. They don't know where he is. They're talking about a body. A body? Alive or dead. Dead. 'Why aren't you looking for him?' Tea shakes out of the cup and scalds my fingers. 'You should be out there.' This is a nightmare. There was blood, they told me. Whoever did this hurt him too.

'Jenna.' Langton smiles. Not friendly. The circles under her eyes look darker than when I saw her last. She's not sleeping. Good. She shouldn't rest till Robert's found. 'We've been over this. Your fingerprints are on the murder weapon.'

Not this again. 'It was our knife, I told you.' I feel sick at the thought of it being grabbed from the block.

'Only your fingerprints, Jenna,' she says.

'The thief must have been wearing gloves.' Yes, that makes sense. 'It was a robbery. We have money and nice things, and Emily must have disturbed them.'

'We've taken exclusion prints. There's no unexplained DNA in the house . . .' Langton says.

Why was Emily home? I hadn't thought of it at all until now. 'She should have been at swim practice. Did somebody pick her up – take her?' It was a kidnap attempt that went wrong. And now they have Robert.

'Jenna,' Langton sighs, cutting me off. I want to shake her. It's like I'm speaking a different language. 'We found the photos on your computer.'

Salinsky is trying his best to hold his face neutral, but it keeps twisting into something ugly.

A cavity opens inside me. I can feel myself teetering on its edge. 'What photos?'

'Images of child abuse.' Salinsky spits the words.

'What?'

'Numerous unsavoury images,' Langton says.

There must be a mistake. 'Emily is a keen swimmer. I have photos of her at meets. In her costume . . .'

'These are not family snaps.' Salinsky's face is twisting again. 'They are hard-core.'

Sick floods into the cavity. They've made a mistake. 'Of Emily?' *Did someone hurt her?*

Langton shakes her head.

Oh thank god. I can't bear the idea that someone would touch her.

'Jenna, here's what I think happened,' Langton is saying. 'You were looking at your images on the laptop in the kitchen . . .'

'They weren't my images,' I say.

'And Emily came home unexpectedly early – we spoke to a Mrs Diane Monkford.' Langton looks at her notes.

Isabel's mother?

'She confirms she brought Emily home early because her period started and she didn't want to go to swim club,' she says. 'She dropped her off just before five p.m.'

Oh Emily. You shouldn't have been there. You poor girl.

'I think Emily found you looking at those photos,' Langton says. 'I think she caught you.'

'No.' I shake my head. That isn't what happened.

'Perhaps you decided to try something on with her?' Langton is talking as if we're discussing the weather.

They are accusing me of . . . 'Of course I didn't!' I clasp my hand over my mouth. Push the chair back. I'm shaking. 'She was fourteen!' I push the heels of my palms into my bruised eyes. Want to push them all the way through.

'But she wouldn't play along would she, and that made you angry.' Langton's words worm between my fingers, burrow into my head. 'I think she said no, I think she fought back – there are defence wounds on the body.'

'I didn't hurt her!' The words rip out of me.

Langton keeps going, the words raining down. 'And then I think Robert came home. He saw what you'd done, so you stabbed him too. You killed him and hid the body.'

They think he's dead? Robert's dead? 'No – you've got it wrong.'

'His phone has been switched off since Wednesday – the night of the murder,' Salinsky says. 'That's two whole days ago. None of his credit cards have been used since.'

Does that mean they're right? No. I won't believe it. Can't believe it.

'You hid his body, didn't you, Jenna?' Langton's voice hardens.

'No, I didn't.' All the hours of questioning yesterday, the court this morning, bringing me here. They've been wasting valuable time. 'You have to keep looking for him.'

'You hid his body and when you came back you realised Emily wasn't dead. She'd pressed her alarm. The police were on their way and you panicked. You stuffed your jumper in the washing machine. Tried to clean up. Make it look like an accident, that you'd just found her.'

'I did find her! I found her like that!' I feel like I've been punched in the stomach. This is a nightmare I can't wake from. Why won't they listen to me? 'I love Emily . . . loved Emily!' Tears burn over my split face. Emily with her little dimple. Her laughter. She and her dad eating blueberry pancakes on the weekend.

'You're not helping yourself,' Langton says calmly.

'You're not helping us!' I scream.

She sighs audibly. Snot bubbles out of my bloodied nose. My darling Emily. My poor Robert.

Langton leans back. 'We've searched the house. There's blood, evidence he was dragged.' *No.* 'If you tell us where Robert's body is—'

'He's still alive!' I scream. He has to be. 'Don't stop looking – please!' They can't stop. Desperation claws through me.

Langton pushes on, each word another brick in the wall. 'If you tell us where the body is it will show willingness to cooperate.'

I don't know. I didn't do this.

'Think on it overnight. Next week you'll be taken to a police station, and we will charge you with possession of indecent images of children. Your solicitor will be present.'

I didn't. I couldn't. I retch, but my stomach is empty. Salinsky moves away, physically repulsed. I have to make them understand. Make them listen. I reach for Langton, grab hold of her hand.

'Let go of the officer, prisoner,' Salinsky barks.

Langton waves him off. Stares at me. I will her to believe me, to hear. 'Promise you won't stop looking for him, please?'

Her face pales but she doesn't move. For a moment we are locked like this, each staring into the eyes of the enemy. Then she pulls her hand away.

'*Please.*' I have to keep trying.

Langton nods at him to go, but as the guard holds the door for them she turns back. Just for a second.

Please believe me. Please help Robert.

They leave.

I didn't do this. There's been an awful mistake. I didn't download those photos ... those disgusting things onto my computer. The words snag in my brain.

I didn't ... but someone did. Someone put those images on my laptop. This wasn't a robbery gone wrong. This wasn't a failed kidnap attempt. Someone deliberately put those images on my computer. They deliberately incriminated me. Someone framed me.

Then

'Hey, boo! I made it – Locke's sheep were out again. I thought I wasn't going to get here in time.' I'd had to reverse and come in via the back lane rather than past the hotel. There's no sign of Phoebe's mum yet. I balance the cake on my two arms, dropping the key and my mobile on the hallway table, and push the door closed with my hip. I can still get it set up before she arrives. 'Ready to surprise our fourteen-year-old!' Emily's already grown and changed so much from the kid I met eleven months ago. And I think I've finally got to grips with her mood swings. Christ, if you'd told me a year ago I'd be acting-mum to a teenager I'd have laughed you out the building. There's no reply from the house. Robert's probably upstairs. 'Hello! Darling?'

Silence.

There should be music on. Robert always listens to BBC 6 when he cooks. There's no bubbling pans, no extractor fan. My skin prickles. Something's wrong. A sense, a smell: something familiar that I can't quite catch. The air's disturbed.

'Robert?' My voice echoes over the silent piano in the lounge. Comes back to greet me, tight. A fine net of tension pulls at my shoulders. The cushions are undisturbed on the sofa, the coasters on the coffee table, my iPad next to them. Did I leave it there? Everything looks as it did this morning. But I can sense it. Something's wrong.

The kitchen door is open. The glass is smashed. The glass is smashed. My brain jolts. The glass is smashed. Jump starts.

Oh my god.

A flash of red on the frame. Blood on the wall. 'Robert!' I scream.

My foot slides on something. My heart is drumming against my ribs. It's liquid. Red. Blood. A scream punches out of me.

'Emily! Emily! Oh my god! Emily!'

She's lying on the floor, curled. Her pastel-pink hoodie blooming red. So much blood. Her fine blonde hair dyed dark with it.

The cake falls from my hands. Everything slows. I'm struggling to get to her. The cake hits the floor. Icing explodes into the air. I grab her, pull her to me.

'Emily? Can you hear me? Emily?' Must help her. Is she breathing? She's wet. Warm. There's so much blood. One of our knives is crimson beside her – I pick it up. Drop it. Oh my god. What happened? An accident.

'Robert! Call an ambulance! Robert!' My voice echoes back at me.

Tears blur my vision. Blink. Blink. Find a pulse. My fingers slip. So much blood. Is she breathing? Please, god, let her be breathing. Pull her face against my cheek. No breath. I can't feel breath. What do I do? 'Hold on, my love, hold on.' The knife glistens. Must get help. What do I do? Drag her to the phone. She's so tiny, but so heavy. Fingers slip. 'Stay with me, baby girl, stay with me.'

The phone hangs from the wall. The socket clean out. Ripped. Who did this? An intruder? A thief? Protect Emily. Help Emily. My brain is stuttering.

'Robert! Robert!' My tears bounce into the blood on Emily's face, run new rivulets. Where is he? Red splashes cover the room, the walls, the table, my laptop, the post, a mug.

Must find Robert. Must get help.

My mind swims, surges, drowns. I feel like I'm turning underwater, everything is upside down. I scrabble for my mobile, pressing 999, before my mind catches up. There's no signal inside the house, only WiFi. Shit. Shit. Shit. Where are my keys? Emily's bag lies to the side of her, blood creeping up it like the tide. My hand searches inside. Books. A hair scrunchie. Metal. Keys.

With one arm I rock Emily. 'Shhhh, shhhhh,' I soothe. 'It's going to be okay.' My tears wash into her hair. I pull her close, as if I could breathe her in, as if I could hold her together, as I press the panic alarm on her keys.

Now

'All right, honey. Try to breathe.' The female guard with the mismatched earrings is crouching in front of me.

The police have left. And I'm shaking. Crying. Someone killed Emily. Someone hurt Robert. Someone has him. Then they set me up so it looks like I did this. Why? Who could be that evil?

'Bad news, was it?' The woman gives my shoulder a squeeze.

Understatement. I manage to nod. My head hurts. I want to curl into a ball and be left alone.

'Have you had anything to eat?' she says.

I shake my head. I want her to go away. I want everything to go away.

'Okay,' she says, patting my knee. 'Let's get you some grub and some water. Follow me. You can't go onto the wing in this state. And trust me, you don't want to spend your first night in seg.'

Segregation? This isn't fair. I try to swallow my sobs. It's getting harder to breathe with my nose like this. 'I thought they'd found him.'

'Who, honey?' she says.

'Robert. My fiancé. He's missing.' What if he saw those horrible images on my laptop, what if he thought they were mine? He wouldn't have believed it. He knows me. He loves me.

The guard purses her lips. 'I'm sure he'll turn up – men always come back with their tail between their legs eventually.'

She makes it sound like he's ducked out for a cheeky pint. I want this woman to see me. Not the thing they're trying to make me out to be. 'I'm Jenna.' I wipe my eyes as I follow her back through the rabbit warren of corridors.

'We're not supposed to give our first names,' she says.

A watery sob catches in my throat. It's like we're not human.

'But it seems to me you be needing a friend right now, honey. I'm Sara.'

'Thank you,' I whisper. I unwrap this small act of trust and hold it to me. Sara. A friend.

She leads me to a room just off reception. I gaze longingly at the door outside before it disappears from view.

'You vegetarian?' Sara says. Robert asked me that once. It feels like an age ago. Like it was another world. Part of a magical night. A dream. I shake my head. 'Any religious or dietary restrictions?' I shake my head again. 'Right. Give me two minutes.' She closes the door as she leaves.

I'm in what looks like another small interview room, it's bare apart from tiny flecks of paper strewn over the floor. The last person in here must have shredded whatever paper they were given. Destroyed it.

Sara returns holding a moulded plastic tray like the ones we used to have at school. The smell of hot food hits me. My stomach growls. I didn't realise how hungry I was. I take it. One compartment contains something brown and liquid, lumps of meat and carrots in it. I snatch up the plastic fork and shovel it into my mouth. Beef stew, I think. It scorches the top of my mouth. It's been microwaved, but I don't care. In the other compartment is a small dry bread roll, cold as if it's been in the fridge. It reminds me of airline food. I dunk it into the gloop and scoop it into my mouth. The bandage over my nose makes it difficult to eat without chewing with my mouth open. But I'm so hungry I don't care. Instinct has taken over.

'That'll make you feel better,' Sara nods.

'Thank you,' I manage between mouthfuls. The food hits my empty stomach. It gurgles a response.

Sara is leaning against the door frame. 'Listen, honey, I'm about to go off shift.'

My fork freezes mid-air. She's going to leave me.

Sara checks behind her. I can see Kev still at the reception desk. She lowers her voice. 'You a smoker?'

'No.' Is she offering me a cigarette?

'Say you are anyway,' she says.

'Officer!' Kev's voice rings out across the reception. Sara flinches. 'Is the prisoner ready yet?'

I scrape the remaining liquid off the tray with my fork. 'Done.'

She smiles at me gratefully. 'Yes, sir,' she calls.

Kev is not happy that I'm interrupting his Sudoku. He takes me through more forms. Sara says good night and I wistfully watch her go. She can leave. The envy I feel is physical.

When Kev asks if I'm a smoker I remember what she said and nod. He hands me a packet. Through the plastic I can see it's Rizlas, some loose-leaf tobacco and a lighter. Why do I want this?

'That's £3.60 off your £5 canteen,' he says.

'My canteen?'

'You had no money on you when you arrived,' he says. 'You are loaned an emergency £5, on your card.' Why have I paid for something I don't want? Was Sara lying to me?

He looks at his watch. 'Legally you're entitled to one phone call.' He glances at the camera. I get the distinct feeling Kev has got in trouble for denying this in the past.

Someone has set me up. I should call my lawyer. It's gone nine. Mr Peterson will be home with his family right now. Lucky sod. I want to speak to Mum. 'Thank you.' I can't help but gush.

Kev doesn't smile. He passes me a card, with a startled photo of me printed on the front. Like the worst passport photo you can imagine. 'This is your ID. Enter your prisoner number to dial out.'

'Thank you.' I don't care that he doesn't seem bothered.

Standing in front of the phone on the wall, my hand automatically reaches for my mobile. But of course it's not there. With pooling dread I realise I don't know anyone's numbers. I know Robert's. My heart twists. I would give anything to speak to him. And I know our old landline at the flat we grew up in. But I never learnt Mum's new one by heart when she moved. I close my eyes and try to visualise my mum's mobile. Or my sister's. Zero, seven, something. I think there's a three toward the end of Mum's, and then a six. 'Excuse me?' I say to Kev, who is back consulting his puzzle. 'Can I Google numbers somewhere?'

He scoffs. 'Inmates are not permitted access to the Internet.'

'What, never? But how do you look things up?' How do you find anything out? My mind swims with all the questions I have about prison. What do I do? What should I expect? What are my rights? What should I be doing about my case? What legal help am I entitled to? My fingers itch for my smartphone. Anxiety laps toward me like flood water.

'Try reading a book,' he says. Then adds with a sneer. 'Though you better behave, only those with privileges are allowed library access.'

Tears prick my eyes. I just want to hear my mum's voice. I want to speak to someone who loves me. Who believes me. Someone who's going to tell me I'm all right. How could I have been so stupid as to not have remembered any numbers? They've just always been there, at hand.

'I haven't got all night.' Kev taps his watch.

I can't tell if he's being deliberately obtuse or just doesn't understand that I'm massively out of my depth here. I shouldn't be here. This is all wrong. Stay calm. Don't panic. And then I think of it: Ness's work. She's a personal trainer at

Star Gym. They have radio adverts with those little jingles to the same tune as 'The Teddy Bears' Picnic'. It includes the number. How does it go? I sing it quietly to myself. '*If you go down to Star Gym today, you're sure of admiring eyes …*' Kev glances at me. Block him out. '*Zero, one, three, eight, six, duh- do, duh-do eight five …*' Got it!

I lift the receiver and dial. It starts to ring. Would Ness have gone back to work? She often works nights. *Please be there. Please*. The ring stops. It clicks to connection.

'*You have reached Star Gym, we're not available to answer your call …*'

Beep, beep, beep, sounds the phone in my ear and it cuts dead. 'What happened?' I stare at the receiver. I wanted to leave a message at least.

'Credit's up,' Kev says.

'What?' I stare at him in disbelief. What credit?

'After your smoker's pack, you only had £1.40 left on your canteen.'

'I paid for this call?' I can't believe he didn't explain that.

'Who else is gonna pay for it, Missy? You expect me to fork out of my own wages?'

He didn't say. 'I didn't even speak to anyone.'

'Not my fault you called a mobile.'

'I didn't! It was a landline!'

'Must have been a premium one,' he says.

'Can I borrow some more money?' I look desperately at the phone. Ness might be there, she might have heard my voice. She might have picked up.

'You've had your maximum loan already.'

I've had five quid!

'You can receive money from outside or earn more for your canteen,' he reels off.

If I can't get hold of Ness how can I ask her for money? 'There's money in my bank account. If I could get online I could transfer some over . . .' The words die in my mouth as his face clouds. *Inmates are not permitted access to the Internet.* He thinks I'm taking the piss. This is madness. Like stepping back in time. No mobile, no Internet. I am cut off from everything and everyone.

Sara would have told me that. Would have explained the rules. I finger the smoker's pack in my hand. Unless that was all a lie too.

A gate off the reception room jangles, and I see another guard unlocking it for another prisoner. For a second I think it's Gould, but this woman is smaller, more feminine, in black jogging bottoms and sweatshirt. Her hair wrapped up in a scarf tucked tight to her head. She doesn't smile.

Kev waves a dismissive hand. 'This is Vina. Your Insider. She's gonna take you to your cell.'

My cell. I'm in prison for a crime I didn't commit. Illegal images were found on my computer. My fingerprints are on the murder weapon. Someone set me up. 'Can I see my lawyer – tomorrow?' I add desperately.

Kev grunts an acknowledgement.

The Insider stares at me. Her eyes are empty dark pools. With a sharp gesture of her head she beckons me and I walk toward hell.

Now

The day it happened, the day I was arrested, I left work early to collect Emily's birthday cake. Deb had left the key for me under the flowerpot out back. I let myself in and picked it up. I drove home. There were sheep on the lane to the hotel, so I went the back way. I let myself in. My brain stops there . . . I can't think about this here, now. I force myself to think about after.

When the police arrived, they kept going on about it being Emily's panic alarm that had been activated. The paramedics had wrapped me in a silver blanket. They wouldn't let me stay with Emily. They wouldn't let me back in the house. All these people in white boilersuits were going in and out. There were tents. They kept asking where Robert was. Cars. Ambulances. Sally arrived, but they wouldn't let me speak to her. They said I sent her a text. I don't remember. Then there was a shout. Salinsky brought out a bag containing my wet sweatshirt. I didn't understand why it was wet. They asked if it was mine. Then they took me to the police station. Took my clothes. The shock has shaken everything up in my mind. I need to speak to Mr Peterson. I need to go over this again. I thought it would be okay. I thought they'd realise their mistake. I didn't know about the images on my computer.

I consider telling Vina that I think someone's framed me, but I don't think she's the sharing kind. She doesn't say anything, but walks, barely lifting her feet off the floor, with surprising pace, down the corridor. It gives the impression she's gliding over tiny bumps. She stops at a table. It's also bolted to the floor. Above it, sunk into the wall, are two huge cabinets.

Making a moist sucking tut with her tongue, Vina opens the cabinets, releasing a musty varnish smell, and pulls things from the deep dark-brown shelves. 'This ya clean underwear, yeah?'

Two pairs of socks that were once white, but now nearer grey, are handed over. And two bras, a similar cloudy colour. The fabric feels soft between my fingers from over-washing.

'Your bedding.' Vina piles folded stiff scratchy sheets into my arms. 'And ya blanket.'

'Thank you,' I manage.

'This ya breakfast pack.' She puts a box down on top.

Breakfast? I've just had dinner. 'What happened to porridge, hey?' I try to sound upbeat. I meant it as a joke, like the TV show. Isn't that what they used to call doing time?

Vina sucks on her teeth again. 'You done bird before?'

I dig my fingers into the sheets. Is she asking if I've slept with a woman before? Kev has followed us, a few paces away, leaning against the wall, absorbed in his newspaper. 'Err, I have a fiancé. A male one. It's a very nice offer but I . . .'

She tilts her head and her eyebrows meet. 'Nah, I askin' if you been inside before?'

Oh my god. Did I just proposition her? Or worse, reject her? 'I'm so sorry . . . I . . .' I'm supposed to be making a good impression. I'm supposed to be channelling the male prisoners. I'm supposed to be acting hard. 'I was kidding.'

'Hmm,' she says. She doesn't look convinced.

'Yeah, it's my first time,' I add.

'You got bread, cereal, UHT, and jam in there.' She taps the breakfast pack.

There doesn't appear to be a best-before date. I wonder how long it's been in this cupboard.

'Don't get excited, it's not up ta much. They only cost the guv twenty-seven pence.' She makes the sucking tut noise again. 'You get cold?' she asks.

My hands feel icy already. 'A bit, yeah.'

'Okay.' She checks Kev hasn't looked up. 'You get any burn?'

Does she mean my surname? Something my mum's mates used to say comes back to me. 'Yeah, I got my smoker's pack.'

'Good. I'll have the Amber Leaf, and you get an extra blanket.' She holds her hand out.

Thank you, Sara. I pass her the tobacco and she drops the blanket on top of my pile.

'Hang on to your lighter, they're worth a bob on eBay after,' Vina says. 'What size you?'

'A ten – twelve?' I say.

'Medium,' she sniffs and selects two white T-shirts, two pairs of bottle-green jogging bottoms, and two matching sweatshirts from the pile.

Thank god: clean clothes. I resist the urge to bury my face in them. I'll wear them tomorrow when I see Mr Peterson. Hopefully I can speak to him before the police do. Tell him someone has set me up.

'An ya toiletries.' She pops another pack on top. 'Including toothbrush.' She gives me a pointed look.

Can she smell the sick from earlier? My cheeks burn. 'Thanks.' It comes out as barely a whisper.

'Arr-right, and we done,' she says, closing the cabinets. 'Done now!' she calls louder for Kev's attention.

The guard tucks his paper under his arm. It's the one with my photo on the front. Did Vina see? She hasn't reacted. 'Now then, *Princess.*' The word stings. 'Let's introduce you to your new cellmate.'

What if it's Gould? *I'll kill you! I'll do what you did to that kiddie!* What if it's someone else who has seen the paper?

What if they want to hurt me? I grip the blankets tight, using their bulk to hide my rising and falling chest. Vina is still beside me. I can hear her sucked breaths. Feel her eyes on me. Kev whistles in front of us, as I force myself to put one foot in front of the other. He stops at the gate. His keys are jangled and he selects the right one. I'm about to be locked up.

I look behind me, desperate for a final glimpse of the outside, but all I see are small flakes of paper blowing across the reception floor. Tiny, torn pieces of something that was once whole.

Now

Who would have done this to me? Who would have put that stuff on my computer, who would have killed Emily? It makes no sense. For as long as I'm here it's too easy to kid myself that Emily's still alive. That she and Robert are living out there, normally; I just can't see them. I'm exhausted. I need to sleep. I need to think. I need to survive tonight.

With each gate we reach, and there are a lot, the noise from the cells grows louder. It bounces and barrels toward us, an indistinct clamour, like walking into a community swimming pool full of screaming kids. Vina doesn't bat an eyelid. I can't imagine ever growing used to this. It's cacophonous. Constant. It sets my teeth on edge. I grip my parcel of blankets like a barrier, hiking it up to shield as much of my face as possible.

Vina is looking at me with curiosity. Is she thinking she knows the face but can't think from where? I don't want to offend her. 'How many people are there here?'

'Fallenbrook was built to hold nine hundred *reprobates*.' Kev draws the word out like he's pulling it from stinking wet mud. 'But we currently got one thousand one hundred and three,' he says.

The number swims in front of me and I try to make it mean something. Mesh it together with the noise I can hear.

'It's inhumane,' Vina snaps.

Surely he meant they'd extended since it was built?

'Animals are treated better,' she says.

'We should never have stopped shipping cons off to the colonies,' he sighs, as if our very presence pains him.

My spine stiffens. 'And then what would you do for a job?' The words are out before I can stop them.

Vina hoots.

'Shut up unless you want to be on basic,' he snaps, but he doesn't look at me.

'She got you,' Vina says with a laugh.

'Don't go getting ideas, Vina.' His voice is hard, angry, trying to claw back control. 'You don't want people to think you're like *her* – it won't end well.'

Does he know about the images they found on my computer? Will that be released in the newspapers? The stringy beef in my stomach flops from side to side. *Pick your battles, Jenna.* I need to change the subject. 'We nearly there?'

Kev doesn't bother to answer. He doesn't have to. The lofty corridors of the old house suddenly splinter up and away into a triple-height wing. It's as high as the whole building. We stop as Kev takes out his key to open the final gate.

It reminds me of standing in front of the lion enclosure in the safari park we took Emily to. Except there you could see trees, and the sky. Here all I can see is acres of sickly yellow paint like congealed custard. Landings run round each floor, nets to catch falling possessions or prisoners strung between them like cobwebs. Along each landing, standing like upright coffins, are metal doors to the cells. Thin windows slash into them so everyone on the outside can see in, and everyone on the inside can see out. I see with relief that they're all locked in. If Charlie Gould is here, she's locked up. Unless she's waiting in my cell . . .

A fat sleek rat scurries along the edge of the wing and I almost scream. Neither Vina nor Kev react. Did they see it? Vina catches my eye. Yes. Yes, they did, and it's normal.

Now we're closer, the words of the prisoners are clearer. They're talking to each other:

'*Our Justine's gonna be five next week . . .*'

'*Starting school, then.*'

'*They do it at four now. Too much too young . . .*'

'*And I told him he's got to step up.*'

'*Beyoncé's twins are in the Mirror. Pretty little things . . .*'

'*Lend it to me in Association?*'

Someone's singing. It sounds like a hymn.

> '*. . . Swift to its close ebbs out life's little day;*
> *Earth's joys grow dim, its glories pass away;*
> *Change and decay in all around I see –*
> *O Thou who changest not, abide with me.*'

And then a sound that chills me to the bone floats from one of the cells. Someone is watching television. The news. '*Gloucestershire resident Jennifer Burns was taken to prison today, after being charged with the murder of her fourteen-year-old stepdaughter. Press are calling the thirty-two-year-old recruitment consultant The Blonde Slayer. Her fiancé, wealthy hotelier Robert Milcombe, is still missing and police would like to hear from anyone who was in the area of . . .*'

Panic swarms inside me like angry wasps. They'll show photos, won't they? Like the newspaper. The other prisoners will know it's me. I dip my head forward, suddenly thankful that Gould has obliterated half my face. I need to change my appearance. I need to hide.

But neither Kev nor Vina show signs of having heard the report.

And though I want to keep my head down, I can't help but look up, up into the lofty, looming wing.

'It's huge.' Despite being a triple-height room, it feels airless, and smells metallic, stale, of cheap, sharp antiseptic. It catches in my throat.

'Stop dawdling.' Kev has the gate open. 'My shift ends soon, and if you're not in your cell by then, you'll be checked into seg.'

Vina pushes me from behind. 'Come on, man.'

I force my feet to move. Three days ago I was safe at home, with the man and the young girl that I love. But someone tore that life to shreds. Each step reverberates through me, up, out into the wing, and echoes back, slamming against me with force. As hollow as I am.

Now

I don't watch as the door is bolted behind me. Can't. I grip my blankets tight. The cell is smaller than the room with the magnetic chair in it. Claustrophobia tickles at my edges. It's narrow, a high barred slim window at one end. A toilet, no seat, stained black from mould, in the corner to my right. Someone has stretched a sheet of what looks like the paper roll on a doctor's couch in front of it from wall to wall, a flimsy attempt at a privacy screen. Someone who is sitting on the top bunk bed in front of me.

Thin, young, only late teens, with black hair pulled back into a severe ponytail, she doesn't look intimidating. But I still can't move. She's wrapped up in blankets, a magazine resting on the pillow over her lap.

'Telly's broken,' she says.

I nod.

'Supposed to have a new one five days ago but they're dragging their heels.' She sounds stronger than she looks. Her green sweatshirt balloons out from the top of her blankets.

'I'm keeping the top bunk,' she says.

'Sure,' I nod. I can't make my feet move. The door is bolted behind me. I'm locked in with a stranger. Voices carry outside. It's still so noisy. I shouldn't be here.

'What you done to your face?' She points at her own pixie features.

My stinging nose bristles. 'Fell,' I say. I can't let anyone know I was attacked, they'll want to know why.

'I usually turn the light off in a bit – this lot wakes early.' She jerks a thumb at the wall, to which she has stuck photos and hearts that look like they've been cut from magazines.

She means the other inmates. I force myself to move toward the bed. The mattress is thin, the frame basic.

The girl above shifts on her bunk and the frame creaks. I can smell her. Radox, and is that a hint of nicotine? I said I smoked. Have they put me in with a smoker? She's still talking.

'The screws can turn the light on and off from outside, like. You know, if they want to do a headcount or you're giving trouble or that. And if you piss them off they leave it on all night.'

They leave the light on all night? Isn't that one of the ways they torture people in Guantanamo Bay?

'But you won't be pissing them off, will you?' She pauses to peer down at me.

My scalp prickles. She feels so close. I want to scream. It takes everything I have to shake my head.

She tuts, dissatisfied with the inadequacy of my response. But my tongue is dry and heavy in my mouth. Huffing, she rolls over, making the whole bunk squeak and rock. Her magazine rustles. I can't look at her. I focus on stretching the sheet over the mattress, piling the blankets up. I'm so thankful for the extra one. Sitting on my bed I have some privacy. I take off the soiled T-shirt and joggies, and replace them quickly with my new set. I put the jumper over the T-shirt; it's too cold to sleep in anything less. I'll work out what to do with the dirty clothes tomorrow. I want to brush my teeth, but I don't want to use the bathroom in front of this woman. Can't face it.

'You done then?' her voice comes from above.

I want to say I need a minute. That I haven't got used to it yet. But I'm too scared what will come out if I speak. I make a noise, a grunt.

The woman above sighs, the bed rocks again and then the power cuts. I panic as everything is plunged into dark. My bed rocks and creaks as she shuffles back into position. For a second I can see nothing. Then the light from the moon begins to trace the room.

People are still talking outside.

'Shut up!' shouts more than one voice.

My heart is hammering in my chest. I roll over, pulling the blankets up tight around me. If the woman above tries to hurt me in the night, I should at least be alerted by the bed moving. But soon I can hear her breathing slow, and the gentle rasp of her snores. I can't really be frightened of someone who sounds like a cat purring, can I?

I screw my eyes shut. How has this happened? How did I get here? I open my mouth in a silent howl of pain. I don't move, don't make a sound, just let the tears wash over me, and into the stiff surface of my pillow.

Now

I barely sleep. Fitful starts throughout the night. Emily runs laughing through my mind. I don't deserve sleep. I don't deserve rest. For as long as I am in here the real killer is free. The real killer may have Robert. What have I done to deserve this? Someone killed Emily and destroyed my life. Who would have done this to us? Someone unhinged that I slighted in some way? You read about people who accidentally cut someone up on the road and the driver of the other car follows them and kills them. Stalkers who target people for random reasons. Perhaps it's someone we rejected from work? There have been people I've interviewed who I wasn't comfortable with recommending to any of our clients. One guy was so creepy, so unnerving in the way he stared at me when it was just the two of us in the room, I wanted to shower myself clean after the interview. No way was I going to recommend him to anyone. Could it have been him? There's something I'm still not seeing. A piece of the puzzle that will make it all make sense.

A cry from one of the other cells cuts into my thoughts and my heart thumps loudly in my chest. I grip my blankets. We're locked in. No one can get out of their cell to hurt me. The girl above me grunts and shifts in her sleep. The bed rocks. And as the adrenaline floods round my body it crystallises my thoughts. Sharpening my focus on the day Emily died. It must be someone we know. Someone who had access to our house. Someone who wasn't expecting Emily to be home. Or someone who arranged to meet her there? But who? My conscience fights with the logic. There's no other way. It has to be someone who knew me and Robert well. Danger must have been close and I never sensed it. Familiar faces twist like funhouse-mirror reflections in my tired mind. Who could have done this? Who did I get wrong? Someone betrayed us.

Somewhere in the early hours of the morning, I guess, when the moans and crying from the other cells have grown silent, I fall asleep.

For a moment when I wake I don't remember where I am. Then it all comes rushing back to me, like the morning after Nan died. I am in a bunk bed in a prison cell. Emily is dead. Robert is missing. Someone betrayed us. And I can hear my cellmate weeing.

I roll over.

'Hey! What about some privacy!' The tiny brunette is sitting on the loo, the paper screen not hiding the fact her rucked up sweatshirt was covering a bump. She's pregnant. They lock pregnant women up? Jesus. She's a kid. 'What, you never seen anyone take a piss before?'

I was staring. 'Sorry,' I mumble and roll over to face the wall. It's a dirty white colour, pockmarked where the paint's given way and the brick is visible underneath. Someone has scratched into it: *Mandi was ere.* I hope you got out, Mandi.

There's a flush. 'All right – I'm done,' the girl says.

I can't believe I slept. 'What time is it?'

'Seven thirty,' she says. 'You did well for your first night – you been in before?' There's a small square of reflective plastic above the breakfast-bowl-sized sink and she's yanking her hair up into its tight ponytail.

'No. First time,' I say. Is it the done thing to ask what someone's in for? I'd quite like to know who I'm sharing a cell with. 'I'm Jenna.'

'Kelly,' the girl says. 'Probs should've said that last night, shouldn't I? I get grumpy when I get tired. And they said you'd be here much earlier.'

I think of the police's accusations and my gut twists. I should say sorry, explain. I'm rooted to the bed.

'So how long you got?' she says.

'Err, I don't know. I've got to appear in court again next week – enter my plea.' I try to remember what Mr Peterson said when we came out the Magistrates' Court. Everything happened so fast.

'Crown?' she asks, and I realise she's referring to the court. I nod.

'They do them over the video link,' she says. 'Saves them staff and bother for going the two hours back to Gloucester.'

So I won't even get to see the outside world? But then I won't have to go back in the sweatbox either, I think with relief.

'That's where they did me,' Kelly is saying. 'The judge did me up right and proper. Eight months. Eight months for nicking a bottle of wine – how was I supposed to know it was over two hundred quid's worth. I mean, who pays that much for a bottle of booze?' I think of Judith and David's cellar, their parties. 'It weren't even that good.' She shakes her head. 'It was probably the hormones, you know.' She turns to me. 'I don't nick stuff normally. But that's what my baby daddy gave me: he's fucked off and I've got a bloody sentence, and a life sentence.' She pats her stomach and laughs.

I don't like to ask how old she is – eighteen, maybe? *Only a few years older than Emily*, I think with a twinge. 'Err, when you due?' I say. Surely they'll let her out before then.

She looks sad for a moment. 'Twenty-first of June. Gemini–Cancer cusp. He'll be trouble.' She smiles.

Four days after I'm supposed to get married. I can't think about that right now.

'So how 'bout you – what you done then?'

Kev's words come to me without thinking. 'Party girl. Drugs,' I say.

She looks warily at my clothes.

'I'm clean.' I reassure her.

She nods. 'You never know who you're gonna end up with in here. Hopefully it's you and me till baby comes – I like to know where I stand.'

I'll be out before then. I have to be.

'You wanna use the bathroom?' She unpegs the paper sheet and holds it open.

I remember the black uncovered toilet bowl. I can catch the sour stench of blocked drains. I feel sick again.

'You got to get a wiggle on,' Kelly says. 'Thirty minutes till Free Flow.'

'Free Flow?' I place my feet on the floor, tilt my head forward. That feels a bit better.

'Yeah, Free Flow, when they unlock for those of us who've got work, education, appointments and that. Happens four times a day. 8.30 a.m. Then 11.30 a.m. back to cell for lunch – we usually get a baguette and a packet of crisps. Delivered to the door, or we fetch it from the wing if they're feeling lazy and we get an extra five-minute walk about.' She lists it off with her fingers. '2 p.m. Free Flow again, then again at 4.30 p.m. so you can get back for dinner. You get that off a tray in the wing, and your breakfast box at the same time. Then we eat in here. So I like to keep it clean, yeah?' She looks at my stained clothes again.

I nod.

'Then 5.30 p.m. it's lock up till 8.30 a.m. again.'

'But what if I don't have education or work?' Anxiety blossoms inside me. The walls close in. This room is about four metres by two and shrinking.

'Well,' Kelly says, 'we're supposed to get an hour's Association once a day. Where you can see the chemist, apply for any jobs or education, have a shower, make phone calls and play pool and that. They also let you out in the yard.' I think of the sky. 'It's supposed to be in the morning. But it varies. They're always short-staffed and sometimes we only get thirty minutes, or nothing at all.'

'So we're locked in for the whole time?' I thought we'd be allowed on the wing. Out for exercise. Even with Association, that's twenty-three hours inside this cell. My throat begins to close. I can't breathe.

'There's roll-call as well – that's when they check none of us have dug a tunnel and escaped.' She laughs at her own joke. 'It happens at random, and they often get us to stand outside the cell for the head count. So you can stretch your legs then,' she says as if this is a genuine bonus.

I shake my head. I can't do this.

'You not had your Induction yet?' Kelly says. Then taps her palm against her forehead. 'What am I saying – it's Saturday, isn't it? Bloody baby brain. I'd forget to put my own head on.'

Induction?

Her face shifts, 'Oh mate, Friday's the worst day to get banged up. You won't get your Induction till Monday now, which means they won't let you out till then. We almost never get Association on the weekends because the screws fuck off with their families.'

'What about you?' I suddenly don't want to be alone in this cell.

Kelly looks sad. 'Sorry, bruv. I'm signed up for the Adventists today, and the Methodists tomorrow. I ain't much one for god-bothering, but it's better than being in here, you know?'

I nod my head dumbly. I'm going to be locked in a cell on my own. All weekend. 'I need to see my lawyer,' I say.

'Come Monday. You got to find the number-one cleaner – they have all the forms. Get them done, and in. Apply for the lot – I did. Anything's better than going stir crazy in here. Am

I right?' She's buzzing around the room. Under the small desk she has neatly folded all her clothes. She catches me looking.

'You lucky I'm here,' she says. 'I disinfected this whole place when I moved in.' She points at the kettle. 'You know how many people have hepatitis in here? Dirty fucks.'

My stomach turns again. I jump up, covering my mouth.

'Oh shit! Get it in the toilet!' Kelly shouts.

I make it just in time. My eyes burn. My throat hurts. I must be ill.

Kelly is buzzing round the cell. 'Trust me to get a puker. Here.' She passes me a plastic cup of water.

'Thank you.' I gratefully rinse my mouth.

'Where's your toothbrush?' she says. I should probably stop her going through my stuff, she said she was a thief, but I have nothing of value anyway.

When she hands me my toothbrush, and some toothpaste from her bunk, I feel guilty. 'The stuff they give you is shit. Borrow mine. You can pay me back when your canteen comes in.' Her thin face is very pretty when she smiles. 'Fifteen minutes,' she says, looking at her watch. 'You gonna be okay?'

I nod. I'll have to be.

'Okay – you can use the bathroom,' she says. It's an instruction as much as an offer. This is a small space and I must smell pretty bad by now.

I focus on getting myself as clean as possible. I rinse my face under the tap, and pull my lank hair back with a spare band from Kelly. I'll owe her for that too. I reserve the set of clothes I slept in for pyjamas for the time being, and change into the spare clean set in case Kev did request a meeting with Mr Peterson.

'Do we get visitors on Saturdays?' I say.

'Thursdays, Saturdays and Sundays, while you're on remand.' Kelly reels it off like a pro. 'You have to get visitors on your cleared list. Same with telephone numbers – it takes a couple of weeks for probation to clear numbers, then you can call those people,' she says.

I should be writing this down, there's so much to remember. I wish there was a handbook or a guide or something. But there's nothing. 'What about my lawyer?'

'Theys can come Monday through Friday. They ain't likely to come in today though.' She shakes her head as I smooth my joggies as best I can. 'Would you wanna be working on the weekend?'

I won't get to see Mr Peterson till Monday at the earliest. That's okay. It's just two days till he can get me out. Just two days till I can explain that I didn't do this. That someone has falsely incriminated me. There are eleven hundred women here. If I keep my head down I can avoid Charlie Gould. The thought of her screaming face terrifies me. I hope she's in seg. I hope I never see her again.

Kelly keeps talking throughout, and from the voices from the other cells, she's not alone. The whole place is gearing up for Free Flow. It's a welcome distraction from my thoughts. God knows how I did it, but sleep has made me feel slightly better. At least mentally. I just need to speak to Mr Peterson and explain the stuff on my computer proves someone is trying to frame me. That someone else has done this.

'Two minutes,' Kelly sings. Her enthusiasm is infectious. She reminds me of Emily, and the thought makes my heart ache.

There's a noise at the door, and the little flap that covers the window is opened from the outside. Kelly looks surprised.

The square jaw and disembodied mouth of a male guard I've not seen before appears at it. 'Burns. Appointment.'

'But it's Saturday!' Kelly sounds panicked.

Kev must have come through for me. 'Don't worry,' I say. 'Ready.' I stand by the door as he unlocks it.

The guard's eyes sparkle with that knowing arrogance of a good-looking lad. His shirt looks like it's deliberately one size too small to emphasise the V of his shoulders and abs. He runs a lascivious gaze up over me, seemingly unbothered by the bruised mess that is my face, and I pull my jumper down as far as it'll go. I follow him as he struts away.

'Hey Ryan – when you gonna unlock us?' a flirtatious voice calls from one of the cells.

'Calm down, ladies. I won't be long.' He winks in the direction of the cell. Is that appropriate?

Kelly and I are on the top tier of the atrium, so I have to follow Ryan down the flights of open stairs to reach the bottom, and he starts unlocking gates. I thought we'd be headed back to the room I met the police in, but we must be going somewhere else.

It's only when we pass the toilet Sara let me use, that I realise where we are. Apprehension swells in my bruised stomach. Kelly mentioned hepatitis. I think of sitting naked on the magnetic chair. Or using the fork Sara gave me. Were those things clean? By the time we reach the door I'm shaking. This is not a meeting with my lawyer. I've been summoned back to the doctor. On a Saturday. As if it's an emergency. As if something is very wrong.

Now

'You're pregnant.'

I stare at him. I hear the words but I can't seem to understand them. It's like they're sounds crashing, like fists against the side of the sweatbox.

'Do you know when you had your last period?'

I shake my head. 'I can't be. I'm on the Pill.' I have been since Ness put me on it at twelve.

The doctor sighs. 'Some women do find it difficult to manage regular contraception.'

What is he insinuating? 'I take it regularly every morning when I get up. Always have done. I tri-cycle my packets . . .' I stop as the implication hits me. I haven't bled for three months.

He looks unconvinced. 'Have you had any sickness or diarrhoea recently?'

My blood runs cold. There was that takeaway we had at Robert's friend's house. We all had food poisoning afterwards. When was that – two, three months ago? If I could just check my diary in my handbag I could work it out. But of course I don't have that. 'I . . . I had food poisoning. I was sick.' I must have vomited the Pill back up before it worked.

'And when was that?' the doctor says, sounding bored.

'I . . . I'm not sure.' I need to see my diary. 'Two months ago, I think.'

'Then – I think – you are two months pregnant,' the doctor says.

That's as scientific as it gets? 'Can't you tell?'

'We'll know more at your three-month scan. I'll put you in the system.'

I frantically count in my head. In seven months from now it'll be October. 'But we're getting married in June,' I say. Seventeenth of June, the happiest day of my life. I won't fit in my dress. *That's a stupid thing to think.*

'Well that's something,' he says drily.

We. Pregnant. I clutch my stomach. There's a baby in there. Part of Robert. He'll be so happy! A younger brother or sister for Emily to— I blink. The breath catches in my throat. Emily's gone. Robert is gone. 'I can't be. Not here. Not now. Not like this.'

Did they know last night? Is that why they put me with Kelly? Is that why I was sick? Morning sickness. Oh god, I was sick in the van. I was thrown around in the van. I was attacked.

'Is everything all right? Will the Pill have hurt the baby?' I was punched.

'The Pill will not harm the foetus.'

'But I was attacked – I fell on my stomach,' I say, desperate.

'There's no reason to believe there is anything wrong, but we'll know more when you've had a scan,' he says.

What happens now? Do pregnant women get convicted of murder? Are people accused of having child pornography allowed to keep their baby? *I didn't do it.* I have to get out of here. I have to get to fresh air. I have to get my baby out of here. I stand up.

'Sit down, Jennifer.' The doctor eyes the alarm on the wall.

I'm not a threat. I'm no danger. I'm in danger. Charlie Gould's words replay in my head. *I'll kill you! I'll do what you did to that kiddie!* She's going to kill me. She's going to kill my baby. Emily's broken, bloodied body flickers through my mind, merges with a photo of her as a baby in her crib. Blood everywhere.

'I have to get out of here.' Before he can stop me, I'm at the door. I pull the handle. It's locked. It rattles.

The doctor is next to the alarm.

'Jennifer, I need you to sit down. I understand this is a shock.'

'This isn't a shock – it's wonderful. It's the best news. Robert will be happy.' If he's still alive. I choke back tears. It wasn't supposed to be like this. We are getting married. Robert's parents would probably prefer us to go ahead before the baby is born, but we could put the wedding back. Wait so Emily can carry her baby brother or sister down the aisle. The image in my mind freezes, shudders, blurs like a damaged film reel. That's not going to happen. That's never going to happen. 'You can't keep me here. You can't lock up pregnant women.' I think of Kelly.

'You're not the first woman to arrive here and not know she was pregnant,' the doctor says. He makes it sound like a personal failing.

How was I supposed to know? How could I have prepared for this?

'And you wouldn't be the first who's thought a jury would view them more leniently if they were expecting.' He peers over his glasses.

I stare at him in shock. 'You think I planned this? I was on the Pill!' My hands cradle my belly. It doesn't feel different. It doesn't feel like there's anything in there. Is it . . .

'I won't ask you to sit again, Jennifer.' The doctor's hand hovers over the alarm.

They bundled Charlie Gould to the ground. Forcefully. Face down. Stomach down. Meekly, I return to my chair.

The doctor blows air out over his face so his thin fringe flutters.

'We'll need to request a hospital visit for you.' He sits back down at his side of the desk. 'Check how far along you are for sure. Check everything is okay. Like I said, I'll put in an application.'

An application? 'Surely I should go now – I was assaulted. My baby could be—'

He waves a dismissive hand to silence me. He's not listening. Not caring what I have to say. How many times has he delivered what should be happy news like this? 'What will happen to the baby?' My voice is shaking again. They can't force you to abort, can they? A wave of nausea punches out from my centre, as if the baby wants to alert me to the risk.

It's not fair. It's not fair that Emily is gone and that I am still here. Me and my baby. Robert needs to know. 'I need to tell my partner.'

The doctor is making a tutting sound. 'You can telephone him this afternoon.'

I wish. Even if Association goes ahead that's not going to happen. 'No, you don't understand. He's missing.' And there's blood. They think I hurt him. They think I killed him.

'Not all fathers are reliable, I'm afraid,' he says.

It makes it sound like he's skipped out on me. I blink. I have to work out what happened in our house, work out who did this. I have to make the police believe me. I have to find Robert. I have to tell him he's going to be a father.

I've been framed. I'm in prison. I'm pregnant.

Then

'I'd kill for a gin, darling.' Robert's mother flops onto her cream sofa. And for a moment, though she is immaculate as ever in a Peter Pan-collared cream shift dress that brings out the golden flecks in her hair, the small woman looks more like her teenage granddaughter than a sophisticated lady in her sixties.

I giggle. 'Have one then – it's gone four.' Robert's dad's drinks cabinet intimidates me. I wouldn't dare touch it myself. It looks like double doors to another room, but the polished walnut front opens out into a built-in bar. Well, it's as big as a bar. They never call it that. Crass, I guess. The doors are lined with polished chrome shelves displaying an array of specialist glasses, shakers, and even little sterling-silver cocktail sticks. On the internal shelves are a wide range of liquors, including at least five types of gin.

I take the vintage Penguin paperback from my handbag and see Judith's eyes light up. Her lips a deep berry-red smile. It's one of the green ones: Agatha Christie's *Death Comes At The End*. One of the only ones she's missing.

'Oh my goodness, Jennifer – you are clever! Where did you find it?' she cries as I hand it to her.

'I promised I'd keep an eye out for it.' I've been looking for weeks. Ever since she showed me the collection she keeps in her dedicated study. The books are the only old things in the whole house. Everything else is shiny and new and flawless – David had it all redone by a famous Swedish designer when they got married. Robert jokes that by the time they finish re-painting it white each year, they have to start again at the other end, like the Golden Gate Bridge. 'I found it in the second-hand bookstore in Cirencester.'

Judith smooths a dog-eared corner. 'How much do I owe you?'

'It was only a pound, please don't worry about it,' I say, embarrassed. She knows I can afford to buy a second-hand book, right? But I see by her face that she didn't mean anything by it. I don't think Judith has a strong grasp of the value of money. I guess she's never had to, growing up in a place like this. David likes to tell people with great pride how he saved the big house and the family fortune after he married her and developed the hotel complex, catapulting them into the social stratosphere.

'Thank you,' Judith beams.

'This calls for a celebration drink!' I say.

The smile drops from her lips and she jumps up, busying herself plumping an already plump cushion. 'Oh, I can't.'

I laugh. 'Course you can. Sounds like you've had a busy day.' She's just finished telling me about the committee meetings she's been attending, the charity lunch at David's Freemasons club, and how she and David are meeting their art curator to look at pieces for the new hotel first thing in the morning. I think it's wonderful they're still so involved in the family business, even after they've retired.

'I'd better not,' she says swiftly. Then returns the cushion to the others, turning it once – I realise – so the fabric grain is aligned with the rest. She gives a slightly forced laugh. 'You know men, darling. Only David is allowed to use the drinks cabinet.'

I hadn't noticed, but now she's said it I guess he does always make people's drinks. I assumed he was being polite. Fetching a glass for his wife, his son, me. 'I'm sure he won't mind,' I say.

'Won't mind what?' Robert appears in the kitchen doorway, wearing a blue-and-white striped butcher's apron, and a white chef's hat.

'Oh Robert, I thought you were your father for a second.' Judith clutches her hand to her chest. He must have made her jump. Something stirs inside me.

'I'm not Robert!' he cries. 'Hurdy-gurdy, gurdy!' He waves a pair of tongs around.

'What are you playing at!' Judith laughs.

'You're the Swedish chef from the Muppets!' I cry.

'Exactly! And that's why we're the perfect match, Jenna.' He swoops in for a kiss. He smells smoky from the barbecue.

'Careful – don't touch the sofa!' I grab the tongs before they connect with the cream fabric. Like the rest of Robert's parents' house it's painfully expensive. It'd be a nightmare to get a stain out. My mum's flat has wipe-clean lino in the kitchen, and swirly patterned carpet in the hallway. It hides a multitude of sins, whereas everything shows here.

Robert loops his arm round my shoulders and pulls me close. 'Sod the sofa, and give me some sugar!'

'Language, please, darling, we don't use jargon in this house,' Judith chides. 'Talk properly.'

Properly? Was that a dig at me? I'm being overly sensitive. She was teasing Robert. That's all. Judith doesn't know anything about where I grew up. And she probably wouldn't care. I have to stop feeling like I'm about to be caught out. Being in this design magazine of a house just makes me feel nervous.

'Oh my,' Judith says. 'I haven't brought in the crudités!' And she dashes out to fetch a dish of sculpted raw vegetables and hummus. Carrot sticks, all perfectly the same length and width, and radishes lined up in neat little rows. This is where Robert gets his precision from. After years of working in the hospitality industry a tube of Pringles isn't going to cut it.

'Lovely!' Robert grabs a cucumber spear.

'Thank you.' I'm still not comfortable enough to help myself, even though the brightly coloured veg is making me hungry.

'David, darling!' Judith trills. She trained at RADA before she met David, and it's apparent in her posture, her voice. She has the presence of someone much bigger than the delicate five-foot woman in front of us.

Through the orangery, I can see Emily turning cartwheels in the garden. Still practising her swim routines, even on land. David appears in front of her, obscuring my view. Robert is the spit of him. David still has the square jaw and full head of hair, but his skin is softer, weathered, like Sally's prized Hermès handbag. I can see Robert will still be handsome in forty years' time. I kiss him. Imagine us together then. Emily, and maybe another kid or two of our own, will be grown-ups. We might even have grandkids.

'Twenty minutes and we'll be ready.' David walks in and takes his wife's hand.

Judith, demure, blushes and looks delighted. Still so touched to receive attention from the man she loves. Couple goals. This is the perfect family. I can't believe they're letting me be part of it.

'Shall I lay the table?' I finally pluck up the courage to offer.

'Oh, that would be lovely, darling,' Judith says.

'Who fancies a Pimms? Probably the last of the season.' David strides over to the polished walnut bar. He opens the door and selects a cut-crystal highball.

I glance at Judith, but she's turned away, straightening more cushions.

'Might as well make the most of it – we'll be onto the mulled wine before you know it!' Robert says.

Judith picks up a carrot stick.

'No, darling,' David says, and she puts it back down. 'We're watching our weight.' He smiles at me.

But Judith is tiny. Barely skin and bone.

'Do we have any cucumber?' David asks.

'Use these.' Robert offers a green stick from the plate.

His mum makes a soft clucking noise and bats his hand away. 'Don't be silly, darling.'

'And ice?' David asks, helping himself to a celery stick and a healthy scoop of dip.

What about his weight?

'I'll fetch the bucket.' Judith smiles at me. 'Could you help me reach down the placemats, Jennifer?'

'Of course.' I feel an absurd pride in being asked to fetch something.

'The cotton ones, darling, for outside,' Judith says. 'And maybe a few of the blankets – in case we get chilly.'

They're in the ancient pine dresser that lines the dining-room wall. I run my fingers along its smooth edge. Reach past framed photos of Robert growing up. Pin neat in his uniform. Wearing a straw hat that's ridiculously cute. It's a far cry from my own school's haphazard attempts at uniformity. I had a jumper, I think, and an old black skirt of Mum's. There's another of Robert, posing with his Masters scroll. Emily, as a baby, in David's arms at her christening, swathed in the white lace gown Robert's great, great, great, grandfather wore.

Outside I can hear Emily singing the lyrics to the latest song she and Phoebe are learning. The scented smoke drifts inside, carried on the early autumn breeze. David is right, this probably will be the last barbecue of the year. And I'm so happy, I think for a moment I might cry. I never imagined a family like this. I'd never seen one. The love, the care, the joy. They're so lucky to have each other. I'm so lucky just to witness it. But they've made me welcome. I feel at home.

It's only when I carry the placemats outside that I see everyone has a glass of Pimms, except Judith.

Now

The same guard, Ryan, is lounging against the wall outside the doctor's room, as if he's waiting behind the bike sheds at school. He gives me a leering grin. 'Cheer up, love, bet I can make you smile.'

But we aren't at school and this isn't some trifling matter. Irritation bubbles over. 'Should you be hitting on prisoners?'

'As if I'd be interested in you.' His lip curls, and his gaze lingers on my unwashed hair.

'I don't want your or anyone else's interest.'

'Bent bitch,' he snorts, and starts to swagger back toward the wing. Did he think that would really work? Does it with others? I'm glad I haven't washed my hair, not least because it makes it look darker than the blow-dried photo of me in the newspaper. I need to do everything I can to not look like that woman – like me – while I'm in here. No one can know I'm the 'Blonde Slayer'. Especially not now.

I slide a hand under my jumper and feel my stomach. Is it bigger? Have I just not noticed? It's puffy, but I just thought that was a touch of IBS. Kept meaning to go gluten-free in the last few weeks, but with Robert's work, the wedding planning and Emily's approaching birthday it's been so busy. I swallow the lump in my throat. I need a bigger jumper. Adding bulk to my frame will help. I want to keep my baby hidden for as long as possible. Being pregnant in prison can only be a weakness. It'll be my secret for now. If I can speak to Mr Peterson, if I can explain that I've been framed, then they can get me out before it really starts to show.

Ryan is a few paces ahead, apparently over my rejection. He's whistling to himself, hands in his pockets. It gives me a chance to get to grips with the layout of this place.

The triple-height wing is in the centre of the building. It's surrounded on three sides, like a horseshoe, with non-prisoner areas that look to be made up of rooms and offices. Through grubby windows in doors I see people slumped at desks, staring at computers. At one end of the horseshoe is the doctor's surgery that we've just left, and at the other end, back toward the cells, are signs for Education, and a Careers Advisor. Some rooms have two doors, one from this side, and one that presumably goes straight onto the wing side of the prison. But we don't take any of these, instead walking the long way round. It feels like rooms have been added, requisitioned and reassigned in a haphazard manner, over time.

'When was the prison built?'

Ryan jumps. He'd obviously forgotten I was here. 'Eighteen hundred and something.' His speech has an affected velvety tone. Like he thinks I will enjoy it.

Chunks of plaster are missing from the walls, and bundles of wires run from plug sockets out here into offices, through doors that are apparently kept open for this purpose. It looks patched. A small dated phone booth hangs on the wall, covered in dust, seemingly unused. A draught pushes at the heavy wooden door to our left, whose sign proclaims Library. It rumbles as we pass, as if something inside is trying to get out.

A scream reaches us as we approach the wing. I flinch.

Ryan looks at me from the corner of his eyes. Runs his tongue over his teeth. 'They used to hang prisoners here.' He holds up his hand as if gripping a noose, goes cross-eyed, and lets his tongue loll from his mouth.

A creak sounds behind us and I can't help but imagine the trapdoor swinging open beneath my feet, the heavy rope tightening against my neck. 'That's awful.' Of course the prison was built before they abolished the death penalty.

He looks delighted at the reaction, a cruel expression obliterating any attractive features on his face. 'I'd have made a wicked executioner.' He makes a chopping action with his hand.

The noise of the wing is almost a comfort, when he unlocks the gate. I don't want to be alone with this man. Kev from the arrival suite is unlocking each of the cells, starting at the far end of the wing, and prisoners are starting to mill outside their doors. Thankfully no one pays much attention to me. What is this? Why's everyone out?

As if he can read my thoughts, Ryan is too close behind me. His breath on my hair. 'Quick smart,' he says. 'Roll-call in five and you don't want to be away from your cell.'

Roll-call – like Kelly said. Do I have to do something – call my name, wear anything? Those women who are outside their cells don't look bothered by anything, and are not all dressed alike. In fact, I see now that many have their own clothes on, among the dark-green regulation tracksuits.

Ryan obviously sees me staring. I feel his hand rest in the small of my back. 'Those are for good girls,' he says. 'Or very naughty ones.'

I pull away, my skin burning from where he touched me. I walk quicker.

'That's it,' he calls. 'Hurry back to your cell – it's one of my favourites!'

I stop. Turn. 'What does that mean?'

'The execution suite was right here in the wing,' he grins. 'Handy, huh?'

A shiver runs through me. This must be a wind-up.

But something tells me from the delighted look on Ryan's face that he isn't lying. 'Over all three floors it was. The gallows suspended in the top cell, the trapdoor in the one beneath. Their bodies dropped into the bottom one. Easy access for outside then.'

'In here?' I can't help but answer. He's got me, dangling, and he knows it. It's barbaric. Awful. People died here, were executed here. Alongside where we live.

'Oh yeah, used to be nicknamed the cold-meat suite. They've been converted now, but no one likes sleeping in the cells we executed crims in.'

I shake my head.

He steps so close I can smell the mouthwash he's used to try to mask the smell of cigarette smoke. 'We try and keep them empty, but with overcrowding it's tricky.'

He looks over my shoulder. Kev has unlocked the bottom two tiers of the wing now. All the doors are open apart from two cells, stacked on top of each other. The two directly beneath number eight. Mine and Kelly's cell. We are in the top of the cold-meat suite. Where the gallows once hung.

'Roll-call!' Ryan booms in my ear.

The squeak of trainers, last shouts, and hushed whispers fill the space, as the women return promptly, standing two by two, outside their cell doors.

'Roll-call!' Kev's voice echoes from the other end of the wing, up on the third floor.

'Any inmate not present and correct in thirty seconds will be sent to seg!' Ryan bellows again.

Kelly's anxious face peers down from the third-floor landing; she's obviously back from church. I sprint for the stairs, taking them two at a time, holding my stomach in case it hurts my child. I shouldn't have answered back to Ryan. I should have let him say what he liked. I can't afford to make any more enemies.

Kev is working his way down the gangway, counting, as I take my place next to Kelly, who is standing outside our room.

So far no one seems to have spotted any resemblance between me and the Blonde Slayer from the news, but how long will my luck last? I can't hide now.

Kev stops alongside us and sticks out his hand, placing it on Kelly's bump.

'Any kicking yet?' he says. Kelly looks like she wants to pull away, but she just smiles weakly and nods. 'Need to know how the little one is doing,' Kev says, his podgy hand still moving, stroking, uninvited, on Kelly's bump. 'We've got a sweepstake running on when the little bastard is coming out.'

Kelly manages a nervous giggle.

Kev lets go, and I see her relax. 'Don't cut it so fine, next time.' He looks pointedly at me, and makes his way, his big fat hands clasped behind his back, along the landing.

'I can't believe he just did that – you okay?' I whisper to Kelly.

She looks like she might be sick, but she tries to sound upbeat. 'Not as bad as when one of this lot cop a feel.' She jerks her head to signal the other inmates. 'Everyone thinks they own you when you're up the duff. No fucking boundaries. There's one on the second landing who's obsessed.'

'Why don't you tell them to stop?' I can't believe this.

'She's a lifer,' she says. 'In for bloody murder. Abi told me. On the alpha course.' She gives a croaky laugh.

A horrible prickly sensation creeps over me. 'What's the alpha course?'

'Anger management,' Kelly says. 'Don't want to go all *fuck off of my bump* on someone who's gonna kick my head in.' She shudders, wraps her own arm round her belly.

I don't know what to say. Images of Gould's elbow jerking toward my face flash at me. And that was when she was hand-cuffed to two guards. People – murderers – walk freely around the wing. Kev is descending the stairs, his heavy lolloping strides making the metal sing tonelessly. He's already a long way away. How long would it take him or the other guards to get to you if you were in trouble? Would they even bother to hurry?

I want to reach out and squeeze Kelly's arm in comfort, but maybe that's unwanted too. Maybe Kelly's scared of me.

I need to request a meeting with Mr Peterson. He'll get me out of this living hell. He has to. But in the meantime I need to learn the rules. I need to stop drawing attention to myself. No one is going to find out I'm pregnant. Not even Kelly. It's too much of a risk. I need to protect my baby. I need to protect me. I need to stay focused.

But as I run through the things I need to fit into Monday in my mind, I can't help thinking again and again of women hanging beneath my feet. I'm not ready to be a mother.

Now

Sunday drags painfully. Kelly goes off to the faith room at 8.30 a.m. and doesn't return till lunch. Lunch itself is shoved in a bag through the hatch in our door, and consists of a chewy roll and crisps. By one o'clock I'm starving again. Is this what it's going to be like being pregnant inside – always hungry? In the afternoon I persuade Kelly to let me have one of her gigantic hoodies – it must be a size eighteen to my twelve – in exchange for some promised make-up when my canteen comes in. She doesn't ask questions about why I want it, or why I'm tearing a strip off the bottom of my sheet to wrap round my hair. I need to find a way to disguise the blonde. Kelly laughed when I asked if it was possible to buy hair dye, and suggested I ask for a fake ID and a key out at the same time. If she thinks my behaviour is odd, she hasn't said. Perhaps that's what everyone does in here – tries to disappear.

That night I can barely sleep, and I'm up with the sun on Monday morning, ready. I have a lot to do. I have to have my Induction, and a letter was delivered to our cell informing me I must attend the video-link room in the afternoon session to enter my Crown Court plea. Then I should finally get to speak to Mr Peterson. Then I can get out of here.

'Free Flow!' Sara's voice is upbeat, almost jolly as it echoes round the wing. I want to thank her for her kind tip on Friday, but I don't think it's wise to imply I'm pally with the guards.

We've all been unlocked already, and it's a relief to be outside the cell. I want to stretch my arms wide. But I don't want to draw attention to myself. And now there's a scramble toward the gates as everyone prepares to move round the prison. I keep my eyes down. I'm hiding in Kelly's supersized hoodie. The strip of bedsheet a makeshift headscarf round my hair. When my canteen comes in I might buy some coffee granules and experiment with a home tint.

'Here we go!' Kelly jiggles next to me, more than ready to go to her job. She's making bags for a high street chain as part of a team in a huge wooden hangar outside the main building – not that I've seen it – for which she earns a nominal amount toward her canteen per week. 'Good luck!' she calls as the gates open and we all hurry to our destinations.

Induction involves me and two scared-looking new arrivals sitting in a hot and dark classroom near the library, watching a video, while a guard, with her feet on a desk, reads the paper. On screen, the upbeat 'Insider' who is clearly a fresh-faced actor, takes us through the prison routine. Kelly is more convincing and more useful.

'Sounds like you need a form to take a dump,' mutters one of the other women as we wait for Free Flow to start up again. I fall in behind the prisoners coming out of the library, as we hurry back to the wing for lunch.

Kelly beats me there. And just after they lock us in again, a hand thrusts two brown paper bags through the door hatch. Kelly catches them before they hit the floor.

'Lunch.' She chucks mine to me.

I can barely eat my ham roll, and I just nod along as she tells me about gossip from her work. I'm too distracted to care what some stranger said to another stranger. This is my chance this afternoon. I can tell the judge someone framed me. That it has to be someone I know. The police can then start looking properly. They can let me out. They can find Robert.

Before I know it, it's Free Flow again. And I'm desperately trying to remember which way to go, and several times have to ask other women the way to the video-link suite. Eventually the crowd thins, and I realise myself and another two women, both dressed in their own clothes – a smart shirt and a dress – are headed in the same direction. None of us talk. I should be in something other than joggies. How's this going to look to the judge?

Kev herds us all into individual rooms before we can ask questions. The door is locked behind me. I sit at the desk in front of a computer. There's no keyboard or instructions. What if I'm supposed to do something and I don't know? What if they're waiting for me and I don't know how to see them? I thought Mr Peterson would be on screen. I thought he would talk me through this.

The monitor flicks on, and the feed is there live. A court-room. A judge. Oh my god. Mr Peterson is talking. Another solicitor – the Crown Prosecution Service. They list the charges. Two counts of murder. *Two.* I want to cry out that I'm pregnant. No one even appears to look at me. Can they see me? It's like I'm not there. I'm not. These strangers are in a room two hours away deciding my case.

Suddenly Mr Peterson is prompting me. I've been asked for my plea.

'Not Guilty,' I say. 'I didn't—'

'Thank you, Ms Burns,' the judge says. 'That is all that is required now. The defendant will be remanded until trial, with no bail posted.'

Until my trial? When is that – no one's said? No bail? I'm staying here. I'm about to open my mouth to say I want to speak to Mr Peterson, when the screen goes blank. Is that it?

I stare at it for a moment. Then I hear the door being unlocked behind me.

'Back to your cell, prisoner,' Kev says.

'I need to speak to my lawyer.' This can't be happening. I didn't even get to tell Mr Peterson I've been framed.

'Fill out a form,' Kev says. 'Like everyone else.'

And I walk back, stunned, toward the tiny cold room that is now my home.

Now

It's been a week since I arrived. A week. I will never get that time back. The hours drag in painful minutes and seconds. I worry about Robert. I worry about my baby. I worry about me. The only way I can fight this is to try to figure out who framed me. Thinking it over, playing it from every angle, retracing everything that has happened in the last year, till I spot the thing that's wrong, the thing that stands out, the thing that will explain all this. And it must be there. There must be a clue, if only I can remember it. I have to keep thinking. And I have a lot of time to do that.

Every Association I'm ready. I've submitted my call-list telephone numbers and my visitors list for approval, and asked to see Mr Peterson. Again. Kelly says I'm unlikely to get work till I'm off remand, and I don't intend to be here that long. I can't apply for education until my two weeks' proba- tion is up, but as there's nothing higher than a BTEC on offer, I've put in for library time instead. Anything to get out of the cell. And on Wednesday my luck changes.

We're grouped around the wing gates waiting after the call has gone up for Free Flow.

'What's taking them so long to unlock?' Kelly is agitated beside me.

'Short-staffed again, ain't they?' answers a slender woman in her thirties, her ginger hair in a high ponytail with a pinned quiff fringe.

'Bloody disgrace,' Kelly says.

'Can't say I'd wanna work in this dump, though,' the redhead says. A bird tattoo is visible on her freckled arm. 'No wonder they all quit.'

'Can't get the staff these days,' I quip.

She and Kelly laugh.

'Here, Jenna, this is Abi,' Kelly says, introducing us. 'Jenna's my new roomie. She's in for drugs.'

Abi gives me the once over. I suck my stomach in. I'm being stupid, no one could tell under this jumper. But what if she recognises my face from the news?

'Stolen goods – but I was set up,' Abi says.

Me too.

'Nice to meet you, Jenna,' she says.

I should have changed my name. At least all the reports I've seen have called me Jennifer.

'Hi,' I manage. Abi doesn't seem to have noticed anything odd.

'Abi runs aerobics classes in Association in the wing,' Kelly says. 'When we bloody get it, that is.'

'We had it twice last week.' Abi holds two fingers up. 'Two measly hours out the cell. Never mind. Shake it off.' She rolls her shoulders vigorously. 'You gotta stay positive. That's the key to getting out of here alive.' She taps the side of her forehead.

Getting out alive?

'Tell her about the programme you designed,' Kelly butts in.

'Right.' Abi's face brightens. 'We got a particular focus on those who want to lose weight. Some of the guards even join in,' she says proudly.

I'm not sure how to respond to this, so I just say, 'Cool.'

'It's good for mental health as well, you know.' Abi looks quite animated now, and I can imagine her shouting encouragement at grapevines and star jumps. 'I've done my Gym

Instructor – Level 2, and I've put in for Healthier Foods and Special Diets. I wanna be a personal trainer when I get out of here,' she says.

'Like Gwyneth Paltrow's got,' Kelly says. 'She's got all these books out the library on running your own business,' she adds, sounding impressed.

And it is impressive. 'What, Gwyneth has?' I say.

Kelly blinks for a split second, then she and Abi both crack up.

'Good one.' Abi claps me on the shoulder. The warm glow of acceptance flows through me. This isn't so bad. Kelly and Abi are nice, friendly. Abi's set up a class. It's going to be okay.

The feeling is short-lived, as Sara's radio crackles and tells us there's a further delay. Sighs of frustration bloom around us. I'm fast learning this is a regular occurrence, as staffing issues seem to be a constant worry. But I haven't got time to waste. Every minute is eating into my meeting time. And we've already lost twenty.

'Why are we waiting?' someone starts to sing. A few others join in.

'All right now,' Sara calls. 'That's enough, girls.'

'Jesus!' Kelly snaps. 'Some of us have work to do!'

'What's keeping them?' Abi says, as another mouthful of crackle can be heard coming from Sara's walkie-talkie.

I shrug. There's been no sign of Gould on the wing – there's no way I would have braved the showers otherwise – but I don't like talking too much out here anyway. I shouldn't have cracked those jokes. Shouldn't draw any attention to myself.

There's another burst of static from Sara's radio and a cheer goes up as she unlocks the gate with a clang. 'All right, girls, off you go.'

Anticipation rises inside.

'See ya later,' Kelly calls, as she disappears off with Abi and the other workers.

I'm following those who have visitors.

As we approach the visitors' hall, nine of us, those with offi-cial visitors, are filed off to one side. My heart falls as I see it's Ryan on duty.

'Ladies,' he beckons, as if he's welcoming friends to a club.

'Looking fine, Ryan.' A woman in her forties with badly pencilled eyebrows runs her hand down his arm, squeezing a muscle on the way.

Most of the group giggle. Am I the only one who finds this uncomfortable? I busy myself looking at the list of prisoner numbers and allotted rooms. Even Ryan's smarm can't dent my excitement. For the first time in ages, I feel hope.

'He's so hot,' a girl, who only looks about seventeen, her fair hair plaited down the side of her head, whispers behind her hand to an older woman wearing plain black trousers and a white shirt.

Ryan winks at the fair girl as we file past. She giggles. How can they flirt with a guard? How can he flirt with them?

But all my misgivings are forgotten when I reach the door. Meeting room 1B. I'm almost excited. Because this is my chance to prove my innocence. Knowing that someone has put that obscene stuff on my computer proves it, doesn't it? Truth will out. The system won't fail me. Everything is going to be okay.

As I place my hand on the door handle, I see Ryan squeeze the bum of the young fair-haired girl as she steps through her own door. My insides clench. He catches my eye and winks at me, as if to say *what you going to do about it?*

And suddenly my faith in the system doesn't feel so well-placed.

Now

Mr Peterson is already sitting in the small grubby room when Ryan shows me in. He's wearing the same pink-and-blue checked tie and hangdog expression on his face from the last time I saw him, fixated on the papers in front of him on the desk. I feel renewed shame at my joggies.

'Clock's ticking. I'll just be outside.' Ryan's voice is silky smooth. I hear the door lock behind me.

Just the two of us.

Mr Peterson doesn't look up: he doesn't look unnerved by being locked in a room with an alleged killer.

He signals with one hand for me to sit, while the pink fingers of his other move his papers around like Tetris blocks.

Though I'm his client, I feel like I've been summoned to face the board.

He looks up, his eyes kind, smiles. 'How are you? I see you've hurt your face.'

Is Ryan still outside? I don't want to be accused of being a grass. 'I fell. I'm pregnant.'

His lip shakes, a wavy line in his upside-down egg face. 'Congratulations,' he says.

I nod because I'm too frightened I'll cry if I speak.

He clears his throat, moves another piece of paper. 'So, the charges have been increased, as a result of new evidence presented by the police.'

The images. The disgusting things they found on my laptop. 'I didn't put that stuff there. I wouldn't. I couldn't,' I say.

If he feels revulsion, he doesn't show it. Is it cynicism, professionalism, or does he know I'm not capable of that? I hope it's the latter. I've worked with clients, and candidates, sometimes, who I haven't liked. But never with anyone who was a convicted criminal. We would ask candidates to disclose convictions. It's a legal requirement for a certain period after they've done time. I remember Becky had a guy once who had a driving conviction for speeding. We chose to reject his application.

'Mr Peterson. I need to tell you something.'

'Okay,' he says.

'I think someone is framing me.' I pause, wait.

He looks unconvinced. 'And why would someone do that?'

'To cover their own back?'

He sighs. 'It seems unlikely,' he says.

'But I didn't put that stuff on my computer – that proves it, doesn't it? That proves that someone else did this.' He must understand.

'I'm afraid it's a little more complex than that. As you say, the obscene material was found on your laptop, which was in your possession when it was confiscated by the police,' Mr Peterson says awkwardly.

'It was in my house but . . . but other people could have put it there.' I'm not making myself clear. It's so obvious to me. 'Someone must have killed Emily, then planted the images on my computer so the police would think I had motive. They are the ones who must have hurt Robert. They must have taken him somewhere. The estate where we live is huge – there are outbuildings, follies. Loads of places you could hide someone.' He could be out there in desperate need of help. My voice is rising. 'I just don't understand how the police could think I did this?' I need to understand. Work it backwards. Work out who did this. On the table, a groove has been dug in by someone repeatedly pushing a blue biro back and forth. An angry underline of their meeting.

Mr Peterson sighs. 'Because on Wednesday, 1st March the police were summoned to Milcombe Dower House, your current residence, shortly after 5.30 p.m. when Emily Milcombe's alarm was activated,' he says. 'And upon arrival at the scene you were found with the dead body of the girl. Several initial observations by the police pointed to your involvement. Further forensic evidence – blood – was discovered that implied Robert Milcombe – your partner – had also been injured, and been dragged from the house. Since then, obscene images of children have been discovered on a laptop in your possession.' He pauses. Watches my hands shake. 'The CPS will disclose their full evidence before the trial.'

'When is the trial? No one's told me.' This can't be right.

'You can only be remanded in custody for a maximum of one hundred and eighty-two days,' he says. 'Before the end of August.'

August – but my wedding, my baby! It's due in October. I can't be pregnant in here all that time.

'We will be notified of your trial date six weeks in advance.' He runs his tongue over his teeth. 'We will work through a strategy as we approach the trial. Try not to worry.'

'The trial date hasn't even been set yet?' August. That's six months from now. But it won't get to that stage, surely? I'll be out before then. I have to be. I need to know what other evidence they have. If I can understand why they think I did this, then I can figure out who did do it. I'm probably the only one who can. Apart from Robert. I keep my eyes fixed on the gouge of biro on the desk.

'You will be notified six weeks before—'

'Thank you. I understand. But, Mr Peterson, on that night . . . after I found Emily. The police questioned me all of Thursday. I was in shock, I didn't take in what they said. Can you take me through everything again?'

He looks up. His gaze unrelenting, and I see that it is cynicism in there. He's a kind man; his gestures, his attempts to get them to shield my face from the photographers, show that. But there's a resilience too, an acceptance of the type of people he deals with. How many of them say they didn't do it? Say they were framed? Abi said it earlier. How many times has he heard this all before. I need proof. 'Please, Mr Peterson. I need to understand it all.'

Mr Peterson rearranges his Tetris blocks one more time, as if they could spell out the answer. I'm locked in a pen-scratched dingy room, with a man whose first name I don't know, but in whose hands my fate rests.

I hold my breath.

Now

The paper crackles like fire in my hand as I walk back to my cell. Our cell. I could be here for six months. Six months. Kelly is back from work. They've started locking everyone in again after Free Flow.

She holds up a mug. 'Cuppa?'

I press the paper to my chest. The facts as they stand. The facts as they've been applied to me. Wrongly. I shake my head at Kelly. I can't take any more input. Any more questions. I have to make notes. My head buzzes. 'Can't talk. I need to think.' What do I need to do? Now I have it here, in black and white: the reason – more reasons – I'm in here and I can't make sense of it. It's so much more than the vile images they found on my laptop.

'All right,' Kelly says huffily. 'Just thought you might be thirsty after your chinwag with your lawyer.'

I cringe at my insensitivity. And my stupidity. I have to sleep in a locked room with this girl and don't know her that well. I don't know what her moods are like, her temper. If she really is dangerous. Kelly pouts, and it reminds me so much of Emily when Robert told her she had to go to bed, or she couldn't go to the disco at the local youth club, that I almost smile through the twist of my heart. 'Sorry. I didn't mean to be short. Thank you.' The words are clumsy, stilted. 'For the offer of the tea.'

'It's fine.' Kelly is curt, her actions still so teenage they're almost comical.

'That meeting was a little bit intense.' I find myself mirroring her language. I almost stick a 'like' on the end.

Kelly softens, her shoulders let go. 'All right, I'll shut up. I've got a new magazine anyway.' She rubs her stomach.

I smile, grateful. I need to study the list that Mr Peterson gave me. The things I now know. The things that make no sense. 'Thanks.'

'You could always talk to Vina, she's well good on all this stuff, you know?' Kelly says.

Vina knows about people being framed? How to do it? Or how to prove it?

Kelly continues, 'All that legal shit. She's read up on it. Better than the dozy bint who they sent for me.'

That makes much more sense. Should I show my list to Vina? The accusation of child pornography is on there. No one can see that. 'Kelly, can I borrow some paper, and a pen?' She raises an eyebrow at me. I know she's got an A4 diary she tears pages out of. But she's already given me so much. I falter. 'Please?'

'Course,' she says softly. 'Ain't like I need it to write shopping lists or owt.'

I want to do something for her. Get her something. Say thank you. 'Can I get my sister to bring in some more magazines?'

'That ain't allowed.' She rolls her eyes.

'How did you get yours then?' The rules are opaque.

'My mum set me up a subscription.' She leans against the metal door frame, seeming to balance her bulk with the backwards slant. 'The local newsagent does it if you give them your prison number.'

'All right, what about if I get her to set up another of those?'

'Really?' Her face lights up.

And it feels wonderful to make someone happy. 'Well you've already given me so much.'

'Yeah.' Her eyes shine. 'I was gonna ask for some mascara when your canteen came in, but this is way better. I'm gonna ask Lillie – she gets *Take A Break*. See if she wants to set up a library: lend 'em out when we're done. For a small compensation, obvs.' Her belly jiggles, as she climbs the ladder.

My grin falls from my face as soon as my thoughts return to the list.

I tear the pages from Kelly's pad as neatly as I can. And I bring them onto my bunk. The bed above gives the sense of cover, a canopy. It makes me feel hidden, protected. I don't want anyone seeing this. I spread open the paper Mr Peterson let me have. My hastily written notes. The words wobbly where my pen shook. The evidence against me.

Evidence I can't argue with.

Now

These are the things I know about Wednesday, 1st March, Emily's birthday. The day she died:

1. *I was forensically covered in Emily's blood and hair.*

I held her. I tried to save her. Of course she was on me.

2. *Emily's fob triggered the alarm. Her blood is on it.*

This I can explain. I pressed her alarm. My keys were in the hallway, too far away. The phone was broken. Her blood was on me.

The paper shakes in my hand. Words like 'forensics' and 'blood' are raw, visceral stings on my heart. I force myself to read on.

This is where it goes awry. Where it doesn't make sense.

3. *I sent a text to Sally saying:* I've done something terrible. God forgive me.

Except I didn't. I have no recollection of that. Am I going mad? No. The message has got to be part of it: part of the fit up. Someone made it look like I sent it.

4. *My sweatshirt, covered in Emily's blood, was found inside the washing machine – halfway through a cycle.*

That must have been when I felt Salinsky's attitude shift toward me on the night of the murder. It must have been the jumper they brought out of the house in an evidence bag. It was then that Salinsky believed that I was guilty. He thinks that I was wearing it when I attacked Emily, and then tried to hide it by putting it in the machine.

When Mr Peterson said that, my heart had leapt into my mouth. Surely the jumper in the machine proves I didn't do it? Why would I take one bloody top off, and then cover myself in Emily's blood again? But Mr Peterson explained it's about the blood spatter on the top. He's going to get our own expert to look at it, but the police believe I took it off to try to alter the implications of the blood pattern by holding it against Emily, and wiping the floor with it. That I then tried to wash away the evidence, and hugged her to cover up my actions and give me a new story. At that point I'd had to take a few minutes because all I could see was Emily and red and I couldn't breathe.

I think of DI Langton's blunt fringe. Her penetrating eyes. Her composure next to her angry colleague. The creases from where she'd pushed her sleeves up to work. If I was assessing her as a candidate for a job I would say she was shrewd, intelligent, organised, in control. There's a touch of the alpha about her. Has she really made this fit? If I were DI Langton, I'd look at this damning list and draw the same conclusions. The enormity of the task ahead of me looms up and threatens to engulf me. I don't know enough about law, about evidence, about how this all works.

Mr Peterson said it was a blue Sweaty Betty jumper. My Pilates top. Where was it when I left that morning? I'd last been at class on Saturday. I'd done a wash the day before – was it in that? Was it on the dryer, or in the basket in the utility room, or upstairs? It's such a mundane thing – I can't remember if my memory of it is from that week or the last. Why would someone else use it? Why that top? And why put it in the wash?

5. *Only my fingerprints (and a few trace smudges) were on the washing machine.*

The police have already confirmed that our cleaner Michelle comes every Tuesday and Friday. And that that Tuesday she cleaned the utility room, including wiping down the washing machine as usual. Of course my fingerprints were on the machine. But why weren't the killer's?

6. *Only my fingerprints were on the murder weapon.*

The word 'weapon' throbs on the page. The buzzing starts in my head again. I know I picked the knife up. Or at least I think I did, in the panic. Trying to understand what had happened. It was there on the floor. Glinting. Slick with blood.

I force myself to remember. Yes, it was one of Robert's expensive Japanese knives. From the block set on the counter. I remember emptying them from the dishwasher Wednesday morning. Robert must have put them in the night before – we were hurrying, trying to get everything ready for Emily's big day.

Keep going. Keep remembering. Keep thinking. I'm the only one who can solve this. I'm the only one – apart from the real culprit – who knows I didn't do this.

I put the knife back in the block. I'm the only person who touched it, besides the killer. They must have been wearing gloves. That explains the lack of prints on the washing machine too.

Someone hated us enough to do this. Who? There were no signs of a break-in. It was someone who had a key. Or knew where we kept ours. Then there's the thing they think gives me motive. The final damning proof.

7. *Obscene images of children were found on my laptop.*

A large encrypted file. Thousands of photos and videos. But no one could think a pregnant woman was capable of that. DI Langton will see that. Mr Peterson will explain. Because they can't possibly keep me and my baby in here. It's got to just be a matter of time.

I close my eyes and think about how when I'm out of here I will paint the spare room yellow, for a nursery. And get a hanging mobile of planes and hot-air balloons, so my baby knows it can go anywhere. Do anything.

A cheer from another cell breaks into my thoughts. Two people finding something to celebrate in here. Then I realise something so obvious it's terrifying. Mr Peterson said there were thousands of photos and videos of child porn on my computer. That the police aren't sure when they were added. Emily was dropped home just before five. I was back just after half past five. There wasn't time to kill her and download that many files. Adding the child porn to my computer wasn't opportunistic.

This was premeditated. And I was the target.

Then

'I can't wait for you to meet Pip.' Robert takes me by the hand as we walk toward his parents' house. The sound of a swing band carries on the crisp autumn air. This is a big deal, his mum's birthday. A chance to meet all the wider family, his parents' friends, people who are important to the business. 'She and Mum have been friends since school. Pip's a riot,' he says. 'And my godmother. I get all my raffish ways from her!' He tilts his Rat Pack-style hat and grins.

'I didn't know you had any raffish ways?' I say.

'Oh yes.' He nuzzles into my neck. 'I'm a real cad.'

I pretend-shriek and run ahead, giggling, enjoying the swish of the net skirt under my fifties-style dress. 'I promised my mother I'd never go out with a cad!'

He runs to catch up with me, grabbing my hand as we reach the house. 'It's not going out with me that you've got to watch, it's going home with me.' He pinches my bum. A pale-blue carpet has been rolled out from the front door, and a doorman in a fifties cinema outfit stands to greet us. I slap Robert's hand away as the guy holds the door, nervous of what he'll think.

'Evening, Mr Milcombe.' He nods to Robert.

'I see Mother persuaded you into a costume after all, John.' Robert loops his arm round my waist.

'The lady of the house always gets her own way.' John smiles.

'Quite right,' says Robert, squeezing me. 'Quite right.'

Off the back of the house a huge marquee has been erected, decorated like a classic American diner. 'Wow!' I say. There's an ice-cream bar, a jukebox, a dance floor, and several shiny Corvettes and Chevrolets are parked up alongside the structure. This is another world. The extravagance, the cost. 'It looks like *Happy Days*!' I say.

'My father doesn't do things by halves,' Robert says. 'Timothée! *Ça va?*' He turns to an elegant couple in their sixties, him with gelled rockabilly hair, her in a wiggle dress. 'Béatrice.' He bends to double-kiss the woman.

'*Mon cher* Robert.' Béatrice rests her hands on his shoulders to return the greeting.

'Can you believe it's a year since we visited the chateau?' Robert beams, at total ease in these surroundings. With these people. 'I must introduce you to my girlfriend – Jenna.' He turns to me, and I feel myself blush. 'Jenna, Timothée and Béatrice make the most exquisite award-winning champagne. We are the only establishment in the country to stock it. It is a great honour.' I nod and smile, unsure of what to say.

'Nothing but the best for David and his family.' Timothée smiles.

After several more rounds of introductions to foie gras suppliers, other hoteliers, an ambassador, and several people from David's Freemasons club, we find ourselves in the relative quiet of the kitchen.

'Mother, there you are!' Robert says to Judith, resplendent in a white satin fifties dress and a little pale-blue cardigan. She is inspecting canapés before they go out.

'Oh darling,' she says. 'Don't you both look delightful?' She takes his hands and grins at us.

'Happy birthday, Mummy.' He hugs her to him.

'You daft so-and-so.' She pats him away. 'Why aren't you out there dancing? Your father spent ages auditioning the bands.'

'It looks incredible,' I say, stupidly. 'You look incredible.'

'Thank you, darling, you are sweet.' Judith blushes.

'We came in here looking for you,' Robert says. 'Where's Auntie Pip?'

'Oh, she's not coming.' Judith turns and stops one of the fifties cinema girls who is carrying a tray of mini hamburgers to align a tiny bun. Her attention to detail is extraordinary.

'Is she sick?' Robert sounds concerned.

I give a little smile to the waitress as she passes.

'Oh no,' Judith says, checking the next tray they're lining up. Tiny striped boxes of popcorn. 'Your father thought it was best she didn't come.'

I feel Robert bristle next to me. 'But it's your birthday,' he says.

'Yes,' Judith says wistfully. 'But you know Pip – she is very . . .' She trails off. Picks up one of the boxes of popcorn. 'Try one of these – they're salted caramel, what do you think? I'm not sure.'

Robert doesn't move, so I take one and pop it in my mouth. 'Delicious,' I say.

'I can't believe he told you to un-invite her.' Robert sounds cross. I feel like I shouldn't be here for this conversation. Can I make an excuse and get out? 'Do you want me to speak to him?'

'Don't make a fuss, darling,' Judith says, alarm flickering in her eyes. 'Pip has always been a bit trying.'

'She's your best friend!' Robert says.

'Oh, we really don't see each other that much any more.' She looks wistful again, just for a second. 'I'm quite happy. Really, darling.'

'Let me talk to him,' Robert tries again.

Judith's hand snakes out and grabs him quickly, startling us both. 'You mustn't, Robert. Promise me you won't?'

A chill runs down my spine. She looks genuinely frightened.

'Okay, Mummy,' he says. 'Don't worry. I won't. I promise.'

The look is gone in an instant, and the smiling ethereal Judith is back. 'Wonderful, now why don't you two lovebirds run off and enjoy the party. Your father will want you out there.'

'Okay, Mummy,' Robert says.

I smile at Judith, want her to be happy on her birthday. 'I'll meet you back outside,' I say to Robert. 'I just need to powder my nose.'

'Miss you already,' he says.

On the way back down from the loo I get lost. The stairs on the left go down to the drawing room and the orangery in the left wing, don't they? Or is it the stairs on the right? It's mad to have more than one staircase. I keep wanting to pinch myself. I can't believe this is real. I lift my fingers to my nose and smell the expensive almond-scented hand cream Judith keeps in this bathroom. Through the window I can see the party in the garden. At least I'm on the right side of the house.

Downstairs there are more closed white doors, and I feel like Alice in Wonderland, unsure of where to go. Voices drift through one. David and Judith. This must be the kitchen entrance, from the other side. I'll fess up. Tell them I got lost.

The handle is cool against my palm. I'm smiling in a bid to laugh off my mistake.

The second I open the door I feel it.

David has hold of Judith's hand. But her wrist is at the wrong angle. Her face is contorted.

They look up. Jump away from each other.

'Jennifer, darling, where did you come from?' Judith's fingers flick up and over her hair, like she's performing a magic trick and is about to pull a card from behind her ear. She's coming toward me, arms open, a swoosh of petticoats and bangles.

'I . . .' I gesture behind me to signal I'm lost. Did I imagine that?

David joins her, his arm looped over her shoulder. Kissing the top of her head. Judith smiles up at him, adoration in her eyes.

'Can you fetch Jennifer a drink, my darling?'

'Of course, my love.' David kisses Judith's forehead again. She blushes like they are just courting. Dating is too modern. Courting implies gentlemanly behaviour. Manners. Flowers and dancing. I made a mistake. I saw something that wasn't there.

'Let's go find one of those waitresses with the Bellinis.' David places his hand on the small of my back.

'Thank you,' I smile.

As the heavy wooden door swings shut behind us I see Judith massaging her wrist.

Now

At the time I'd thought I was mistaken, seeing David hurting Judith. As if I'd brought elements of my own dysfunctional childhood, and projected it onto Robert's home life. But what if I wasn't? I know David is hardworking and excessively proud when it comes to the company and the family name. And he holds those around him to the same high standards. He's created the perfect brand, and he's never tolerated anything that doesn't fit with that vision. Pip had to go, despite being Judith's oldest friend. Was that a one-off or was David violent toward Judith regularly? Someone's framed me. And it was planned, because whoever put that stuff on my computer wore gloves. And they used my jumper to mop up the blood to ram the implication home. David is smart enough, but is he really capable of it? Of hurting his own granddaughter?

'You bored yet?' Kelly's head appears from above.

I jump, bunching the papers together. I can't let her see them. It's all there, the horrible things I've been accused of. The words flash up at me like burning coals. *Obscene. Children. Murder. Blood. Forensics.* I shove them under my pillow.

I try to sound carefree. 'Yeah, had some stuff to figure out.' *Like whether my future father-in-law framed me for murder.* That's ridiculous. But is it? A month ago I would have said it was ridiculous that I would ever be locked up for Emily's murder. For child porn. And David had access to my computer. Once, I came home and found him alone in our house. He'd let himself in, and he was there, bold as brass, using my laptop in the kitchen. Said he had to do some work while he waited for Robert. What if that was a lie? If he was covering up what he was really doing? But David wouldn't hurt Emily, surely. He loved her. Didn't he? I think of Judith rubbing her wrist. David might have had a funny way of showing love.

'Earth to Jenna!' Kelly said. 'Did you hear any of that?'

I look up as she lowers herself down. 'Sorry, no – I'm feeling a bit tired actually.'

'You all right?' Kelly drops onto her haunches to look at me with concern.

I feel the paper burn hot and angry behind me.

'You not gonna puke again, are you?' She looks worried.

'No.' The nausea, at least, has eased off this last week. I hadn't had it earlier in my pregnancy, otherwise I might have cottoned on sooner. It had obviously been triggered by the van ride, or the stress of that first day. Whatever the reason it had waned, it was a relief.

For a second I think about telling Kelly about the baby. About the list of evidence from Mr Peterson, about my doubts about David. But the look on her face when Kev ran his pudgy hand over her stomach makes me stop. It's too risky. No one can know. Thank god I have stopped being sick: I'm already panicking about what to do when my bump starts to show. I don't think I could hide my pregnancy from my roommate if I was hurling every morning.

'Good magazine?' I say, changing the subject.

Kelly beams. 'Oh yeah. You would not believe what Cheryl Cole's been up to.'

Kelly talks on and off about celebrities all afternoon. Your typical teen girl. Except she's locked in here. I nod and make polite noises, all the time thinking about David. Spinning backwards and forwards between certainty and doubt. He did have opportunity. But he couldn't really hurt Emily, could he? Unless he lost his temper. Unless things got out of hand.

'I really want a contour kit, you know,' Kelly says happily as we head out for dinner. 'Like that photo I showed you of Kim Kardashian's one. But they're not on the canteen. So Abi and I are gonna do what we can with what we got.'

'Sounds good,' I say, scanning the line of women queuing at the kitchen trolley for Gould. Still no sign. Maybe she's not coming on the main wing.

I'm so busy surreptitiously checking the chatting and laughing women approaching to join the back of the queue for Gould, I don't realise Kelly has stopped talking. She has a pensive look on her face. And is watching Vina, who is balancing her plastic tray of what looks like brown curry and rice in one hand, and a pack of loose-leaf papers in the other, on the way back to her cell.

'You okay?' I say.

'Mind if I join yous.' Abi arrives to the side of us. Her red hair in a topknot today, her green prison trousers low on her hips to reveal her abs.

I glance at the small woman behind us, who has the wide-eyed petrified look of a new arrival.

'She don't mind,' Abi says, waving her hand dismissively and turning me back to face her.

I try to give the lady behind a reassuring smile.

Kelly stops staring after Vina, and looks at me. 'What are you writing?'

Her question startles me. Did she see my notes after all? I fight the panic rising in me. The cacophonous sounds of the hundreds of women around us fill my ears. Not here. Not now. 'I . . . err . . .'

'Not another book?' Kelly says.

'What?'

'You writing one too?' Abi slaps her hand against my shoulder, grinning.

'Look, bloody Vina's got a load of paper – I bet she's doing one,' Kelly points, looking miserable.

I don't understand what's going on. 'Not a book,' I manage. 'Notes. 'Bout my case.'

Abi's face is still alight. 'Want to see mine?'

'Err, sure,' I say.

Kelly folds her arms and pouts.

Abi sprints off to her cell, her bun bouncing.

'Wish I hadn't brought it up,' Kelly says.

Abi returns clutching a bundle of what look like clear plastic folders. 'Here.' She passes them to me.

I see that each page is full of neat bubble-shaped black handwriting, little hearts above the 'i's. Abi has encircled each paragraph in a different colour of pencil and shaded it in, then added intricate borders round each one. Tendrils of flowering plants, ribbons, scrolls of paper, bouncing balls, and bubbles border each page, carefully coloured by hand. This is hours of work. And they're not in plastic files, but each page, the number written and decorated at the top, has been laminated.

'Wow!' I say.

Kelly seems to be fighting with her grumpiness and her clear impressed pride. 'Look at this one.' She turns to one page whose coloured border is made up of hand-drawn monkeys dangling, topsy-turvy, hand-to-tail from top to bottom.

The two women in front of us have turned around to look as well.

'That's really good,' says the taller one.

I see Kelly's smile falter.

'Wish I could draw like that,' says the one with a tight-gelled ponytail.

'Did you do all this?' I ask Abi. My handwriting is barely legible.

She nods and beams. 'It's my book. Have you read *The Secret*?'

I have a dim memory of a self-help book. 'No, but I think I've heard of it,' I say.

'Well, it's all about visualising what you want. The law of attraction.' Abi has become incredibly animated.

I scan some of the words on the laminated pages: *ask, believe, receive*. But Abi is fast turning pages, back to the front, where the title reads: 'About Me'.

'This bit is like my introduction. My story. I was abused for years by my dad, all kinds of different abuse, the whole lot.' She turns the pages over and over, and I realise all the drawings that border this section are monochrome. 'I won't go into it, won't get emotional.' Her voice gives slightly. Kerry puts an arm round her.

The words slap against me.

'Then I was in care and that,' she says, turning the page. 'That bit's about my mum. She's a user.' She flips more pages over and we're back in the brightly coloured section. 'And like, I tell other people's stories,' she says.

'There's one about that boy never believing he would get to go on holiday, like travel, and that he wasn't worth it – but how he kept hoping, clutching this little stone that his mum gave him. Then he's holding it one day and his brother calls and says he's getting married to a Spanish woman and he's taking him to the wedding in Spain,' Kelly says excitedly, all her earlier antagonism apparently forgotten.

'That one always sticks in people's memories,' Abi says. She turns the page again. The words are now a series of positive affirmations. Almost like incantations, filling the pages. 'The number-one governor liked that bit.'

The words wink up at me from the plastic.

You deserve to live a full life.
You deserve to be loved.
You deserve to be happy.

A lump forms in my throat. 'It's amazing,' I manage.

We soon reach the front of the queue. Kelly and I head back to our cell with our trays of now cold food. Abi heads to hers to safely deposit her book.

Kelly and I perch on the edge of my bed, eating in silence for a moment. The smell from the curry has already started to hang in the air. We all eat in our cells, and with the window opening less than an inch it's hard to keep it smelling fresh in here. But I don't care as much right now. Abi's story, the things she's been through, what she's survived, those positive things she was still able to write, have warmed me more than this dhal.

'Do you not like Abi's book?' I ask Kelly, as she scrapes her tray with her plastic fork.

'Course I like it,' she sighs. 'It's just everyone already likes Abi because she does the aerobics classes, and she's going to be a personal trainer when she gets out, and then she's written this amazing book as well. I was always crap at everything at school.' Kelly suddenly looks small, and I remember just how very young she is.

'Those bags you make for work must be pretty good if they sell them in high-street shops,' I say.

She sighs again. 'It's just following a pattern, anyone could do it. It's not like writing your own book.'

I think about the look she gave Vina. The empty diary Kelly let me have the pages out of for my notes. She'd said something then too. She wants to do this. 'Well, why don't you write your own book then?'

'I couldn't do that,' she says.

'Why not? You're smart and funny and entertaining,' I say. 'You're always making me and Abi laugh.'

She looks doubtful. 'But what would I write about?'

'Well . . . what about a story?' For a second I feel like I'm back in Sally's office, coaching a prospective candidate again.

'Nah,' Kelly shakes her head. 'I wanna do something help-ful – like Abi. Make some good out of all this.' She signals the cell with her hands.

'Okay, well then what about self-help, or a guide of some sort?' I look at the make-up on her face. 'A make-up guide?'

'Maybe,' she sniffs, looking more like her usual self. She picks up the diary she gave me earlier and opens it. 'Might write a few ideas down.'

I smile. 'Good plan.'

After lock-up, Kelly sits on her bed, her pen scratching away in her book. After an hour or so I hear her abandon it in favour of the fluttery turn of one of her magazines.

I'm still staring at my own notes. My own story. *You deserve to be happy.* Not until I find who did this to us. Someone framed me. Someone who planned it and wore gloves. Someone who had access to my computer. Someone who had access to my house. Someone who was close to us. Could it really be David? Could he kill Emily, and hurt Robert? His own granddaughter, his own son. And if so, where is Robert now? DI Langton's words about no activity on Robert's cards, about his mobile being found at our house, spring into my mind unbidden. A small gasp escapes my lips.

'You all right?' Kelly says from above.

'Cramp,' I say quickly.

Robert is not dead. I won't believe it. David had opportunity. He had access. He was strong enough to force Robert to go. He knows where our knives are. My mind swings between incredulity and suspicion. Because why would he do this?

What possible motive could David have?

Then

I hear the car door slam as I'm getting out of the bath. It's David's car. Emily is storming away from it, a look of thunder on her face. What's happened? She should be at school.

'Do not walk away from me when I'm talking to you, young lady!' David flings his door open and shouts.

Instinctively I duck behind the curtain of the dressing room. It's only been a month since I moved in, and I don't feel comfortable witnessing a family row. I peer through the gap in the curtain.

Emily rounds on him, hands on hips, her voice high and indignant. 'It has nothing to do with you anyway. Dad should have come and got me!' I've never heard her talk like this, let alone to David.

'As I'm the one who pays for your school fees, I'm the one they ring when they threaten to expel you!' he roars.

Expel her? Oh my god, what's happened?

'It was just one puff, for god's sake.' Emily throws her arms up in exasperation. 'It wasn't even my joint!'

Oh crap. David looks livid.

'The school have a zero-tolerance policy. What do you think would have happened if I hadn't been there to smooth things over? You would have been out.' His voice is threateningly calm.

'I don't care! I don't like the damn school anyway,' Emily says. I know that's a lie, she's just caught in the moment. Not enough to swear though, Robert's parents are funny about that. She's still watching her limits.

'You ungrateful little madam.' David marches toward her, pounding his feet into the gravel, and for one horrible moment I think he's going to raise his hand.

Emily does too because she shrinks backwards. And when Robert's Range Rover comes screeching into the driveway she races toward it. He jumps out, and she runs into his arms. 'What's going on? Dad – why didn't you call me?' he says.

'Your daughter,' David runs his hands through his hair, 'has been caught doing drugs.'

Robert suddenly thrusts Emily away from him. 'You stupid girl!' I clasp my hand to my mouth. I've never seen him like this before. It's panic, I realise.

'It was just one puff, Dad. I've never done it before,' Emily cries. 'I promise.'

He lets her go and she stumbles back. Still shaking. He can't have meant to hurt her. He turns to David. 'You should have called. *I'm* her father.' Robert sounds venomous. I hold my breath.

'You were in a meeting, and your daughter needs to appreciate that the world doesn't revolve around her.' David and Robert stare at each other for a second. I can hear Emily snivelling.

'Robert,' David says, warningly. As if it's him who has been caught with drugs.

Robert almost spits at Emily. 'Go to your room!' I've never heard him sound so angry. The hairs on my arm stand up. I want to make it better. I want him to calm down. 'You'll be punished for this.' She runs into the house, slamming the door behind her. The glass in the windows rattles as she thumps upstairs.

'You should have called me,' he says to David.

'Don't start,' David snaps. 'I warned you this would happen. This is because of *her*.'

Her? Who's her?

'I knew this would happen when she started dressing like that,' David says.

Like what? She dresses like a normal teen.

'And you should have stamped out that ridiculous vegetarian notion as soon as your mother told me about it,' David snaps. 'They need to understand how lucky they are. They're like cattle. Give an inch and they take a mile.'

Did he just compare teenagers – or women – to cattle?

Robert sounds like he's pleading. 'Lots of teenagers experiment, Dad, it doesn't mean anything. She's a kid.' There's the man I love. There's the voice of reason.

David shakes his head, as if he's not listening. 'You defied me once and we're still paying for it. I sometimes think it would have been kinder to start afresh completely after her mother.'

Defied him? Paying for what? What does he mean?

'She's a good kid.' Robert sounds hurt.

David points a finger at him. 'If this had got out, if she'd been arrested – then what? I play bridge with the Chief Commissioner. Imagine how embarrassing that would be for us. For the company. You need to keep your house in order, Robert. If you're not up to the job . . .'

'That's not fair. Everyone makes mistakes,' Robert says.

'You make mistakes,' David says. 'And I clear them up. It's got to stop.' His voice is so cold I shiver.

What mistakes? What's he talking about? I can hear Emily sobbing in her bedroom.

'Yes, Father.' Robert looks at the ground.

I burn with embarrassment for him. Is this how it looks from the outside when Mum and I fight?

David exhales, walks over to his car and drives off. Robert stands there for a moment, looking up at the sky. I don't know what to do, but I want to go to him. I want to ease his pain.

Pulling my dressing gown and trainers on, I go downstairs as quietly as possible. The last thing Emily needs now is a witness.

Robert is still outside, looking out over the fields, as I step quietly across to him. 'Hey,' I say softly, wrapping my arms around him from behind. 'Sorry – I was upstairs.' He stiffens. All families have their rows. David will calm down. It's not that big a deal. 'She's a good kid – I bet she didn't even inhale!' I go for light-hearted.

He forcibly shrugs me off, and turns away. 'You don't know anything about it,' he snaps, and kicks his car door shut with such force I fear the window will shatter.

My heart is thumping in my chest. I said the wrong thing. I made it worse.

He sighs. Runs his hands through his hair, just like his dad does. 'Sorry,' he says, and looks up with an apologetic smile. 'Teenagers – hey?'

I loop my arm round him as we walk back into the house.

Now

I'd excused it in the past as his wanting the best, but David is a bully. Did he and Emily have another row? Did he hit her this time? I keep thinking over that day. The *her* David blamed for Emily's experimentation could have been me. I'd just moved in – maybe he thought I made her act out. Maybe that wasn't the last time she did drugs. But how can I prove any of this? My mind whirrs with it all. At least I've got a distraction today. My probation period has finally ended, the relevant forms have cleared, and Mum and Ness will be able to visit for the first time. I get up and dress before Kelly leaves her bed. Carefully facing the wall at all times, so she can't see my stomach. My bump is certainly protruding now; it's like my baby was just waiting for me to be told before it put in a proper appearance. My lower abdomen is firm, rounded. I'll have to keep the big baggy jumper Kelly gave me on at all times. Until I can get out of here.

Kelly's staring at one of the photos she has stuck on her wall. A little old couple sit on a bench, small and curled by age, her with fluffy set grey hair, him with a gummy smile and two walking sticks leaning against his knee. Her grandparents.

She must have seen me looking, because she suddenly points and says, 'My mum and dad.'

The shock must show on my face.

Kelly sits up and grins. 'I'm the surprise baby. They thought they couldn't have kids. Mum thought it was the menopause – but it was me.'

I think of my own surprise baby. 'Bet they were delighted.'

'Dad bought the whole pub a round after he got up off the floor,' she laughed.

'They coming today?'

Her smile faltered. 'No. It's a bit far for them with Dad's legs now. And Mum don't see so well since her diabetes got worse.'

I can't believe I put my foot in it, and after Kelly was down about Abi's book as well. 'I'm sorry.'

'It's fine.' She forces a smile. 'They still come once a month. Gotta save up for the cab fare. Two more weeks,' she says.

Everything is carved into units of time in here. Measured out in painful seconds. 'It'll soon be here.'

Kelly gives her best impression of being okay, but I keep my excitement at my own potential visit under wraps until Free Flow.

The visitors' centre is like a school assembly hall. Windows, high up the triple-height walls, presumably out of reach of us inmates, pour natural light onto us. The daffodils will be blooming in David and Judith's garden, but from in here I can't see anything but the grey spring sky. With its pale-lemon painted walls, it has a more airy, cleaner feel than the rest of the prison. In the diagonally opposite corners, there are two doors. One through which we prisoners have just filed. And another through which the visitors will enter. Abi grins eagerly in front of me. Her hair down, freshly cleaned and flowing around her shoulders today, she's not wearing her regulation trousers, but smart black leggings. There's an excited, expectant air to the room, that even the horrid stained red tabards they've given us all to wear cannot dim. Brightly coloured homemade artwork and streamers decorate the walls, between the regulation posters instructing visitors they'll be prosecuted for smuggling in banned items.

'Ladies,' calls Ryan. He's gelled his hair into a quiff at the front so that it looks like it's constantly pointing which way he should go. 'Ladies!' The lively chatter hushes. 'It's a busy one today, so take your seats quickly.'

Vina, who is at the front of the queue, with a brightly coloured hair wrap I've not seen her wear before, leads the way, walking to a table at the far end of the room. We all follow.

Each table is small and oval. They're evenly placed, remind-ing me of taking GCSEs. I'm three rows back, toward the middle. I take the one chair that's on my side. They're padded, and blue, like mass-market cheap conference chairs. But this is the first time I've sat on anything cushioned since I've been inside, and it feels ridiculously comfortable. Opposite me are two more chairs, where my visitors will sit. If they come. *Please let them come.* Every chair has been tethered to the floor by what looks like a taut metal rope. Have they always been like that or were they added after trouble?

Ryan walks among us, checking nothing's out of place. 'You're allowed to stand up – and give a cuddle to your visi-tors,' he says with a leer. There's a few saucy cheers. 'Once at the beginning of the session and once at the end of the session. The rest of the time you are to keep those booties pressed firmly against those chairs.' He gives me a sly look.

I drop my head, wishing I hadn't when I catch a whiff of the stale sweat that has soaked this tabard. I can smell the previ-ous wearer's distress. I think of these chairs flying through the air.

Ryan is still going. 'It's been explained to your visitors that they are able to purchase hot drinks and snacks for them-selves, and for you lucky lot, from the tuck shop.' He points at the counter in the corner by the visitors' door.

A woman, not a prisoner I'd say from her skinny jeans, bouffant blow-dried hair and smart blue apron, waves cheerfully from behind a small shelving display of flapjacks, chocolate bars and crisps. My stomach growls.

'Kiddies are free to play in the corner,' Ryan says. There is a selection of children's toys, the bright joyful plastic jarring with their home. It doesn't matter how nice they've tried to make it look: children are about to visit their mothers in a prison. What does that do to a kid?

Ryan is making his way down the next row of tables now and he pauses at the table of the timid-looking woman who stood behind us in the dinner queue yesterday. 'And,' he said, 'young children are obviously allowed a few extra cuddles. Just try to stay seated please.' He nods at her kindly. Maybe he's not all sleaze and cheese.

'You got kids?' a curvy woman to my left asks. I fight the urge to rest my palm on my belly.

'No.' I shake my head. Not yet.

'It never gets any easier,' she says. Then, leaning in as if to tell me a secret, 'My Rhianna thinks this is where Mummy works. Marc is old enough not to fall for that. He don't come with my mother any more.'

'I'm sorry,' I say, at a loss at what else to add.

She shrugs. 'Only three more months left and then I'm out.'

The thought of not seeing my child is like guy ropes fired into my flesh, pulling at my stomach. 'And he won't come at all?'

Her gaze drops to the floor as if it's too heavy to hold up. 'He feels guilty. He's got to get over it.'

'For not visiting?' Everyone's barriers are down in here, like we're all sharing the same moment. Like how strangers chat in the ladies' loos in restaurants and bars.

'For putting me in here,' she says.

My shock must show on my face, as she continues.

'He had hash in the house. Dealing,' she whispers. 'But it's my name on the lease, see? I had to prove that I never knew it were there.'

I'm staggered. This can't be right. 'But that's not fair. What did your solicitor say?'

'Bloody useless.' She shrugs again. 'It's better this way, though. Cause I said it was mine. If my boy goes into juvie now . . .' she shakes her head. 'This way he's got a shot.'

'But you didn't do anything.' I know she loves her son, but this is too much. She shouldn't be here. Punished for a crime she didn't commit. And separated from her family. Her son doesn't even have the decency to visit.

'I keep putting him on my visitor list. One day he'll come,' she says.

Will Ness and Mum come? Mum would never believe the things they're saying. But what about Ness? Could they have shown her the images they found on my computer? Forced her to confront what they think her sister is? Dread bubbles in my stomach and I try to breathe deeply and release it. Like the Mindfulness app I'd been using for insomnia outside taught me. *Release.* I don't want whatever chemicals or hormones panic produces passing to the baby. I want the baby to be calm. It's going to be okay – the police will work out who really did this. Mr Peterson will tell them my concerns. They won't keep an innocent pregnant woman locked up. This *will* be over soon. *Release. Release. Release.*

Ryan's radio crackles and we all look up as the far door is unlocked from the other side, and Kev appears.

The woman to my left practically strains in her seat. The energy in the room is electric. A mass of final tugs at the hems of tops. Fingers run through hair. Creases smoothed. As the first of the visitors start to enter the room, a snake of men, women, children clutching the hands of their fathers, their older siblings, their nans, women all around me start to wave.

'Mummy!' cries out one little boy in a bright-blue *Frozen* jumper.

'Hello, darling!' calls a woman toward the back, the hard lines of her face lifted into a look of pure joy.

Beside me, Rhianna's mum looks as proud as if she's the mother of Mary in the nativity play. I follow her gaze to that of a large older woman, who is clutching the hand of a tiny girl in a pretty pink dress and shiny shoes. The girl shyly looks up and across at her mum. I can't help but smile. Emily wouldn't wear pink at all. *Urgh, I'm not a girly girl, Jenna!* My chest aches.

Behind the woman at the back are several opaque windows through which I can see moving shapes. Private rooms. How do you get one of them? I lean toward Abi, who is bouncing excitedly in her seat and waving at a guy in a tight blue T-shirt and Adidas track pants who is walking quickly toward her, a huge grin on his face. Must be her boyfriend. 'Who's in those rooms?'

Abi doesn't let the smile fade from her face, but her words hiss out from behind her teeth like a ventriloquist dummy. 'That's where they put the kiddie fiddlers. Twisted fucks.'

My hand clutches at my stomach. Before I can say anything more, I catch sight of Ness and Mum and I have to fight back tears.

Now

Mum's face is set like it used to be before her NA meetings. A grim determination pushes her jaw forward, making her head seem more prominent on her sinewy frame. She's tucked her hands into the sleeves of her jumper, and walks with purpose, as if daring anyone near to get in her way. It's a fragile front. And I know I can't tell them. Learning I'm pregnant in here would be a tipping point. She's been clean for nineteen years, but we've all been holding our breath, aware addiction is the uninvited guest that never leaves.

Next to her Ness looks pale, drawn. Her eyes anxiously comb the room till she meets my own stare. She's normally so pulled together, all perfect brows, and a dazzling smile. But she's still in her gym work uniform and her usually glossy hair is scraped back into a greasy ponytail. I've done this to her. I've ground those dark circles under her eyes. I've threatened Mum's health.

'Oh Jenna,' Mum cries, and I'm only half up as she folds me into her. The sickly-sweet perfume she's tried to use to mask the smell of cigarette smoke burrows into my sinuses. I want to collapse into her, curl up on her lap. Will she feel the heartbeat of my baby as we hold each other?

'What happened to your face?' Ness reaches for my cheek, her fingers cold against the greening bruises.

I can't say. 'I fell. It's not as bad as it looks.' Mum's eyes swim with worry. It's too much.

Ness sniffs. 'All right,' she says. 'But if I find out that anyone in here did that to you . . .' she points at my face.

'I told you. It was an accident.' I cut her off fast. Glance at Abi quickly, but she's gazing rapt into the eyes of the guy visiting her, their fingers entwined across the table.

'We're gonna get you out of here, love.' Mum's hands shake as she reaches behind her for the unmoving chair.

Kev is looking at Ness. She follows my gaze, and turns to glare at him. He looks away.

Instinctively she runs her hand over her hair. Tugs at the sleeve of her hoodie.

'They searched my bag on the way in.' Ness is holding her handbag tight.

'They did it to all of us, love,' Mum soothes her.

'They didn't take your bloody yoghurt though, did they?' Ness is prickly. She gets like this when she's upset. And having your sister accused of murder is upsetting.

'They said you can have it back after,' Mum said. Adding, in an astounded voice 'They wouldn't let me bring in my pack of tissues.'

Ness tugs at the chair. It doesn't move. 'And you didn't get groped.'

'What?' I look at Kev. Can they do that?

'It wasn't personal, at you,' Mum says. 'Random checks, that's what they said.'

I glare at Kev: how dare he?

Mum follows my look. 'It was a lady officer.' She pats my hand, reassuringly.

'Scum,' Ness says, loudly.

I feel the word ripple through the tables around us. I need to get her to calm down. Ness's temper is legendary. 'Please, Ness, it won't help.'

Ryan is fast approaching, his eyes narrowed. Heat rises up my face.

Clocking him, Ness's demeanour changes. 'I wouldn't mind if he'd given me the pat down.' She raises her eyebrows suggestively.

Ryan slows. Appraises Ness's tight, toned figure. 'Nice of your two sisters to come visit you, Jenna,' he says, in his affected silky voice. He winks at Ness as he passes.

'Typical Ness!' Mum laughs. Her face relaxing for the first time since they arrived. If only it wasn't because of Ryan.

'It's not all bad in here then.' Ness leans in conspiratorially, her thirsty eyes still on Ryan. 'I wouldn't mind doing hard labour with that one.'

Mum hoots and playfully bats her arm.

'He's a sleazebag, trust me,' I say.

'A bad boy in uniform.' Her eyes twinkle.

Urgh. I give her a look. She really does want to stay away from that one.

'Oh all right.' She rolls her eyes. But her face has lost some of the tension it had when she arrived. She looks herself again.

The woman at the table behind Mum and Ness is being visited by someone I presume is her mum. The older lady is wrapped in a faded tan mac the same colour as her skin. Four children cling and crawl over her. The nauseating smell of a ripe nappy wafts over. And smoke. Mum is obviously not the only one who had one last fag before she summoned up the courage to come in.

'It took us ages to get here.' Mum frowns as she looks around the room.

Ness shoots her a look.

'You didn't drive?' Great timing of Ness's car to break down again.

'Car's been nicked.' Ness rolls her eyes.

How much bad luck can one family have? 'When?'

'I didn't want to tell you.' She picks at a crack in the table veneer with a painted nail.

Mum looks guilty.

They didn't want to add to my burden. But maybe a healthy dose of mundane reality is what I need. 'What did the police say?'

Ness purses her lips. Mum starts fiddling with her hands. 'I told her,' she said, without looking up.

Oh no. 'Ness?'

There's a plastic slap and a yell as two kids career into each other with brightly coloured toys in the corner. Ness turns to look, her face shifting into something akin to disgust. She tuts. Would she be like this with my baby? No, she's stalling.

'Ness,' I say again.

She turns her palms skyward. 'I was a little behind with the insurance, that's all . . .'

'It's illegal to drive without insurance!' I hiss.

'Well dur, why do you think I'm not blabbing my mouth off about it?' She glares at Mum, who is smiling at the little girl from the table behind.

This is all we need. Another member of the family getting in trouble. It'd only take the press to start sniffing round for dirt on my family. She's basically handed it to them on a plate. 'Why on earth isn't it insured?'

'We haven't all got buckets of cash sloshing about,' she snaps.

I sigh. 'I would have lent you the money.' I would have paid for her if I'd known. Now I can't do anything to help. My throat runs dry.

'It's fine, it's just for a few months till I get a few things sorted . . .' she trails off. 'Except some fucker nicked it. Probably someone in here.' She raises an eyebrow and mimes scoping out the room.

I giggle despite myself. Catch hold of her hand. 'Thank you for coming anyway.'

Mum beams.

'I love you so much I even used public transport,' Ness says, the twinkle back in her eye.

'I need to talk to you about that, actually.' I tug at my tabard, the material stiff between my fingers.

'The car?' Ness's face shifts. And she glances back at Ryan. Who keeps smiling over at us.

'No. It's a bit awkward. Can you transfer me some money?'

Both Mum and Ness look shocked. For a long time it's gone the other way. To Mum at least. Ness and I sending her top-ups for her benefit. Keeping her buoyant. Away from that desperate place that might pull her under again.

'Of course, love,' Mum says. I know she hasn't got two pennies to rub together. 'How much do you need?'

'It's all right, Mum, I've got it,' Ness says. 'I'm paid at the end of the month – I'll transfer some in then.'

The end of the month – it's only the 11th today. Things must be tight if Ness wasn't insuring her car. Neither of them will have enough to cover legal fees. But I need cash for in here. 'I can't access any of my bank accounts,' I say. 'I need a small transfer for things in here.' More food for me and my baby. I'm starving and tired on the standard three meals. Perhaps I can even get some vitamins.

'No problem,' Ness says.

'I can pay you back as soon as I'm out,' I say. 'And I need you to set up a magazine subscription for my cellmate.'

Ness's eyes narrow in suspicion, as her gaze flickers over my bruises.

'She's great,' I add quickly. 'Helped me out with a lot of stuff I needed.'

'All right.' Ness is still watching me like I might be hiding something. I am.

'You're my daughter, I want to help.' Mum's eyes are milky pools.

I take her hand, warm and papery in mine. 'You have. You came,' I say, emotion in my voice.

She tuts. 'That's not much,' she says.

'You were just moaning about the three buses we had to take,' Ness says. She means it as a joke. I try to keep my smile fixed. When did they set off? Did all the other people here also struggle on public transport?

Mum is looking intently at her hands.

'What is it, Mum?' I say.

'Nothing,' she says.

Ness sighs. 'She can't afford to come up all the time, and I can't get the time off work.'

'Wow,' I say. 'Talk about breaking it gently to me. So – what? You're not coming to see me again?' I can't believe this.

'Course we are.' Mum tuts at Ness.

'There's no point giving her false hope,' Ness says.

'I understand that you won't come three times a week,' I say. I guess it was unreasonable to expect them to come quite that frequently.

Ness's face falls. *Oh no. Not even every week?*

'It's fine,' I manage.

'We're gonna come every month, love,' Mum says, giving me a smile and squeezing my hand. 'Every month.'

Once a month. Four weeks on my own in here. I feel my bottom lip tremble. I can't show them I'm upset. It's okay. It's three hours away, and without the car it's hard. It costs money, I get that. 'That'll be great.' I try to sound bright.

'I'll try and get up a bit more than that, if I can, okay?' Ness says. 'And you can always call us.'

I think about the very public shared phones in the wing. I don't know if I can do this. 'Have the police spoken to you?' They exchange a look. Fear crawls across my skin. Is this what this is about. 'What is it? What have they said? Have they found something? Did they . . .' I glance at the children at the next table. Lower my voice. 'Whatever they said they found it's not true. I didn't put that stuff . . . I couldn't . . .' Bile tickles the base of my throat.

'What have they found?' Ness says.

I stare at her. They don't know. They haven't been told. Maybe they're not allowed to know. Breach of court or something.

I have to talk to Ness alone. 'Mum, could you get us some tea?' My stomach rumbles again as I point out the counter.

She pats my hand. 'Course, love. Anything you want. You want a snack as well?'

'Please.' I nod my head keenly.

She looks torn between wanting to stay and being pleased to be doing something practical. 'What about you, love?' she asks Ness.

'Herbal tea if they've got it,' she says. 'None of that funny plastic milk.'

I smile. Ness would have refused to eat the breakfast box I greedily devoured this morning. Mum nods, glancing back at us when she reaches the counter.

'What's going on?' Ness leans toward me.

'I need you to speak to Robert's parents. I need you to ask them to come and see me. They need to know that I didn't do this to Robert and Emily. God knows what the police have told them.' And if David is somehow involved in this I need to see him. I need to look him in the eyes. I need to know if he's lying.

Ness nods. If I can get them to visit, I can ask them to lend me money for a lawyer. A better one. Mr Peterson seems nice, but I need more than that to get out of here. If David is innocent they'll have to help. If he's not I'll know by his reaction. 'Robert's parents have connections, money,' I say.

'You have money,' she says.

'It's mostly his. I've spent all mine on wedding things.' Sorrow and guilt burn inside me. I splashed out on an extravagant vintage watch for Robert. All my savings gone in one go. I just wanted something to equal his contribution.

'Only thirty minutes left,' I hear Abi sigh next to me. We're already halfway through the session. There's no time for emotion.

'I need better legal representation,' I say.

Ness looks doubtful. 'The five-oh can't really think you did this – it's a mistake. Or like one of them tricks to smoke out the real killer, like you see on the telly?' she says. She looks desperate for me to agree.

I lean toward Ness. 'I think someone else is involved.'

Her eyes widen.

'What?' Ness's face has moved from shock to confusion.

I glance at the people either side of me. Rhianna is snuggled on her mum's lap, her big eyes watching me with interest.

'I think someone is framing me.' It sounds absurd. She's going to think I've lost the plot.

I see the lady behind the counter pass Mum some takeaway cups of tea.

Ness nods slowly, still absorbing this news. 'Like in *Making a Murderer* on Netflix – you think it's one of the pigs?'

The words hit me like Gould's elbow. *Of course.* I'd seen how the American police tampered with evidence to make it fit their theory. That guy was wrongfully sent to prison for eighteen years. My stomach falls away. Is that what's happening here? 'I don't know.'

'You remember Carly from our block?' Ness says.

Mum starts walking back toward us.

'They fitted up her man for a newsagent that was done over.'

Most people on the estate distrusted the police. A fair few had good reason to. You were often pre-judged for being an Orchard resident. I can't imagine that DI Langton could or would do something like this. But what about Salinsky? He hates me. He would have had ample opportunity. He could have planted the pornography after that night, to make it seem like I had a motive. To make the crime fit me. But this isn't America, it's Gloucestershire. It's the UK. The police aren't fitting people up for murder, surely?

Mum appears next to us, handing Ness the cups to distribute, while she pulls packets of food from her jeans pockets. 'I got you one with chocolate in it, like you used to like when you were wee.'

'Thanks.' I open it eagerly. I can't believe I didn't spot the signs sooner. The last couple of months I've been snacking like crazy. Supplementing my meals without even realising I was doing it. And now I'm back down to three a day. I can't imagine there was any nutrition in my cardboard breakfast. I should've got Mum to get me some fruit.

'They feeding you in here, love?' Mum looks at me concerned. I realise I've eaten two thirds of the flapjack already.

'Yes, sorry.' I force myself to put the rest of the flapjack down. 'Does anyone else want any?'

Ness is peering at me like she used to when I said I'd already done my homework, but hadn't.

'Nah, you're all right.' She pushes the packet back toward me.

The bell rings. 'That can't be it already?' I look up with alarm.

'Will all visitors please say their goodbyes and exit the hall. Residents, remain seated,' Kev shouts.

At the table to the left, Rhianna's mum is hugging her daughter to her. The little girl is crying. 'Shush, my baby, shush,' she says. 'It's okay, Mummy will be home soon.'

'Come on now, Rhianna, don't make a fuss,' the older woman says. She pulls the kid away with both hands as she tries to bundle forwards onto her mum, desperate not to let go.

Abi is clutching her partner tightly, her face buried in his shoulder.

I swallow the lump forming in my throat. Pull Mum into me.

'I don't want to leave you here.' Her voice wavers.

'It's all right, Mum,' I force myself to say.

'It's okay,' Ness says, gently peeling her off. 'With no WiFi and dodgy food it's like a new age retreat, isn't it?'

Mum tries to laugh.

Ness looks at me imploringly, but I've already plastered a grin on my face. 'I'm going to market it when I get out.'

'The Bang Up Diet,' Ness says, and Mum properly laughs this time.

Kev starts shouting again and the exit door is unlocked.

'Let me have a squeeze.' Ness leans over Mum to pull me into her. Ness is taller than us both, and so strong from her work at the gym that I instantly feel small and safe in her arms.

I whisper into her ear. 'Promise you'll speak to Robert's parents?'

She rests her cheek on the top of my head. Strokes my hair. 'I'm gonna sort this,' she says.

And then I have to sit down and watch them go. Seeing them made me feel normal, like everything might be okay. But seeing them leave is crushing. When am I going to see them again? Not till April? Another month closer to the wedding. My heart pinches.

The whole room deflates around me as the last visitor disappears through the door, and it is locked from the other side with a loud, finite clunk. Abi looks exhausted, as if the effort of behaving happy and upbeat has drained all her reserves. Rhianna's mum is quietly sobbing at the table next to me. And the woman behind us is reaching out absentmindedly with her hands, as if she might pull her children back and into her arms.

Gripping the table to give myself something to hold on to,

I keep thinking the same thing. *I'm innocent. Let me leave. I'm innocent. Let me leave.* If the police have done this I'll prove it. And if they didn't? I think of Robert's parents. I imagine David sitting across from me. I need to look him in the eye.

I need to know if it was him.

Now

Even with my thin pillow between my back and the wall I can feel the damp cold seeping through the bricks. Kelly has the one chair at the small bedside unit we have. Because regardless of the fact she doesn't know I'm pregnant and my back is aching too, she is still more pregnant. An ever-expanding, ever-tense beach-ball predicting my own future shape. Rain drums against the window. Both of us working on our own projects, to the background music of prison shouts and squeals. Hundreds of tellies turned up to try to block out the emotions. Hundreds of voices raised. Kelly's biro scratches against her pad.

What do policemen do on the cop shows when they have a suspect? They have forensics, and specialists, and technology, and all the things that are damning me. But Langton and Salinsky must have missed something. Or I have. Something that only I would spot is wrong. That's why they haven't seen it yet. I need to go back over everything. Before it becomes the list of horrible accusations from Mr Peterson. When it was still just a day. I force my mind back. Back to my arrival home. No, before that.

I left the office early, at 4.30 p.m., probably just after. I start a timeline. Write down everything I know.

Left office: 4.35 p.m.

I drove to Deb's to collect Emily's cake. They'd already left for their week in Cornwall, so I went round the back. Deb had left the key under the third terracotta plant pot, as usual. I remember looking at my watch – it was gone five. I was stressed about getting home before Emily. She was due back from swim club at 5.30 p.m. Robert and I were going to get everything set up before she arrived. Emily's gone to swim club every Wednesday since I've known her. It was her favourite. She named the pop band she'd formed with her friend Phoebe after it: The Tumble Tucks. Even when she had a cold, she insisted on going, putting Vicks onto her nose clip, much to my alarm. In summer she'll be at their holiday swim club Monday to Friday again. *Would've been.* I close my eyes and I can see all her swim medals and certificates fluttering round the edge of her pin board. But she came home unexpectedly that day. She could have disturbed David. Or maybe he arranged to meet her? She could have bunked off swim club easily enough by saying her period had started.

I force myself not to dwell, to go back to where I was. In Deb's kitchen: picking up the cake. She'd left it covered on the side, with a card and a present for Emily. I put the card and present in my bag, and then carried the cake back to the car.

Once you're out of Deb's village, it's mostly lanes to Robert's house, to our house. Time was against me, and as I came round Pears' bend, Locke's sheep were out again. No point beeping them, it only makes it worse. It took fifteen minutes to double back on myself and come in the back entrance. I kept looking at the clock. I remember being relieved at the time that there were no other vehicles on the narrow road. No need to stop, reverse back to the last passing point, slowing me down more. No more delays in getting home. Mr Peterson said that if there had been someone on the road, someone who had remembered passing me, then there'd be someone to corroborate my timings. As it was, it was only the sheep.

Arrive home: 5.30 p.m. The back gate was still open, so I thought Phoebe's mum hadn't dropped Emily off yet. She always closed it after she'd said goodbye. And I remember being elated at that. Because it meant I'd beaten them back. If I'd had even the slightest inkling then what had happened I wouldn't have got out the car. But I had no idea at all. I picked up the cake, balancing it with one hand to unlock the door. I dropped my keys and fob on the hall side table. And then . . . then . . . then I knew something was wrong.

I stare at the paper. Unable to re-visit what happened next. The cold terms on Mr Peterson's evidence list have done nothing to reduce their impact. Everything speeds up and slows down.

Emily was still warm when I held her. I cover my mouth and breathe deeply, try not to alert Kelly. I need to stay focused. How long does a body stay warm for? I swallow. If I only had the Internet. Just two minutes and I could look this up. But I've got nothing and nowhere to check. I could try the library, but where would I look? I doubt very much that they keep books on decomposition. Had the murderer only just left? Was David disappearing with Robert out the other gate as I was coming in? I think of the anger between Robert and David after Emily's school found her smoking weed. David pushes them all so hard. David and Robert could have been fighting again. Was there a struggle? Did something go badly wrong? David would know which way to go to get away without being seen. Under my jumper, I cup my stomach as if to protect my unborn child from my growing suspicions. David could have done this.

Now

The day after Ness and Mum visited, I applied for a library session. A week after that I was allowed a morning in the draughty, double-height room lined with panelled shelves, hundreds of books, and three humming grey plastic computers that look older than the ones they had in my naughties school. My excitement at getting online was squashed again by the librarian, Helen, a vivacious woman in her forties, with cropped bleached hair and a ready smile. She confirmed that, no, these were sadly not connected to the Internet either. It really is banned everywhere. If I was outside I'd check Milcombe Estate's finances with Companies House. I've never seen any indication that David is running out of money – in fact, the opposite – but it's often a motive, isn't it? You read about insurance fraud and things all the time. Maybe he planted the pornographic images to try and break me and Robert up, to keep me away from the family fortune? Or to stop the wedding. And something happened and Emily ended up dead and Robert missing. Or hidden. I don't know.

The library has a small number of books on pregnancy, and if I sit behind the stacks at the back, it's possible to read without being seen by anyone else. I can't take them out because Kelly or one of the others would notice. You're never alone in here. As far as Kelly and anyone else knows, I'm in for drug-related offences. And I am definitely not pregnant, nor the Blonde Slayer. Luckily no one seems to have recognised me, and the news has moved on.

Each week since then I've been here, sitting in the corner, breathing in the dust from the hard floor, and watching March slowly thaw through the window. The faint smell of coffee is with me at all times from where I comb a thick tint of it through my hair while Kelly is at work. I wash in the sink when she's out too. My bump is bigger, not just a little pouch at the bottom of my stomach now, but rising. It's impossible to use the showers, which have no privacy screens, and are always busy in the short Associations we get. I've taken to wrapping my blanket round my shoulders, like a poncho, to hide my growing stomach and boobs. Luckily the prison is so cold nobody seems to have questioned this.

Today is my twenty-seventh day in Fallenbrook. Nearly a whole month. According to the books, at three months my baby is 7.4 cm long. That means I should still be able to hide my pregnancy. At four months you're bigger, and the baby begins to move around. And I can definitely feel bubbles and flutterings in there. I think the doctor's wrong – or I made a mistake about when we had food poisoning – and I'm more than three months gone. I can't help but imagine my baby turning this way and that, trying to get out. Like me. We're both locked in. Counting the days, the hours. The seconds. I'm wading through treacle. Everything is slow and hard, and seems to involve multiple forms.

There was the form applying for my first scan appointment, which has still not come through. And the form to apply to see the doctor to chase my scan. And the form yesterday trying again, because I still haven't heard anything. Under my blanket I cup my belly.

I'm so sorry I haven't had my scan yet. That I haven't seen you and checked you're okay. And that I haven't been able to eat hard

*cheese, yoghurt, and leafy greens to get you the calcium to grow
your teeth and bones. Please be okay. I'm letting you down already,
baby.*

Even if my money had come in from Ness already, I
haven't seen anything suitable on canteen to buy. Kelly
doesn't seem to have any folic acid or vitamins, and I don't
want to upset her by asking about it. If it wasn't for her and
Abi, and Vina, who has taken to talking to me about the
Criminology degree she's trying to take, I wouldn't know
how anything worked. I wouldn't be surviving. Those girls,
this library, and the patch of sky I can see out the window
sitting here, are keeping me going. That and my unborn
child.

There's been no word from Ness, and without any money I
can't call her. But in the meantime Kelly has shown me how
to apply for telephone numbers to be added to my approved
list. It's humiliating that I can't just call up whoever I want,
and David and Judith have rejected my application. At first I
thought it was a mistake – I'd added Sally's office number and
that came back rejected as well. So did Becky's, and Deb's. I
thought maybe I filled out the form wrong. But then none of
them replied to my visitor requests either. They can't really all
think I did this. Can they? It's like I vanished from their lives
the moment I came inside.

But two weeks have gone by and I heard this morning
David and Judith have rejected it again. That could be a sign
of guilt. The more I think about it, the more I think David
could be capable of this. And what about Judith? What
lengths would she go to for her husband? She is definitely
scared of him. Vina is writing about female prisoners for
one of her course modules. She told me fifty-seven per cent
of women inside have a history of being abused by their
partners. That there's a lot of evidence to suggest a large
number of women could have been coerced into

committing their crimes. Could Judith have been coerced into helping David? Could they both be involved? It sounds mad. It feels mad. I don't know if the amount of time I'm spending alone, inside my head, is driving me crazy. If I'm seeing things that aren't there. I can't discuss my suspicions with Mr Peterson till I have something more concrete. I need to speak to David and Judith to ask for money, but also to see if they are lying. I've realised over the last month that I don't know them at all.

'Hello, love – do you want a biscuit?' Helen's smiling face appears over the top of the stack, brandishing a packet of supermarket-brand biscuits. My hand lurches away from my stomach like it's been scalded. I drop it over the book I was reading, the photo of a pregnant woman throbbing beneath my palm. I can feel a draught on my belly – is it uncovered? I daren't look down in case Helen looks too.

'Errr . . .' My brain won't function. *Please don't notice.*

'I've got some left over from a poetry class this morning.' Helen glances at the book I'm covering but her face doesn't change.

Did she see? Has she guessed? 'Err . . . thanks.' I reach quickly for the biscuit – I am actually starving.

Helen presses the packet forward. 'Why don't you take a couple. Keep your strength up.'

Oh god. She knows. No, don't panic, she's just being kind. I manage a 'Thanks' as I take three and sweep my other arm up at the same time so the blanket flicks round me tight. My stomach gurgles. When I look up Helen has gone, and I hear her asking a woman who is reading legal books at the small table to the right if she'd like a snack.

My heart's thumping. That was too close. It's getting harder and harder to hide. And Helen isn't a threat. What if it was someone else, someone who is dangerous? I could bind my stomach with strips of my bed sheet. The thought makes me feel sick. That would restrict my baby. Hurt it. I have to get some money, I have to get a better lawyer, or new evidence, or prove who did this.

I have to get out of here.

Now

'Yes!' says Kelly, as they start unlocking the doors on the walkway below. 'Association is go!'

I grin. I'm feeling far more confident after unpicking the
waistband from my size 18 hoodie this morning while Kelly
was out at work. Now it hangs down like a giant box over my
size 12 frame – hiding my bump. I should have thought of this
before.

The noise and excitement levels rise as women are released
and people begin to make the most of the precious hour.
Some head straight to the showers with their flip-flops, towels
and shampoo, others greet and gather friends round the pool
table, some queue for the yard door to be opened. That's
where I'm headed when Vina stops me.

'Hey!' she says. Today her hair is up in a plain cream calico
scarf. 'Was wondering if you'd check my latest essay? You
know, for spelling and that.' She clicks her tongue.

'I'd be delighted to.' They're really fascinating to read, and I
keep hoping I can find out if she's come across any cases
where people have been framed. And, more importantly, how
they proved it.

'This module will be eighteen credits.' She almost smiles.

'Any news on funding?' Vina has applied to take the full
degree while she's inside, but apparently competition for
funding is fierce. I know she's been sentenced, because she's
been at Fallenbrook for two years, but I don't know how long
she's got. I don't know what she did. Some of the women tell

you, and some don't. Vina is one of the private ones. Kelly said she heard it was death by dangerous driving, but I think you can't tell what's gossip and what's not.

A raucous round of laughter explodes from a cell behind us. Vina shoots them a dirty look, clicks her tongue again. 'Hooch,' she says.

What? 'Alcohol?' I breathe. 'Where did they get that from?' Someone must have smuggled it in.

'Made it,' Vina says. 'You never wonder why it's so hard to get fruit in here? That's what they make it out of.'

I shake my head, astounded, yet again, at the ingenuity of the women. 'Don't the screws know?' I whisper, checking that the officer is well out of earshot.

Vina checks where Kev is herself before replying. 'They brew it in the sanitary bins – the guards never check there.' She winks.

'Oh my god!' The disgust must show on my face, because Vina does laugh at this.

Then her smile freezes into a rictus grimace. She stares past me. Others have stopped talking as well, and are turning toward the gate.

Oh god. I thought it was okay. I let my guard down.

Hushed panicked whispers burn the word through the wing lightning fast. I feel the name before I hear it: *Gould*. My nose prickles at the memory of the pain.

I have to get out of here. Our cell is all the way upstairs. I can't cross the now silent room to reach the metal stairway. The voice of someone blissfully unaware and singing in the shower, the run of water, floats through the unnatural silence. People are coming out of their cells to see what's happening. The singing stops abruptly. Gould is here.

Why haven't I put my hood up? Why haven't I kept my face covered? I don't want to turn around. Don't want this to be real. I try to make eye contact with Vina, as if to will her to understand that whatever Gould might say – I didn't do it. But Vina, like everyone else, is looking behind me.

I hear the squeak of Gould's trainers on the ground. And other steps. Clipped. She's not alone.

Sara calls out, 'All right, ladies, stop your gawking.'

The relief at hearing her voice reduces my fear enough for me to turn, albeit while tucking myself as much out of sight behind Vina as possible.

Gould isn't wearing the regulation sweatshirt and joggies I've been assigned. Instead she's managed to get hold of new clothes: civilian. It's still a tracksuit, but it's red. For danger. Designer, you can tell. She obviously wasn't waiting for her canteen to come in. But then she's been inside before, according to the papers. She knows how things work. She probably has an ongoing account here. I would laugh if I wasn't too busy holding my hands together behind my back trying to stop them shaking.

She walks with that same relaxed bounce that makes her look like she's strolling onto a dance floor, not walking into the UK's largest female prison wing. Sara, by contrast, has a tense efficiency to her gait. Her eyes roam quickly back and forth across the room as if she's waiting for something to happen.

Gould stops, and, not expecting it, Sara has to take two half-steps backwards to keep alongside her. Gould, her dark eyes laconic, inspects four women who are sitting round a table, plastic cups of tea in front of them.

I'm not the only one holding my breath.

'I know you?' Gould points at one woman, whose ginger hair springs away from her head in an unfortunate manner that resembles a kid's clown.

The woman stands as if she's been called to attention by a sergeant major. 'Annie.' She delivers her name like it's roll-call.

'Clive's sister.' Gould nods.

'Who's Clive?' someone whispers behind us.

'Don't know,' comes the hissed response.

'Good man, Clive.' Gould is inspecting Annie like she's thinking about buying her. Perhaps she is.

'I haven't got all day.' Sara taps her foot. 'Let's get you settled in, please.'

Gould turns her eyes on her, her face so ferocious and full of hate that I nearly run forward to shield Sara. The crowd audibly inhale. But Gould's fierce glare breaks with a cheery 'Sure thing, guv.' She makes the final word sound dirty. A few women giggle, but it could be from the tension.

Sara holds her own, signalling with her hand that Gould should go first.

Gould walks on. Sara's tapping boots alongside. The inharmonious jingle of the keys.

They'll reach us in seconds. I could run now: get me and my baby to the stairs. To our cell. To safety.

Vina steps aside as Gould and Sara pass. I hold my breath, but she doesn't even glance at us.

Maybe she's already moved on from our encounter? She presumably fights all the time; violence is an everyday occurrence for her. Maybe, just maybe, she's forgotten about me? I pity the person who has to share her cell, though. And you can already tell it will be *her* cell. The one next to us is empty. *Please not there.* The thought of her being just the other side of the wall makes me feel sick.

But for once things go my way. There are a few whispers from the walkways above, but people are quiet, almost reverential, as Sara stops on the ground floor to show Gould her new home. Two along from us, but two whole glorious floors below. *Thank god.*

As Gould disappears inside, the room erupts into conversation.

'*She runs Bristol.*'

'*She did over my Danny's cousin. He was in hospital for six days. He never grassed, though. Too scared.*'

'*Her kids go to that fancy school. The lad got a Boxster for his seventeenth.*'

'*I heard she cut off a man's cock and choked him on it. Apparently he'd cut her up on the road.*'

As I walk through the excited, chattering women, Sara comes out of the cell and the woman who identified herself as Annie walks over to it. I usually say hi to Sara, but I don't want to hang around listening to the gory details of Gould's life. Maybe she has forgotten about me, but it's not worth risking getting back on her radar.

Upstairs, Kelly is excitedly hopping about, making her bump and topknot shake. 'Did you see her?'

Gossip, born of boredom, is the only real currency we have left in here. I get that. But I'm not about to gush about the woman who smashed my nose in. Who put my baby at risk. I'm staying out of it. I nod, and fold myself into my bunk, hugging the blanket to me. Picking up the novel I was pretending to read earlier.

But Kelly isn't done. She bounds after me. 'Did you see her trainers? And that top was lit.' Her eyes are sparkling with excitement, as if Gould is a celebrity.

'How you getting on with your book ideas?' I want to talk about anything but this.

Kelly squats down beside me, her bump resting against my arm. 'You still feeling rough?'

'No, I'm fine,' I say, too curtly.

She doesn't seem to notice. 'What do you reckon will happen with her and her man locked up, to her gang and that?' She whispers excitedly, as if she's sharing a secret from *EastEnders*, not discussing a real woman with links to drugs and prostitution. 'Do you think there'll be a turf war?'

A shadow appears in the doorway, blocking the light. Kelly turns to shout at the intruder, then stiffens.

Gould is standing there. I sit up, banging my head against the bottom of Kelly's bunk.

Gould smiles, lazily. 'I think I'll be all right running it from in here, don't you?' She looks at Kelly expectantly.

Kelly squeaks. 'Yeah, course.' Pushes herself upright, takes a step back. Laughing nervously. 'I wasn't saying anything else. I mean you . . . you're you. You can, er, do anything.'

Gould remains, casually leaning against the door frame. Behind her, the bulk of Annie stands, scowling in at us. 'Thought I'd familiarise myself with my new surroundings. I don't like any unpleasant surprises.'

Her eyes pin me to the bed. I want it to suck me under. To make me disappear. *Don't show fear.*

Slowly, I force myself to swing my legs over the side, and stand.

Gould's lip curls in amusement. Her skin is flawless apart from a smattering of freckles. My nose is still tender four weeks later. I feel the pressure pushing in, making it hard to breathe. Should I tell her I'm pregnant? Would it make a difference? How do you negotiate with someone like this?

Gould springs forward, and I jump. But she's only walking about, in her dancing, bouncing way. Moving round our cell, uncomfortably full with three in here. She bends and picks up Kelly's diary. Flicks through the pages. My notes, the list of evidence against me, is face down next to my bed. *Please don't pick them up. Please.* Gould sniffs. Puts Kelly's book notes back down and turns her attention to her.

She points at her stomach. 'When you due?'

Kelly swallows. 'Two months.'

'What you called?' Gould tilts her head each time she speaks, as if her chin were jabbing at Kelly like a pointed finger.

Kelly, nervous, speaks quickly. 'Dunno yet, I like Brandon if it's a boy . . .'

'What's your name, not the kid's, muppet?' Gould turns to Annie as if she can't believe anyone would be this daft. Annie makes a noise like a grunting laugh. Kelly looks like she might cry.

Anger burns inside me.

Kelly has both her hands on her belly, as if she is covering the baby's ears. She clears her throat. 'Oh right, yeah. Kelly.'

'Well, you make sure you watch out for yourself, *oh-right-yeah-Kelly*,' Gould says, and Annie laughs again. 'If you need anything while you're in here you just let me know, yeah?'

Kelly looks confused by this seemingly altruistic offer. But she nods.

'I look after those that come to me,' Gould continued.

Oh god, it's a recruitment drive. She wants Kelly, so I'll be vulnerable in this cell. She hasn't forgotten, she hasn't moved on at all. I swallow.

Gould steps toward her. Kelly bumps into the unit behind. Gould reaches out her hand, running it over Kelly's stomach. Kelly looks like she's not breathing.

I step toward them, but Annie's hand is hard and firm on my shoulder. Holding me down.

Gould is still stroking Kelly's bump. Her voice silky. 'I can get you and your baby there some things you might need.' She sounds almost excited, as if she is enjoying Kelly's clear fear.

Then she stops. Turns, looks around the cell as if imagining redecorating. 'Make things a little bit easier in here.'

Gould has only been on the wing for ten minutes and already she's asserting a new order. One in which she's at the top. My heart starts to hammer. Annie knows it, that's why she's acting like a henchman.

Kelly says nothing. All the colour has gone from her cheeks. This is my fault. She should have sailed under Gould's radar. She should have been safe just gossiping about her.

'All right then,' Gould says, as if she were a school teacher who'd invited us to read when we'd rather play in the sandpit. Disappointed, but forgiving. 'You just give it some thought.' She pats Kelly's bump once more.

She's going to run things from in here. That's what she said. And that means she's going to run this place too. There's been no offer to me. No invitation to participate. I am out in the cold. How many others would sign up?

Gould turns, sniffs again, and strolls, hands in pockets, out. Annie follows her.

As Gould reaches the threshold she pauses, taps the air with her finger, and purses her lips as if she's forgotten to tell us something innocuous. Blood rushes to my ears.

Gould turns and looks directly at me for the first time. Her eyes hard stones. The hairs on the back of my neck stand up. Her words are leaden with menace. 'I'm watching you, Blondie.'

Now

Since Gould's arrival over a fortnight ago I've spent as little time as possible out on the wing. But today I have to risk it. The money Ness sent in for me finally arrived, and I now have phone cards. They bang against my leg as I walk quickly back to the ground-floor landing, bumping in my pocket against the new lipstick I bought Kelly. She's been quiet since the incident in our cell, and I had to tell her Gould knew me because of my drug-taking. I'm not sure she believes me, but she hasn't pushed the point. She's been nothing but kind to me, and this is how I repay her: inviting someone like Gould into her life.

I haven't seen Gould about since then. But I've heard her. She talks in that lazy drawl, but her laugh is high, tinny, almost manic. I've learnt to move as soon as I hear it. Like an early warning system. And I've certainly felt her presence. Already others have joined Annie in her gang. You see them in pairs or threes during Association, passing between cells, industrious, purposeful. I don't know what they're running – messages, contraband, weapons? I don't want to think about it. They have started to roll the sleeves of their tops up on one side. Just a couple of times. It's subtle, but it's a signifier. I'm not the only one who's noticed. The woman who just sold me my cards checked my left sleeve before she spoke. It looks like Gould has favourites, ranks even. Annie apparently only leaves her side for meals, and there's a small wiry woman, her left sleeve rolled, who I suspect is queuing up for all Gould's food. She certainly isn't deigning to queue herself, which is a relief. I can't skip meals with the baby.

The wing is busy, as ever. Some women are just sitting around chatting, some are playing pool or table tennis. A group near me are plotting how to make a banoffee pie.

'Luce, you get the bananas from your mate in the kitchen. Sandy, you're owed a packet of biscuits, right? Kay, you and Fran club together for the condensed milk. I'll heat it.'

'How ya gonna do that?'

'It's easy. Stick the tin in a bowl of water, strip the plug off the kettle, get your two wires and: buzzzzz! You electrocute it and it turns into Dulce de Leche.'

'What's Dulce la doobery?'

'Like a caramel sauce. What do they teach you kids at school nowadays?'

They all laugh.

No sign of Gould or any of her goons though. They're probably in one of the cells. I need to move quickly.

There are eight telephones in the wing. Sprinkled, two at a time, throughout the ground-floor landing. They have a mere suggestion of a cover for the illusion of privacy, like each handset is wearing a large plastic deerstalker hat. Everyone can hear everything. And, like everything in here, half of them are broken. The first two, the furthest from Gould's cell, are both missing their handsets, the wires hanging down like tails of stray dogs. One of the next two is the same. The other has an out-of-order sign hanging off it. One of the wall-mounted units of the next pair is hanging off. Four women wait at the one that is in use, behind a woman who is crying softly into the receiver, mumbling in what sounds like Polish.

Which leaves the two closest to Gould's cell. They are both occupied, and a line of three has formed behind them. But I can't wait – Association will be over before you know it. It's my best option. I pull my hood up, hunching my shoulders so

I disappear as much as possible into it. Rounding my back to try and counter my ever-growing bump. Turning myself inside out.

It takes twenty minutes to get to the front of the queue, to get hold of Ness at work, and get her to call me back (like Kelly taught me to – it saves money). And now I can't believe what she's saying.

'They got their lawyer on me.' Ness is raging at the other end.

'What?' Why do they have a lawyer? Surely that implies guilt?

'I did what you said and tried calling them. They screened the call and next thing I know I get a call from some stuck-up woman telling me I have to cease and fucking desist or whatever.' Ness sounds far away, like she's screaming from the end of a tunnel.

Panic rises in me. David and Judith won't talk to Ness. They believe what the police have said. Or they're hiding something. They did this. Behind me there are already four more people waiting to use the phone. One of them I recognise as Rhianna's mum from the visiting room. Another, a pretty Asian lady, is reading a book while she waits. They are all pretending not to listen to me, but there's little else to do. I have to watch my words. But if they won't even talk to Ness then I have no choice.

'I haven't got long,' I say. I turn my back toward the woman tapping her watch pointedly behind me, and try and curl my whole body round the phone. 'Ness, I need you not to freak out, okay?'

'What's happened?' Her voice moves from righteous indignation at David's lawyer being set on her, to concern. I can picture her gripping the phone in her hand so tight it creaks.

'It's going to be okay, but . . .' I lower my voice to a whisper. Please don't let anyone else hear. Please don't let Gould hear.

I think of her hand on Kelly's stomach, on her baby. The sound her voice made.

'What is it, Jenna?'

'I'm pregnant,' I whisper.

There's silence on the other end. Did I say it too quiet? I should be shouting it joyously from the rooftops. This is all wrong.

'Ness, you still there? Did you hear?'

I hear her swallow. 'Pregnant? Is it his?'

The words slash at me. 'Of course it's his! How can you even say that?'

'I don't know ... I thought maybe ... Look, it doesn't matter. Wow. This is a lot to take in,' she says.

The floor feels like it's opened beneath my feet, and I'm hanging by a thread. 'What did you think? You said, "I thought" then you stopped.'

'I didn't mean it,' Ness says. 'It's just a shock.'

The thread stretches thinner. I fight to keep my voice calm. 'You think I'd sleep with someone else?'

'No. Course not. I just mean, like, accidents happen. You know? People make mistakes.'

'I would never cheat on Robert.' How could she think that? Then I realise. And the thread snaps. I'm falling. 'You think that's what this is about? You think that's what happened.' My own sister suspects me. 'What do you think, that we had a fight or something? Fucking hell, Ness.'

'No. No. No. I just meant if there was someone else then they'd be a suspect, you know?' Her words slippery like dirty wet bin bags.

My own sister thinks I'm capable of this.

Ness is back-pedalling. 'You said someone set you up. That would be a motive, wouldn't it? If you were having an affair?'

I want to scream at her. 'I'm not. I haven't. You're supposed to be helping me!' For the last few years it's been me who's bailed Ness out. Bailed – the irony! I've lent her money when she couldn't make rent. When she couldn't pay off her credit card. When she wanted to get a boob job.

'I'm sorry. I'm trying,' she says. 'This is a lot to get my head round.'

Behind me the woman tapping her watch coughs. 'Your time's up.'

I nod. Hold my finger up for one more minute. Swallow my rage. 'Ness, you need to tell Robert's parents. This is their grandchild. They'll have to talk to me then.' I think about Judith massaging her wrist. I need to look them in the eye. It's the only way I'll know if they're involved.

'Okay, okay,' she sighs. I imagine her rubbing her hand across her face. Pushing her fingers into her eyes like she does when she's tired. It's not just me who's struggling to come to terms with this. 'Jenna?' Her voice is smaller, fragile.

'I'm still here.'

'Look after yourself, yeah?' she says.

'Sure.' The receiver is heavy like my heart, as I replace it onto the cradle.

Now

I feel guilty as soon as I walk away from the phone. Ness is struggling to deal with this insane situation too. And it's not her fault she's needed to borrow a bit of cash here and there. I got to go to uni, I got to get a graduate role. Ness never had that. Times are tougher for everyone. Everything is getting more expensive, and even with Ness's increased responsibility at the gym, wages haven't gone up. And I've been shielded from it by Robert. I've been lucky. Until now.

Someone steps out in front of me, and I pull up sharp. A woman. Broad shoulders, broad hips. A mass in a black tracksuit. I wasn't paying attention. I should have been alert. Her left sleeve is rolled. Too late.

'Hello, Blondie.' Gould is leaning against a doorway to a cell. Behind her, a lank-haired sinewy woman who has the recognisable concave look of an addict is bent double, clutching her stomach. Annie looms over her.

Did Gould hear me on the phone? Does she know about my baby?

Black tracksuit woman leers at me.

'Why do you keep covering up your hair?' Gould's voice is velvety, her dark eyes twinkling malevolently, as she reaches up and pulls the hood of my jumper down.

Every muscle in me clenches.

'It's almost like she don't want to be recognised, isn't it, O'Brien?'

O'Brien, the woman in the black tracksuit, lets out a laugh. Has Gould told her what I'm accused of? Do they know? No. It would be out. I would have been . . . I would know.

I swallow. In the corner of my eye I see Vina watching us. *Don't show fear.*

'Not very chatty today are we, Blondie?' Gould says, circling round me. Each time she calls me that she lingers on the 'Blonde', drawing it out, threatening to add 'Slayer' to the end.

I grip my phone card tighter.

Gould notices. 'What's that you got there?' She grabs my wrist, her hand cold, and yanks it out to see. A few more people on the wing are watching now. 'A phone card? You obviously been talking to someone. But not me.' She pushes her freckled face into mine, twisting my wrist. 'Why's that then? Am I too old for you?'

No, no, no.

'Please,' I whisper.

She laughs, pulls the card from my hand. 'What else you got, hey? O'Brien.' She signals with her head.

Gould still has my wrist in her claw. O'Brien thrusts her fat hands into my pockets. Pulls out my other telephone card. My only means of communication with Ness.

'I'll have that.' Gould pockets it, her eyes taunting. Daring me to object. She grins.

O'Brien's podgy hand opens to reveal the red lipstick I bought for Kelly. Gould takes it. 'A present. For me?' She looks at it. 'I usually don't use cheap slut shit like this.'

There's a gathering crowd around us now. Eyes peering, glassy, expectant. A groan comes from the cell Gould came out of. People are whispering. Watching. Wanting to see who has pissed off who. Waiting to see if it's going to kick off.

'That's mine.' I reach for the lipstick with my free arm, but O'Brien grabs that too and twists it behind my back. 'Ow! Let go.'

'Now, now, Blondie. Did your mother never teach you it's rude to snatch?' Gould takes the lid off, turns it so the smooth red lipstick rises. 'If you want to share, you just have to ask.'

She steps toward me. My nose pulsates with the memory of the attack. I struggle, but O'Brien grabs both my arms and uses her doughy bulk to hold me still. My stomach feels exposed, vulnerable.

Please don't let my bump be visible. Please don't let them see. 'Please!'

Gould's hand comes up and silences my cry. She squeezes my chin like a vice, pulling me forward, holding me still. My top hangs down straight from my breasts. Her grip is so tight my jaw hurts, and my lips are smooshed together. Her face has the same excited look it did when she touched Kelly. I must look terrified. I feel shame burn over me as she presses the lipstick into my face. People are just standing watching, like it's a sick sideshow.

I catch Vina's eye – her mouth frozen in an exclamation *oh* of horror. Some people are whispering, pointing. More are coming over. Vina makes a move toward us, but her roommate stops her. No one is going to say anything. No one is going to help me.

Humiliation flowers through me and I feel my bladder contract. Gould presses the lipstick harder into my face, I feel the oily product split, spread against my cheek. Gould jabs with the end. In. In. In. Like she's punching holes in paper.

Please don't hurt my baby. And I close my eyes against it all as she draws what feels like a jagged joker smile, her breath heavy. Fevered. Fear trickles through me.

What is she going to do when she has finished with my face?

Now

'Roll-call!'

I have never been so pleased to hear Ryan's voice.

'What's going on here?' he yells, as those who'd gathered around us scatter. Gould and O'Brien release me at the same time, Gould casually putting the lid back on the lipstick and dropping it in her pocket.

I take my chance and run.

'Whoa there.' Ryan puts his hands up as I nearly career into him. 'What the fuck is that on your face?' His plucked eyebrows rise in disgust.

Behind me Gould and O'Brien have melted into the crowd.

'I . . . I . . .' My voice is shaking. My legs are jelly. I just want to disappear.

People are staring at me.

'Get that crap cleaned off,' he says. And booms: 'Roll-call!'

I pull my hood up. Scrub at my cheeks with the back of my hand. I need water to wash it off. I feel dirty. Soiled. All around me people are looking and pointing. Rhianna's mum is smirking to her friend. Vina steps toward me. I can't look at her. I run. I have to get away. I have to get out.

But there's nowhere to go. My heart smacks against my ribcage like a trapped bird against a window. I haul myself, my thighs screaming, up the stairs.

Women push past, trying not to laugh.

'You all right?' A long-nailed hand reaches for me, but I can't talk. My skin burns with shame. I have to get away. I have to get to my cell. I have to hide.

'Roll-call!' Ryan screams again, as I make it onto our landing. And see Kelly, aghast, as I lurch toward her and into position.

'What the fuck?' she hisses under her breath. 'What happened?'

But I can't answer, I can't speak. I look at my sad prison trainers and blink back the tears as Ryan does the head count.

Of course, today they let us out to collect our lunch bags. I don't go. Kelly comes back from an afternoon session at the library at dinnertime with two trays of what looks like chilli.

'Here,' she says quietly. 'I told them you weren't feeling well.'

I keep the covers tight round me. 'Thanks.' Everyone – apart from Gould, it seems – is supposed to collect their own meals. Apparently it's to stop theft of food, or contamination. By which they mean people might spit in it. Or worse. But I suspect it's another way to check we're where we're supposed to be. An unofficial head count.

Kelly sits down next to me, and starts to eat. After a while she says, 'We started a new design today. Beaded. Going to be big this season. Apparently.'

I nod. Force myself to lift the plastic fork to my mouth. My hand shaking.

'Looks like bronze is gonna be big too. Bronze beads, bronze fabric, bronze clasps . . .' She trails off.

I can't bring myself to look at her, to see judgement, or worse, pity, in her eyes.

Kelly sighs, rests her fork against the stale roll on her tray. 'What did you do to piss her off?'

I can't tell her the truth: that Gould believes I'm a child killer. That she seems to be enjoying toying with me. I keep chewing.

'I mean, one of the Spice Goblins downstairs owes her money and they just got turned over.' Kelly phrases it like a question. 'They didn't get – that, whatever that was. She signals at my face, and the towel next to my bunk which still bears smudges of red lipstick.

I swallow a particularly dry mouthful of bread. 'I think she was improvising.' I try and smile.

Kelly's not buying it. Her brows still knitted in concern. 'Hmm.' She picks her fork back up. Pokes a bit of cheese into the chilli. 'You got to find a way to make this better.'

'Yeah, I'm not really sure Charlie Gould is the type to sit down for a friendly debate and shake hands after,' I say.

Kelly gives half a smile. 'No. I guess she's not.'

It's awful, and true, and I am stuck, but I still feel a tiny bit better from having made Kelly smile.

'Kel, is there any other way I can get a message outside if I haven't got any phone credit?' I've been playing it over all afternoon in my mind, along with what happened. Going round and round on the same things. I need to know how Ness gets on. I need to tell her to make another transfer, if she can manage it. Explain why all the money she sent has already gone.

'You can send a letter.' She talks with her mouth full. 'Yous get two free stamps a week on remand. Drops to one after.'

'Do I?' No one told me I can write to Ness. I won't be overheard that way. I can tell her I made a mistake with my money. That I need some more. 'And can people write back?'

'Oh yeah,' she says, chewing. 'They read them and stuff, so you can't have anything dodgy in them, like.'

I'll tell Ness to reply that way. To tell me what Robert's parents say.

As soon as I finish my dinner I start to write. Kelly returns my tray, seemingly pleased to see me at least upright in bed.

In the end the return letter doesn't come. There's no message from Ness. But there is a visiting order.

David and Judith Milcombe are coming to see me.

Now

The voice wakes me. A woman's voice. She's downstairs, must be the floor beneath us.

'Hello? Hello? Hello?'

It sounds like she's out of her cell, but how could she be? Like she's looking for someone. Someone must come soon. Her cries sound pitiful, painful.

'Hello? Hello? Hello?'

It sounds like it's getting closer. I sit up, my hand against the wall. It's wet. Sticky. Something's wrong.

'Hello? Hello?'

The voice is nearer now. More urgent. More insistent.

I try to swing my legs off the bed. But there's no floor. And I see what made the noise. A trapdoor in the floor. A rope hanging down.

The woman starts to scream, desperate cries. 'My baby! My baby!' I need to help her, but I can't get off the bed. And the walls are running wet with blood. And they're closing in on me, tighter and tighter, crushing the edges of the bed. The metal buckling, screaming. The woman is crying. And the blood is pouring over me. Emily's blood. The walls are pressing against me. I must save my baby. I must stop them from coming.

I wake with a start. Slick with sweat. My blankets piled on top of me. No one is screaming. It's a dream. Another one. They've been coming for days now, taking savage chunks out of my nights.

'You all right?' Kelly mumbles sleepily from above.

'Bad dream.' My tongue is stuck to the roof of my mouth. My heartbeat going like a train. My baby. What if I can't do this? What if I'm not a good mother? What if what happened in my childhood – all that chaos from Mum's addiction, the times I found her covered in sick, unconscious, the times she let strange men into our flat, the time she sold all the furniture for drugs – what if that's in me? Like a genetic code. What happens if I fail my child?

I feel Kelly roll over above me. 'Hate those,' she says. Her breathing slowing rhythmically again. I don't go back to sleep. Instead I stare up and out the window as the cold night slowly cracks and fades into the dawn. Finally, when Kelly begins to stir more frequently, I roll over and pull the papers out from where they're hidden under the bedside table. A photo of Emily in her school uniform that was published in the newspaper grins at me. It's an older one – they obviously wanted to make her look as young as possible to up the horror of the story – but it's the only one I have. Under that is my list of evidence the police have on me. I add another pen scratch to the tally of days I've been in here. Not that I need to write it down. I carry it with me all the time. The numbers are better than the memories. Today is my forty-eighth day in Fallenbrook. Forty-eight. *Keep breathing.* Overcast April days make shadows in the chipped brick over the door, a grinning devil's face. This time last year Robert and I met. We had our picnic outside in the evening sunshine. We're supposed to be getting married in two months. The doctor is definitely wrong – I am too big for three months. And I still haven't had a scan. The one date I had booked was cancelled when Kev was off sick. Short-staffed. I've started chasing with the forms again to get it rearranged but no one seems to care. *Keep breathing. It's okay.* Because today I can finally do something about it.

Today I can take my first solid steps to getting out of here. Because today is the day David and Judith visit.

I wait until Free Flow is properly underway before I come down from our cell. This is my life now, fearfully peering round corners and over landings to check for Gould or anyone with a rolled-up left sleeve. If the coast is clear I dart out, head down, walking as quickly as I can without drawing attention to myself. I haven't visited the library since the attack. And, though I feel sick at the prospect of seeing Judith and David, and even worse at the prospect of seeing Gould, I can't help but feel relief for being out of our stale cell. It's not only in my dreams that the walls have started to close in on me.

I'm hyper-alert the whole way to the visitors' room. But no one gives me a second glance. I hear snippets of conversation as I pass.

'*They're bringing in the smoking ban. Nationwide. All prisons.*'

'*They ain't stopping me.*'

'*It's everyone, even the screws.*'

'*The number-one governor said we'll be getting patches, and we can buy vape.*'

'*Fucking stupid idea.*'

'*What about our rights?*'

I've obviously missed a serious development in prison policy while I've been hiding away. Can they really be banning smoking inside? Yeah, I'm pleased to stop breathing in second-hand smoke and worrying about the damage to my baby. But what about the damage from a pissed-off lag going through withdrawal? Does Gould smoke? This is what everyone is talking about now. They have moved on from me and the lipstick incident.

Sara is on duty in the visitors' room. Her shirt crisp and white, her hair up in an intricate plaited number. She gives me a smile and a wink as she hands me what looks like not a bad tabard.

'Thanks.'

She nods and I move along the line. As we wait to file in I see Rhianna's mum is in front of me again. Her hair clean, and fresh lipstick on. 'Hey? Your little girl coming in today?'

Her lip curls and she looks at me with undisguised disgust. It's then that I see her left sleeve is rolled.

'Here we go, girls,' Sara calls.

I swallow the panic down as we file in. *Roll your shoulders, pull your stomach in.* I tug at my tabard so it balloons out away from me.

Rhianna's mum purposefully picks a table away from me. Does she know what I've been accused of, or is she just demonstrating her loyalty to Gould? There's no time to worry before the door at the other end of the room is unlocked and I see them.

Judith's delicately coloured bob is shaped like a helmet round her head, as if protecting her from her environment. She has expensive hair. Ness always jokes we have Croydon hair. Fine, flyaway, split ends. The kind that collapses against your head no matter how expensive the blow-dry.

David has his arms around Judith, as if shielding her from this reality. I can see they have tried to dress down. He's gone all gin and tonics at the country club, and she for a simple cotton dress, but they have that unmistakable air that comes with the super-rich. It's in their private health-maintained posture, Judith's subtly nipped and tucked skin, their cruise-liner tan, the way they hold themselves confidently, as if they belong everywhere. Except, of course, they don't belong here. They're attracting looks from the other visitors. An elderly gent in a cream blazer, blue shirt, and slacks, who has been seated by Kev already, is watching them keenly. Then there are myriad jeans and puffa jackets, striped track pants, children in tatty Disney dresses and superhero jumpers. And us, the prisoners, in our regulation tabards.

My hair is a muddy brown from the coffee granules, and I only have my tent hoodie to wear, but I've tried to make myself as presentable as possible. The shocked look on Judith's face tells me it's not been wholly successful. David does a double-take, as if he were about to walk past me.

Up close, Judith looks pale under her make-up. The recent events have shaved layers off her, leaving her seemingly translucent. You can almost see her anxious heartbeat pulsing through her veins. Her pain reflects my own back at me. *I can't do this. I can't breathe.* David looks stoic, his jaw set, as if he's about to enter a board meeting. He guides Judith through the tables, and out of the way when a child that's clearly missing its nap time flops from its gran's hand and falls at her feet. David wrinkles his nose, as if he's just avoided treading in something nasty. He's a bully and a snob. Judith hasn't taken her eyes from me. I want to stand, but I can't till they reach me.

David tries to pull out a chair for Judith, but it's chained to the floor. Judith looks astonished.

'Thank you for coming.' I'm up now. Will it look weird if I don't hug them? I hover. Reach my arms up.

David makes a noise like an elegant grunt. Judith looks alarmed. I let my arms drop. Sit down. Heat flushes my cheeks.

David takes out a cotton handkerchief and wipes the seats before they sit. Folds his hanky carefully over on the contamination. Puts it on the table.

Judith's mouth is slightly agape. She's leaning back in her seat, staring at me. They don't speak.

I study David's face for clues, look at his hands as if they might be bloodstained, but all I can feel is their judgement of me. I wish I had something other than my joggies and shapeless hoodie to wear. I wish I was in my own clothes. I wish we were meeting in private. I wish this wasn't happening at all.

I've been rehearsing what to say for days. How I'm going to test him. Test her. Look for lies. Discrepancies. Make them reveal what they know. Make them help me. But now they're here, the words churn in my mouth.

David and I go to speak at the same time.

'I needed to—'

'I didn't want Judith to come.' He folds his hands in his lap.

'Is there any news on Robert?' He could have been found – unconscious, suffering from amnesia or something – and no one thought to tell me. He might not know about Emily. 'I'm so sorry about . . .' I can't say her name out loud. 'For your loss.'

Judith looks startled. Her eyes dart from me, my hoodie, my hair, round the room, back again. David squeezes her shoulder.

'You didn't give us a choice,' he says.

A chill spreads over my skin. No news of Robert. Judith is raw with grief, it pours from her, but David is suppressed, curled, like a waiting snake. His voice is dangerous. I force myself to push on. I wasn't raised to discuss money in public. 'I appreciate this must be hard for you.'

David scoffs.

'Just tell us where he is – please?' Judith's words spill out in a high-pitched cry. She clutches for the table, for my hands. Her eyes are wild. Scared.

She thinks I hurt Robert. Unless it's an act . . .

'I don't know. I promise you, I didn't do this.'

David's face is a tense scowl. He gently pulls Judith back, as if he's holding her together. Maybe he is.

Bile sloshes through my stomach, and I imagine it curling, hissing round my baby. I shake my head. I have to make them believe me. 'I could never hurt Robert. I could never hurt Emily.' Her name crumbles into dust in my mouth.

'Is it his?' Judith stares at my stomach.

The second person to ask me that. I hold the anger down this time. 'The baby is Robert's.'

Judith looks up at David. Panic in her eyes. 'It can't stay here.'

Yes. This is my way in. 'I need your help. I need money. Just a loan. If I can get a decent lawyer I can get them to listen to me.' I think about telling them about the files, or that I think I'm being framed, and then I think about David bending Judith's wrist back. Of him arguing with Emily. Of him using my laptop without my permission. He could have done this. He could have put me here.

His face is as unyielding as stone. 'If there even is a baby.'

The words slap me across the table. Judith lets out a mewling sound and clutches at David's shirtsleeve.

You think I would have a baby here deliberately? No. That's not what you mean. You mean I'm lying. That I've created a phantom baby. He doesn't trust me at all. Has he ever? Was he always waiting and watching and sowing seeds of doubt? I think of the day Emily won the county swimming cup. He was so proud. He hugged her. He loved her. But his type of love is twisted, controlling, rotten.

'It's convenient, isn't it?' he prods. 'You get arrested and then suddenly you're pregnant.' His voice is rising. I glance nervously around. No one else must hear this. 'Did you think it would make people sympathetic? You probably get a cushy ride in here now, huh?'

'You can ask the doctor.' I don't know if they can. I don't care. 'I didn't plan this.'

He snorts. Judith's pain flutters between us like a moth at a flame.

I lean forward, speak as clearly as I dare. 'I'm pregnant. It's Robert's child. You can help me or not. But it's your grand-child.' I need them to accept it. I need money. A great lawyer. Bail. I can go to the hospital normally. I can eat properly. I can care for this baby. I can find Robert. I can find out if David did this. I dig my fingernails into my palm.

David nods. 'Okay.'

I exhale. He's going to help. He's going to get me out. Does this mean it wasn't him? Or that he's feeling guilty? 'I'm happy to go with a lawyer of your choosing,' I say. I bet they have barristers among their set.

'No,' David says.

I stammer. 'Okay. Then I'm sure I can find one.' Ness can Google it for me.

'I'm not giving you any more of *my* money.' Specks of his spittle land on my face. His voice is icy. 'I hired a private investigator. Did you really think we wouldn't find out about you?'

Panic breaks free inside me, pulling hard and fast on my ribs. My lungs fight to keep breathing. My chest screams.

What do they know?

Now

David shakes his head. 'I know all about that criminal hothouse you came from. A delinquent estate full of illegal immigrants and god knows what kind of other people.'

I grip the table, trying to hold on. 'I thought Robert told you?'

'The dregs of society.' David wrinkles his nose. Judith starts to cry. 'You're just a money-grabbing little tart with a filthy drug addict mother.'

I look to Judith. 'He said you didn't care.' Judith looks away. And I realise. It was Robert who didn't care. Robert who has never been judged based on where he was born, where he grew up. Robert who never had anyone form opinions on him, on his character, before he'd even spoken.

'People like *that*,' David looks round with a sneer, 'are a drain on society. It'd be kinder to put them down.'

'How dare you talk about my mum like that!' Fury pours out of me.

'Be quiet, woman.' David's voice is glacial, all traces of the jovial guy at the family barbecue gone. 'You have taken everything from us. Everything.'

'No.' I shake my head. The chatter of the room drops away, and it's just him and me, and hatred in his eyes.

'I will see you rot in jail,' he says.

'No.' I clutch my stomach. The baby. 'I loved ... love Robert. Loved Emily!'

'He should have listened to me when I warned him about you.' David stands.

He warned Robert about me? What did he say? What did Robert say? He never told me. He always said they liked me. He shielded me from this.

'You will not keep that baby.' David's words explode between us.

Abort? They can't force me.

'You can't look after it in here.' Judith throws her arms up.

'You won't ruin another of my grandchildren,' he says. 'We will have the baby.'

David's words break like waves over me, winding me, holding me under. They don't think I'm ever getting out.

'A baby can't live here,' Judith says, imploring, desperate.

There's still some connection in her eyes, I haven't lost her yet. 'I'm its mother. You can't—'

'We will raise it,' David says, pulling Judith brusquely to her unsteady feet. 'I have already spoken to our lawyer. We have started proceedings.'

What proceedings? What does he mean? 'The baby's not even born yet.' I clutch my stomach. The thought of being separated from my child, separated from the last part of Robert I have . . . no.

'You have to see this is for the best?' Judith says.

'A child belongs with its mother.' The words come rushing out. I think of Emily and her lost mother. Would she still be alive if her mother had lived? Could her mum have protected her more than we did? But I'm in here. I'm alone. 'Ness can help.'

'And what kind of upbringing would *she* give a child?' Judith says.

David jabs toward my stomach. 'That baby is mine.'

Panic floods like dirty water through me. He's already started proceedings. He means custody. He is going for custody of my baby. David with all his money and his high-powered lawyers, and his beautiful house and parkland, and opportunity, and freedom. Him out there. Emily and Robert are gone and he wants my baby.

Judith looks at me. Swallows. If there's any doubt in her mind, she can stop this.

'Come on, Judith,' David says. 'We shouldn't have come to *this* place.'

'Please Judith, don't do this.' I jump up and reach for her arm. Judith screams. 'I didn't do it – please!'

'Sit down, prisoner!' a shout comes from Kev. He and Sara start toward me.

I throw my arms up in surrender, my jumper rucks, exposing my stomach. If they tackle me they could hurt the baby.

Judith looks shocked. David pulls her away.

The whole room is silent. Faces turned toward me. The guards stand a metre away like I might explode and take them all down with me. I want to disappear. To collapse into nothing. Instead I see the women around me, several with their left sleeve rolled, turn their gaze down to my swollen belly. *Pregnant.* My secret is out.

Then

'What do you think?' Ness turns her phone toward me. On the screen is a photo of a ripped topless guy.

'Well, you obviously both like going to the gym,' I say. 'What does his bio say?'

'Too late – I swiped right,' she grins, tucking a swathe of her red hair behind her ear.

'Do you even know his name?' Even when I was single I wouldn't have gone near Tinder. But Ness has always been more ballsy than me.

'I'm not interested in his name.' Her sleeves are pulled down over her hands, and she cradles her tea. 'Says he's less than two miles from here – if it works out we could be neighbours.'

'You haven't even met him and you're already moving in.' I push the coaster toward her. Robert doesn't like rings on his table. *Our table*. I have to stop separating things out like this.

'Oh yeah, don't want to rush into anything.' Her rising eyebrows disappear behind the mug.

I feel my cheeks flush. Was that a dig about me? I take my own mug to the butler sink and empty the rest of my coffee away – suddenly it tastes bitter. I flick the tap on, but I've still not quite got the hang of it and it gushes out, splashing up over my sweater. I'll have to change. 'Drat.'

'I just want to find a decent guy, you know?' Ness says. She looks wistfully round the kitchen and I feel a pang of guilt that I've got Robert, when her exes have hardly been the best bunch.

'You will. Maybe it's this guy,' I grin, pointing at her phone.

'Knowing my luck he'll be a penniless plonker with roid rage,' she laughs.

That pretty much describes her last boyfriend. I tread carefully. 'Maybe it's good you're looking further afield.' Away from the losers she meets through her friends. 'A fresh sea to fish in, and all that.'

I expect her to crack a joke, or tell me to shut up, but instead she looks up and holds my gaze. 'Do you ever think about Mum's crappy men?'

I try not to think about that time at all. When Mum quit drugs she thankfully quit men too.

Ness pushes on. 'They say that you unconsciously mimic your parents' relationships, don't they?'

I remember one of Mum's recurrent boyfriends. If you could call Carl that. He showed up whenever there was money in the house, and they would get off their tits in the lounge while Ness and I stayed hidden. The amount of times I did my homework to the background sounds of him smashing up bits of our flat . . . Ness would never date anyone like him. 'You aren't doing that,' I say.

'Yeah, well, not if you're anything to go by,' she grins. 'Though maybe you take after your dad.'

I laugh. Ness and I dealt with the fact we don't know who our dad is – or even if he's the same guy – years ago. We always had each other. That was enough.

'You got any biscuits?' Ness says. 'Or is this swanky kitchen just for show?'

I cringe at the word 'swanky'. 'Cookies – that cupboard.' I point to the larder.

Ness opens the off-white painted wooden door on the array of groceries Michelle organises so neatly. 'Wow,' she says. 'You expecting the five thousand? There's more in here than I've got in my entire kitchen.' She shakes her head.

This is the second time Ness has been to the house. I prepped her the first time so she wasn't too shocked. She still wolf-whistled when we pulled into the drive, Mum silent in the back seat. I thought it best they see the place when Robert and Emily were out. Let them get used to it. We've been out as a five for Sunday lunch. And when Emily's been at swim galas in their direction we've met up. They know Robert. But I still didn't want them judging him. I think that's why I haven't showed them his parents' place yet – I brought them in the back gate. Tried to keep it low key. I want them to be comfortable over Christmas. Our first family Christmas. I'm going to do Nigella's turkey with all the trimmings, and I've been collecting little bits of make-up and Lush bath bombs for a stocking for Emily. It's going to be perfect.

'What the hell is this?' Ness holds up a packet of dark green sheets.

'Seaweed – it's healthy, you'd like it,' I say.

Ness wrinkles her nose. 'No fucking chance.'

The back door opens from outside, the icy November air seeming to suck all the warmth from the room.

Judith stands there in her Barbour jacket, her eyes wide. Did she hear Ness swear? They're not keen on bad language.

'Judith!' I force a bright smile onto my face.

'Oh,' she says. 'I didn't realise you had company.' She stares at Ness, who now has hold of a tin of foie gras as well.

I dry my hands quickly on the tea towel. 'This is my sister Ness. Ness, this is Robert's mum.' This wasn't supposed to happen. What is she doing here?

'All right?' Ness says.

Judith's gaze falls back on the tea towel I've just abandoned. I pick it up and hang it properly from the hook. 'Hello.' Her smile is tight. 'Goodness, it looks like a jumble sale in here, darling.' She snatches up Ness's jacket from the back of the kitchen chair.

A nervous laugh forces its way out my mouth. She definitely heard the swear. I hold my hand out for Ness's puffa, wishing it was something a little less urban. 'Of course – my fault. I didn't show Ness where to hang it. She just stopped by to talk about Christmas plans,' I say. 'All the planning – hey? Why do we put ourselves through it?' What am I saying? I don't even mean that. I'm looking forward to it.

Judith looks perplexed. 'We've always taken Christmas very seriously in our family.'

I look at Ness in desperation.

The sound of crunching feet on the gravel outside heralds my saviour. Robert appears behind his mother. 'Ness!' he says. 'I didn't know you were coming over today. You staying for supper?'

He skirts Judith and hugs my sister.

She hugs him back. 'Nah, got to get back for work, but I was in the area so I thought I'd stop by and say hello.'

'Emily will be gutted to have missed you.' He smiles.

'Plus I've been checking out your local meat market,' Ness says.

Oh no.

'Jennifer never said her family were in farming as well?' Judith's face has given slightly.

'No fear,' Ness says. 'I couldn't be doing with all that mud and cow shit. Bleurgh.' She grimaces.

Judith frowns, looks as if she's about to ask for clarification.

I glare at Ness. 'Who'd like a cup of tea?' I say before she can start explaining the finer details of Tinder.

'Oh, I'd love one.' Robert pauses next to me, squeezing my shoulder and kissing the side of my head. Instantly I relax: warmth radiating through my muscles. He looks into my eyes. He gets it.

Within minutes he has Judith and Ness sitting round the

reclaimed wooden table and has managed to find the one thing they have in common: outdoor activities. They're happily comparing the best walks they've done in the surrounding areas, Ness talking about step counts and miles, Judith talking dogs and views.

Just for a second, I allow myself to believe it's going to be okay.

Now

'I can't believe you never said.' Kelly has her arms folded over her bump.

News has obviously travelled about my showdown in the visitors' room. My head's spinning from what David and Judith said. A week after Judith met Ness our Christmas plans were cancelled. Robert said it was because Emily wanted to spend the day with her grandparents as usual, but I never believed that. Emily didn't like being up at the big house. I always suspected Judith and David were behind the sudden rearrangement. But this? Taking my baby. The look in David's eyes. Robert always said you didn't want to be on the wrong side of his dad.

'After everything that's happened! After Gould came in here, and I didn't sell you out!' Kelly's face has the hard glaze of self-protection. 'You lied to me! You're a fucking liar!'

Adrenaline must have fired me up during the confrontation with David, but now it's spilled out of me and there's nothing left but heavy exhaustion. The baby rattling around inside an empty tin can. I can't deal with this. 'I only just found out.' *Four weeks ago.*

Kelly's face shifts from accusation to delight. 'This is brilliant. We can be birthing partners!' Is it her hormones, her age? Her mood shifts liquid from one extreme to the other.

I ache. My limbs are heavy, sore, as if I can't quite stretch into the stiffness.

She opens her arms wide and grabs me for a surprise hug. It's the first kind physical contact I've had in days. I feel her arms around me, like she's holding me up. Remnants of a plan float through my mind, but I'm too tired to action them. Each one makes me want to cry. That feeling of spiralling out of control, as if everything is about to overwhelm me. I need to speak to Mr Peterson. I need to speak to Ness. They can't take my baby, can they? I have no idea how this works. I thought I would be out before the baby arrived. *I will see that you rot in here*. The ridiculous notion that David knew I was pregnant before I did comes to my mind. That he somehow engineered this whole thing to get my baby. To control my child. I cling to Kelly, her back arching away as her bump presses against mine. A picture of two babies, palms up, pressed together, with prison glass between them.

'I'm just so tired.'

'I know, love,' she says. 'That first trimester's a killer. Here.' She helps me into bed.

I don't tell her I think I'm into my second, that I should have had my scan, that I've been so frightened of anyone finding out I haven't fought for my baby's rights. That I've already failed my child. I should get up. I should be working on a new plan. *A baby can't live here*. I haven't even asked Kelly what her plan is. I can't believe I never asked her. What happens? Can they take my baby away? I haven't seen any babies in here. Is there a special place new mothers go? I think of Gould and the rolled left sleeves. But as Kelly tucks the blanket in, like Ness used to, I let go. My limbs sink into the mattress. I shiver. Suddenly cold. As if my encounter with David and Judith has literally chilled me.

Kelly tuts. Pulls the blanket off her bed and adds that on top of me.

'I . . . I need to make a call . . .' I can barely lift my head.

'Shush,' she says, smoothing my brow. 'You have a kip. You'll feel better after that. I'll let you know if Association starts.'

I would nod but my head is too heavy on the pillow. 'You're gonna make a brilliant mum,' I mumble, before my eyelids close and the lights go out.

In the darkness I see Judith. Small, and fragile, her eyes are desperately searching mine for some clue as to where her lost boy is.

Then

Robert's phone goes to voicemail. Damn it. I leave a breathless message, scraping a brush through my hair as I park up at ours. 'Sweets, it's me. Sorry. I got held up with my last client. Then I had to call the florist back. Your dad told her he wants different buttonholes – which is fine, but it means we need to change the bouquets.' Why on earth did we think we could arrange a wedding in four months, even with holding it at David and Judith's house? But Robert's a romantic, and he's right, there is something magical about getting married on the one-year anniversary of our first date. I take my suit jacket off and fling it into the back seat – no time to change into the dress I'd been planning to wear. 'I'm guessing you've already gone ahead to your parents'. All the lights are off in our house. 'So I'll see you up there in a few minutes. Sorry!'

When I hang up I see another missed call from Ness. Dammit. I keep meaning to call her back. No time now. I fire off a text: *I'll call you later.*

She replies immediately: *You said that three weeks ago. Forgotten what you look like.*

No kiss. Great. She's angry at me too. I need to try to involve her in the wedding prep more. Robert and I are just always so busy.

I stomp up the drive. I hate being late for David and Judith's dinners. They always make me feel like it's incredibly rude. Which is a bit rich given I know they made Robert cancel our

Christmas plans with Mum and Ness. Something which Ness clearly still hasn't forgiven me for.

I force a smile onto my face as I reach the house. No point knocking – they won't hear me in the dining room. I head round the back and let myself in the side door, taking my shoes off in the boot room. I smooth my hair once more, try to straighten the creases on my blouse and skirt and take a deep breath.

I hear the raised voices as soon as I step out of the room. I pause in the empty kitchen as the word 'wedding' reaches my ears.

'But we have planned everything for April the fifteenth,' Robert says. 'The invites are about to go out.'

'Well you can un-plan everything,' David retorts. 'Rushing into it like this.'

My breath catches in my throat. Is he saying we should cancel the wedding?

'It's our anniversary,' Robert says.

'It's a gimmick,' David snaps.

My hand's shaking. Do they not want us to get married? I knew this was moving too quick for them. They only met me in October, the surprise engagement happened on Christmas morning. I saw David's face after I unwrapped the ring and Robert dropped down on one knee.

'Darling.' Judith sounds pleading. 'We're not saying it's not a lovely idea, we're just asking you to push it back by a couple of months. You have to understand, these things take time – we need to make sure the right people can attend.'

What people? This is our wedding, not a work function.

'It's a Milcombe wedding. You have to give them warning. Timothée and Béatrice will need to come from France.'

'It's only Bordeaux – they can use their damn private plane,' Robert snaps.

'Do not use that crude language in front of your mother,' David retorts.

'Sorry, Mummy,' Robert says automatically.

'Don't you think June is better?' Judith says. 'The weather will be nicer. We can use sweet peas in the bouquets.'

I'm allergic to sweet peas.

'It'll give you time to dissuade her from this ridiculous idea of her having anyone other than Emily as a bridesmaid,' David says. 'Bridesmaids are supposed to be that – young maidens. Not women in their thirties.'

Ness?

'It's her sister,' Robert says.

'So uncouth,' Judith says.

I realise I'm twisting my hands together in anger. This is my wedding. They are discussing my wedding without me. Undoing all our plans. Is this a ploy to delay things so Robert will re-think? No, that's crazy. This is Robert's family. They love him. They want us to be happy. They've just got carried away thinking about the business. The big Milcombe wedding. Robert will put them straight.

'There's no negotiation, the wedding is taking place in my house, I am paying for it, and I say it takes place on the seventeenth of June.' David's words are emotionless, like he's closing a work deal, not discussing the wedding of his only son.

I hold my breath. *Please Robert, fight back. Say no. We can get married anywhere. In a registry office. In Vegas. We don't need money. We can run away.*

'I'll talk to Jenna,' Robert says.

A tear rolls down my cheek. I wish he would stand up for himself. Once we're married I'm setting new boundaries: they can't go on interfering like this. I swipe the tear away. We just have to get through the big day. It's a tense time for everyone.

I take a deep breath. Steady myself. Then close the boot-room door with a loud bang, as if I've just arrived. 'Hello!' I call. 'Anyone here?' My voice bright, as if everything is fine. As if my heart is not breaking inside.

Now

'Burns!'

I jolt awake. Ryan's square jaw is pressed against the flap in the door.

'Whass happening?' Kelly mumbles from above. How long have I been asleep? The morning sun streams through the window. My stomach rumbles. I missed dinner.

'Appointment. Move it, prisoner,' Ryan says.

What time is it? Appointment? Are the police back – have they realised that something doesn't add up? Has Mr Peterson been contacted by David?

'Is it her scan?' Kelly's skinny legs, still wearing socks, dangle from above. 'Have you had your scan yet?'

My scan! The timing is funny. Sara was in the visitors' room yesterday – she, like everyone else, will have heard that I'm pregnant. Did she push for me to have my scan? I think she's the type to. I should have trusted her earlier – I should have told her. I'll thank her. Under my blanket I run my hand over the taut mound of skin.

'None of your business, prisoner,' Ryan snaps. 'Move it, Burns.'

Kelly's bump makes her bum stick out as she clambers down. 'He's just grumpy because his favourite *receptacle* got released.' She raises her voice as she pulls her hair back into a ponytail. 'Only the druggies will shag him now!'

The door hatch slams shut. I haul myself out of bed, pulling my jumper off freely in front of Kelly.

'Oh my god – you popped already!' Kelly says, grinning at my bump. 'You're bigger than I was at three months.' She circles me, admiring my skin. I laugh, run my hands over my baby. It's a huge relief to be able to share this with her.

'Err . . . I reckon I might be further along than that,' I say. Then add, as if in explanation. 'I was on the Pill.'

'Ah, mate,' says Kelly. 'That happened to a girlfriend of mine – she got to five and a half months before she realised. Her baby daddy freaked.' She shakes her head.

'Robert will be thrilled – I know he will be.' I hug my bump. Kelly squeezes my arm comfortingly.

There's a thump on the door. 'Hurry up, Burns, I don't have all day!' Ryan yells.

I hurriedly start pulling on clothes. Wash my face in the sink.

Kelly follows me round like a chick behind its mother. 'Fuck, the shitter's backed up again,' she says.

I don't look at the pan.

Kelly bangs on the door. 'You hear that? Our toilet's blocked again. You need to get the number-one governor to sort it out. That's the third time this month.'

Ryan grunts from outside.

'The scans are mind-blowing – like, there's a little human in there.' Kelly passes me my shoes from under the bed. 'I cried at every one!'

By hiding my pregnancy from everyone in here, I've been hiding it from myself too. I've been waiting, in limbo, for DI Langton to show up and say it's all a mistake and I can go home. But my baby's been growing all this time, my body changing. I should have pushed for my scan earlier – what if something's wrong? What if it's my fault for not facing up to it sooner? Could the lawyers find out? David could use it against me. Argue I'm an unfit mother. I think of his cold rage yesterday. His control. It's all about that, always has been:

controlling Judith, Robert, Emily. Everyone has to dance to his tune. Has anyone stood up to him before? I remember Emily, hands on hips, rounding on him. Oh Emily. And suddenly I can picture it all: Emily standing up to him, David losing his temper, lashing out. Robert running in, and David killing him too. The only witness.

Kelly is oblivious, as she bounces round the room. 'She's ready.' She bangs on the door again. Ryan unlocks it. 'Good luck!' She hops from one foot to the other as Ryan closes it in her face.

The wing is empty, only the murmur of early risers coming from the locked cells. And my fears about David filling me up like liquid. I squash them down. Now is not the time. Now is about me and my baby.

Seeing the wing like this reminds me of the first night I arrived. No one peers out the hatches, I guess most are still asleep. I wait until we're through the gate and heading along the corridor before I speak. It'd be too easy to be overheard in the wing. Ryan's strutting, as if his shoulders are so big he can't help but swagger.

'Is Sara taking me?'

Ryan, who clearly isn't a morning fan, manages only a fraction of his usual suggestiveness. 'Prefer women, do you?'

He unlocks the next gate. Weak sunshine pools on the floor. We're getting closer to the reception. To fresh air. My skin tingles.

'It's just me, Kev, and you,' Ryan says.

What?

'If I had to pick a threesome partner, Fat Kev wouldn't be my first choice,' Ryan laughs.

He's joking, surely? Just trying to make things sound sexual when they're not. 'This is my hospital appointment – for my scan?'

'No flies on you, are there?' He swings the key chain like a pendulum off his finger.

'But Sara's a woman.' They can't let two men take me. That can't be right.

'If you can call that thing female,' he sniffs.

Irritation rises in me. 'This isn't funny. Sara should be taking me.'

'Buggers can't be choosers.' His whitened teeth like marble tombstones. 'Me and Kev are stuck escorting you.'

But I don't want them here.

Ryan drops his arm over my shoulders. 'Let's try and make the best of it, get to know each other better,' he purrs into my ear. My flesh crawls. 'Road trip!'

He drops his arm just as we round the corner to find Kev waiting. His paunch looks more like a pregnant belly than mine. Dangling from his hands are handcuffs.

No.

'Arms out, prisoner,' he says.

For so long I have wanted to go outside. To feel the air on my skin. To see the sky. The birds. Trees. Normal people. But not like this. Not in a bottle-green prison hoodie and handcuffs.

'I won't run.' There has to be another way?

Kev scoffs.

'Come on, Burns.' Ryan nudges me. 'It'll be kinky.'

'No cuffs, no appointment.' Kev ignores Ryan.

I swallow the bile rising in my throat and hold my arms out. The metal cold, permanent, humiliating, as it snaps shut onto me.

Now

Handcuffed between Kev and Ryan, I want to die walking into the hospital.

The two women behind the desk stare at me. I say nothing.

'Which way is the maternity ward, love?' Kev asks the one on the right.

She moves her stapler toward herself. 'Down the hall, up to the third floor, and at the end of the corridor.'

I focus on the cracked rubber floor. Tiles covered in circular indentations.

'Oh my god, what do you think she did?' the receptionist hisses to her colleague as we walk away.

'Do you think she's one of them serial killers?'

'Maternity. I bet she's a prostitute.'

A man pushing an empty wheelchair swerves round us.

'And on my tax money,' the woman harrumphs, as we disappear round the corner.

'Here, they've got a Costa,' Kev says.

I see the feet and legs of people grouped round tables turn toward us. A small boy in a blue T-shirt is yanked back to safety.

'You know how much sugar is in those drinks?' Ryan says.

'Hasn't done me any harm. The sign says it's this way.'

'What about you, Burns?' Ryan shakes the arm of mine he's holding. 'Bet you like a bit of something sweet? Bet you'd love a cake, huh?'

They both laugh.

I don't respond.

'I like those little wafer biscuits they do that melt on your latte.' Kev draws a circle on his palm with his finger. I imagine that each circular indent on the floor is a wafer crumbling under my feet.

They keep on like this for a few minutes. Banal small talk, ignoring the deplorable cargo between them.

For a split second I think it's Sally. But why would she be in the maternity ward? It's not her, of course. Just a woman with the same handbag and similar hair. An apparition conjured by my mind. A further humiliation: someone I know seeing me led and shackled like an animal.

The nostrils of the woman with Sally's handbag flare. Protectively she wraps her arm over her swollen stomach.

I would not hurt a child.

I would not hurt you.

I just want to be with Robert.

I just want Emily back.

I just want my baby.

Is that why Sally has rejected me? Left me to face the trial of imprisonment all alone? Because I stopped being Jenna her friend and became the mythical Blonde Slayer, something to fear and despise?

Ryan steers me to a blue plastic chair at the far corner of the room, while Kev speaks through the glass hole in the wall to yet another receptionist. Mercifully, there is no one else in here, and I can't hear anything of what this one says. The receptionist finishes with Kev and closes her window like a guillotine falling. I try to hide my handcuffs in a fold of my jumper.

'How long we got to wait?' Ryan says.

'They've got someone in there already.' Kev hitches his sagging belt up his waist.

'Bloody hospitals.' Ryan looks with disgust at the posters advertising a free app that monitors your baby's movements.

'There ain't enough staff for Free Flow till we get back.' Kev arches his back, flashing us the sweat patches on his white shirt.

'Again? Bloody hell.' Ryan spreads his legs out wide. I move mine away. Try to make myself smaller.

'Another two resigned last week,' Kev says.

'Poofs.' Ryan flicks a bit of lint from his trousers.

For a moment no one speaks. The clock ticks on the wall. I risk a look up and out the seventies-style window. A slither of blue sky curled through the clouds. *Not enough for a sailor's suit.* That's what Nan used to say. A swift darts past, a brief flash of freedom.

'Here, why don't you go get yourself one of them lattes and those wafer biscuits you like?' Ryan says.

Kev looks interested.

'I'll be all right with her.' Ryan jerks a thumb in my direction.

I know straight away I don't want to be alone with Ryan. I try to speak. My mouth is too dry. My throat pinched closed.

'You sure?' Kev wasn't asking me.

No.

'Course, bruv.' Ryan leans back, lets his other arm stretch over the top of the chairs. Relaxed. Proprietorial. 'You deserve a little treat after we've had to slog down here so early.' A persuasive smile. A reassuring flick of the wrist.

Kev ambles off. Already imagining his coffee.

A chill curls up my ankles like a snake.

Instinct tells me not to make any sudden movements. We are alone. The receptionist's window is down. I can't see her through the opaque glass. I'm handcuffed. And Ryan's leg is pressed against mine.

I try to peel myself away, just a millimetre, so I can't feel his weight pushing against me.

'Where you going, Burns?' His left arm is round me in a second.

I freeze. My body rigid. I can feel his pecs against my arm, his breath in my hair, on my face, in my ear. I want to scream.

'If you were just a little bit more friendly,' he purrs, 'things could be a lot more comfortable for you.'

He pushes a strand of hair slowly off my face. Fear surges through me. If I scream will the receptionist come? My chest expands.

As if reading my mind he says, 'Now don't think about doing anything stupid. You don't want to be face down on this floor, do you?' He lets his finger lazily trace down my cheek, my neck. My skin screams. 'We wouldn't want anything to happen to that baby, would we?'

His finger is still going, down, over my breast, round my nipple. My whole body contracts, as if trying to close him out.

The sound of the glass partition sliding up slices into the air.

He springs away from me.

I gulp for air.

'Ms Burns!' the receptionist trills.

'Come on.' Ryan grabs my arm roughly and pulls me to my feet.

My knees are weak. My legs shaking. My hair falls into my eyes. My bound hands can't push it back. I want to pull away, run, but I can't function.

'Come on.' Annoyance in his every thrust. And he forces me into the sonographer's room.

Now

Blue floor. White faded walls. No window.

'Good morning, Ms Burns.' The sonographer, a jolly woman with vanilla ice-cream swirls of hair, turns to greet us with a folder in her hands.

She frowns at the sight of Ryan, who's still gripping my arm. He gives her his best winning smile. Her face doesn't alter.

'You can wait outside,' she says. 'Ms Burns, if you just pop yourself up onto the bed we'll take a look at how you're doing.' She pats the white sanitary paper that's unrolled down the bed.

'I've got to stay with her at all times,' Ryan says.

My cheeks burn. He makes it sound like I'm a threat.

'I see,' the sonographer says, pulling the sliding door behind us.

Please make him leave.

Ryan still has hold of my arm. The sonographer catches sight of the handcuffs glinting on my wrist.

'Those will have to come off,' she says.

I smile at her. *I'm no threat. I won't hurt you. I won't hurt anyone.*

Ryan huffily undoes the cuffs.

I rub at my wrists. Swallow. Try to get some moisture into my mouth.

'Okay, dear,' she says. Her hand cool and gentle on my arm. 'Up you get.'

The paper crinkles as I lie down. Ryan is staring, a smile on his face. I want to scream at him to get out. *He touched me.*

The sonographer glances at him, her face darkening. She puts herself between him and me. 'We just need you to uncover your tummy. That's it,' she says gently. I pull my jumper up and over my mound, careful not to let anything else show. I stare at the ceiling, try to imagine Ryan is not here. That Robert is. No. That's too painful. Just focus on your breath. Just breathe. The sonographer rolls the waistband of my joggies over.

She makes a hmmm noise.

Something's wrong. The prison van, Gould, the stress, the lack of proper food, no vitamins – I haven't protected my baby. 'Is everything okay?' My voice wavers.

She looks at my notes again. 'It says here this is your three-month scan?'

'Well . . . erm . . . it is. It's just I'm a little further along, I think. I was on the Pill. And I didn't know I was pregnant.' Ryan tuts and I want to cry. I'm babbling. Desperate for her to understand that I do care about this baby. That I can be a good mother. 'I wasn't able to come before. I would have if I'd been able to.'

Ryan says nothing to back me up. I refuse to look in his direction.

'These things happen,' the sonographer says, smiling, before writing something in my file. What's she written? Is something wrong that she's not telling me? Is she saying I'm not fit to be a mother? Could David get hold of this?

'Okay.' She clicks her pen shut. 'Let's take a look then, shall we?' She points. 'You'll be able to see baby here on the screen. And I'm afraid this will feel a bit cold, dear.' She squirts icy gel onto my skin, and presses the probe onto my stomach so firmly I worry it's going to hurt the baby. *Please let my baby be okay.*

But out of the grey swirl on the screen comes a head, a body, hands, feet, and nothing else matters. 'Oh my god!' *My baby.*

The sonographer beams. 'There the little one is.'

I reach my fingers toward the screen. *My baby.*

'Ms Burns,' the sonographer says. 'You are right to think that you are further along. The foetus is far more developed than it would be at twelve weeks.'

'The doctor thought I was seventeen weeks.' A blush comes to my cheeks as I add, 'I know I had food poisoning after a takeaway with friends, but I . . . err . . . I haven't been able to look at my diary to check what date that was.'

The sonographer nods. 'I think you are closer to twenty.'

Oh my god. Twenty weeks? But that's five months?

'Here, see: you can clearly see the heart, brain, limbs, digits . . .' she runs through the list.

It's magic, like Kelly said. A huge surge of love and wonder flows through me as I look at my baby. Our baby.

'Do you want to know the sex?' the sonographer asks.

I nod.

'You see here?' She points. 'I believe you are expecting a baby girl. Congratulations.'

My lip shakes and a tear falls from my cheek. 'Is she . . . is everything okay?'

'There's no sign of anomalies from what I can see.' She pats my arm reassuringly. 'But because this is your first scan, I'm going to get the obstetrician to come in and take a look. Is that okay?'

I nod. My baby girl. There. 'Oh!' We watch as my daughter lifts her thumb to her mouth and starts to suck.

'Lovely,' beams the sonographer. 'Ready?'

I nod again. My eyes fill with tears. I could laugh. Giggle. Nothing else matters. I have a baby daughter, perfect, growing inside me.

The sonographer hands me some tissue to wipe myself and leaves to find the obstetrician.

'Five months then,' Ryan says. I don't look up. That's September. That's awfully close to when my trial could be. 'That change who the father is?'

I pull my jumper down over my stomach. Shielding my baby from this man. 'It's my fiancé's.'

'Your fiancé?' Ryan scoffs. 'I ain't seen him on your visitor list.'

My eyes swim again. Robert should be here, not this horrible stranger swinging handcuffs on his fingers.

The door slides open and a woman in her fifties, her hair a soft choppy red, and glasses on a string round her neck, enters, followed by the sonographer.

Ryan tucks the handcuffs back in his belt.

'Now, Jenna, I'm Mrs Picken, your obstetrician. You can call me Mary if you prefer. I'm just going to take a look at you, okay?' She pulls on plastic gloves.

I nod. Pull my jumper back up and wish Ryan had the shred of decency needed to look away.

Mrs Picken measures from my pubic bone up. 'This is your fundal height,' she says, her voice clipped but friendly. 'This tells us that baby is twenty centimetres in length, which means you are indeed twenty weeks gone.' She nods to the sonographer. 'I would suggest a due date of September the seventh.'

I reassure myself that will be after my trial. Mr Peterson said it had to be before the end of August. I could be out by then. Or I could be convicted of murder, and David could have my baby. No. That won't happen. I have four months till my baby is due. Four months to get out of prison. Four months to fight David.

Mrs Picken feels around my stomach with her hands. 'And did your midwife not say anything to you, Jenna?'

'My midwife?' I stare at her. 'I haven't seen one.'

Mrs Picken's face clouds.

'I didn't know I was supposed to ... I didn't know how.' Should they have done other checks? Is anything wrong?

Mrs Picken turns to Ryan. 'Who is responsible for this woman?'

'Well it ain't mine,' he says lazily.

She rounds on him. 'She is legally entitled to maternity care. Why has she not seen a midwife?'

The smirk falls from Ryan's face. His ears tint. He shrugs. 'Not my department.'

'Well then you need to speak to someone whose department it is.' Mrs Picken turns back to me. Her voice softening. 'Have you had your blood tested for Rubella immunity? HIV, hepatitis B, syphilis?'

'I ... I ... the doctor did some tests when I arrived at ...' I don't want to say prison. Why did he not tell me I was entitled to see a midwife? Did he just not care? Was I just not worth it? What about my baby?

'Okay.' Mrs Picken puts a reassuring hand on my arm. 'And how long have you been incarcerated for?'

It's such a brutal word. Jagged. Cold. 'Seven weeks.'

She nods. 'I think we'll do a full bloods screen again. Just to be sure.'

She means it's long enough inside that I might have caught something else. I clutch my stomach.

'A word, please.' Mrs Picken signals for Ryan to follow her outside.

He glances at me as if to say something, but decides against it.

I hear her voice rise as I get dressed.

'You have no jurisdiction within my hospital to insist on being in the room with a patient who doesn't want you there. Everyone has a right to privacy.'

My face burns. I can feel where he touched me. He deliberately came in here to watch me undress. To humiliate me. Because he could. I feel a rush of gratitude for Mrs Picken. For the sonographer. For the fact they're sticking up for me. For their kindness, their professionalism. The gift that they have given me. For a few precious minutes here I wasn't a prisoner, but an expectant mother. A human being. Ryan is being told off because of me. But soon the handcuffs will be refastened. The shame yoked to me once more for the return to Fallenbrook.

A new emotion burns inside of me: anger.

Now

'You know we're supposed to get an extra carton of milk and some fruit each day?' Kelly is wildly gesticulating with her arms, furious about my scan.

I've been an idiot. 'I never even asked what I was entitled to.' Kev's presence made the journey back bearable. Ryan seemed to sulk. He did tell Kev the doctor was a stuck-up bitch, but disappeared off to smoke as soon as we got back. Kev, seemingly still upbeat after his Costa, escorted me back in time for lunch. It's a relief to be out of those cuffs.

'A fluffy told me.' Kelly is pacing our cell, taking bites out of her baguette.

They literally speak another language in here. 'Sit down, you'll get heartburn. A fluffy?'

'One of them charity birds. I said to the screws I should be getting fruit – that my baby needs the vitamins and shit, and they told me some crap about budget cuts.' She stuffs the rest of her sandwich into her mouth, pulls her diary from our bedside table and opens it to pages of neat writing. 'That's what I've been writing my book on, see?'

How To Do Your Bang Up Banged Up is written across the top in biro. I flick through. It's tips and tricks all based on what you can get hold of and what you can do inside. My eyes hungrily grab the information. I turn to the page headed Diet & Exercise.

'I got Abi to help me with that bit.' She watches me read about Pilates moves to stretch and strengthen.

Save up on your canteen and get some lavender oil. You can rub it on your skin during pregnancy. Helps stretch marks and it's calming so it stops you doing your nut inside.

'This is amazing, Kelly, why didn't you say?'

Her cheeks flush and she shrugs. Kicks the floor with the toe of one trainer.

You can ask the screws to leave the room during labour and when you're breastfeeding.

'Seriously, this is really really good. I don't know half this stuff!'

'Yeah, but they don't listen to me, do they?' she jabs a finger toward the wing. 'And then I get all riled up and angry, you know?'

I think about the way I froze at the hospital. How I didn't stop Ryan touching me. Even the good ones like Sara calling us 'girls'. Even if they don't mean to, they infantilise us. They dehumanise us. I nod.

'I ain't finished yet,' she says, tapping the book. 'But you reckon it's coming along good?'

'More than good – I would have loved to have been given this when I found out I was pregnant. You should speak to Education or Helen, the librarian; this is good enough for a prize, mate.'

She hides her grin while retightening her ponytail.

Thinking of the woman with Sally's handbag in the hospital, I say, 'I thought I saw a friend of mine today. None of my mates have been to see me.'

Kelly sounds sad. 'Yeah, that happens.'

'I've got this one friend – Sally. She was there the night I was arrested. I think the police stopped her talking to me. She won't let her number be added to my call list.' I suddenly can't believe how they have all dropped me. Nothing. Not a word from Deb, Becky, Sally. And it's Sally who hurts the most. They can't all believe I did this. *But the police found child pornography on my laptop – presumably they searched my office computer as well.* She will know. I feel sick.

Kelly puts an arm round me. 'Honestly, bruv, you're not alone. No one wants to know you when you're inside. Screw 'em!'

I turn the pages of Kelly's writing. All the clever things she's found out. All the time I spent in the library and I don't have half of this. I was busy thinking about nurseries, hanging mobiles, kidding myself that my fantasy life still existed. When it's shattered beyond recognition.

'Roll-call!' comes the yell from outside.

'Urgh,' sighs Kelly.

But as I'm closing the book I catch some words that detonate panic inside me:

You can apply for a place on a Mother and Baby Unit, where they let you keep your baby for up to 18 months. But there aren't enough places for everyone. Nowhere near.

'Come on!' Kelly heads to the landing.

And you got to take your case to the Admissions Board with the governor to find out if you can keep your kiddie. No one seems to want this meeting to take place and the screws drag their heels. If you don't get a place then they either give your baby to family or the social.

'Is this true? Do we have to fight for a place on a Mother and Baby Unit?' I'm due in September: I'll either be free, or convicted. Would they let a convicted killer keep her child? The worst-case scenario threatens to overwhelm me.

'Roll-call! Hurry up!' The shout comes from the landing. The door bolt is unlocked.

Kelly looks nervously over her shoulder. 'Yeah. Come on. The screws will already be pissed at you after that doctor ripped them a new one.'

'How many places are there?'

Kelly snatches the book from my hand and drags me out onto the landing. 'About sixty, I think.'

'Here?' How many women have I seen in here who are pregnant? Ten, maybe. How many more are hiding it, like me?

'Nah,' says Kelly. 'In the whole country. More than half have already got lags in them.'

We step onto the landing.

'Shut up, you dipshit,' hisses a prisoner to our right. Ryan is scowling as he walks toward us, doing the head count.

Sixty. In the whole country. And half are gone.

'If you don't get your act together quicker, prisoner,' Ryan booms, his face in mine, payback for earlier, 'I shall dock privileges from the whole fucking landing.'

I wipe my cheek as he storms off. 'Three hundred, three hundred and one. Stand up straight, prisoner!'

'Fucking morons.' The woman next to us glares.

And then I notice her left sleeve is rolled up. My mouth runs dry.

Now

The computer monitor flickers and Mr Peterson's face appears, frozen mid-word, before it jumpstarts again.

'Hello? Mr Peterson?'

'Can you hear me?' he speaks at the same time as me. He has the same tie on as when we last met and I wonder if he only owns the one.

I'm back in the same room I was for my Crown Court plea, ten weeks ago. Ten weeks ago when I thought I would be out at any minute. The number-one cleaner recommended a twenty-minute video call was the quickest way to see my lawyer. 'I'm here.' I blended into a bustling group of Bengali women who were on their way to Education to get out of the wing unseen, but I'm here. 'I can hear you.'

'Good,' he says. 'How are you doing?' I presume he is in his office: behind him is a filing cabinet, piled high with folders. The room doesn't look big, or light, he may not even have a window.

'I'm five months pregnant.'

His eyebrows flicker but it could be the dodgy monitor. 'Yes, you said.'

'I'm further along now.' I've been on at the doctor to get me and Kelly the extra snacks we're entitled to, to make up for his earlier abject failure to get us maternity classes. 'My baby is due on the seventh of September.'

'How lovely, they'll be the oldest in the year. Statistically more likely to do well at school.' He smiles, and I wonder if he or his own child has a September birthday.

'Mr Peterson, I need to know when my trial date is. And I need to know what my rights are, with regards to my baby. If I'm still here . . .'

'Jenna,' he tries to interrupt me.

But I don't have time for this. '*If* I'm still here and there isn't a Mother and Baby Unit place for me.' I fight to keep my voice steady. 'Can I pick who looks after my baby on the outside?'

'That is a decision for the board and Social Services to take. I'm afraid I cannot advise you on that,' he says.

'I'm not allowed legal representation?' I can't believe I have to argue to keep my baby without legal support!

'There are a number of charities that can provide advocacy,' he says, riffling through papers on his desk. 'If you can get hold of someone at Birth Companions, they may be able to help.'

'And how am I supposed to do that?' I need to speak to Ness. She sent more money in response to my letter, but I haven't been able to call her as I risk bumping into Gould or one of her goons each time I leave the cell.

He sighs. 'I know they're not able to cover every prison. I'm not supposed to comment on this, Jenna.' He rubs the bridge of his nose. 'But you should prepare yourself: those who have a record of cruelty against children or child-related offences are not given places on Mother and Baby Units.'

It suddenly feels like I'm on a ferry and the room is rocking. 'But I didn't do it!' David will not get my child. He will not.

Mr Peterson pauses. Clears his throat. 'With regard to your trial date, as I've explained before, you cannot be remanded in custody for longer than one hundred and eighty-two days.'

'Yes, but when will it be?' I can't keep the tears from my voice. This is mine and my baby's life, and he just keeps saying he doesn't know.

'Jenna, I understand you're frustrated, but I will not be notified of your trial date until six weeks before it is due to take
place—' The screen freezes again.

'Oh for fuck's sake!' I try the door to the room, but I've
been locked in. I rattle the handle. 'Hello? Hello! Can anyone
hear me – the computer has gone off!' I wait but hear nothing.
Ryan escorted us in today and I saw him eyeing one of the
new young girls. He's probably locked in a room with her
now. I shudder. I try the handle again. 'Hello!'

There's no response.

Back at the desk Mr Peterson's face is still frozen. There's
no keyboard, no buttons I can try. No restart. I look around
the room. And see a small camera in the left corner. I wave at
it frantically. Nothing happens. I can't see a light on it. Perhaps
it's a dummy. Or unmanned. I don't have time for this. The
stupidity of prison: on one hand you have too much time,
enough time to count every brick in your cell, but not enough
time to talk to your lawyer.

I rest my forearms on the desk and let my forehead slump
onto them.

'. . . Jenna? Hello?'

I jump up. 'I'm here! I can hear you!'

'Sorry about that.' Mr Peterson looks flustered. 'They've
been digging up outside our offices all week and I wonder if
they've hit a cable or something.'

'No problem,' I find myself saying. Though it obviously is.
Poor WiFi is a minor inconvenience for him; it's a matter of
keeping my baby for me. 'Look, I think we need to take a look
at Robert's parents – his father in particular. David. He's
controlling, manipulative, almost certainly violent. He could
have done this.'

Mr Peterson looks stunned.

'We could ask the police to investigate him, or you could
investigate him?'

Mr Peterson shakes his head almost imperceptibly, but his jowls wobble. 'The burden of proof lies with the prosecution – we only need to challenge their evidence.'

'But if we could prove that David did this, we could find Robert. I could get out of here . . .'

'Jenna.' Mr Peterson sounds sad but firm. 'That isn't how this works . . .'

'But the police think I did it – they aren't looking for Robert. They aren't helping me. David is threatening to take my baby!' Hysteria screams from my every word.

'He has threatened you?'

'Yes – well, no. He wants custody of the child.' I dig my fingernails into my thighs.

'Jenna, you're upsetting yourself,' Mr Peterson says. 'Think of the baby.'

'I am!' He's talking to me like I'm a child, or an idiot. I feel so powerless.

'Look, you've got to trust in the justice system,' he says. 'We should hear about your trial date over the coming few weeks.'

My shoulders droop. I'm suddenly incredibly tired. Heavy. 'We were going to get married on the seventeenth of June, but I'm going to be in here, aren't I?'

'I'm sorry, Jenna,' Mr Peterson says, his eyes sad. 'I really—' And the screen goes blank.

What happened? Has the WiFi gone down again?

The lock turns in the door. And Ryan opens it. 'Time's up.'

'But we haven't finished.' I point at the screen. I haven't told Mr Peterson David must have been wearing gloves. How the perpetrator had to have had access to my laptop. That David had ample opportunity for that. I didn't explain my evidence. I did it all backwards.

'You booked a twenty-minute slot and your time's up,' Ryan says with a smirk. His hair gel glints in the strip lighting.

'But the WiFi wasn't working!' I can't believe this.

'Life's a bitch,' Ryan says. 'Now stop arguing, inmate, unless you want to go to seg?'

I close my mouth. In my mind, I hear David laugh. Entitled, confident, unbeatable.

Now

It's another two days before we have Association, and another three until I can get out to call Ness. It's a Thursday and perhaps Gould has visitors, because she doesn't seem to be around. More inmates have rolled up their left sleeves, more whispering seems to be taking place in cells and in corners, the vibe has shifted. Or perhaps my nerves are just hyper-sensitive to any risk. I feel raw, prickling. My baby makes me vulnerable, and now everyone knows. I head for the nearest working phone as swiftly as possible. No point tempting fate.

A woman answers and after a tense sixty seconds where she's not sure she can find Ness – and I have to listen to the thudding dance music and clang of free weights and shouting that echo through the cavernous gym my sister works at – she's finally here.

'How you doing? Sorry I can't get away this week – if visiting was on any other days but Thursday to Sunday, you know? That's our peak times.'

'I know – it's fine.' It's not. But what can I say? Ness works at one of those proper old-school gyms where professional bodybuilders train. It's not a part-time thing for these guys. It's spread over three floors, with a floor for weights machines, a floor for free weights and a boxing ring. She loves it. 'Look, I haven't got long – but I need to talk to you,' I say, glancing around for any sign of Gould or her crew. Waiting to use the phone is a squat woman in her sixties, maybe older, her face a sag of defeat. She reminds me of a sad toad in her green prison jumper. I wonder what she did.

'What's wrong?' Ness says, obviously cupping her hand over the phone, because the background noise her end dims slightly.

I can't believe I'm having this conversation in front of a stranger, with Ness at work, over the telephone. 'You know I said in the letter I sent that David and Judith came but it didn't go well?'

'Stuck-up cunts,' Ness says.

'Well, yes.' I push on. I don't know how to say this. Toad lady behind me clears her throat and starts pointedly tapping her foot. I cut to the chase. 'He wants my baby.' The words hurt.

'What?' Ness says, and I can tell she's leapt up.

'I'm gonna try – but – but . . .' Oh god. I hug my stomach, my child. 'Ness, I probably won't be allowed to keep my baby. Not in here.'

'Fuck,' says Ness.

'And David has said he is going to go for custody.' My voice cracks. Tears blur my vision.

'No way,' says Ness. 'No way are they having it.' Her voice is rising, she's gonna blow.

'Ness, listen to me. You know the social won't let Mum have her with her record . . .'

'Her?' Ness's voice is suddenly awestruck.

Tears are coursing down my cheeks now, but I can't help smiling. 'I'm having a girl. A little girl.'

'Oh my god – a little girl! We're having a little girl!' she shouts as if to the gym behind her. Someone cheers.

I laugh. I didn't know how Ness would take this; she's never shown any real interest in kids. Maybe she doesn't realise the enormity of this. If I go down for murder . . . I could go down for years. The floor shakes. That won't happen. I will find out who did this. I will find out if David did this. I think of Ness plaiting my hair for school, of her barricading us into her room when Carl or Mum's other waster mates came over, snacks at the ready, helping me with my homework. How she has always been there for me. 'Ness, will you look after her?'

'Oh Jenna,' she says.

'I know it's a huge thing . . . it's just I can't let him have her, and she can't go into care.' I feel like a knife is twisting in my gut. 'Ness, I think he did this. I think David did this. He's controlling, dangerous.' My voice cracks.

'Christ. The sick fuck.' Ness exhales.

She believes me. She knows David. She's met him. She recognises he's capable of this. A racking sob escapes my mouth.

'Don't cry. It's going to be okay,' Ness says, soothingly. 'Of course I'll look after her. You're my sister. We're family, yeah?'

'Family.' I nod and swallow the painful lump in my throat. My shoulders shaking. My face wet, crinkled.

Toad lady coughs again.

'All right!' I snap at her. 'Sorry,' I say into the phone.

'We got this, Jenna. We got her. A baby girl!' Ness says. 'Fuck – I better clear out the flat.'

I laugh despite myself. 'We'll need to win the social over,' I say. It's going to be hard convincing them that Ness, a single woman in a one-bed flat, is a better option than David and Judith in their fifty-acre parkland mansion.

'Don't you worry about that,' Ness says. 'I don't drink, I don't smoke, I don't do drugs, I've got my own place, a proper job, I'm not Mum.'

'I know,' I say.

Toad lady loudly clears her throat and I glare at her. 'I'm gonna have to go, Ness. I'll write – I'll give you all the details.'

'Listen, Jenna, don't let the bastards get you down, yeah?'

'Yeah,' I manage.

'I've been asking around – seeing if anyone knows anyone that can help. There's a barrister who comes here – and I've been setting up one of them FundMe pages to raise funds for legal costs. I'm on it, okay? Don't worry.'

'Thank you, thank you, Ness,' I manage.

'I love you,' she says.

'Love you too,' I whisper.

I run past toad lady and back into our cell. Kelly is still out in the yard, doing Pilates with Abi in the late April sun. This time last year Robert and I had just started dating. We were supposed to be getting married. Emily was supposed to be our bridesmaid. How has everything gone so horribly wrong in such a short amount of time? I flop onto my bed, pull the blanket round me and cry for Emily, for Robert, for my baby, for Ness, for Mum, for everything that might have been.

Now

Time slows down when you're inside. Hundreds of grains of sand falling through an hourglass, weighing you down with the hopelessness of it all. I daren't venture out the cell unless I have to, because of Gould. Instead I watch the light on the wall stretch and grow like my stomach. The days are lengthening, first the May light filling our tiny box cell, then the heat of June. The building is no longer cold, but dripping with sweat. Each un-openable window a magnifier of the sun's heat. It's like living inside a greenhouse. We are both counting now. Kelly is due on the 21st of June. Four days after I was due to get married. And I still haven't had any contact from my so-called friends. I torture myself with that when I can't sleep – which is most of the time. I'm just driving myself crazy thinking about it all. It's as if I'm dead. That's what I've realised. I'm dead to those on the outside. Worse than that. Because if I were dead they could mourn. And this way I guess they are ashamed. I feel their embarrassment like a scald. I have tainted everyone's lives. I wrap my hands round my bump. But my child is innocent. I am innocent.

I have sent a letter to Mr Peterson listing my concerns about David and Judith. Documenting examples of David's controlling nature. Listing how I unpacked the knife from the dishwasher, and how our cleaner Michelle had been the day before, so the lack of other fingerprints must mean the person who did this wore gloves. I've listed everyone else who had access to my laptop. Explained that I didn't send the text message to Sally. Walked him through how my phone could have been synced to another device and any message sent would have still looked like it was from me. I've asked if they can check which device the incriminating message was sent from. I told him David and Judith have masses of land, follies, outbuildings – they could be hiding Robert, keeping him captive. How the police have to keep looking for him. My baby needs her father. I know he isn't dead, he can't be. I have asked Mr Peterson to pass it on to DI Langton. I have kept a separate list about David for the Mother and Baby Unit board. I cannot allow him to take her.

I run through it all over and over. Again and again. Looking for the loose thread that will unravel the secret. I feel it's close. I can almost touch it.

As the time drips closer to our wedding day, I don't know if I can cope. I spend more and more time in bed, though I know I should be exercising. I should be having dress fittings, deciding the table plan, having a hen do, spending time with friends and family. Has someone cancelled the church? And the caterers? I picture Judith sobbing into the phone as she tells guests not to come. This should be the happiest day of my life. I dream of confetti that turns into hail, bridesmaids with their left sleeves rolled, and me standing alone in the cold dark church in my dress.

On the 17th of June, the day of the wedding, I stay in bed all day. Kelly sits on the floor next to me, stroking my hair.

And then I get up.

Because I can't wallow. I am part of this world now. I have learnt the rules and I know how to play. Now I just have to learn to win.

My trial date comes through. The 3rd of August. I have a new deadline. I have six weeks to prove that David did this. I have six weeks to prove that I didn't. I have to keep going.

I'm fighting for my and my daughter's life.

Now

I hear the guard below yell: 'Free Flow!'

This is it. Every venture out from our cell starts with a scope to check Gould's not in sight. I've managed to stay below her radar for months now. Since the obstetrician had a go at Ryan, the guards are being a bit more understanding about the pregnancy. Kelly tells them I've got pubic pain, and fetches my food for me. We've occasionally even got an extra apple. We've also had some antenatal classes with a midwife. She does us and a handful of other scared-looking expectant mothers in here. There's enough turnover inside that Kelly and I are the only ones who've been to every class. Most memorable was Kelly's 'Hell no way, motherfucker!' at the sight of forceps. But most classes just leave me more anxious. How can we develop a birth plan in here? We're not even allowed to pack a bag for the hospital. Some of the other mothers have been transferred out to other prisons far away from their families, but with available Mother and Baby Unit places. Transferring, as a rule, seems to happen quickly, with little warning. We were woken last week by the screws waking the sixty-year-old lifer in the next cell and telling her she was being moved to another prison. She had ten minutes to pack her stuff and go. Her mate came looking for her in Association. They'd had a cup of tea and put the world to rights every day for the last six years. There'd been no goodbye.

Sitting alone in our cell, I fantasise about Gould getting transferred out and being free again. How stupid is that? I'm in a prison inside a prison. But she's still here. Her claws dug deep into Fallenbrook.

During yesterday's evening roll-call I watched six women come out of Gould's room. It's against the rules to have that many inmates in one cell, but Kev didn't seem to notice. I think he's frightened of her. I don't blame him. Everyone knows she has things: cigarettes, chocolate-covered biscuits, good tea bags, a radio, a television, a hi-fi, fresh milk, make-up, hooch. And that's just the soft stuff. The screws don't even have pepper spray. She has all the power. Abi pops in to see me every now and then, helps me with some Pilates moves. And she says the rumour is Gould's stockpiling tobacco, so when the ban comes into effect she will have the only supply. Two-thirds of the prison smoke, and though being smoke-free will be good for my baby girl, I can't see how it's going to work. Seven hundred and fifty tobacco addicts – some with severe anger management issues – all going cold turkey at once. Not smart. Gould is just playing the market. Because everyone in here wants something. And more and more people are getting themselves in debt, doing favours, being recruited, rolling their left sleeves up. I've lost count now.

I can hear Annie's grunting laugh coming from a cell under-neath. She never leaves Gould's side. I can't see them, but now's as good a time as any to risk it. Because this visiting order could be the first good news I've had in months.

Despite the heat I've got my hoodie on, and I pull my hood up, shove the paper into my pocket, and walk as quickly as possible. A woman's yellowed hand claws round a door as I pass, her dead eyes peering out. She wavers like a zombie. Spice. I've had a crash course in the artificial weed since I've been in here. More powerful, and more addictive. Abi explained people were spraying it onto children's paintings and either posting them or bringing them in, crumbling it, and smoking it. Everyone seems to know someone who died of a heart attack the first time they smoked it. But they still do it. It's an escape from the boredom, the fear, the self-loathing that comes when you spend twenty-three hours locked in a cell. I have to stay positive for my baby – bathe her in happy hormones. But I can see why so many are tempted to oblite-rate themselves. It seems to be getting worse. More prevalent. I pull the fabric of my hoodie up over my mouth and nose, to stop inhaling it. I see another woman, slumped in a stiff, crooked position against her bed as I pass. Someone has upped the supply in here. And I bet I know who it is. But if Gould's busy with that, perhaps she's grown tired of torment-ing me.

I manoeuvre my bump past the couple sitting, holding hands, on the top of the landing steps. The guard on duty, a new one I haven't seen before, is at the other end of the wing. He either doesn't know about those high in their cells, or he doesn't care. What is one guy going to do anyway?

A woman, pretty, surprisingly young, freckles decorating her neckline like beads, stops on her way up so I can pass. Watching me go, her unlined face impassive. Her left sleeve rolled. I hurry on.

When I reach the ground floor there's still no sign of Gould. A few women are playing pool. I nod at Abi, who is showing a woman with long black hair how to stretch her hamstrings.

'Thought you'd left?'

Vina's voice makes me jump. She's holding her books. Just stepped out her cell. It's bathed in white light from the sun behind her. It must be hotter than ours.

'No.' I try to smile without lifting my head up too much. I don't want everyone to see my face. 'Been unwell,' I say.

'Oh yeah.' Vina nods knowingly.

Behind us someone laughs uproariously and I jump again, remembering the last time I stood here. The lipstick pushing into my cheek. All the eyes on me. My baby kicks in my stomach, urging me to keep moving. I wave my phone card. 'I've got to get going. Before I miss the phone.' I can see the nearest one, the one furthest away from Gould's cell, is currently free.

I go to step away, but Vina grabs hold of my arm. 'Hell is empty and all the devils are here.'

'What?' I stare at her.

'Shakespeare,' she says. 'Look after your baby.'

I watch for a second as she disappears into the white light of her cell. What was that about? But bickering breaks out over a pool shot and the cacophony of the wing rises around me again; I haven't got time to dwell.

'Star Gym,' the gruff voice on the other end shouts. I can hear the familiar boom of base from the music and the clang of free weights in the background.

'Is Ness there please?' I look at the piece of paper in my hand. I didn't recognise the name on the visitor request. E. Matthews. Ness had said she'd been talking to people about my case, trying to find someone to help. Maybe this was them – and they were coming to see me? This could be my chance to expose David. But I have to get hold of her to check.

'Who's calling?' the man at the gym shouts. The times I've called before, no one's asked that.

I swallowed. 'Err, it's her sister.'

'Jenna?' he replies.

'Yeah.' I brace myself for abuse. Ness has persuaded the gym owner to put the gym on my cleared-caller list – but they can't have been thrilled with an alleged child killer ringing in.

'How you doing, love?' the guy says. 'Ness keeps us all up-to-date with your news. We're all rooting for you. I've given her my sister's little one's old cot – it's a nice one, Ikea.'

'Oh.' My lip shakes. A mix of emotions rush through me: happiness, sadness. I want my baby with me. 'Thank you. That's really kind.'

'Bloody cops,' the guy says, and I can imagine him shaking his head. 'Listen, love, I'm sorry but your sister's gone to the wholesaler's. Can I get her to call you back? Does it work like that?'

Not really. 'Don't worry. I'll try her again later.'

'She should be back by seven,' he says.

'Great. Thank you.' We'll be back locked in our cells by five thirty. And the next visiting slot is tomorrow. Perhaps this person is the barrister Ness mentioned, and they've taken the time to come and see me. I can't turn them away. I'll approve the request.

'Listen, you keep your chin up, hey, love?' the guy at the gym says.

I say goodbye before my voice breaks. There are people out there who believe me. It's enough for today.

The arm grazes my nose as it passes my face fast, a hand planting into the wall to bar my way. The soft languorous tone at odds with the unambiguous physical threat.

'Hello, Blondie, long time no see.'

I look up into the face of Gould.

My insides turn liquid.

Now

Gould is the other side of Annie's arm. Leaning against the wall, her hands casually in her tracksuit pockets, not even bothering to check if there's an approaching guard. Behind her the pretty freckled girl I'd passed on the stairs stands watch, ready to alert them to any incoming trouble. She must have turned round, followed me, gone and found Gould.

As if reading my mind, Gould lets a smile stretch across her face. 'I thought you were hiding from me?'

I'm nothing, I'm no one. I'll stay out of her way, if she can just let me be. I fold my arms protectively over my bump. Gould's eyes twinkle. I find my voice. 'I never told anyone about my cards – the lipstick.' She attacked me, she humiliated me, she stole from me, and I haven't grassed her up.

'You haven't told anyone?' She sounds amused.

'I don't want any trouble.' My voice wavering. Across the way a woman I recognise from the library is laughing with her friend. Her eye catches mine. She clocks Gould, then Annie, then Gould's freckled scout. She looks away after that. Turns so she's facing the other way. Give her a minute and she and her friend will be gone. No one wants to cross Gould. Where's the guard?

'How's your young cellmate?' Gould licks her lips.

My stomach twists, as if my baby is trying to pull as far away from Gould as possible. My own breath rebounds onto my face from Annie's arm. 'She has nothing to do with this.'

As Annie drops her arm, Gould steps toward me with a light bounce. Her face is mere centimetres from mine. 'With this?'

She's still grinning. Two of her teeth on the bottom row completely overlap, like a shark's. 'You think *this* is a thing?' She taps herself before slapping her hand against my chest.

The hollow thud echoes round my head. Shakes my heart.

'You think,' her voice falls lower, her smile drops, 'that I give a fuck about you, Blondie? That you are – *what*, some kind of threat?'

No. No that's not what I meant. I try to shake my head but she's so close now I smell the spearmint on her breath.

'You.' She jabs a finger hard into my chest. Jab. Jab. Jab. Again, punctuating her words. 'You are fucking scum.'

My swollen breasts scream. My arms tighten over my bump, hugging myself. Protecting my daughter.

Gould glances down, her lip curling into a deformed smile. 'You and your filthy scum bastard child.' My arms are pushed apart, thrust by the flat palm that grips my stomach, holds it like a melon in her hand. My baby. And she starts to squeeze.

Images flash through my mind. The baby inside the amniotic sac on the midwife's video. Water balloons falling from the Orchard Park estate block landings. The slow-motion shiver and shudder before they burst in mid-air on the first bounce.

And I'm still an Orchard kid.

Before either of us know it, my fist is up and in the side of Gould's face.

Her jaw gives as my knuckles force her mouth apart, spit flies out, her head shudders away. Her yell, an elongated low roar of pain and surprise, as everything slows. And I'm punching through her like Ness taught me.

And I'm not hiding any more. I'm hitting and kicking and clawing like I can rip my world apart from the inside. Like I can set myself free.

But my second punch doesn't land before Annie intercepts it. Gould bounces back like a Weeble, her neck pulling back readying for a head butt. The freckled girl is a blur when—

The alarm sounds.

A loud, piercing explosion of noise.

Everyone jumps up.

People pour from cells.

The thud of the running guard on the landing above, from the other side of the gate. *Code 3*.

We stop, fall apart, as if we were holding each other up. Turn, to see Kelly.

Her eyes wide. Aghast. Staring at me. At my bump. Her fist against the red panic button on the wing wall.

After that, everyone runs.

Now

'I can't sleep!' Kelly almost screams in frustration. Her bulk, a week from her due date, rocks the whole bunk.

I've been awake for hours. A few tossed minutes, restless in the middle, Gould's face leering toward me, her teeth multiplying till she was a mass of incisors. I'd hit her. I'd punched Gould. In the confusion of the alarm everyone had scattered. I didn't see which way she'd gone. I just got Kelly and got out of there. Sprinting, adrenaline still wrapping round me, getting us up the stairs before the shit hit the fan. There'd been an immediate lockdown. Everyone's cell had been spun. And no one said anything. No matter how much the screws screamed and bellowed, revealing that the camera at that end of the wing was out of order, a fact I'm sure Gould will have stored. But still, no one said who'd pressed the alarm. This should have been a good thing, but it made me fearful. You didn't snitch. You didn't sell people out. Because there was a different code in here. A different punishment system. I hit Gould. Kelly sounded the alarm. What the hell had I been thinking?

'This is all I need!' Kelly kicks at her covers, rocking the bunk again.

I roll my own basketball stomach off the wafer-thin mattress. My body aches. I rub my eyes with one hand, my back with the other. Purple bruises, shaped like fingers, are starting to show on my stomach. The knuckles on my right hand are red raw. If David had seen me yesterday it would have confirmed his every last suspicion. *Animal.* Or rather, animalistic. She threatened my baby and something had taken over. Something that was bigger and more powerful than me. Sure, I'd known how to fight because of where I'd come from. But I'd fought because of who I am now. A mother. And I would do it again. I will fight David till my dying breath. 'Want to get up and do some stretches?'

Kelly harrumphs as she prepares to descend. She can't really do it without my help now, and I worry she'll try when I'm in the library and hurt herself. It's not just the rubbish mattress, her size, or even the fight or the alarm that's stopping her sleeping. Today, finally, she presents her case to the Admissions Board for a place on the Mother and Baby Unit. I quell rising panic at my own lack of date. Maybe I won't need it. It's six weeks till my trial. I could get out in time. But I'm no closer to proving David did this. I hoped the police would come and see me again after Mr Peterson gave them my letter, but I've heard nothing.

'Let's go through it again,' Kelly says. Her face, puffier now, dark circles under her eyes from lack of sleep.

I need to be present for her now. To put all thoughts of David and Gould and alarm bells ringing out of my mind. 'You're going to explain that your parents are too old to look after the baby outside. That you're in for a non-violent crime.' I start to list the points we've drawn up.

'That I've kept my nose clean since I've been inside,' she says, blowing her nose. Then laughs.

A clean record she almost lost yesterday because of me. Gould saw it was her who triggered the alarm. Kelly needs this. She needs to get out of here. I force a smile. Pull on my oversized hoodie that only hides my bump if I hunch forward now. I have my own visitor today. The one Ness sent. Thank god my nose isn't plastered across my face. Or worse. Kelly stopped that. 'You're going to tell them you have a job that you have kept and worked hard at. And you have been supportive and caring to other inmates, and have shown great tenacity and skill by writing an informative and transformative guide for other pregnant inmates,' I end with a flourish.

Kelly blushes. And though I want the day to hurry up, more so than ever now, I try not to think what it will be like when she goes. They will take her straight to the Mother and Baby Unit from hospital. I won't get to see her or the baby, unless I get to join her there. And that's not likely. Either Ness will have my baby or I will be out. I can no longer work out which is my best chance.

I help Kelly apply her make-up and do her hair while she deep-breathes and re-reads her notes. She can just about get into the black dress she has for court, though it does look a little tight over her boobs. Then I focus on tidying myself up for my own visit.

Kelly is pacing by the time we hear the unlock starting downstairs. It takes nearly forty minutes for them to get up to our cells.

'I can't do this.' She tugs at her hair.

I don't know if she's thinking about the alarm and Gould. How she denied her her prey: me. But I behave as if she's not. 'You can. You've prepared. You've got a brilliant case, it's going to be fine.' There's not much room for me to move with her prowling like a cat, so I ease myself onto the one plastic chair we have.

'Promise?' Her eyes are wide, pleading. Sometimes she reminds me so much of Emily it hurts.

'Everything is going to be okay. I promise.' I smile.

Something twinges in my lower back. A small spasm. Did I once promise Emily the same thing? I quash the feeling as the bolt on our door slides across. 'Good luck!' I call, and we slide straight out. Kelly with her head held high as the new guard escorts her, me trying to melt into the crowd, unseen, on my way to the visitors' room.

Now

The visitors' room is only half full. Most people attend the afternoon session – it gives visitors longer to get here. By the time I passed the library it was comparatively quiet, only Ryan giving me his now customary scowl as he filed the handful of us in. It meant I could get my favoured table. Over to one side, next to the outer wall. The opposite corner to the door, the opposite end to the kids' play area. Away from Ryan, who's joined Sara by the entrance. It's as close to privacy as you can get in this glorified school hall. It also means I can see who else is there. I'd known an ex-SAS guy who liked to sit with his back against the wall, where he could see all the exits, when we went out. I've adopted the same strategy. But there is no Gould, no Annie, no one with a rolled left sleeve. I flex my bruised knuckles. If anyone recognises me as being involved in the alarm punch yesterday, their faces don't register it. The few other prisoners present don't look my way at all, all caught up in their own anticipation for visitors. Their own excitement.

Ryan circles once more, checking we are all in position. Sedate. He winks at two of the women, who then shoot evils at each other. The bell rings and the visitors start to file in. An older man with sea-captain white whiskers, encased in a brown suit, is walking toward my corner. Is this Ness's contact? He looks a little eccentric to be a lawyer, but perhaps he's a private investigator, or someone else who can shed some light on who put me here. Ness said it was someone she knew from work. He looks a little old to be going to a gym, but his shoulders are broad enough to suggest he still keeps in good shape.

I smile, and he gives me a funny look, then stops at the table three rows in front of me. The woman he is meeting turns and glares at me. Great, now they think I was coming on to him or something.

I'm still staring at my hands when a shadow falls between me and the strip lighting overhead.

'Jenna?'

A woman.

But this can't be.

Oxygen expands my chest, but doesn't manage to get any higher.

I know her face straight away. Those eyes.

I jerk backwards in my chair, the tether reminding me where I am. That this is reality. This is happening. The oxygen tries to push its way up my throat, but my body doesn't seem to want to respond to basic instructions. Neither does my brain. It's as if everything is suspended in that one breath. And we are both floating. The image of a photo on a bedside table colliding with the flesh and blood before me. I am looking at a ghost.

In front of me stands Emily's mother.

Now

Did she have a sister I didn't know about? Another relative who looked just like the photo Emily kept? My eyes rake over her for clues. She is a small, pale woman, her face pushed tight into her skin. Lines that hadn't been in the smiling photograph. I always thought Emily had been the spit of Robert, but now I see their daughter held herself in the same way as her mother, the slight tilt of one hip. And she had her mother's eyes. I would have recognised those eyes anywhere.

'I thought you were dead.'

If she is surprised by this her face doesn't register it. Her eyes – Emily's eyes – pick over me intensely. With a sickened jolt, she takes in my bump.

I pull my jumper out to try and hide its rounded shape, as if it were obscene. It is, in the face of another mother's loss. Another of Robert's children. Robert who thought his wife was dead.

'Sit down, please,' Ryan calls, as he turns into our row.

Still clutching her bag with both hands, as if she might throw it forwards at any moment, Erica Matthews sits without looking away. E. Matthews.

'You killed my baby.' The words are reedy hisses from her thin lips.

A wave of anger rises in me. I loved Emily. The girl who thought her real mother was dead. 'I would *never* have done anything to hurt her. You – you're supposed to be dead.'

The pressure of her eyes, Emily's eyes, bore into me. The bubble of air in my chest begins to hurt.

We stare at each other, as if neither can believe the other is there.

Then the bubble pops. 'You look like her.' A tear slides over my cheek.

Her face crumples, the fine lines a well-worn path into anguish. Her whole body vibrates with a shudder of pain.

She isn't making any noise, and no tears come, but she is crying. I recognise the shell of someone wrung dry from emotion. When the pain is still there but you have nothing more to give. Grief has shaken her dry. And I understand that. We share that. 'I'm so sorry,' I whisper.

'I didn't know if you would see me.' Her voice is shrill, teetering on the edge of hysteria.

'I didn't know you were alive.' This is madness. I've fallen into another world, where everything is flipped. Instinct tells me to comfort this broken woman, but I also want to grab her, shake her till answers come out. I settle for practicalities instead. 'I'm not allowed to get up.' The shame at the words pinches my cheeks. 'But they do hot drinks – tea, a sugary one, might make you feel better?'

Her face looks even more hollowed out, but she stops shaking. 'Nothing will make me feel better.'

I know that feeling. 'I thought you were dead.' If I keep saying it, it might make sense. 'Emily thought you were dead.'

She flinches at that.

I give her a moment. Fight the urge to scream for an explanation. The happy burble of visitors and prisoners drift around us. A child giggles in the background.

Erica Matthews seems to be struggling herself, her fingers tighter still on her bag. I can see the grooves in her knuckles through her skin. 'When is it due?'

The familiar guilt floods through me. As if I asked for this. One moment of hope in the whole quagmire. 'Seven weeks.'

She doesn't respond.

'I didn't know until I arrived here. I haven't been able to tell Robert.'

'A replacement for my daughter?'

'She would have been a sister for Emily.' Emily is irreplaceable. *How could you rob her of her mother? How could you ever hurt her? How could anyone?*

She is still staring at me, as if I might metamorphose into a different version of the truth. But she abandoned Emily. How many nights had Emily cried over her dead mother? And Robert over his dead wife. Something niggles at the back of my mind. An irritating fly. I remember the case of the canoeing guy in the news a few years ago – how he and his wife faked their own deaths. Lied to their own children. It was an insurance scam, wasn't it? Money. It was about money. 'Why does everyone think you're dead? It's cruel. Despicable.'

Her hand flies to the locket that dangles from her neck. 'It was for the best. For Emily.'

How can she trot out such glib responses? After everything she has done to the people I loved. 'You didn't even know her – how do you know what was best for her?'

Her hand wraps tighter around the necklace, holding it against her chest. 'I knew he would get to you.'

The floor shifts. He would get to me? Robert? Did Robert know she was alive? No, surely not. 'Who?' He would have said. He wouldn't have lied. The fly buzzes inside my head. 'What do you mean?' My words hang in the air, beckoning the thoughts I never want to entertain. Never want to let in. Emily is dead. Emily's mum isn't. Did Robert know? Had he lied to me? Had he lied to his daughter? To our Emily. If he had, then I didn't know him at all. And worse, if he was capable of that, what else was he capable of? *We've found traces of his blood.* But no body.

Where is Robert?

Then

I hear the front door slam from the kitchen. Robert's voice a fraction after it.

'We do not slam doors – show a little respect. We've spoken about this before, young lady.'

Oh no, another row. I lift my magazine up, as if I can use it as a shield.

'You are so embarrassing!' Emily cries. They must both be in the hallway. There's nowhere for me to go without being seen. 'No one else's parents stayed for the party.'

I knew this would happen. No teen girl wants their dad there when they're with their friends.

'I don't care what other people's parents do,' Robert snaps. 'I just want to make sure you're safe.'

Oh Robert. He lost his wife when Emily was still just a baby, of course he's over-protective.

'It was Phoebe's birthday! It was all girls, not a mass orgy! Her mum was there the whole time!' Emily yells.

'Right. That's it,' Robert says. 'No more car shares with Phoebe this month.'

'You're joking, right?' Emily says. 'Her mum drives!'

'No,' Robert says. 'Until you can learn to behave like an adult I will drive you to and from school. I will drive you to swim club, and I will wait until you are done. You will go nowhere without me.'

Dammit. There go our plans for date night.

'And I'm confiscating your phone,' he says.

'I hate you!' Emily screams. I hear her stomp up the stairs, before her bedroom door slams shut, shaking the rafters of the old building.

I jump as Robert appears in the kitchen, frantically jabbing at her smartphone.

He still looks gorgeous, even when he's stressed. 'Hey?' I try.

'Hang on,' he says without looking up. 'I'm just installing an app on her phone. I want to know where she is at all times.' He pushes air out of his reddened cheeks.

Whoah. Spyware? That's a bit much. She's just testing her boundaries. 'You sure that's the best idea, sweetie?' I rest a hand gently on his arm.

His eyes bore into me as he looks up from under his fringe, and I pull my hand away like it burns. 'I think I know my daughter better than you,' he says.

'Of course. Right.' I have to turn so he can't see I'm hurt. Is it always going to be like this? If he wants me to live with them, he has to take my opinion on board sometimes. It can't always be him and Emily, and me on the outside. 'I was just trying to help.'

I hear him sigh, and put the phone down on the table.

'Sorry,' he says. The softness back in his voice, as his arms snake round me, and I feel him nuzzle into my neck.

It's just going to take time, that's all. I hug him back. 'I remember what it was like being a teenage girl, you know?' Though my challenges were a bit different than smartphones and birthday parties at recording studios.

'Yeah, and I remember what it was like being a teenage boy.' He runs his hands through his hair, with such a perplexed look I can't help but laugh. He grins back. 'How about a cup of tea?' he says. 'For us oldies.'

I switch the kettle on, and see the app uploading symbol on Emily's phone. She's a good kid. He just needs to trust her.

'I wanted to talk to you actually,' Robert says, sifting through the *Telegraph* for the business section.

'Oh yes?' I aim to sound flirtatious. We need something to dissipate the tension.

'We should talk about money,' Robert says, settling himself into a chair.

Ever since he gave me the key and asked me to move in, this has been the unspoken thing between us. I don't want to have this conversation while he's in this mood. I'm dreading telling him what my mortgage is. I've always been proud of the two-bed flat I bought on the assisted-buying scheme. First homeowner in my family. Yet it feels silly now, like playing at being a grown-up, compared to here. If I cut back on some things, maybe cycle to work, I could scrape together an extra hundred or so. That could go toward my contribution. I want to live here with him and Emily. I want it to work so much.

I put the tea down in front of him decisively. 'Yes, we do. I don't think I can cover half the mortgage for this place, but perhaps I could cover the bills instead?'

His eyebrows go up. This is excruciating. But I'm younger than him, and I don't own my own business. I feel the annoyance rise in me.

'I send home part of my wage to Mum. They keep cutting back her benefits. She's got herself involved with one of those awful payday loans. The APR was over three hundred per cent. She didn't think people would rip people off like that. Ness and I only found out when they cut off her electricity.' It comes out in an angry rush.

'Jenna.' His voice is all serious, a hint of the same tone he used with Emily. 'There's no need to get so worked up. Why didn't you come to me before?'

Because I didn't want to embarrass Mum. Because I don't ever want her to feel like she's failing. She fought hard for us when we were younger. To get better, to be there for us. Anger surges in me. 'You didn't notice.'

'Well that's not fair, is it?' he says.

'No,' I concede.

'Jenna.' He reaches for my hand. 'I don't expect you to pay me rent. For a start there's no mortgage on this place, the family own it outright.'

It takes a second to process the words. But of course there's no mortgage – this is inherited wealth. I just didn't think. But I'm not a charity case. 'I want to be an equal in this relationship.' I want to be listened to when I try to talk about Emily.

'You are,' he says. 'But you're my girlfriend. How would it look if people found out you were paying to live here?'

I don't really see what it has to do with anyone else.

Robert pushes on. 'Maybe it's time to get rid of the flat, to show my parents that you're committed, fully.'

Committed? I falter. This conversation is moving quicker than I wanted it to. 'I don't want anyone to think I'm some kind of gold-digger.'

He gives me a slightly strained smile. 'It's just not appropriate for you to have another place. I want you here, with me and Emily. Where we can keep an eye on you.'

Keep an eye on me? He sounds like he's talking to Emily again. 'But what will your parents say?' I know how this looks.

Robert smiles as if he's won. 'Actually, Mother suggested I set you up with a little allowance, so you can get your hair done, and clothes for corporate parties and things.'

Have I not been wearing the right things so far? I feel myself flush.

Robert mistakes my embarrassment for relief. He pats my hand. 'That's all settled then. I knew you'd see sense.' He picks up his newspaper again and leans back. 'I'll instruct our solicitor to put your flat on the market.'

Panic suddenly gushes up in me. 'Don't do that!'

He looks up quizzically.

I scramble to cover it up. 'I mean, I'll talk to the agent. You've got enough on your plate with work already.' I'm not sure I want to get rid of it. I'm not sure what I want. Ness might want to rent it or something. Why do I feel like I was just outmanoeuvred?

'Of course, darling,' he says, looking at the paper. 'Whatever makes you happy.' And I realise he sounds just like his father talking to his mother.

Now

'The papers said you were engaged. You must have known what he was like.' Erica stares at me with Emily's eyes.

I dig my fingers into the chair.

No.

I won't believe it. This woman knows nothing about us. About Robert. He couldn't have lied about this. She did this. She abandoned them both.

Erica licks her lips, the dry white flecks greedily sucking up the moisture. 'He's dangerous.'

'No.' I won't listen to these lies. I turn to signal for Sara or Ryan, I don't care, I just want out of here. 'You're lying.'

'He paid me.'

I stare at her.

'He paid me money to disappear. To stay away.' She is massaging the locket between two fingers. A photo of Emily inside? 'He threatened me.'

I think of the newspaper I found discarded in the library. With me and Robert on the front. And the photo of Emily in her school uniform on the inside. The photo I keep under the little bedside unit Kelly and I share. 'Why would he do that?'

She looks up, sad, but different. Pitying. 'I wasn't suitable.'

It's lies. 'You were her mother.'

She winces at my use of past tense. 'I had an accident when Emily was a baby. I was carrying her downstairs – tired – I hadn't been sleeping. And I slipped. I didn't want to hurt her.' Her voice wavers. She takes a breath. 'I held onto her, so I couldn't break my fall. My arm broke in three places. My shoulder dislocated. They had to fuse it together with metal.' She runs her hand over the outside of her arm, as if tracing the join. 'I was in hospital for weeks and in a lot of pain.'

What did this have to do with Robert? He would have looked after her – she was his wife. He was – is – kind. Caring. The thought that this woman is mad comes to me. Delusional. She's blaming Robert for her faking her own death. For her deserting her child. Could she be behind all this? Presumably Robert stashed the spare key in the same place he had when they'd been together? It wasn't the kind of thing you randomly moved. Or maybe she still had her own key. She could have been inside our house without us knowing. At my laptop. With Emily.

Erica takes another breath, as if shaking off a memory. 'I wanted to get home from hospital – to Emily and Robert – as soon as I could. And of course we had private care. I discharged myself before I should have. I can see that now. But I wanted to be with my baby.' A tear rolls down her cheek and she swipes at it. Is it part of an act? 'To cope with the pain, the doctor prescribed me strong medication. I needed to take them just to get up, to make food for Emily, to feed her. And . . . well. I became dependent.' Her hand shakes slightly.

I watch the tremor. Look again at the way her skin is taut over her skull. How her depleted, fragile frame reminds me not of strong-muscled Emily turning cartwheels, slicing through the pool, but of Mum. Addiction doesn't care where you're from. It doesn't give a fuck what school you went to, or how nice your house is. It can take root anywhere. Shoots spring up. And soon it's obliterated everything. Would I really have wanted Emily to go through that? To find her mother passed out, covered in her own piss and vomit. To tend the cuts and bruises from the latest man she'd let treat her body like a punch bag in exchange for a high. Ness used to barricade us into her room to keep safe. Would I have wanted her to have my childhood? Smiling, happy, innocent Emily. 'I'm sorry.'

Erica nods, a look of resignation on her face. 'I passed out one day. While I was bathing Emily. Robert was out. And he came home to find her screaming in freezing water and me comatose on the floor.'

'Oh my god.' I think of the shape of Mum on the sofa. Ness screaming into the phone. The blue flashing lights of the ambulance. Robert must have been terrified. Angry.

'She was okay. But only because I was lucky.' Her agony at what she did clings to every word. 'After that I got help.'

I nod. But it isn't that easy.

'I went cold turkey. I don't take anything any more – not even paracetamol.' She fingers her locket again. It is a talisman. A reminder. Rosary beads for staying clean. 'I've been clean for twelve years. Even now,' she adds the last words painfully, 'I feel so guilty.' She looks up, Emily's eyes pleading. 'I hate myself. I was weak. Easy to manipulate.'

The word cuts through me.

But Erica can't stop now. I can see she has to get this out. It's a confession. An accusation. 'He used that against me. He threatened to have me sectioned.' Bile blossoms in my stomach. 'He told me I would hurt Emily . . .' She trails off, her fingers fluttering around the locket. 'Maybe I would have.'

Robert had always been good about Mum. But then he'd never seen her sick. Never left his baby daughter with her. 'Robert understood, surely?'

She smiles sadly. 'Of course. But it wasn't him I had to worry about.'

The hairs on the back of my neck stand up.

Erica isn't telling me Robert had done this – how could I even think that? How could I have doubted the man I love? How could I even begin to think he would be capable of this?

Guilt hangs around me like spice smoke. 'Erica, who threatened you? Who paid you to disappear?'

Erica looks up with Emily's eyes. She drops the locket, as if she doesn't want to taint it with the name. And I know what she's going to say. Who she's going to say. My darkest fear. The man who has taken one baby from its mother, and who now wants to take mine.

'David. David did this.'

'You have to go to the police – you have to tell them what he's like.' I reach for her hand, desperate.

She lurches backwards. Fear in her eyes. Shakes her head.

'He's going to do it again.' I have to make her understand. 'He's going to take my baby.'

'I can't,' she says.

'You can, you have to. You know what he's like. You know what he's capable of!' Is she? Does she? I search her face for any sign. 'I think he might be involved in this . . . in what happened to Emily.'

'No,' she says, shaking her head vehemently. Tears flying out. 'No. He wouldn't. Robert would've protected her.'

'But don't you see: Robert is missing. He was hurt. There was blood.' I force myself to confront this. 'Did Robert know? Does Robert think you're dead?'

She blinks rapidly. As if the smoke is in her eyes. Her guilt fogging her sight. The truth floating just in front of her.

'Robert knows I'm alive.'

Then

Laughter greets me as I carry in more crisps. A slight wobble in my walk, the wine's hit me harder than I thought. Ness and Robert are by the fire, gripping glasses of red. Robert in his cable-knit jumper, Ness in my cashmere cardi. It's such a relief to see him relaxed after the last few weeks. He's been stressed about Emily, work. I just want him to be as happy as he's made me.

Right on cue Robert's phone rings, and his face falls.

'Dad,' he says, getting up. 'I'll call him back from my study.'

'Take your drink,' Ness says. 'Sounds like you might need it!'

'Wise lady, this one.' He winks at me, and picks up the glass.

'Salt and vinegar or cheese and onion.' I offer the crisps to Ness. Not quite the same standards as Judith's artful presentation, but I'm learning.

She takes a handful of each and looks at the grand piano. 'I love this room.'

'Me too,' I say, pulling my blanket over my knees. I could just go to sleep right here, right now in front of the fire. I still can't believe this beautiful building is home. 'It's so cosy.'

'It's like something out of a posh hotel.' She sips her drink. 'You're a lucky girl, Jenna.'

I smile, then I think of Judith and David and it falters.

'What is it?' Ness says. 'Trouble in paradise?'

I check Robert closed the door on his way out. I probably shouldn't say anything, but it's Ness. It doesn't count. 'Nothing like that. I just don't want to let him down, you know?'

Ness reaches for the bottle to top us up. I forget to say I'm not drinking red. 'What do you mean? Nothing's happened, has it?'

I consider telling her about David and Judith and the real reason we've postponed the wedding to June. But I don't want her to think less of Robert. He's trying so hard to please them. 'No, nothing's happened. It's just – this place, Emily, the business, his parents – I feel a bit out of my depth sometimes. I'm probably just tired.' I haven't been getting much sleep.

'Pfft,' Ness says. 'Looks like you're doing great to me.' She crunches a crisp. 'You've always smashed everything you've done. You know that.'

I squeeze her knee. 'That's 'cause I learnt from the best. I just . . .' I think of the photo of Robert's first wife in its polished frame. How he won't talk about her, because it still hurts. I can see he will always love her. 'I just want to get it right for him, you know? I want everything to be perfect. Robert and Emily have had it hard in the past. And they deserve everything to be perfect. Me to be perfect.' I really have had too much to drink.

'You already are Miss Perfect,' Ness says. And throws a crisp at me.

I catch it and laugh. The vinegar bitter on my tongue, reviving me.

'That why me and Mum haven't seen you so much recently?' Ness says, suddenly serious. ''Cause you're here playing happy families.'

I've been busy with the wedding and Robert's work commitments sure, but it's not been that bad, has it? I did cancel our last lunch when Robert needed me to take Emily to band practice. Maybe it has been a while. The time just goes so fast. 'Sorry,' I say guiltily. 'Robert's been very busy at work, but things will be better once the wedding's out the way.' I squash the feeling I shouldn't be thinking of the happiest day of my life as something to get off the list. All brides feel overwhelmed.

'Right,' Ness says, curtly.

I throw my arms round her. 'Please don't be cross with me.' Not you as well.

'All right, all right,' she says. 'Just as long as you've still got time for your sister when you're a fancy married lady.'

'Promise,' I say. I rest my head on her shoulder. She strokes my hair like she did when I was little.

The door opens. 'I need more wine,' Robert says, his own hair ruffled from where he's been tugging at it.

'You okay, darling?' I pour the bottle for him. Can't David leave him alone for one evening? It's gone ten, for god's sake.

'Fine. Fine,' he says. Then shakes his head. 'He was supposed to have retired last year. I'm ready. I've proved myself. But it's never going to be enough.'

I freeze, Robert's obviously had too much too. He very rarely says anything negative about David.

'Shots?' Ness says, breaking the awkward silence.

We all laugh.

'No way – I'm too old for that,' Robert says, the light back in his eyes.

'Shut up,' Ness says. 'You're only a few years older than me. If you're old, then I'm old. And I'm *not* old.'

'Not a day over twenty-one,' I say. 'Which would make me . . .'

'Jailbait,' Robert cuts in.

'Hey that's my sister you're talking about.' Ness laughs. 'Well, I'll have something stronger even if you won't.'

Ness pours more drinks. I know it's time to make changes. Tonight is a new start. I'll be more organised. More on top of things. Better able to support Robert to becoming head of the company. No more cancelling get-togethers with Ness and Mum. I'll make time. I can be the perfect partner and surrogate parent for Robert and Emily, and still be a good sister and daughter too.

Now

Robert knows I'm alive.

I thought Robert was a tragic grieving widow. That Erica was this impossibly perfect first wife I had to live up to. I supported him. I loved him. I was worried about him. I wanted to make him happy. I gave him and Emily everything. And he used that to manipulate me.

Unless Erica lied. I know nothing about this woman. An hour ago I thought she was dead. I keep playing her words over in my mind as I walk back to the wing. With only a handful of us, we got out quickly, early. The rest of the prison hasn't gone into Free Flow yet. I can hear classes still packing up. I need to speak to her again. I didn't ask her how to get hold of her. Stupid. Stupid. Stupid. She could have been round the corner, a few miles away, and I never knew. I never asked her why she came. Though her eyes had that look, like Judith's, looking for her child. She came for answers and she left me with nothing but questions.

I turn around, make to go back. But where am I going to go? Erica is already the other side of many locked doors. Possibly already outside, on her way home. Away from this place. The walls of Fallenbrook are tight around me, the corridor the inside of a long snake, its skin impervious to shouts. No one else has come out of the classrooms yet. If I'm fast I can make it.

In the hallway outside the library is the old wall-mounted phone booth I saw on my first night here. The induction video told us we're only supposed to use the ones on the wing. Use of any unauthorised communication device means an automatic spell in seg. I've got to risk it. I pick up the handset – there's a dial tone. I check over my shoulder and dial fast. It connects.

'Hayworth, Morrow and Peal,' announces the clipped voice on the other end.

'Can I speak to Mr Peterson, please. It's urgent,' I say. If anyone catches me – if Ryan catches me – I'm in so much trouble. My heart's pounding.

The library door vibrates, a seal broken somewhere else. A door opening? The corridor will be full any minute. Anyone could see me. The chattering voices of a class packing up.

'May I ask who's calling?' the lady says.

'It's Jenna Burns,' I say urgently. *Please be there. Please.*

'Please hold,' the voice says, and Vivaldi's *Four Seasons* starts up in my ear.

I can hear voices in both directions. Doors and gates being unlocked.

'Hello. Jenna?' Mr Peterson's voice.

'She's alive – Robert's wife. She's alive. She could have been here. She could have done this.'

'Whoa, slow down,' he says.

I can't, I glance over my shoulder.

'Who is alive, who are you talking about?'

'Erica Matthews. Robert's wife – I thought she was dead. Emily thought she was dead.'

'Hang on,' Mr Peterson says. There's the sound of rustling. 'Yes, here she is. The police confirmed her alibi.'

His words take a second to register. 'You knew? You knew she was alive?' What kind of lawyer is he?

He sounds matter-of-fact. 'I had no reason to suspect *you* didn't.' His words rub salt into the wound of Robert's lie. Did everyone know but me? 'She was in Sydney, Australia when it happened. She's lived there for twelve years.'

Twelve years. David had contacts in Australia. He sent her there. He sent her as far away as he could. Presumably DI Langton and DS Salinsky didn't fly out to Australia – presumably it's easy to lie about an alibi over the phone? 'I need to see her again,' I say. If what she's saying is true I have to convince her to help me. To tell the board and the social what David is like. If she's lying she could be guilty. She could be the one that did this. She said she'd heard we were engaged – did she come back to get her family? To stop me from having them? Did she and Emily fight?

'I'm afraid I don't have contact details for her,' Mr Peterson is saying. The noise from the library grows louder, closer. I have to go.

'Thank you,' I say, and hang up.

I'll ask Ness to find Erica. Ask her to come and see me again. Or if I had an address, I could write to her.

Inmates stream from the library. I put my head down and get moving.

My head's spinning. Am I in shock? My skin feels cold. I need a tea, with sugar. I need to think. David blackmailed Erica, paid her to disappear. That's what she said. I think of David's rage at me. His threat to take my baby. I gently massage my stomach, away from the tender bruises. He is a man accustomed to getting his own way. He sent the mother of his own granddaughter away. He's more than capable of incredible cruelty. Had he been trying to get rid of me? Had Emily stood in his way? Or what if this isn't about me at all – what if Emily found out what he did to her mother and confronted him? If David's temper got the better of him he could have lost it. Robert could have disturbed them. David would have had no choice but to get rid of him too. Or at least keep him quiet somewhere, hidden. A shudder runs through me. Otherwise people would find out what David did, that his daughter-in-law was an addict, not a tragic early death. That he had blackmailed her into leaving. What would he do to stop that coming out? Motive. Erica is motive. My baby kicks inside. A gentle poke, as if to remind me I'm not going through this alone.

But it only serves to remind me instead that soon she will be here, and I am no nearer to being able to prove any of this. *Robert knows I'm alive.* Robert had lied to me. Or Erica had. He had told me his wife was dead.

I stop suddenly in the corridor.

His wife. We were engaged. We were going to get married. Erica only knew about the engagement from the papers. Mr Peterson had said ex-wife. You don't divorce dead people. Robert divorced her. She was telling the truth. Robert knew Erica was alive.

David must have forced Robert into it. David is dangerous, Erica knows that. I can persuade her to come forward – to tell the police and the social what he's like. It's supporting evidence. I just have to talk to her again. What happened to Emily can't happen to my daughter.

I need a stamp.

I start to run, turning left away from the wing and toward the canteen.

The orderly in charge of post is Nicky. She's still dawdling, not keen to get back into the wing. I don't blame her. The first time we met she introduced herself as 'Nicky – death by dangerous driving.' As if it was an unusual surname, rather than a crime. She likes to call it like it is, that's what she says.

'Can I get a stamp, please?' I say breathlessly. My bump makes it so much harder to run. I need to do more squats with Kelly. Keep strengthening up. Aside from that I sound surprisingly normal given I've just met my fiancé's dead wife. 'It's for a legal thing.' Erica can save my baby from David. The hope takes seed inside of me. 'Bit of good news for a change, you know?'

Nicky fixes me with her beady eyes. 'Good news? From what I heard, you're not gonna be out for a long time.' An unattractive smile spreads over her face.

What?

My arms and legs tingle. *Gould.* The punch had slipped my mind with everything else. How could I have been wandering around as if nothing's happened? Nicky tells it like it is. 'I . . . I don't know what you mean.'

'Don't play innocent with me, madam.' She peels the stamp off the roll with a long, yellowing nail. Presses it firmly onto the envelope. Looks up, her eyes shining. 'Your secret's out.'

The floor turns to jelly beneath my feet.

She knows.

Her cackling laughter chases me as I sprint toward the wing.

Now

For a moment I think Nicky's wrong. Then I hear it.

There's noise coming from above. Shouting. Voices. I look up. There's a clump of people, a gathering crowd on the top floor. Outside our cell. *Kelly*. She'll be out of the board presentation now. She'll be here. Gould saw her press the alarm. She knows she did it.

I run up the stairs as fast as I can. Holding onto the rail so I don't slip. My bum and hips forced out behind me. My breath painful squirts now.

The upper walkway is thronging with people, women, shouting and trying to see what's going on. Why haven't they called an end to Free Flow?

'*What is it?*'

'*What's happened?*'

'*What's going on?*'

'*There'll be trouble.*'

'*Go back to your cell.*'

Voices swim round me. I pass two women who are hanging back from the inner group, a mix of excitement and wariness in each of their faces.

Then I reach the knot, women whooping and craning over the heads of those in front. Hands on shoulders, up on tiptoes.

I tug at the first arm I reach. 'Out my way. Let me through!' They peel off from those in front of them, so that I'm soon in the throng. Surrounded by green hoodies. 'That's my cell. Let me through,' I shout.

A woman turns to stare at me. Steps back. And then another does the same, a look of disgust on her face. I feel my muscles tense. Someone tuts. Another clicks their tongue with disgust.

The more the space grows around me, the more the dread seeps in. They're moving away like I'm diseased. Contagious.

They know. But how?

And then I see it.

Writ in blood-red letters, above our door, like a twisted inversion of biblical scrawl: Nonce.

I'm frozen for a second. The whispering hisses of the women around me fall away. All I can hear is the rushing blood in my ears. *Nonce.*

Kelly, frantic, still in her black court dress, has a wad of wet tissue in one hand and is trying to scrub at the letters. She looks up, her hair wild about her face. 'I can't get it off! I can't get it off!'

I step toward her, take the tissue from her hand. Silence has descended around us, as the gathered women wait for the fireworks.

'Why have they done this?' Kelly cries. 'Which one of you did this?'

'It's her!' One of the women stabs toward me with an accusatory finger, her face a mask of outraged disgust.

Another, in anger, more than disgust, shouts: 'She killed her stepdaughter!' Too late, I see her left sleeve is rolled.

Kelly staggers backwards, away from me, her mouth open.

'I didn't . . .' My words are lost under an ear-piercing whistle.

'What the hell is all this?' Kev's voice booms as he bustles into the crowd.

'Nonce!' shouts one woman, leaping up next to her friend.

'Paedo!' comes the called reply.

'Smother her in her sleep!' shouts someone. There's laughter.

'Shut up, and get back to your cells – Free Flow's over,' yells Kev. His face is an angry red, he obviously hurried up the stairs and he found it harder than me. 'What the hell is going on here?'

But no one moves. There's only one of him, and so many of them. Alarm radiates through my body.

I'm holding the red-stained tissue. Kelly, a step away from me, is shaking. Looking at the floor.

Kev looks at the tissue in my hand and the words on the wall, puts two and two together and comes up with five. 'What the hell is the meaning of this?' He turns on me.

Why on earth would I mark myself out like this? 'I didn't do it!' I say.

'That's it, you're on basic,' Kev screams.

'But I didn't do it!' I say. This isn't fair. They should be investigating this, protecting me, protecting Kelly. 'Do you understand what that word means?' It's a death sentence.

'Shut up, unless you want to end up in seg!' he bellows. 'Now find yourself a mop and get that muck cleaned off.' He swivels, and the gathered women take a step back. 'All of you! Free Flow'll be finished any minute. Unless you want to go into lockdown!'

He stomps along the walkway, making the metal ring out. But no one pays him any heed. If people hadn't seen before, they are looking now. Up and down the landing inquisitive heads appear, whispering faces. Below us people crane up to see. Pointing. Those who can't read the word being told by those around them. Whispers, shouts, spreading faster than cockroaches through the cells. *The Blonde Slayer. Killed her own stepdaughter. Kid was only fourteen. Murdering paedo scum.*

And there, on the ground floor, in the middle of the wing, ringed by cat-calling cronies, smirking with triumphant hatred: Gould.

Now

Kelly is still staring at me. Her body shaking. Her arms wrapped around her belly. She came back from her Admissions Board session to this.

I take a step toward her. 'Kelly . . .'

She steps back; her nostrils flare.

I swallow my hurt. The rejection. Tell myself it's not personal. 'Please,' I say quietly. 'I didn't do this.'

'I know you wouldn't paint that . . . that . . . word yourself,' she explodes. 'What, you think I'm as thick as Kev?' Her arms flail and she steps toward me now, like a drunk arguing with their mate outside a club. Prods two fingers into my chest. 'Don't you lie to me.'

I step back. Hold my arms wide. I don't want to fight her. She's heavily pregnant. I'm slightly less heavily pregnant, for god's sake. I want to cry. 'I didn't do what they said. I didn't do it. It's a set-up.'

Kelly's face is still twisted in anger. Behind me, doors creak. People are watching, listening. There is no privacy in here. No secrets.

I step toward the edge of the landing, my arms still open, offering myself like a sacrifice. I raise my voice. 'I was framed. Someone set me up. I didn't do it.' David, Erica, and Robert's faces swim through my mind.

People say it all the time. I was set up. I didn't do it. Nicky's blunt up-front admittance a way to dispense with the questions, the doubt, the worry. Can you ever really trust anyone in here? Can I trust anyone on the outside? People laugh. Jeer. The whispers rumble on. *Lying bitch*. Right now I only need one person to believe me.

I turn back toward Kelly, whose arms are back down by her sides. Her breath is still ragged, and her lips are parted, but the rage has gone from her face. We've shared some things in here. Softly I say, 'I promise, on my baby's life, I didn't do those horrible things.'

I'm still holding my arms out, my chest heaving from the exertion of the last few minutes.

Kelly sighs. Tugs at her dress where it's ruched round her belly. 'I'll see if I can get a broom,' she says. 'We can get it off with that.'

I want to hug her. I want to cry. I want to thank her for having faith in me. Instead I walk into the cell and run the tap into the kettle, my hands shaking the whole time.

Now

It takes several minutes and several refreshes of the tiny kettle to get the word off, even with the broom moving in time with the clunk of the doors being locked below, one cell at a time, working up toward us. The silence between us only broken when Kelly turns and snarls at the clumps of women grouped not far from us.

'What you looking at – get out of it!' she says. But they only laugh and jeer. Tell her not to get her knickers knotted. I daren't look away from the wall long enough to see if they have rolled left sleeves or not. But now, it isn't just them I have to be fearful of. Now everyone knows.

Kelly, clearly thinking the same, says, 'They'll be up here in a second. I'll take the broom back. You get inside and make a cuppa, yeah?'

'How did the hearing go?' With everything that's happened this is the first opportunity I've had to ask.

She bites her bottom lip. 'All right. I think. My mum came – said her and Dad weren't fit enough to have a kiddie, though they would have if they could. And that I should be allowed to keep him.'

I nod. There isn't really anything else to say.

Kelly straightens up. 'I'm supposed to be told the verdict within twenty-four hours – but you know what this place is like.' She looks at her watch. 'They'll bring lunch round after this, I reckon. You stay put.'

Today's events have given Kelly a new efficient tone. Perhaps it is donning the court dress rather than these pyjama stand-ins. Perhaps outside she was always getting on with things. Which begs the question, which one is the closest to the real Kelly? The decisive pro, or the child-like anxious thing that snaps when cornered? A bit of both, probably. We all reveal different sides of ourselves to different people. Like David. Like Robert.

After lunch I make my excuses and lie down with my eyes closed, the adrenaline dribbling out of me with the remainder of my energy. *Nonce*. Has my situation got a whole lot worse? Or am I just panicking? I think of the whispered looks. The jeers. The rumours might die down. Something else might save me. Tomorrow is the day the prison goes no smoking! That will distract people. People aren't happy about it, with the possible exception of Gould, who is nicely placed to capitalise on the new market.

And then there is Erica. Erica, who is very much alive. Mr Peterson said the police had checked her alibi, but the woman had fooled everyone into thinking she was dead for twelve years. Surely she could get someone to simply give her a false alibi? How long has she really been back for? And did Emily know? Did Robert know? Every time my thoughts turn to Robert, my insides writhe like they are full of black mist. I am angry. Angry at him for lying to me. To his daughter. And frightened. We'd fallen in love fast, hard, quickly. But was it too quickly? Was Robert trying to replace Erica while his parents were away? Had we rushed into this? How well do I really know him if he could lie to me about something like this? How much can I really trust him?

Then

'I was thinking of inviting Sally over this Sunday for lunch,' I say, as I clear the plates from the table. I feel like it's been ages since I had a proper chat with her. We used to go out for drinks after work all the time, but I'm so busy picking Emily up after school and going to work dos with Robert that we haven't managed it in months.

'No can do,' Robert says, putting the vase of lilies back on the kitchen table. 'We're spending Sunday with my parents and the Boyles.'

'Are we?' I don't remember that.

'It must have slipped your mind,' he says, kissing the top of my head as he passes. 'Besides, don't you see enough of Sally at work every day?'

I really don't remember him saying anything about the Boyles. And the thought of spending another weekend at his parents' makes me squirm. Things are fraught between Emily and her granddad. She won't want to come and play happy families. 'That was my thinking, actually. I've been so busy, lately – I haven't had a proper catch-up with Sal forever.'

'Oh well,' he says. 'I'm sure she'll cope.'

That wasn't really what I meant. 'But I'd like to see her.'

He stops rearranging the stems of the flowers, dusts the pollen off his hands and perches on the side of the table. He has the same look on his face as when he's about to talk to Emily about 'appropriate clothing'. I stop too. There's no point trying to escape these conversations, it's just something Robert has to do. Sometimes I think he forgets I'm his partner, and not another daughter, but I don't want to upset him. 'Darling, I think it's time we had a little chat about work, don't you?'

'What about it?' I try to keep my voice light. I don't want to row. I think about the perfect first wife in the photo upstairs. Feel her spectre of judgement hanging over me as dishwater drips from my hands and onto my top.

He takes hold of one of my hands and tenderly wipes the bubbles off, cupping it like he does when he's talking to important older female suppliers. 'The thing is, darling, Sally takes advantage of you.'

'What?' No, she doesn't.

'She wants too much, takes too much, and it's stressing you out. You've barely got a second to yourself.'

But that's because I'm in a relationship now, I suddenly have a teen I'm responsible for, I'm planning for a wedding. My life has changed, that's all. 'No, it's not that,' I say.

He squeezes my hand. 'It's because you're so kind-hearted and generous that you don't see it.' He tucks a strand of hair behind my ear and taps my nose with his finger. Like you would to a cheeky child.

'Sally would never—'

'I'm not the only one to notice,' he says meaningfully. Who else has noticed? Who else has said something? We saw Ness last week, did she say something? 'Wouldn't you like a bit more time for yourself – for us?'

I'm not the one booking in dates with the Boyles. 'I guess with the wedding and stuff, things have been a little hectic.' Maybe I have been neglecting him. Anxiety catches at my stomach, stitching together the familiar knot. I just want to make him smile, make him happy. Make him look at me like he does when I get it right.

'This is an important time for me at work, you know that.' I nod. I know he needs my support. 'I need to prove to Dad that I'm capable of running the company.'

'You are,' I say.

'You know how important the company is to me. And Dad would never be able to do it without Mum.' He holds my stare. A thousand unspoken words about being as good as his father between us.

'I know. I do. We can do this.'

'Good,' he says, dropping my hands. He turns back to the flowers, moving the vase by half an inch to the left. Checking the line. 'I think three days is enough to start with.'

'Three days?'

'Yes,' he says, fixing me with a smile that makes me gooey inside. The knot loosens. He still loves me. It's going to be okay. 'Tell Sally you'll drop down to three days a week for now. It'll give you more time to plan for the wedding. And it'll give her time to find a decent replacement.' He stoops to kiss me. 'Not that you're replaceable of course.' And he walks out the room.

I stand there, shocked. What just happened? I don't want to go part-time. I didn't realise that's what he meant. I go to call after him, but something stops me. He's under so much pressure right now. I can't add to that. I can't bear to disappoint him. When did I start biting my tongue? I'm protecting him from more stress. I think of Judith up at the big house, manicuring, preening, perfecting her gilded cage. Delighted to be on David's arm at events because she's out of the house.

Suddenly I feel like I'm standing in a stranger's house, not in the kitchen of the man I love. *This is my home.* I think of my flat, still sitting empty: I haven't called the estate agent yet. Everything is happening so fast. Am I ready for this? I force myself to face the question I've been avoiding. Is this what I really want? I love my job, I love earning my own money, I love my independence. On my left hand, my ring finger is weighed down by the diamond. Am I ready to be Robert's wife? To love, honour and obey.

But I do love him. I love him and Emily so much. I have never felt as happy as I do when we're together. And every relationship involves compromise, doesn't it? That's just what this is. Robert is not your average man, he needs a wife who will support him and the business. Plenty of Emily's friends' mothers don't work. It's normal in this world. I squash the panicked thought of a life full of charity lunches and organising Robert's shirts.

Going part-time is actually the best of both worlds. I get to keep what I love doing, and I get to be with Robert. I can do this. I just have to try a bit harder. I can be as good as Robert's first wife. The diamond flashes tiny yellow and red dots in the sun, like it's spitting flame. I'll talk to Sally tomorrow.

I get up and straighten the dishcloth on the enamel hook. This is for the best.

Now

Robert ground me down. He played on my insecurities to get what he wanted. Why did I ever think that was okay? I was lulled, I was in love, I wasn't aware it was happening. That the water was slowly rising around me. Was Robert always like that? No, not at the beginning. It started when his parents returned from their cruise. That's when things started to crack. Everything he suggested seemed reasonable at the time. And I wanted to believe. I close my eyes. I face up to the thing I have been avoiding. Robert is like David. A horrible thought detonates in my mind. Robert had the means, the access. He had an explosive secret he was keeping from all of us. Maybe Emily did find out about her mum. But she didn't confront her granddad, she confronted her dad.

But Robert just wanted everything to be perfect too. His anger at Emily was always when she didn't conform to that. He had a very fixed idea of what was appropriate and good. David's idea. David instilled that belief in both Judith and Robert. Robert was frightened of him, and that made Robert scary too. I think of how I didn't want to upset Robert. How I couldn't bear to have him disappointed in me, how I needed, desperately, to be back in the warm basking glow of his approval. I think of how David uses money, terror, and love itself as weapons to control those closest to him. How Robert has learnt from the master. How did I never see it? I dismissed the warning signs. Robert's childhood was just as dysfunctional as mine. More so, because all the damage in mine was out in the open, and the malignancy that festers in the Milcombe house is hidden by wealth and privilege.

How far would David and Judith go to protect their son, their name, their perfect life? Even if Robert did hurt Emily. An accident, surely. An escalation. I don't know. I don't know what I believe any more. Erica is back from the dead. Robert lied. Far enough to get him cash and a new phone and onto a private plane to Bordeaux? Far enough to cover up his crime? Far enough to frame me?

Kelly clears her throat, jolting me back to the present. 'Sorry,' I say, sitting up.

She's back in her tracksuit now. 'They called Association,' she says.

I can hear them unlocking below. 'Right.'

She scrubs at a mark on the floor with the toe of her trainer. 'I think you should probably stay here, you know. Till things calm down. They're late today – so they'll probably run it into dinner. I'll try and bring yours back. All right?'

I nod. Grateful. Return to my thoughts. Close my eyes. Think about Emily, Robert, David, Judith, Erica. Did being with me make Robert realise how much he missed Erica? Did Robert put the child porn on my computer to get rid of me? But something went wrong. That's what I keep coming back to. Something went wrong. Emily wasn't supposed to be home that early. Emily wasn't supposed to die.

The door opens and I jump. How long have I been lying here?

Kelly is gripping two trays of what looks like chilli. Again. 'The idiot on the trolley almost wouldn't give me yours.'

My stomach growls as I take it, suddenly ravenous. *Nonce.* They can't starve me, can they? It wouldn't be allowed. They had to give Kelly my tray. I don't want to think what will happen when she leaves for the Mother and Baby Unit. I shove my plastic fork in and begin shovelling the cold bland goop into my mouth. Pausing only to lend a steadying hand to

Kelly as she lowers herself down, legs hip-width apart, till she's sitting next to me.

We eat in silence for a minute. Me grateful it's companionable. That she trusts me. That she's standing by me.

Then something hard catches between my teeth, and almost skids backwards into my throat. I gag, my palm open to catch the spatter of chilli and the solid thing. Is it a pip, a stone of some fruit that's found its way in? No, it's bigger than a pip, squarer, glinting. I pick it up to rub off the sauce and it slices into my skin. Blood springs from my thumb.

'Bloody hell!' shouts Kelly, as I drop the foreign object onto the floor, with the unmistakable gritty crunch of glass hitting concrete.

Oh my god.

'Fucking hell, is that glass?' Kelly puts her own fork down.

I'm already working mine through the chilli, finding more glinting lumps.

'What the hell are they playing at?' Kelly says, as I produce another shard that looks like it was once the bottom of a jar of sauce.

'They aren't playing.' I swallow. It must have come from the kitchen – no glass is allowed on the wing. *Nonce.* News travels fast.

'They could have killed you!' Kelly's voice rings round our cell. Her own chilli squashed flat against her tray, no concerning anomalies in that. No wonder they didn't want to hand my tray over to her. This one was meant just for me.

Have I swallowed any already? No. I would have felt it. I grip my throat. They don't need to starve me. They can get to me any way they want. I'm locked inside a prison with real murderers, sadists like Gould, and they think I'm a child killer. Our door has been marked. *Oh god.*

And at that moment the very same door swings open forcefully into the cell.

Now

Kelly and I stare at Ryan, who is standing there scowling.

'Did I disturb your dinner?' he says.

My heart is still thumping. I imagine glass moving through me, slicing into my insides, cutting my baby.

'Someone's put glass in her food!' Kelly is veering between outrage and panic.

Ryan walks toward us, squats down onto his haunches and looks at the pieces that have been stirred into my dinner. 'Looks like an accident to me,' he said.

'An accident?' Kelly cries. 'Are you fricking mental? That's deliberate – you're supposed to be looking after us. You're in charge of our welfare and all that.'

Ryan gives me a withering look. 'I think Ms Burns is more than capable of looking after herself.'

I put the tray down on the floor. What else might be in it? Things I can't see? Drugs, bleach, or things that are more readily available? Like bodily fluids? I try not to gag. Hepatitis, syphilis, HIV, all the things the doctor had tested for. All the things, all the germs people could have.

Ryan picks up the tray. 'I've heard some pregnant women get like this.' He nods in my direction. 'Lose their appetite and stuff. I'll take it away for you.'

And dispose of the evidence.

'What are you doing here anyway – what do you want?' Kelly glares at him.

'I'm an officer and I'm allowed to carry out spot checks if I have reason to believe prisoners have contraband in their cells.' He kicks over the pile of library books we have next to the bed. Kelly's handwritten pregnancy guide falls from the top, loose pages fluttering out.

'We had a full search yesterday,' Kelly says. 'We got nothing we ain't supposed to have.'

Ryan nudges the books with the toe of his boot, looks at the small collection of personal-care items we have on the top of the bedside shelves. A rollerball deodorant each, some tooth-paste, a loo roll. Then he shrugs like he can't be bothered. 'Oh yeah, and there was this.' He hands Kelly a letter. An official Fallenbrook stamp on it. Internal mail.

Kelly looks at me, her mouth an O.

Is it the decision of the board already? In one afternoon? Is that a good or a bad sign?

'Oh my god,' Kelly says, tearing into it like it's exam results. It is.

But as Ryan strolls out, apparently bored, I see something flash across his chiselled face. Something like amusement.

And my stomach collapses in on its own emptiness.

Now

Kelly screams. Her tray flies across the room and splatters against the wall. She is up and pulling at the beds. The mattress tumbling into both of us before I can get to her. A whirl of hair and ripping sheets. A wail pouring out of her.

'Kelly! No! Kelly!' Jesus Christ. Ryan will be back here in two seconds. They'll be carting her off to seg.

The shelves tip and the deodorants skid across the floor.

Her nails catch my skin but there isn't time to think, before I get my arms around her from behind. Reaching forward over my bump, being careful not to hurt hers. I clamp her arms by her side, dimly aware I've done this to Mum before. Holding her still. Stopping the chaos.

'You're all right, you're all right,' I say, expecting her arms and legs to wheel and her head to come smashing back into my nose. But she goes limp. Her body, my centre of balance off, tipping us forwards so I am holding her as if she were hanging just off the floor.

'No, no, no, no, no,' she is saying. Tears pouring down her face.

Oh god. 'You're okay, you're okay.' I gently lower her onto the floor, ready in case she roars back up, but she doesn't. Instead she curls like a comma over her stomach, in the chaos of our cell. I lower myself next to her. Stroke her hair, her arm. Curl myself into her, spooning around her as best I can with my own bump while she sobs.

Outside I can hear the noise of prisoners returning their trays after dinner. The skip and clang of movement on the landings as people make use of their last free moments before lock-in. The gossip, the bartering, the thousands of tiny deals that are negotiated and struck to survive in here. The shared stories, the sadness, the hope. And we still lie on the floor.

Eventually I manage to get the mattress back onto Kelly's bunk. To get her onto it, to get her settled. Standing on my bed, my own bump pressing against the metal frame as I keep my arms round her. My back screaming at me to move. But I stay there till her sobs subside, her breathing slows. Only then getting down.

I have mere minutes to right the upturned books and unit. To tidy as quickly as I can before they check the cells before shift change. And it is only after all this, when our cell looks the right way up again, that I pick up the letter Ryan has delivered and read what I already know.

To Prisoner AF160299,

Thank you for presenting your case at the Admissions Board. Your application has been carefully considered, but I am afraid on this occasion we are unable to offer a place on a Mother and Baby Unit. As there is not a suitable family alternative for your child to go to, arrangements have been put in motion for your baby to be taken into social care upon arrival.

My eyes mist and I stifle a sob. I don't want to wake Kelly. The letter reads like it is discussing bin collection, or a council tax increase. Not taking her baby away. Kelly, who is smart and hardworking, and trying to do her best. Kelly, to whom I had promised everything was going to be all right.

'Keep it down!' shouts Ryan, the distant sound of a fist hammering against a metal door.

I get into bed and stare at the springs of the bunk above. They are going to take Kelly's baby away. I have to help. There has to be another way. Something we can do. Something.

Just after 4 a.m. her contractions start.

Now

'It's not that bad,' Kelly says, rubbing her lower stomach. 'Just like period pains. I don't know what all the fuss is about.'

I don't point out that I think this is just early days, that she probably hasn't dilated much yet.

Kelly starts pulling on the T-shirt she wears to work.

'What are you doing? Don't you think you ought to stay here, or at least let the doctor know? We can see if Sara's on today – tell her,' I say.

'No screws,' Kelly says. There's a flatness to her voice. Her eyes have lost all their sparkle. It's as if a shutter has come down since last night. As if she's distanced herself from what's happening. We read about this in a specialist pamphlet from the midwife. Women who are not going to be with their babies after birth don't always bond. They create distance. Kelly is in shock. Kelly is in labour. Everything is happening too fast. How can they only just have had the Admissions Board? It's too stressful. A sliver of ripped sheet hangs down from the bed. It's barbaric. There's no time to adjust. No time to appeal.

Kelly is heading for the door. 'I really think you ought to tell someone, Kel.'

But she doesn't stop.

I follow her out, my heart leaping into my throat the moment I cross the threshold onto the landing. A scratching sensation inside.

'Kelly, please?'

But she doesn't turn around. I see her wince on the stairs.

Below, several women are dancing in a conga line, singing to the tune of Tequila:

> '*Tobacco! It makes me happy!*
> *Tobacco it feels fine!*
> *Tobacco when the doors are open!*'

The smoking ban has started. As Kelly disappears through the gate I go back into the cell.

She doesn't come back at lunchtime.

I have eaten all the snacks we have. Tried to focus on our library books, but the words blur on the page. I need to find out what's happening. I haven't spoken to Ness yet about Erica. I didn't even tell Kelly. With everything that happened last night it didn't seem like the right time. *Oh yeah, Kelly, funny story: I just met my fiancé's dead wife.* I can already imagine what Ness would say, and it would include the words lying and bastard. And I'm not sure I'm ready to face that. I still love Robert. I just don't know if I trust him. I have to be strong. To stay focused. To get me and my baby out of here. Because I know now: if they aren't letting Kelly keep her child, they sure as hell ain't going to let the Blonde Slayer keep hers. And I would rather die than let David get my daughter. I need comfort. I need kind words. I want my mum.

I look at my watch again. Surely someone will tell me about Kelly? But of course they won't. The staff owe us nothing in here. Ryan sees you as either someone to shag or someone to screw over. I don't think Kev sees us at all. Definitely not as human. But Sara, I thought she was different. If she was here, if she knew what was happening with Kelly, she would tell me.

I stand up. I can't cope with this any more.

I pull on my big hoodie, pull the hood up, and wait for Association. Kev unlocks my door without a word. I slouch my shoulders forward to try to lose my bump in the folds of the jumper and leave the cell.

And finally I get a break. Because there's Abi, at the other end of the landing, chatting to a woman in a vest top and baggies.

I walk quickly toward them, making sure my face is hidden within the jumper. Abi will know what's happened to Kelly. Abi has her finger on the pulse of the prison.

'Yeah, it might be your hip flexors,' Abi is saying to the other girl. 'Like, pulling on your knee. Do they feel tight? Try this.' She folds her leg back, and pulls her foot against her bum into the stretch.

The other woman copies, her foot getting nowhere near her bum.

'Tuck your pelvis under, you wanna feel it pull here,' she says.

I'm almost upon them before they see me.

I grin. But it falters as Abi's features drop into a scowl.

'Err ... I wondered if you'd seen Kelly, or heard about where she is – she hasn't come back,' I say.

Abi turns to face me and my heart stops. The left sleeve of her T-shirt is rolled. 'Abi – not you too?' I stare at her, dumb-founded. Abi is clean. She's one of the good guys. She knows me. She knows Kelly. The other woman releases her foot, looks nervously between us, unsure what the hell is going on. 'You saw what they did to our cell?'

'*Your* cell.' Abi's jaw is set. Defiant. 'I've told Kelly she should have nothing to do with scum like you.'

She has? For a second I think that's what's happened – Kelly has transferred to a different cell. But her stuff, her magazines, her photos, she would never leave them. 'I just want to know if she's all right.' I think of the colourful deco-rated pages of Abi's book, and how they seem so alien to this granite-faced girl.

Abi's head is tilted back, so she's peering through slatted eyes at me. Divide and conquer, that's what Gould is doing. Except soon there won't be anyone left on my side.

'Fine. Forget it.' I turn to walk back.

'She's at the hospital,' Abi says. I pause. 'They took her in this morning.'

'Thanks,' I say.

But Abi has already turned around, and I get the feeling that was it. One final moment for old times' sake. But now I'm on my own.

Now

It's three days till Kelly returns. Sara, helping her, one arm round her, easing her into our cell. Her hair is lank against her face, and she looks pale, hollowed out, older. Her eyes ringed in shadow so they look like sockets. As if the life has been sucked from her.

I jump up from the bed as quickly as my bump allows. See Kelly's eyes rest on it sickeningly. Oh god. I don't know what to say. What to do. 'Should she . . .? Is there nowhere else – a hospital wing?' I look at Sara imploringly.

'This ain't *Harry Potter*,' she says, kindly. I know that. I know there's no hospital wing. I know that if you have a mental health issue, if you have a breakdown, they take you to seg. And that's no place for Kelly in this state.

Sara puts down the plastic bag she's been carrying. 'Here you go, love,' she says, patting Kelly. 'Jenna here will look after you.'

Kelly shuffles but doesn't sit. I wonder if she's had stitches. How we're supposed to keep her clean. Sterile. Someone must be coming. Someone professional must be being sent to help.

Another rendition of the Tobacco song starts up outside.

'Drat,' says Sara, looking over her shoulder. They're stamping them out as fast as they can. She looks at me. 'Put the kettle on – stay with her, yeah?'

And she's gone.

Silence fills the room. Kelly stares ahead at a spot on the floor, as if it hurts for her to look at me. Which it probably does. They've taken her baby. They've actually done it. This is actually real. They take babies away from mothers.

'He had hair,' she says, without looking up.

I swallow the lump in my throat. I don't know what to say. How to help. She should be talking to a professional. I move across the room and switch on the kettle like Sara said. Has she done this before? Seen women separated from their newborns?

'Black,' Kelly says. 'Like one big curl.'

My heart breaks.

The kettle noisily shakes itself on its cradle.

Kelly hasn't moved. Her voice even quieter. I struggle to hear it over the jiggling kettle. 'They only let me keep him for four hours. I didn't have anything to give him. Nothing for him to remember me by.'

The kettle clicks.

Her voice is barely a whisper. 'Not even a nappy. I had to borrow money off the screw to buy some in the shop.'

I put my arm around her. Her shoulders are slumped.

'They handcuffed me in the ambulance.' She closes her eyes as if she can squeeze the memory out.

'I'm so sorry, Kelly. I'm so very very sorry.' But the words do no more than the steam that's rising from the kettle. They're nothing but vapour. Gone like her son.

Kelly shudders under my arm. Did she get to hold him? To tell him she loved him? To give him a name?

After a long time in silence Kelly shifts. And I help her shuffle backwards till she's perched on the edge of the bed.

I re-boil the kettle for something to do. Pick up the plastic bag Sara left behind.

'What is this?' I say, pulling out some bottles, the bag still weighty. I thought it was her overnight bag, but I realise Kelly is still in the same clothes she left for work in. She's had no fresh set, no pyjamas, no clean underwear. She had nothing with her.

A tiny flicker of something, the girl I used to know, the woman Kelly was before, flits over her face. 'Breast pump.'

'Breast pump?' The words are cold stones in my mouth.

'It's the only thing I can do for him now.'

She's going to express. That's what the bottles are for. And someone is going to take the milk to him. To her baby.

I put the bottle top we use as a plug in the sink and fill it with boiling water. Tears course silently down my face and I try not to let my shoulders shake as I wash the bottles for her.

Behind me Kelly stares at the floor.

Now

For three weeks Kelly only gets out of bed to express and use the toilet. She stops eating, until I tell her her milk will stop if she doesn't keep her calorie count up. The idea that she is helping her son is the rope that is leading her through the darkness. And no one comes. On the first day I went to see the doctor, said she needed psychological help, comfort, something. He said if she had a problem she could come see him herself. I get her meals as best I can, checking both our trays carefully before eating. After I found dead cockroaches in both our dishes word obviously got out. Abi brings up at least one tray a day for Kelly. She won't come in the cell while I am inside though. And I'm not about to loiter on the landing when I don't need to.

The screws, in a rare moment of empathy, have taken to sticking their head in to count Kelly as she stares up at the ceiling during roll-call. Though it is apparent she isn't about to run off. And Sara comes most days to collect the bottles of milk.

'She needs help,' I say quietly, as she collects the bottles from the sink, where I store them in cold water to try and fight the sweltering July heat. I've been in this cell for one hundred and thirty-three days and I think it's just getting hotter. The length of time weighs on me along with the sweat. There are only two bottles today, down from three, and I'm already beginning to worry what will happen when it drops to one. And then below that.

Sara glances at Kelly, whose unwashed hair is beyond the greasy stage, and, I've noticed, starting to come away in wisps on the pillow. 'It's a tragic thing – it's going to take her time,' she says, quietly.

A tragic thing the prison had full control over. Kelly's baby hasn't died. This is not some awful accident of fate. She is in limbo, a malformed grief for a child she's been denied. A child who is out there, drinking its mother's milk, living, breathing, growing. And it feels so frustratingly simple to fix. They could make all this stop. They could give Kelly her baby back. But they aren't going to.

'And how are you?' Sara says.

I realise I've been rubbing my lower back.

I'm thirty-two weeks pregnant. Screaming inside. Terrified about what will happen to my child. Devastated that Emily's dead. Reeling that her mother is not. Fearful of David. Scared my fiancé is still missing. Scared that he had something to do with this. And unable to talk to my lawyer because he's with his family at Center Parcs for the summer holidays. 'I'm fine.'

I don't know if she believes me. Anything we might have had at the beginning when I arrived – those small crumbs of kindness – had been just that. Scraps. Sara isn't bad, but she is one of them. Because you couldn't be one of us and just act as if what is happening to Kelly is okay.

'Ryan's going to pick the milk up tomorrow,' Sara says.

I nod.

'The weekend,' she says, by means of explanation.

I presume it is a big deal to get both a Saturday and Sunday off when you do shift work, but I can't bring myself to be happy for her. Ness, realising that phone calls had dried up, has sent a letter saying she and Mum are going to come up next Thursday. Mum has apparently been incapacitated with bad asthma. I push away the idea that this might be a euphemism. That the pressure of this situation has tipped her back over the edge. I named Ness as my guardian of choice, and the social has been to see them both. It is a preliminary for the Admissions Board hearing. Presumably they've been to see David and Judith and their spacious and luxurious home as well. *Please don't have failed me, Mum.* I hate myself for the thought.

'All right, so I'll see you next week,' Sara says.

I nod.

It is only after she's gone that I see she's left several packets of noodles, and some bananas.

'Roll-call!' The shout wakes me. Early today. I hope that doesn't mean they're going to pull another search. They've been picked up since the smoking ban came in, and everyone is fed up about it. It's stupid really, because the smell of both cigarette and spice smoke wafts freely from the cells on two and three landings. They could round up the smokers straight away. But they are presumably after the supply. Not that that should be too difficult to track down. But wherever Gould has stashed her stockpile, they are yet to find it.

'Move it, ladies!' It's Ryan's voice yelling. 'Roll-call!'

Kelly hasn't moved above. I don't know if she is asleep. She has been at times, because that's when she makes horrible sounds, thrashing about in her nightmares. Thwarted screams emanate from deep down inside her, as if they've got lost on the way up. Then she'll gasp for air. I'll ask if she's okay. And she won't answer. Because she isn't.

I jump up, pull my joggies and big jumper on, and leave the cell.

Immediately I feel the eyes on me. The air shifts, grows ripe with expectation. *Did someone just whisper Blonde Slayer?* I can no longer tell what is paranoia and what is real threat. The two women in the cell to the right peer through narrowed eyes. As if they are about to hiss like cats. The pretty freckled girl from the stairs seems to now be in the cell to our left. Why have they moved her? She is one of Gould's – could she have somehow engineered that? Has she been moved to watch me? That's daft. It is just as likely her toilet has backed up and this is the only spare cell. Stretching her bare arms up and moulding her bed-head hair into a bun, she catches my eye.

The globule of spit lands a centimetre from my foot. Not just paranoia then.

'Wakey, wakey!' Ryan has reached the end of our floor.

I do not need to be blamed for this. I smear the yellow spittle into nothing with my trainer, and keep my eyes down. Twenty-seven hours and thirty-two minutes till I get to see Mum and Ness.

'It's against our human rights!' A voice rises at the other end of the platform. There is a low rumble of agreement.

'If I'm not allowed a fag, you ain't,' Ryan says. I sneak a look to see he has a confiscated packet of tobacco in his hand. The woman who is arguing with him is in her early sixties. Her hair already coiffured into the tight, close curls my Nan used to favour for special occasions. She is wearing black trousers, and a blouse, and looks more like an office manager than a criminal. Though by this point I know any ideas I'd had about what a criminal looks like were nonsense.

The woman looks like she is going to add more, but instead she purses her lips and Ryan continues down the line. It is a punishable offence to be caught with tobacco. She is lucky he hasn't taken her privileges away. She is lucky she isn't sent to seg. There are murmurs up and down the landing, but Ryan ignores them. Continues to swagger along. My skin tingles. Something bad is going to happen.

Now

'Good morning, sunshine.' Ryan pauses and looks appraisingly at the skimpy vest top of the girl who spat at me. 'You're all present and correct,' he says, in the direction of her breasts.

She giggles. Actually giggles.

Most of the women are staring forward, or at the ground, lost in their own thoughts. Counting down to when they can get back in their cells, on with their days. Below I can hear another officer counting the women down there.

I only look up for a second, but it is enough. Ryan tucks the tobacco into the pretty freckled girl's pyjama bottoms like it was a twenty into a stripper's pants. And she flicks it out of sight with her wrist.

I don't look away quickly enough. Ryan's eyes catch me. It must show on my face. I look at the ground.

I didn't see anything. I don't want any trouble.

He swaggers over, exaggerating the stance his muscles require. The feel of his finger running down my body shudders through me.

'What's up, Blondie?' he says.

I stare at the ground. Wrong choice.

His voice hardens. 'Where's the other mother?' The freckled girl laughs. He's grinning at his own joke. His teeth-whitening needs topping up.

You know where she is. Where she's been for the last three weeks, since you lot took her baby away. 'She's not well. She's in bed.'

He steps toward me, and instinctively I bump backwards into the wall. He has to lean over the top of my bump to get his face close to mine. His arm brushing my stomach. My hands feel clammy. 'Last time I checked you weren't a doctor, Blondie,' he says. 'And,' he pantomimes looking around, 'I don't see your stuck-up friend from the hospital here right now, do you?'

I swallow.

'So, let's get the other mother up, shall we?' He pushes past me and kicks open the cell door. 'Oh Mummy!' he calls.

'Stop!' Oh my god.

'Mummy, mummy, mummy,' Ryan calls. He marches over to the bunk. Kelly a tiny bundle in the covers. His foot catches the breast pump, and a bottle goes skittering across the floor. Revulsion colours his face. 'Urgh.' He shakes his foot as if it has been contaminated.

'Stop it, please.' I reach toward him, to pull him away from her.

He looks quite comical for a second, balancing on one leg, his face a grimace. I've seen him be nice to those with kids in the visitors' room. He isn't bad. He's just out of his depth. He hasn't had the training. And I can see there is little difference, only the smallest of veils, between those who are on his side and those who are on ours.

'Please,' I say quietly. 'She needs to rest.'

The bottle is still spinning on the floor. Slowing and slowing like a dark version of the teen's game.

I bend to pick it up. A booted foot comes to rest on top of it before I can get there.

Kelly has still not moved, has not made a noise.

I looked up at Ryan. Nicotine has made marble veins on his teeth. How much of this is withdrawal, fear at what I've seen, payback for the bollocking he received at the hospital. 'She's not doing any harm,' I say quietly.

His grin widens. 'Do you know what we do with these?' He flexes his foot on the bottle and a bit of creamy liquid escapes.

A sour taste fills my mouth.

His voice is full of delight now. 'We throw the disgusting muck away.'

Kelly makes a noise like a mewling cat.

No.

'Playtime's over.' Ryan reaches for her.

'No! Don't touch her.' I jump up, try to grab his arm. But my bulk unbalances me and I tip forward, two hands up, into him. Ryan throws his own arms up to break his fall, but not before his face connects with the side of the metal bunk. A chunk of whitened tooth flies out like spit.

'You bitch!' comes a scream from the doorway.

'Fight!' roars another voice.

'*Fight! Fight! Fight!*'

'Fucking hell.' Ryan spits and wipes his face with the back of his hand.

Christ. I hadn't meant to hurt him. 'I just wanted you to stop . . .'

His training kicks in. He swings round. I step back. Arms up.

Protect the baby. Protect the baby.

He swings at me. I fold over my belly.

'She's pregnant!' someone shouts.

Ryan's radio crackles. An alarm squeals from it. He grabs me, roughly turning me.

'Don't resist!' a woman screams.

'*Fight! Fight! Fight!*'

'I'm pregnant!' *My baby!*

His hands force my arms up behind my back. The floor looms up. He is going to put me down on my stomach. Like they had Gould.

'I'm pregnant!' Panic vibrates through my every nerve ending.

But he rights me, pulling my arms tighter, higher behind me. A rip at the top of my chest. Muscle. Tendon.

He is yelling, shouting. 'Get the fuck out the way!'

Another voice. Kev. 'Move it! Back to your cells. Now.'

My arms are screaming, my belly thrust forward. A target. Kelly? I can't see her. A blur of faces.

Ryan's eyes next to mine. Spittle on my face.

'You're going to seg, prisoner!'

Now

It's not like it is in the movies. The dirty dark cell with the one lone voice, coaxing you into madness. The cells are no more or less clean than the normal ones. But they're smaller. And they smell. Of fear. And the noise is constant. Because seg isn't just where you go for seven days after you accidentally attack an officer. It's where you go if you're not very well. There's no infirmary. *This isn't Harry Potter.* If you are having a mental health episode and you are a danger to others or to yourself they put you here. Here where the lights are always on, where there's nothing but a bare bed and your own thoughts.

Someone framed me. Someone who had access to my house. Someone who had access to my laptop. Someone who wore gloves. Someone who planted child pornography on my computer. Someone who expected Emily to not be in. Someone who knew our routines. Someone who killed her and tried to make it look like I did it. Someone who made it look like I'd sent an incriminating message to Sally.

David is controlling, he clashed with Emily, he was angry she wouldn't conform to his expectations. Angry she would turn out like her mother, an embarrassment to the Milcombe name. He wanted to start again, wipe the slate clean. He wants my baby.

Judith is frightened and snobby. She would do anything for David. She's bought into the lifestyle, upholding the perfect-family myth at all costs. She's completely under David's control.

Erica is alive. She colluded in the faking of her own death, abandoned her child, her husband, and allowed herself to be paid off to leave. She's an addict. A damaged woman. I suspect the spare key is hidden in the same place it always was. Or she could still have her own key. She could be jealous, revengeful, she could think I replaced her.

And Robert. Robert knew where everyone was supposed to be and when. Robert, who wants to both please and over-throw the man who has spent his whole life controlling him. Robert, who lied about his former wife being dead to his own child, to me. Robert, who is so like his father. He could have planted the images to get rid of me. Killing Emily must have been an accident. I think of him shaking her shoulders. A moment of anger. Or maybe it was the other way around? Maybe he and Emily fought again, he lost his temper, lashed out. And to cover up what he'd done he implicated me. Or David or Judith did it after he'd fled. And now he's in the wind. The cherished son, gone, until I'm convicted.

It is two weeks until my trial. Two weeks until I have to convince the jury it wasn't me. And if I can't? In seven weeks my daughter is due. In seven weeks they will take her away like they took away Kelly's son. And I'm trapped in here. Unable to speak to anyone. Unable to do anything but cry.

The woman next to me has been throwing herself repeat-edly against her door for over ten hours. At least I think it's that long – they took my watch off me. But I can see through the hatch into the cavernous double-height wing, and I've watched the light brighten and fade. Evidence that the sun rose and fell. And she's still going. It must be her because the bed is screwed down. Again and again and again. A regular drum beat of bones against metal. So desperate to escape her own mind she's trying to break out of her own skin.

Food comes under the door on a tray. No cutlery. At least here I don't need to worry about bugs or glass. It's a tiny consolation in the pool of darkness that I float in. The noise does that to you. The continuous clamour cushions you, pushes you out of yourself. Some people scream abuse. Some cry. And some, like the woman in the next cell, try to break themselves apart.

Closing my eyes doesn't bring sleep but faces. Emily. Robert. Mum. Ness. David. Judith. Becky. Deb. Sally. Erica. Mr Peterson. DI Langton. There is an artwork by Tracey Emin listing all the people she ever slept with. I saw it at the Tate. This metal box is an artwork to all the people I've failed. All those I've let down. I hope they told Ness and Mum not to come. I hope they didn't travel all this way to be told no. I hope Kelly is okay. I hope she is eating.

'*Tobacco! It makes me happy!*' Someone starts to sing, then laugh, then cry. Is it me? The noise outside has merged with the noise inside. White noise like the lights in here. Burning into me. Nowhere to hide.

My name is Jenna Burns. I'm not guilty. Someone killed my stepdaughter. Someone who came into my house, who used my laptop, who knew things about us. About me. Someone framed me. But I didn't do it.

I didn't do it.

I'm innocent.

I'm innocent.

I'm pregnant.

I'm innocent.

The words match the rhythm of the woman's pained throws.

I'm innocent.

And somewhere, deep inside, my body says *enough*. A core survival technique, not for me, but for my unborn child. The baby it is my job to grow and protect and deliver safe into the world. And it is as if two small hands close over my eyes and then my ears.

And finally, sleep takes me.

Now

My shoulders begin to relax as we leave the bangs and howls of seg behind. I never thought it would feel spacious in here. That I would be so grateful for the custard-coloured walls surrounding me. If I stretched out both my arms there would be metres till I hit the wall. I could run between them. Muscle memory urges me to do it, to jog, to skip through this place. Thank god I am out of there. Though the smell lingers in my nostrils. Half a whiff on the still air to drag me back. I wipe my nose with the back of my hand. But that smells of it too. The antiseptic, metallic smell of fear. I need a shower. Though showers are risky.

Kev opens the gate into our wing and I almost cry with relief at seeing other faces. Half the cells are unlocked, Association is early today. I pass Vina with her breakfast box. Feel the eyes of the others on me.

'Blonde Slayer,' someone hisses.

But I don't care. It's human interaction, albeit hostile. At least I can move, walk, breathe.

The regular clunk-click of the doors being opened – opened! – makes me want to dance. Click my fingers like it's a song.

There's a shout from above. Different. Distinct. Not the normal banter. Kev freezes next to me. He felt it too. We look up. Suddenly the alarm sounds. High-pitched and piercing. Like before. Another mistake? Faces appear, some with tooth-brushes still in hands. Foam mouths open, asking 'What's happening?'

Kev's radio explodes into crackles of sound. The words punching between static sizzles, desperate to be heard.

'*Code . . . Oh god . . . the door's barricaded . . . I can see blood . . . Not a drill. Code Red! Red! Red!*'

And Kev is running.

'Suicide,' says a woman near me. And people turn to look at her. Nodding. Pale.

'Code Red!' The radio is still screaming. 'Cell eight.'

No.

There's a whoosh of movement, like everything is racing away from me in a blur. And I am running too, one hand to steady my bump. We all are. Toward the noise. Toward the screams. Toward my cell.

A clump of women have stopped down the gangway and I can't see.

'Let me through!' I half push, half weave through them. Their bodies soft, hard, warm. Someone's tea splashes against my arm but I barely feel it.

They've stopped at a discreet distance. Kev is already there. And the guard from the crackling radio message. They're outside. The wrong side. And it takes me a moment to work it out. Kelly's barricaded herself in.

'We need the big red key,' Kev is screaming into the radio.

'Hold on, love, hold on,' the radio guard is shouting. Pulling at the door.

The group of women behind me are quiet, or I've blocked them out. Blood whooshes into my ears. Round and round my head.

No.

I run forwards. Throw my shoulder against the door. Push with the radio guard.

'Kelly! Can you hear me! Kelly!' The noise is coming from me.

I flip open the viewing panel. Something is blocking it. The bed is end up. But I can see feet. And a red smear on the floor.

Behind us Ryan pushes through with a hand-held battering ram. It's absurd. Red. Coloured-in like a child's toy.

A sob comes from someone. From me.

'Kelly!' I scream.

The radio guard's hands are on my arms, pulling me back. I've not seen him before. That's what's going through my mind. I don't know his face or his name. He must have started while I was in seg. But it doesn't matter.

The thought interrupted as they swing the battering ram at the door. The noise echoes through the wing. No one speaks. No one breathes. Bang. Bang. Bang.

On the third attempt the door gives, there's a scrape, a crash. The radio guard's grip tightens on my arms. I hear his breath shorten. Kev pushes past Ryan. Pushes the bed frame that's been leant against the door aside.

The radio guard's fingernails pierce my skin.

On the floor lies a sharpened toothbrush, next to the tiny, crumpled body of Kelly. Open next to her is her book on pregnancy in prison, the handwriting disappearing in her pooling blood.

Now

If I hadn't been in seg.
   If I'd been here . . .
   If I'd tried harder.
   If.
   Oh Kelly.

Kelly's parents are coming to Fallenbrook today. To the memorial. Her friends are to show them the places their daughter worked, lived, if you can call it that. Before she passed away. As if she had happy times in here. *The exaggerated pout. The tinkle of laughter. The blush at her writing. The fear on her face when she pressed that alarm. The panic at the word scrawled on our door. The empty shell that came back from the hospital.* Guilt has spread through me, filling every cell of my body until it's all I can feel and see and breathe.

Abi has been chosen to meet them. They've put me in a different cell. Next door. I asked to be close. So I can imagine she's just the other side of the wall. I'm on my own for the time being. I don't know what happened to the pretty freckled girl. I don't care.

My stuff is untouched in a box Vina brought for me. My food comes via one of the guards. They eye my stomach like an unexploded bomb. The priest and the imam tried to talk to me, but there are no words. I watched the police visit through the door hatch. Forensics, as they deconstructed and took away the final parts of Kelly's world in clear plastic bags. And

I thought of Emily and Robert. Of how everyone I care about gets hurt. There's no special clean-up team in here. Vina, her hair in a calico wrap, her sleeves rolled up, arrived with another inmate with a bucket and mop. They cleaned Kelly's blood from the floor and walls. The other woman crying, Vina reciting prayers. I run my hand over the rough, cool bricks.

I see her when I close my eyes. Curled on the floor. Like Emily. Sometimes they're curled together. The yin and yang of my pain.

The spiky burble of the wing dips outside. They're here. Kelly's parents.

And suddenly I have to tell them how special she was.

I lever myself up. Open the door.

It's like stepping into a vacuum. The women are all standing as if it's roll-call, but with heads bowed, hands clasped, like a funeral procession is passing. Because that's what this is. I can hear the sniffs and snuffles of tears. Kelly's work friends, women from the antenatal classes, people she chatted to in the wing. We won't be allowed to attend the real funeral. We won't be allowed to say goodbye properly. To the girl I slept next to for the last four months. The girl whose breathing I heard last thing at night and first thing in the morning. The girl who kept me going in here.

I knew Kelly's parents were too old to take on her son, but seeing them underlines it. Her dad is bent over two sticks. Wisps of hair cling to his hollow face, his lips suck over his teeth. Despite the July heat, her mum is in a thick black woollen suit and high-necked white blouse. She shuffles, her feet barely lifting off the ground. It will have taken them an age to get up the stairs. Behind them, the governor, stiff in his uniform, buttons gleaming, stands solemnly. I can't stop staring at him.

This is your fault. You could have prevented this. You had a duty of care. You headed the Admissions Board. How can you take a baby from someone and offer them no counselling? No support?

Who cares about funding and budgets and all this crap when you're talking about people's lives?

The baby kicks hard inside me and I grip my stomach. An *ooof* of air escaping. People look.

'Cellmate,' someone says.

Kelly's dad's bottom lip trembles.

I step forward. 'Mr and Mrs Allen, I'm so sorry for your loss.' I try to choke back the tears.

'You,' her mum hisses, pulling herself upright, her face tight with suffering, her mouth seeping anger. 'You did this.'

It's like being slapped. 'What?'

Some of the women behind murmur. The governor's usually hangdog face has unfurled in shock.

Kelly's mum steps toward me, stabbing a finger in the air. 'It's all right for you, with your money and your fancy lawyers.'

I want to tell her she's wrong but I'm too horrified to speak. I clutch my stomach with my hand.

'You people get away with murder.' She spits the word. 'You filled her head with a load of nonsense. Told her she'd get to keep her baby. You lied to her.'

'No,' I say.

The governor jolts into action. The threat of an imminent PR disaster plays distastefully across his face. 'Try not to upset yourself any further, Mrs Allen,' he soothes.

She rounds on him. 'We've lost everything. Our grandson. Our daughter.' She breaks down.

Her husband reaches an arm round her. 'It's all right, Mavis,' he says.

'My baby,' Mrs Allen howls, doubling over. Her pain echoes off the walls.

The governor takes her by the other arm, and they move, slowly, shuffling, away.

The other women stare at me. Their eyes accusatory.

'She did this on purpose,' someone whispers.

'*Drove her to it.*'

'*Blonde Slayer.*'

'*Who gave her the weapon, hey?*'

The murmurs rise and swell into vivid, painful white noise.

I stumble back into the cell. Force the door closed. The box catches under my foot, spilling its contents. Among my things are Kelly's magazines, splashed with blood. I grope for the bed. Pull myself into it. Her mum's wail still coursing through me.

I lied to Kelly. I told her she would get to keep him. That she would get out of here. That it would be okay. I gave her hope. I killed her.

I close my eyes as Kelly and Emily spin like they're turning in the pool. Over and over each other, laughing, crying, screaming. And the water turns red.

Now

'She wouldn't want you sat in here torturing yourself.' Sara puts the tray next to me on my bunk.

'Thanks for the food.' I don't look up. My eyes are gritty from lack of sleep. My limbs cement.

'You may as well be in seg still.' She shakes her head in exasperation.

The irony hasn't escaped me. Punishment for sins.

Sara rocks back on the heels of her prison boots. Makes a show of looking round my cell. 'I'm guessing your family don't live that close?'

My stomach twinges, as if my daughter is reaching for a hug.

She squats down on her haunches, her uniform trousers turning shiny where the fabric pulls tight. I don't meet her eye. 'You can't let the other women get to you,' she says, quietly.

But this isn't secondary school, and I don't get to go home when the bell rings.

She places a hand on my knee and I flinch. But she pats it, and my disloyal skin relaxes under the touch. No one has touched me kindly since . . . since Kelly hugged me.

'It's a pack mentality in here,' she says. 'We both know that. But we also know people say stupid things when they're scared. But not because they believe them.'

'I'm not so sure about that,' I say, meekly. Plenty of people accept I killed Emily. I think they have no issue believing I drove Kelly to harm herself too.

Sara sighs. 'If you won't do it for you, do it for your baby.'

That's a low blow.

'You need exercise, pump those nutrients round. You need a bit of comfort and conversation. It's not good for you cooped up in here all the time.' She sounds like Deb telling her kids to stop playing computer games.

'I am in prison, in case you'd forgotten,' I say. It's the longest sentence I've said in days. But I meet her eyes for the first time.

She smiles. 'I'll escort you from the wing to the visitors' room and back. Nothing is going to happen to you.'

And I nod. Because I do want to see Ness. To hug her. To have her hug me back. To tell me it's all going to be okay. I blink back tears.

'I'll see you five minutes before Free Flow,' she says briskly, bracing her hand against her own knee to right herself.

Even the visitors' room feels different today, as if the strain of the grief that's running like a vein through the prison has soured the sunshine-yellow walls too. Though the other prisoners aren't talking to me, some not even looking at me, I can feel we all carry it. The air is brittle. Kelly's death has shocked everyone. Rhianna's mum glares at Sara as she deposits me at the back of the line.

There's a murmur up the line as they see me.

'*She shouldn't be here.*'

'*Not right.*'

'*Are they taking the piss?*'

It reaches the woman at the front, her red tracksuit shining like wet plastic under the strip lighting. Gould. A ripple of panic passes through me. But she doesn't turn. Stays talking to Annie, who has seemingly arranged for someone to visit her at the same time. Is this how they're getting the stuff in? Passed under the table at visiting? In the last embrace? But I doubt Gould would be doing her own dirty work. She likes the sharp end of the business only when it's something she can poke people with.

I wonder who is visiting her? It can't be her husband, because he's banged up too. But it could be her children, siblings, a parent. It's odd to imagine her with family, to think of her in any kind of loving home, and perhaps that isn't the case. But everyone has someone that loves them, right? Everyone has people who care about them, who they care about. Even Gould. My heart twinges.

I head for my favoured table, in the furthest corner from the door the visitors enter through. Now more than ever I need to keep an eye on the whole room.

I stare pointedly ahead, as a shiny red-track-suited figure takes the table next to mine. It's coincidence, that's all. Of course Gould would want the best vantage point for the room.

She clears her throat.

I flinch.

'Jumpy, Blondie?' Her high-pitched laugh peals out as they unlock the door, letting the visitors in.

Don't look. Don't rise to it. I force myself to smile as I see Ness, my skin tight like a drying face mask. She looks tired, but she's done her hair and make-up today. That must be a good sign. A muscular man with a faint silvery scar on his cheek overtakes Ness and joins Gould. She doesn't stand to greet him but stays relaxed in her chair as he fidgets like a boy summoned to the head teacher's office. I cling to Ness. She smells of the gym, fruity shower gel, hairspray.

'You okay?' she says, quietly.

I keep holding her. I've written to her over the last week. She knows.

A child starts to wail by the tuck-shop counter. I look up to see his screwed-up little face and in his pudgy hands a squashed plastic cup which presumably used to contain tea.

There's a flurry of activity as the cafe lady and Sara rush to get wet tissues.

'I'm sorry about your friend,' Ness says.

She doesn't know about Kelly's parents, or the others, or what everyone is saying though. Doesn't know how I feel. I force another smile. 'Thanks for coming.'

Ness arranges her puffa coat, the chrysalis leaves of padded brown fabric peeling away to reveal her black and orange activewear underneath.

'Looking good,' I say.

She grins. 'Oh yeah, three hours on an air-filtered Megabus will do that for a girl. I reckon that Gwyneth Paltrow should give it a try.'

And it's almost like it was before, except of course it never will be again.

The man at Gould's table explodes in a violent hacking cough. His body jerking with each wheeze and splutter.

Gould doesn't move. 'What you staring at?' She eyeballs Ness.

'What *you* looking at—' Ness starts to retort.

'Leave it,' I hiss. 'It's fine.' She doesn't know who this is, doesn't know the danger she's in.

The child by the counter is still crying, but is now being gathered up into the arms of the adult accompanying it. Sara is sorting through her keys.

'Who's this then, Blondie?' Gould says.

I will Ness not to reply. 'No one,' I say. I still don't turn and look at Gould full on. We're not supposed to talk to other people's visitors. We're not supposed to interact. But Kev and Sara are both occupied with the screaming child, Sara preparing to take them out.

The man visiting Gould is still now, looking at me and Ness, a quizzical look in his eyes. Almost like he's seen something he recognises. He has: fear. At least that's what I'm radiating. I want to curl in on myself and Ness, shield us both from Gould's relentless gaze. Ness is still brazening it out, her chest puffed, her hands flat on the table.

'You better have good news, Stan.' Gould switches her attention back to the guy, and he immediately returns to jiggling his knees. This is a disorientating tactic of hers. With a bit of luck she was only using me and Ness to wrong-foot him.

'Who is that?' Ness's shoulders are still back, but she's got enough street smarts to sense threat and speak quietly.

'It doesn't matter.' I won't say Gould's name, I won't risk attracting her attention again. I need to get this out. I need Ness to help me. 'Listen, I've been doing a lot of thinking, and it has to be someone I know.'

'What does?' Ness says, confused by my change of direction.

'The person that did this to Emily, that did this to me.'

Ness's pencilled eyebrows rise. She sits back. 'David?'

'Yeah, maybe.' Can I voice my concerns about Robert? I still haven't told Ness about Erica. She might think I'm losing it. I need proof. 'I just keep going over it – changing my mind.'

'I don't think you should be stressing yourself out like this in your condition,' Ness says, concern in her face.

Sara is unlocking the far door to take the poor screaming kiddie out.

'What else have I got to think about? Since Kelly . . .' I can't say the words.

Ness closes her hands over mine. They're warm, the callouses from where she lifts weights press against my skin. 'I know, sweetheart, I know.'

Next to me Gould's voice cuts through into my thoughts.

'. . . you better not be,' she snarls at coughing Stan.

I shake my head, try to get rid of the intrusion. Ness glances at Gould.

My thoughts lurch back to Robert. 'The more I think about it, the more I think it was someone else, not David.'

Ness leans toward me, her eyes wide, but what she's about to say gets lost when two things happen.

A woman toward the front grabs for her young daughter, who, wriggling and crying out, tries to run back to the toy corner. The woman cries herself, a horrid, painful yelp at the rejection of this three-year-old who doesn't understand why Mummy wants to hold on to her.

And Gould slams her fist down on the table, shouts, 'You better be fucking kidding me!' and jumps up.

Ness starts back, as do the couple beside us. Gould's voice is so venomous it sends shockwaves through the room, only dented by the screaming child and wailing mother at the front. Anger and love and loss ripple through us.

Kev, alone in the hall, clearly doesn't know which way to go. The little girl has almost broken free of her distraught mother, who stumbles out of her chair to hold on to her.

'Back in your seat!' the officer shouts, clearly deciding this shrieking noise is the one to focus on.

Gould leaves her table and strides toward him. 'Leave the poor fucker alone,' she shouts. 'You lot not done taking kiddies away from their mums?'

Stan, the guy she just shouted at, looks confused. But something billows through the room. A clarion call to Kelly's loss.

'Yeah!' Rhianna's mum stands up.

'Sit down!' barks Kev. There are now three prisoners out of their seats. His eyes flit around the room. Where's Sara?

'We got rights too!' Gould shouts. Stan stands nervously.

I can't believe she cares about this woman and her kid. She's reading the room.

'*Tobacco! It makes us happy!*' someone starts to sing. Half the room erupts in laughter.

Gould isn't laughing though. Her eyes are taking in

everything: the doors, the lack of Sara, the number of rolled left sleeves. I grab Ness's hand.

'We demand respect!' Gould shouts.

I open my mouth to shout a warning to Kev, but my words are buried under the noise. Women around the room are shouting their support of Gould.

'*Respect! Respect! Respect!*'

'*Tobacco! It makes us happy!*'

'*You can't take our kids!*'

Another child starts to cry. Several of the visitors look scared. Ness's face is unreadable.

Kev blows his whistle. The noise slices through the chanting. 'End of session. All prisoners to the wall. All visitors out!' he bellows. For a split second it looks like it's worked.

Then all hell breaks loose.

Now

Everything happens at once. A number of visitors rush toward the exit. Prisoners shout their dissent. And Gould jumps up onto a table.

'They can't treat us like animals!' she bellows.

'Move!' I drag Ness backwards as a wave of support carries women toward Gould. The wriggling child is screaming in its mother's arms. The woman who brought her in, presumably her gran, is holding her arms out for her, crying.

Kev, boggle-eyed, is still blowing his whistle. He releases the door through which he's herding visitors out and makes toward Gould. There's no sign of Sara.

Someone sticks out a foot and Kev trips, clattering down between chairs. Someone screams. People laugh. Gould, with the agility of a cat, springs down from the table and grabs at him.

I turn away, expecting violence, but no: Gould holds up her hand. In it are his keys.

He looks up at her, mouth opening and closing like a fish, as she holds the circle of metal in her hand, the long chain extending back to his belt.

'Back-up required in the visitors' room.' Ryan appears behind us, screaming into his radio. He punches the alarm on the wall.

Ness and I cover our ears as the sound pours into the high-ceilinged room. Heads swivel to look backwards. Women swarm. People fall. Chairs shake on their metal tethers.

'Respect! Respect! Respect!' continues the chant.

Kev has staggered to his feet. Gould yanks hard on his chain, and Kev, distracted by Ryan's attempts at pulling back prisoners, lurches forward belly first.

Ryan barrels past us, and makes a grab for Kev. Ness is torn away from me. I'm thrust sideways, bashing my hip into a table. Ooof. I cup my stomach.

'Jenna!' Ness screams.

The room fills with shouting: 'Respect! Respect! Respect!'

Gould's hand smacks into Kev's nose. Ryan's face a snapshot of shock before Annie's bulk obscures him from view. Stan is hightailing it toward the exit. Gould pulls at a chair, snapping off an arm, which she hurls toward him.

Missiles. Weapons.

'Go, go, go!' Ryan screams at the remaining visitors. Some of the women are helping them toward the door. The gran of the screaming child has her in her arms, head down, running between the chairs.

Ness finds me, hauls me up. Behind us is the locked door back to the wing. In front of us is the brawling mass. 'Go!' I scream. She has to get out.

'Not without you!' Her arm snakes round my side. Pulling.

Someone tips the display of flapjacks on the counter. A ride-on toy truck flies up in the air and smashes into the window. Glass rains down. There are screams. And cheers. The brittle air has snapped. They're destroying the place.

My stomach contracts, like a belt's being pulled tight around my waist. I have to get out.

Two prisoners are helping Kev, who has blood spilling down his face and his white shirt. They are almost at the visitors' door. Ryan has it open, waving them onwards manically with one arm.

Only two people without tabards are in the room now. Ness, and a woman who's still sitting, seemingly frozen in fear, at a table on the right.

Annie's kicking at the tether of a chair and it breaks free. She hurls it toward Kev and those supporting him.

They duck and it splinters against the wall, inches from the door.

Ryan looks up. Catches my eye. A look of horror. Sympathy.

'No! Wait!' I scream.

But as Kev staggers through, Ryan pulls the door closed after him. I imagine I hear the key turn but I can't have.

Several women reach the door seconds after, tugging it. But it doesn't budge. They hammer on it.

'No!' I say.

Ness's face is frantic. My heart is racing. My baby's heart is racing.

'Lockdown!' shouts someone near us.

'*Respect! Respect! Respect!*'

Someone lights a cigarette as a huge cheer goes up.

I still have hold of Ness's hand. She's shaking. I'm shaking.

'We're locked in.'

And Gould has the keys.

Now

This can't be happening. Can't.

Rhianna's mum pulls over the tea urn with a mighty crash.

It's happening. Gould is in here. People are losing their minds. I can no longer tell who has a rolled left sleeve and who hasn't.

'We need to find cover,' I shout in Ness's ear. We get behind the pinboard that shields the small number of tables used for over-spill legal visits in the corner. I can't see the other civilian who was in here. If we just stay put someone will come. They have to.

The room is in chaos. Leaflets and posters are being ripped from the wall and shredded into confetti. Anything that isn't tied down is thrown. Another window smashes to a loud cheer.

Gould is leading a group of chanting protestors, waving the stolen keys in the air. Oh god. She's unlocking the door back to the wing. Surely back-up will arrive now?

'*Respect! Respect! Respect!*'

'What the fuck is going on?' Ness looks as shocked as I feel. My heart racing in my chest, the blood drumming a warning beat in my ears.

'It's . . . it's been coming for a while.' Because it has. 'They're angry.' There were staffing issues, lockdowns, cancelled classes, the smoking ban, the repeated searches, and Kelly. But it might not have tipped if it weren't for Gould. A ring-master of chaos.

Gould finally finds the right key and pulls the door into the wing open.

'Open fucking sesame!' she shouts.

Half the women swarm through the door. The other half are still joyfully trashing the room. Weeks of frustration and grief rent chairs from the ground, free metal legs from seats.

'What do we do?' Ness asks.

'I can't believe they locked us in.'

A woman, her face twisted with rage, holds a lighter to the posters on the wall. They smoulder, then flare, the flames climbing the artwork and streamers like tiny red monkeys.

'Oh my god,' says Ness.

Someone screams. The flames lick the polystyrene ceiling tiles. Flicker. Flicker. I daren't breathe. Then they ignite. Black smoke billows down. Thoughts of Grenfell Tower flash through my mind. This place is government-owned. Last renovated god knows when. For god knows how little money. No one wants to spend money on prisoners, do they?

One of the tiles breaks free and floats down, a balloon of flames. The woman with the lighter still in her hand begins to cough.

What have you done?

Then everyone is screaming.

The cushions of the tethered chairs light like tiki torches.

There's only one way out. Ness's fingers are rigid, cold in my hand. We're running. Arms over mouths.

Pandemonium blocks the doorway, as women pull frantically at each other, swing punches to get out.

'Go, go, go!' I scream as more flaming tiles fall.

Rhianna's mum has the chair Annie broke free and is throwing it up again and again at the windows. I drop Ness's hand. Run for her.

'The bars!' I shout. 'You can't get out that way.'

'I got to get out!' Her face a horror-film still.

The glass shatters above us, and oxygen pours into the room. The flames lurch toward us. The heat builds. It takes minutes. Minutes.

Get out.

Gould is nowhere to be seen. Long gone with her goons back to the wing. And what will happen there? I've seen prison riots on the news. The realisation catches me fresh in the chest as I cough. This is a riot. We are in a prison riot. Why is no one coming? Why have they not opened up the other door?

Looking behind me, the flames curl around the wall, as the felt pinboards burn. There's no way out that way.

Ness runs at the pile of people in front of the door.

'Calm down,' she barks. 'One at a time. One at a time or we all fucking die.' Her voice carries over them all.

People aren't listening though. She begins pulling back those who are pushing forward, those who are bottlenecking the door. It seems to work. The pressure on the front end gives, and four or five women disappear through.

Rhianna's mum throws herself at the wall, clawing with her hands, trying to gain purchase to get to the window. It is never going to work. She's stuck in a broken, desperate pattern, a misfire in her fight-or-flight biology.

I reach for her. 'We've got to go!'

She screams; her arms flail into me. I lurch backwards to protect my bump. It feels like the belt from before tightens around me. Like a squeeze of period pain. It must be the stress. The smoke. The lack of air.

'Come on!' Ness shouts.

I try again with Rhianna's mum. 'Listen to me! This way!' Grab hold of one arm before it smacks me in the face again as she jumps at the wall. 'It's going to be okay.' I dodge the other arm, her frantic face. 'It's okay. We can get out the door. The door,' I repeat louder, firmer.

Her eyes break away from the window and swivel to the door, a second before it hits home and her body does the same thing. Her hoodie rips the nails on my hand as she breaks free and sprints. Another tile falls. The ceiling is crackling now, like pork belly on a barbecue.

'Jenna!' Ness screams. Her eyes are streaming in the smoke, and half her face is covered by her T-shirt. I pull my own up, the fabric sucking into my mouth. We need to wet them – that's what they say for fire safety, isn't it? But the sink and water are now behind a wall of flame.

Ness has got most of the women through the door. I join the remaining two as we hurry out. I take her hand as we stumble into the corridor. Huge gulps of air.

'Is everyone out?'

'Yes! It's clear!' Ness yells from behind her T-shirt.

I grab the door.

'What are you doing?' she shouts. 'We've got to go.'

But we've got to stop the flames. This is a prison. It's a metal door. That must count for something. I swing it shut on the hellscape that a few minutes ago was the visitors' room.

Ness pulls me by the hand. Run. Run. Run. My heartbeat drums the survival instinct into me. Everyone is running. Away from the fire. The alarm is ripping through the prison. There are screams, crying, frightened moans. There must be guards out here. Saviours. To bring things under control. But I can hear voices billowing toward us. Shouting, singing, and above it all the steady chant of: '*Respect! Respect! Respect!*'

Have the officers lost control of the whole prison?

Now

I rip off my tabard and pull up my hood. Ness copies with her own top.

'Keep your hands hidden.' I point at her painted nails.

She pulls her sleeves down over them.

'And . . .' I wipe at her expensive make-up with my sleeve. Think of the times she wiped my face as a kid. No one can know she's not a prisoner. Gould spoke to her. She saw her. If she realises she's in here now . . . The word 'hostage' convulses through me. I grip my stomach.

'You okay?' Her eyes, smudged from the smoke and my handiwork, make her look like a concerned clown.

'It's just a stitch. Come on, let's keep moving.' I want as much distance between the fire and us as possible. Everywhere smells of burning plastic.

We race down the corridor past the classrooms. Inside, people are dancing around with computer monitors lifted above their heads.

'Shit,' breathes Ness.

Behind us the library doors burst open. A huddle of women hurtle past us, whooping. It's all unfolding so fast.

Through the glass windows of one of the classrooms I see the pretty freckled girl. She spots me at the same time, drops the folders she's strewing about the place, jumps the desks and hammers against the glass at me.

'Move!' I say, as she shouts at the others behind her in the room. Where do you hide in a prison? *Oh god, Kelly. You showed you could successfully barricade yourself in your cell.* 'We need to get back to my cell. It's the safest place. We can wait it out.'

'Okay.' Ness squeezes my hand.

In front of us, Rhianna's mum is laughing hysterically with another woman. They're opening and closing office doors. 'They're all gone!' she cackles. 'Not one of the cowardly buggers left!'

How has this happened? Gould. Has she been planning this or did she just seize an opportunity? Were her followers prepped? Had there been a signal? I should have stayed in my cell. I think of Kev's bleeding face. Stan running for the door. He knew Gould and he'd run. Anything rather than be locked in with her.

My bump makes me tire quicker than normal, but I'm still stronger than when I came in. My legs more powerful. *Thank you, Kelly, for all the Pilates you made us do.* Ness is puffing rhythmically, used to jogging. If not quite in these circumstances.

'Like running from the cops on the Orchard,' she says, catching my eye.

'Not far now.' We pass through another unlocked gate. Gould has done a fine job.

Suddenly the alarms stop sounding around us. The sound was so loud that it still echoes through my head. My heart pumping in time. Is it over? But no . . . I can still hear shouts. I skid to a halt as the wing comes into view. Ness pulls up next to me, panting. Not from exertion – she's too fit for that – but anxiety. Or adrenaline. Or both.

'Christ,' she says.

The wing opens up before us like the mouth of a snake.

Groups of women are running along the landings, heaving what they can over the side. The metal nets strung between the walkways droop with furniture, blankets and fire extinguishers. Overhead someone emerges from a room, a computer monitor above her head, before she smashes it down onto the ground. Another cheer goes up.

The flash of two officers' helmets makes my heart surge, but they're being worn by a woman I recognise from the library and another inmate. They must have pulled them from the offices. Which means they must have had access. A loud cheer comes from above as two women heave a metal filing cabinet up and over the parapet and it plunges into the nets. Gould's unmistakable high-pitched laugh floats above them.

This is it. I run up the nearest staircase, pulling Ness behind me. 'This way. Keep your head down.' Hopefully they'll be too busy entertaining themselves to notice us. Thank god my cell is this end of the wing. Other people are still in their rooms. Nervous faces peer out, watching everything unfold. Several doors are closed. Other people had the same idea as me. Find a place of safety, hide, wait for a response.

I'd seen video footage of riots inside the men's prisons last year. Cheering, shirtless, staggering men, wrecking the place. They too had gone for the safety nets, but I realise that what is happening here is different. Those heaving things up and over aren't doing it in a random fashion, but focusing on one spot. The netting is drooping under the combined pressure. Soon it will snap, and fall onto the net below, and then that one will give. Is this the difference between men and women? Our violence feels more choreographed.

The top-floor landing is empty. Thank god. Gould is directing the attack on the nets from the other side. I try to stoop, hide my bump. *Please don't look. Please don't see us.* But she doesn't turn. Her back is to us, red shiny arms marshalling the women carrying more ammo out of the surrounding offices. With all the noise and activity no one pays any heed to us. I pull Ness, with a sweaty hand, into my cell.

I push the door closed. Everything is how I left it. But there's no time to think. Ness is panting, staring round the room, taking in the box of my things on the floor.

'What is this?' She picks up the list of things I know about the person who framed me.

'We need to block the door,' I say, struggling to get purchase on the bed, as I reach beyond my stomach and plant my feet behind me.

Ness is still staring at my notes.

'We need to keep you safe.' With my bum in the air, I manage to heave the bed across the floor. The scrape of the legs scream at me to hurry. Ness turns at the noise.

'Stop!' she says. 'I'll do it.'

The bed shifts away from my hands as she moves it with ease.

'Just like when we were kids, huh?' Ness places it in front of the door, the hatch just visible under the top bunk. And I remember the times we barricaded ourselves into our rooms when Mum's horrid friends came over. How we'd watch telly and I'd do my homework. And I have the bizarre feeling we've always been headed to this point.

'If we flip it up, it'll properly block it. But we won't be able to see what's going on.' I drag the small cabinet and chair over, ready, so we can pile them up if necessary. My breath catches and my stomach twinges. Oooff. *Breathe*. I steady myself.

'You all right?' Ness takes the cabinet.

'Think it was the running.' I exhale. 'I'm fine. Put that on top of the bed, away from the door – so we can see as soon as help arrives.'

Ness deposits it as instructed, claps her hands together to dislodge soot and dust. She looks around. 'It's not too bad in here, is it?'

'You try sleeping next to that toilet in this heat and then get back to me.' It's a relief to smile.

Hopefully it won't come to that. The guards will regain control soon. There are non-inmates in here. Even if they are prepared to let us fight it out amongst ourselves, they can't let innocent people get hurt. This is an almighty screw-up. I'd never have believed how fragile the ecosystem of a prison was if I hadn't seen inside one. You think it's this impenetrable fortress. Top-brass security. *Porridge*, *Escape from Alcatraz*, *Shawshank Redemption*, all those shows are nothing like the reality. The officers aren't super cops, they are human. I think of the fleeting look on Ryan's face before he closed the door. Half of them barely out of school, and there aren't enough of them. Fallenbrook is a wreck of a building, reworked and reworked over hundreds of years till it's no longer fit for purpose. All the offices we passed. Mixed in among the cells. Weakening what should have been a ring of steel. The events of the last half-hour have this aching, hollow feel of something that was always inevitable.

I try to slow my breathing. They will have a plan. A strategy. We'll be out soon.

'It's okay, little one, we're gonna be all right,' I whisper to my bump. I have to protect my family. Me, Ness and the baby.

Outside the viewing hatch, the rioters show no signs of relenting.

Now

There's a flash of brightly coloured headscarf and Vina appears on the landing opposite. 'Guys, come on – this isn't a good idea!' She has her arms open wide like she's preaching. Or facing a firing squad.

'Christ, she's got balls.' Ness's breath tickles my ear.

My muscles clench.

'Shut up, Vina,' someone shouts.

'This isn't gonna help anyone,' Vina tries again. 'What they gonna think when they see this mess?'

'They're treating us like animals!' shouts one young brunette, her fair face twisted into rage.

'And you behaving like animals,' Vina says. 'You think this gonna change their mind?'

'Fuck off, Vina-Vagina.' Annie looms into view.

'Yeah, fuck off, grandma,' says the young brunette. I dig my nails into my palm.

'I'm trying to help you, missy. You don't think this'll add to your sentence?' Vina's face is stern.

Annie suddenly charges at her.

I inhale sharply. Put my hand up as if I might grab her out of harm's way, the door cool against my fingers. Vina stumbles backwards as Annie stops right on top of her. She stands at her full height, bending her face down so it's in Vina's. Vina holds firm. Hands on her hips. Defiant.

'Christ,' Ness exhales.

'We've got to help her.' I reach for the door handle.

'No.' Ness grabs my arm. 'Think of the baby.' My heart hammers against my chest like it's trying to hammer against the door.

'We said: fuck off,' Annie says.

The shouting has died down now, everyone's watching.

'We?' says Vina.

Step down, Vina. Walk away.

'*We* run things now,' says Annie. She smiles. Then, quick as a flash, headbutts Vina in the face.

'No!' I jump up.

Ness's arm holds me back.

Vina's nose explodes She flies backwards and falls with a sickening clang onto the metal walkway.

Her cellmate runs forward to help. 'You fucking maniac!' she shouts at Annie, who's grinning and looking round the wing.

'You hear that? *We* run things now,' Annie bellows.

'Yeah!' the freckled girl appears, a riot vest over her joggies. 'You either with us or you're in our fucking way!'

'You're either with us or against us!' cries another.

There are more jeers. The pretty brunette looks momentarily unsure as Vina's cellmate helps her up and away. But it's only a second before she too has her fist in the air.

You're either with us or against us. Thank god no one heard me cry out. Thank god we got back here. Blood rushes through my ears. 'Fucking hell.'

Ness looks stunned. Pale.

'I'm so sorry, Ness. I got you into this . . .' She shouldn't be here. How long before the guards get control of the prison again? How long will we have to hang on for?

'Shush,' Ness says, preservation taking over.

If we just keep quiet. Just keep our heads down, we can make it out of this.

A face appears the other side of my window. Millimetres from my own. Gould. Instinctively I shove Ness so she falls out of her line of sight.

'Boo!' Gould says, with an ugly grin.

Ness plants her feet on the floor, and pushes her back against the bed, wedging the door shut.

'You can't get in!' I shout as Gould leers through the glass. Every fibre of my body screams to run.

'I don't need to get in, Blondie,' Gould laughs. She bangs the bunch of keys she took from the guard against the pane. 'You need to get out.'

No.

Getting off the bed seems to take an age. Ness rolls to the side. I grab at the metal frame to pull it back into the cell. Try to get to the door, try to get it open.

I hear the key turn in the lock, my guts twisting in sync with it.

I tug at the handle, but it's too late. Gould is already walking away. I hammer on the door.

'Let me out!' I scream. But either no one hears or no one cares. *You're either with us or against us.*

Ness is next to me, pulling at the handle. 'No, no. No!'

Don't panic. Keep calm. My stomach twangs like a snapped guitar string.

Why's she doing this? Is she gonna come back for me? I made it too easy for her. I backed us into a corner. 'I'm sorry, I'm so sorry.' My stomach flexes. I grip my baby. My baby, my sister. We are locked in here because of me.

'There must be another way out!' Ness says.

'It's a fucking prison cell.' My pelvis squeezes. I hold my sides.

'Fuck!' Ness punches her fist hard into the wall. And again. And again.

'Stop!' I grab at her arm. She throws me off. I've never seen her like this.

She shakes her hand, her knuckles raw from the impact, one bleeding. 'Okay,' she says. 'Okay, we just need to keep calm.' She's not talking to me, but herself.

'Ness, you're scaring me.' I swallow.

She looks up and for a second I see something vile flicker in her eyes. She's a stranger. Then she shakes her hands as if she's flicking something off. 'I don't like being locked in,' she says. And she's Ness again. Her face a mix of worry and fear.

'They can't keep us in here.' They can't. I swallow the doubt bubbling inside me. I run the tap, douse my towel in cold water. 'Here, put this on your hand.' The bunk beds are still in the middle of the room, a monument to chaos. We circle them like we're on a twisted merry-go-round.

Ness looks embarrassed. 'Ta.'

Outside, those who were either caught up in the moment with Gould, or too afraid to be against her, are still busy piling things over onto the mesh netting. A mound of blankets is building on the end not bending toward the floor.

I've never known Ness lose it like that. How much pressure has the last few months put on her? I need her to be all right for the baby. When we get out of this I'll talk to her. Check she's okay. *If we get out of this.* I shake off the panic slithering up my spine.

Thwarp, thwarp, thwarp. A sound comes from overhead. Outside. The window is too high to see out clearly. 'Helicopter?' I say.

Ness shrugs. Is it the police? Or could news of the riot be out already? I know some of the women have illegal phones – what would I do if I had one now? I'd call for help. I'd call someone. Turning my bump sideways, I try to tilt my eye against the hatch window to see the payphones in the wing, but can't get the angle.

Another TV screen smashes on the floor outside the cell and I jump. If the news is out, maybe the helicopter is a TV one.

I switch our TV on, flick through the channels. It's nearly lunchtime. I ignore the curl of hunger that spasms inside me.

Is that what Gould is going to do – starve us? Don't think about that right now. The adverts are running on ITV. I look at my watch, flicking back to BBC One, which is still finishing off *Bargain Hunt*.

'You wanna watch telly?' Ness sounds incredulous.

Back to ITV, just as the news starts. 'Shush,' I say. The newsreader is serious-faced as she runs through the headlines. An issue with the shadow cabinet, a car bomb in Afghanistan, and – this is it.

'*Rioting breaks out at Fallenbrook prison, as inmates seize control of the main wing . . .*'

The newsreader's words play over images of the prison taken from above. The building a rectangle of grim rock in the barren landscape. The helicopter is filming us. The footage switches to a ground angle. There are people on the roof! A woman, her face covered with a makeshift bandana, is bent, lifting and chucking off the slate tiles like they're junk mail on the doormat. There's a studied rhythm to the destruction, a hypnotic count, as if the prisoner, and I think I recognise her from my corridor, is trying to deconstruct the place one brick at a time. On the other side of the building, the fire brigade can be seen hosing down the smouldering visitors' hall, its ceiling a charred crater. Dull smoke lazily drifting up.

'Fucking hell,' says Ness.

'*Communication from inside the prison, allegedly from inmates who have access to mobile phones, state that prisoners are unhappy with recent events at the institution, following one inmate taking her own life.*' The newsreader's words sting, despite the surreal aspect of watching her speak about us.

What would I think if I was watching this at home? I try to remember what I'd thought when I'd seen that footage before. It would be karmic if I'd judged those rampaging through wings, but I don't remember feeling that. I don't remember feeling anything. It hadn't concerned me. It hadn't had anything to do with my life. And now here Ness and I are, trapped, as it unfolds around us. While others, watching at home, perhaps tut momentarily, before returning to their own lives. What would Judith and David think if they saw this? Would they watch, aghast, as they ate their lunch at the kitchen table? Would they worry about me, or the baby?

As if on cue, my stomach tenses. As if my body knows it should hold on tight to its precious cargo. I rub it with my palm. Getting worked up won't help.

The news has moved on to cover an MP visiting a local factory.

'They didn't say there are innocent people in here!' Ness's voice is panicked.

Innocent? Then what am I? 'I'm not the only one with a telly – maybe they don't want to inform the prisoners. So they don't think they have hostages,' I stammer.

'Fucking hell.' Ness exhales again. 'Or they don't know that I'm stuck in here.'

'They must – there's a check-in, right? You have to show your passport?' Right. That has to be right.

Help has to be coming.

Has to be.

Now

I make tea. Because what else do you do in a crisis? We're not going anywhere.

We sit on the bed in the middle of the room, sipping quietly. I feel calmer. Ness has stopped fighting it too. It's a comfortable silence. The type you can only share with people you love. The noise of the riot outside is just flickering background shouts and chants.

'If I have to be locked inside a prison protest, I wouldn't want to be with anyone else,' I say.

Ness gives half a laugh. 'Trust us.'

The absurdity of it. 'It's just like when we used to barricade out Carl,' I say.

'Yeah, except I'd rather take my chance with this lot than him.' She grins.

'I wonder what happened to him?' Did he sober up? Did he know how much he scared us as kids? He wasn't nice, he would smash things up, sure, but I wonder if we overreacted. If we liked our own secret space that he and Mum couldn't enter.

'He's dead.' Ness tilts her head to crick her neck.

She must know through the estate grapevine. I feel a stupid pang for having missed out on that. I kept telling myself I was too busy to get back there. Telling others. Too busy for a takeaway. Too busy for drinks. I was so focused on my job, my new life, and then Robert, Emily. Too practised at that fob-off. *I'd love to but I'm booked then. Let's get together soon though.* I thought I'd found new friends, my people, the ones who truly got me in the way my mates from the block never could. But where are my new friends now? I've had no contact from Sally, from Becky, from Deb, from any of them. I should have made more effort with my old friends. What I'd give for a mug of wine on the sofa and a takeaway chippie with them now. I'm sad even for Carl, not to know that he'd passed on. He wasn't so very different from Mum. 'Poor man.'

Ness jumps up. Plants her plastic cup firmly on the cabinet. 'He was an evil bastard.'

I blink. Shocked. 'It wasn't him though, was it? It was the drugs. It messed him up.'

'Ones like that are messed up already.' Ness's words have the air of finality. This is not a debatable point. I don't want to upset her again. I need her to stay calm.

'Course,' I say.

'You were just a kid,' she says. 'You didn't know half of what he did.'

'Sure.' I just want her to sit down. Calm down. I saw more than she knew. More than she likes to admit. Ness has always seen herself as my protector, but she was just a kid too. It's just having seen people in here, having known them, I can see how things could go wrong. We both know what drugs do to people. The hunger that overpowers everything else, even love for others. But it's not their fault. It's not Mum's, or Erica's, or anyone else's. Some people have the addiction gene. But it's not really them behaving like that. They're a puppet to their own addiction.

'Life is wasted on some people!' Ness spits.

Did Carl OD? More than possible.

Ness flops down onto the bed, her anger drained. She scrubs at the floor with the toe of her trainer. And for a moment we listen to the squeak of the rubber against the concrete.

Without looking up, Ness says: 'Do you think about her much – Emily?' And I realise why she's angry. What this is about. Carl gambled his own life with drugs, Emily was an innocent.

I don't think I'll ever be able to go swimming again. The smell of chlorine on her hair. It's too evocative. Too hard. 'Always,' I manage.

I squeeze her hand. She gives half a smile, the one I recognise so well, the one we all give when we're trying to be brave. Recollections peek like sun rays through the grey clouds of loss. One day, I hope the clouds will fade and we'll be left only with the happy warmth of our memories. I cling to that.

'I just keep thinking of her in her pink hoodie.' A tear slides down her cheek. Ness swipes at it with the back of her hand. 'Stupid, huh?' She shakes herself, as if she can cast off the weight of the loss.

My breath stops somewhere in my throat. The whole room shifts. A shard of ice slots into the remaining gap of the puzzle.

Ness, oblivious, rolls her shoulders, shakes her arms, pushes herself up off the bed, starts to pace.

Inside of me something is screaming. Something is shrieking. I can't speak. I feel like everything's tilted and I'm sliding, falling.

'You got any more tea bags?' Ness picks up the kettle and sniffs it.

She looks at me, waiting for an answer. My body gives an involuntary shudder. This can't be right. It's the stress. The situation. The baby.

Peeking out from under the notes on evidence against me is the photo of Emily I tore from the newspaper.

Ness follows my gaze, the kettle still in her hand. It must show on my face. I feel like it's carved into my chest. Illuminating my whole body. I see it flicker behind her eyes.

She *knows*.

Now

In her pink hoodie. Emily didn't have a pink hoodie. She didn't wear pink: scorned it as too girly. I hadn't really thought of it at the time. There were so many more important things, so many more terrible things, that had filled my head. But it was there, in the background of that awful memory, the one that replays in my nightmares: Emily was wearing a pastel-pink hoodie over her uniform. I'd never seen it before. We hadn't bought it for her. It must have been new.

The belt contracts around my waist and I reach for the wall. Am I steadying myself from the pain or the realisation? The hoodie must have been a birthday present from her friends. I wish I could see it now, examine it. Could I be wrong?

I exhale slowly.

'You okay?' Ness is still holding the kettle. Ness. My big sister. The one who has always been there for me. The one who protected me when we were growing up.

I need time to think. 'Fine.'

Ness fills the kettle at the sink. There has to be an explanation.

Think about the hoodie. What can you remember of it? There'd been a symbol on the breast, a logo, the one Emily and Phoebe had designed for their Tumble Tuck band. Emily didn't wear pink, but Phoebe did. It must have been a gift from Phoebe for her birthday. Could Phoebe have anything to do with what happened? No, she's a child. That's a crazy thing to think. This is crazy. My mind claws for answers.

Ness shuts the kettle lid with a snap, like a bubble bursting. 'You sure you're feeling all right?'

A pit opens inside my stomach, me and my baby teetering on the edge of it. About to be dragged down. There has to be a reason. A simple explanation.

She walks back round the room, plugs the kettle in. Flicks the switch.

'How did you know her hoodie was pink?' I wait for Ness's response. The sentence that will clear all this up. I'm still gripping the wall.

'What?' Ness looks confused. The water in the kettle starts to bubble.

'How did you know Emily's hoodie was pink?' I force the words out. Try for a laugh. 'It was new. It must have been a present.'

'Pink, purple, whatever – it was just an expression.' Ness looks at the window. 'They could pull these bars out with that helicopter. Get a ladder up.'

My mouth runs dry. Ness is my sister. We survived our childhood together, we grew up together, she practically raised me when Mum couldn't. I know that when she lies, her right-hand little finger thrums. It's a small and tiny tell, as if she can control every part of her except there. As if the physical pressure of lying has to escape somewhere, like steam rattling a saucepan lid.

And her little finger is shaking.

Bile twists in my stomach. I feel it slosh round my baby. I imagine the small child pushing it away. I run to retch over the toilet.

'Jesus!' Ness shrieks.

Her hand is rubbing my back. I feel myself stiffen. She's lying. Lying about Emily's hoodie.

I pull at my hair, as if I might free the pressure of my own thoughts.

Ness, mistaking it for pain, starts to make soothing sounds. I gag again. Ness knew where we kept the spare key. What the alarm code was. She could get into the house.

There must be an explanation. I'm about to ask, when a contraction squeezes across my stomach. The strength of this one turning my inner pain into a moan.

'Was that a contraction? It's too early, isn't it? Breathe.' She puts a hand on my shoulder.

Her touch scalds my skin. I grit my teeth as the cramp radiates over my stomach. 'You know what Emily was wearing when she was killed. You were there.' I need her to explain. To make this all right.

Ness hesitates. What does she know? What did she see? Robert flashes through my mind.

'Jenna, you've got to understand, I . . . I didn't mean for any of this to happen.'

Happen. Happen?

She starts to snivel.

She has to explain. Tell me she saw someone else. Tell me it wasn't her. I grab her shoulders and shake her. 'What did you do?'

'It was an accident.' She looks into my eyes. 'I didn't mean to hurt her.'

I pull the world into me, as everything collapses like a black hole. All the oxygen gone. My star has died. I can't breathe.

Ness reaches for me.

'Don't touch me!' I turn to run but there's nowhere to go. I back me and my bump against the wall. I need to be away from her.

'Jenna, you've got to listen to me. It was an accident. She went for me, she wouldn't stop screaming.' Ness comes toward me.

This can't be happening. This can't be real. Memories

tumble in my head, like Emily turning in the pool. 'Why would she do that? You got on. She looked up to you!'

'She just went crazy.' Ness's eyes are like a frightened animal's. 'She was kicking and punching me. It was self-defence. I just grabbed for the nearest thing to defend myself!'

'A knife! You grabbed a knife? You stabbed her, Ness. Is that what you're saying? You did this?' I think of the blood in the kitchen. Emily slumped on the floor. 'Why were you there? Why did she hit you?' My mind feels like it's stuttering, misfiring, like it can't keep up. Ness killed Emily. She was there . . . With the blood. In our house. Our home. The contraction starts from low down and squeezes up over my stomach like it's a tube of toothpaste. The power of it bends me forwards. Stops the words. All I can do is try and breathe.

'You okay? Is it the baby?' Ness steps toward me.

It's too early. I'm only eight months gone. I smack her hand away. Robert's blood was in the kitchen. Robert was there—

A flash of light interrupts my thoughts.

A lighter flares through the door hatch. The pile of blankets on the mesh net high now, like a mound. A bonfire.

No. Annie is holding a lit rolled newspaper.

'Oh my god.' Ness is breathless beside me.

Annie lets the flaming newspaper fall. It turns in the air, and drops onto the blankets below.

My throat closes. Fire. It ripped through the visitors' hall in minutes.

'No! We're locked in!' The door is cold, immovable. It barely rattles under my fist.

The grey blankets billow, catch. Flames burrow down into the rest. My whole body convulses, like my baby is hammering her fist against the inside of me, desperate for us both to get out.

People run from their cells. A woman passes our door in a blur.

'Help! Let us out!' Ness hammers against the door.

Us. Emily. I didn't mean to hurt her.

As the smoke curls its sickly perfume under the cell door I could just close my eyes on it all. Don't find out. Don't ask. Don't face the horror. Let it burn. Let it all burn.

My stomach clenches. Hardens under my skin. A rock. My daughter screams at me to move. Run. Fight. For Robert. For Emily. For her.

I grab a book and bang it against the door. 'Please! Someone help! I'm pregnant!' I scream.

Through the smoke, flames dance among the remnants of the blankets, slithering down onto the piled debris like a snake uncoiling.

The landing's empty. Everyone's fled to the roof. No one can hear us.

No one is coming.

Now

'We're going to die.' Ness sounds frightened, small.

I want to hug her. I want to punch her. 'What were you doing at my house?' I register the taste of tears, salty and smoky.

Ness runs at the wall, jumps, catches hold of the window-sill. Tries to scrabble up. But there's no escape. Neither of us can fit through the bars. 'Help me!' she screams.

Me. Me! How can she think of herself now? After what she's confessed? I grab her waistband and pull her back. She careens backwards into the bed. The room looks shaken. Everything turned upside down. Everything broken. I'm coughing. My eyes watering. Ness looks fearful, then angry. She jumps up. Her fingers thrusting into my tender chest.

'This is your fault,' she screams. 'Why couldn't you let me have one good thing?'

I know Ness gets angry. She can be a bit selfish but this? Not this. 'Why did she hit you? You must have done something.' I push her. And again. Hard. 'What did you do?'

I don't see the backhand coming. Perhaps it's the smoke, or the fact that I never believed Ness would actually hurt me.

The impact is sudden. An explosion against my cheekbone. My centre of balance, wriggling somewhere new and unsure in my stomach, tilts me sideways. As I fall, I realise I didn't think this was real until now. I was wrong.

Her trainer comes toward my face. I deaden the blow with my arms. I feel the bone flex, chip, maybe snap. A sickening twist inside of me.

'You always get everything! Everything!' Ness is screaming.

Spittle rains down on me, breaking the tightening film of smoke on my skin.

'The house! The money! The fancy fucking job! You got away!'

Anger fires me and my voice up. 'I've worked hard for what I've got. For where I am!'

'You had it easy,' she spits. 'I took the hits. I protected you.'

We were both on the Orchard as kids. We both went through stuff with Mum. 'I was there too.'

'*You were there?* You were there!' Hate swirls round her with the smoke, making me breathless. 'What do you know?'

What do I know? The ridiculousness of it. The childish teenage idiocy. I know what it's like to be locked in a prison. 'I know what it's like to fear for my and my baby's life.' A contraction rips through me again. It's too soon. I pant in smoke. Cough.

She shakes her head. Her eyes look dead. She's no longer shouting. 'So do I.'

What? She has lost her mind. It's a breakdown. A psychotic episode.

'I killed my baby.' Ness's words are flat.

I can't breathe. 'What baby?'

'Carl's.'

The name comes at me from the side. In the wrong place, the wrong time. Carl who we barricaded the door against. Carl who is dead from an overdose. 'Mum's boyfriend?'

'He forced me.' Her words are without emotion. Fact.

Rape. No. It's like my history is being broken down and re-shuffled around me. A baby. 'When?'

'You want details?' She looks up, incredulous.

No. Yes. I want this to stop. To go back to this morning when I understood the world. When things made sense.

A tear cuts through the grime on her face, and falls onto the dirty floor. 'It was the first time they were together.'

She means when he was with Mum. But she would have been . . . my mind is slowed by the smoke. The shock. Twelve. She would have been twelve. I was six. I dry heave.

'Mum was out cold. You were asleep in your bedroom. I didn't want you to wake up. Didn't want you to see. Didn't want you to be next.'

I cover my mouth with my hand.

'After that I started sleeping in your room. Blocking the door.'

It was when she dropped out of school, got work collecting glasses in the working men's club, and at the taxi rank. Was she getting money to get away? 'Why didn't you say something? He should have been arrested.'

Ness looks almost pitying. 'Who would I tell? Mum was off her face, Gran was gone. Who would believe some kid from the Orchard estate? Who would care?'

I think of the broken women in here. The chaotic childhoods that shattered them and never quite let them gather the pieces of their lives together again.

A baby. She said there was a baby.

She stares at my bump. 'I thought the social would take you away for sure if they found out.'

My stomach hollows out. She didn't want me to be next. She didn't want me taken away. Twelve years old and she was wrestling with all this. Younger than Emily. *Emily.* A thread begins to draw between these two children, Ness damaged and young, Emily privileged and gone.

With a shaking hand Ness pushes her hair off her wet face. 'There was a woman three blocks down who said she could help. There was a man. A doctor, apparently. But he was a crook. It went wrong. The people at the hospital said it was an infection. Or the stuff he used. Something. I've tried again since then, but they all say the same thing: I can't have children.'

'Oh Ness. I'm so sorry.'

She half laughs. 'Sorry? You've never even asked if I wanted kids, have you? You only care about yourself.'

The words sting. 'I didn't know . . .'

'It's all about you.' She pulls her hand away from me. Her words hardening. 'Jenna and her university place, Jenna and her brilliant job, Jenna and her rich boyfriend. I should have had all that. Would have if I'd not been looking after you.'

'I was just a kid.'

'Even Mum.' She shakes her head. 'She was so gutted when you left the Orchard she followed you up here. She left me. After everything!'

Bitterness explodes around me. I think of Mum, desperate to make up for how she was, trying to give us money she doesn't have, hugs, love. 'Mum would be devastated if she knew what had happened.'

'She knows!' Ness's words detonate between us. 'You took it all. You took him.'

Him? Who? And then I see. Ness and Robert on the sofa in front of the fire. Ness hugging Robert in the kitchen. All those texts, trying to meet up. She didn't want to spend more time with me, she wanted to spend more time with him. Ness is in love with Robert. *No.* 'Where is he?' My voice shakes. I force myself to repeat it. My throat cracking with tears, pain, heat. 'Please, where is he, Ness? Tell me?'

Her hair is wild about her face, her eyes black smears of mascara, and she looks at me with such hatred it hurts more than the kick. 'It's always about you. Clever little fucking Jenna.'

No. I shake my head, back away. The door cold against my bare arms, the smoke thicker now.

Bang! Someone else is banging on the door. On the other side!

'In here!' I shout.

Vina's face, bloodied and half-masked by a torn sheet, appears at the hatch.

'Stand back!' she shouts. And I see in her hands the big red key – the battering ram!

'How did you get that . . .' But then I remember the open offices – the inmates running around with riot helmets on. And I can see a strip of sharpened metal, wrenched from the bottom of the frame, tucked into Vina's pocket.

'Get back!' she yells.

I jump clear as there's a huge clang. And another. And on the third, the door busts inwards.

Smoke rolls into the room. Red flashes of heat behind it.

'We need to go!' Vina's eyes are streaming. 'Up onto the roof.'

But Ness grabs hold of my other wrist, hard.

'What are you doing?' I try to shake her off.

Her face is calm now, still in the smoke. 'It's over, Jenna. I'm not going back.'

'What the hell are you doing – we have to get out,' cries Vina.

Ness shakes her head, her hand surprisingly cool against my skin. 'No. She's not going anywhere.' There's a flash of silver. And before I can stop her, Ness has the makeshift blade from Vina's pocket.

I feel the sharp edge press against my neck.

Now

'You hate me.' My words are free from emotion. *It's all about you.* A growing acceptance is flowing through me, warming me with the flames.

The whites of Vina's eyes are reddening. She looks between Ness, the metal, me.

'I love you,' Ness says. 'You're my little sister.'

But I'm not listening any more. My mind is wading through each sharp object that's been thrown at me. 'It can't have been an accident,' I say.

Ness's hand squeezes my arm tighter. 'I told you it was. She attacked me.'

But there was the jumper and the knife in the dishwasher. 'You were wearing gloves. You put that stuff on my computer.'

My fingers begin to tingle.

A flaming cabinet slips from the netting and erupts as it crashes onto the ground below.

Vina starts. 'We have to get out of here!'

But Ness isn't listening to her. It's like there's just two of us now, seeing each other for the first time. 'I should have been his girlfriend, not you,' she says.

'But you aren't,' I say.

I feel my pulse push against the metal at my neck.

'I just needed him to see me,' she said. 'I didn't mean for all this to happen. But if he'd seen those photos on your computer he wouldn't have been able to look at you. And I would have helped him grieve. Helped him recover.'

'You'd do that to me?' My Ness. My sister. My protector.

'You had money, you'd get a good lawyer. You'd have been fine. You always land on your feet.'

Vina stares at us transfixed. The battering ram is limp in her hands. My bump, my baby between me and Ness.

'What about Emily? That doesn't explain what you did to her.'

'I was checking your laptop. Some of the photos were open when she came in. I didn't think anyone would be there.'

Oh god, Emily saw the child porn. I feel sick. 'But you didn't have to hurt her.'

'She went off on one. Started screaming about calling the police.' Ness's voice rises. 'She had the phone.'

Emily with her strong sense of right and wrong. Emily with the confidence that comes of private education. I remember the phone socket hanging, ripped from the wall in the kitchen.

'I had to stop her,' Ness says. 'She wouldn't stop screaming. I just needed her to calm down. I just meant to frighten her but she struggled.'

She fought back. *Emily, you were so brave.*

The metal digs in. Stings. Something dribbles down my neck. I can't tell if it's blood or sweat. I don't care any more. Everything I thought I knew is gone. And I feel so tired. So heavy.

I close my eyes. 'And Robert?'

Ness flinches. 'He's fine.'

She's got him. Alive. My arms feel heavy. My body too.

'We need to get her outside.' Vina is talking over me.

'No.' Ness swipes forward with the metal blade. 'I was going to have the baby. I was going to raise it with Robert. He was going to love me.'

'You're fucking mental.' Vina coughs.

There's no point fighting. I just want to sit down. Lie down. Close my eyes. The air feels like it is pushing down on me.

'She's going to pass out! You're going to die!' Vina shouts.

'Leave us alone!' Ness shouts.

And she's shouting at the barricaded door of my bedroom. Carl is on the other side, grunting, crashing about. But it's okay because we're in here together and nothing can hurt us.

The contraction starts low, and tightens fast, up and over my stomach like a vice. I scream. Buckle forward. Ness drops the metal. Vina swings at her. Ness lets go of my arm. Stumbles backwards. Internally I'm shifting, pushing down. My baby. My baby.

I gulp in air. Smoke makes me cough. And I'm awake. Everything sharp. The pain makes me whole. Strong. Powerful.

'Run!' I scream.

Vina is already on her way. Me too. We sprint down the landing, arms up against the smoke and the heat. Toward a pile of furniture. A makeshift ladder. A square of light flickers down from above. Something sparks to our left.

Vina is there first; she scrambles up onto a large filing cabinet, reaches down for me.

I turn.

Ness is behind me. Running. There's a snapping sound as the last of the metal netting between the landings gives and tumbles its prey down into a fiery ball. The struts buckle. Ness grabs for the edge of the walkway as the section she's on tips and slides.

'Ness!'

Then she's falling.

'No!' I strain against Vina's hold.

I feel the vacuum. Ness twists like she's turning in water.

Our eyes meet.

Then the backdraught explodes upwards.

'Ness!' I scream. As Vina pulls me by my arm, up into the daylight.

Beneath us everything is engulfed in flames.

Coughing. Coughing. Can't breathe.

'Ness! Ness!' Vina's whole body is stopping me. Sliding on the roof tiles. 'I've got to help her!' I scream.

'She's gone, she's gone,' Vina says.

'No!' I love her. I have to help her. 'Ness!' I scream. 'Ness!'

'She's gone.' Vina holds me tight.

I feel my knees buckle. But she can't be gone. She's my sister. She raised me. She . . . she . . .

I see Ness's face smiling as she produces paper-wrapped chips from behind her back. She's brushing my hair for school. Telling the lads on the corner to do one. Singing to me when Mummy is sick. Turning the telly up in my room so we can't hear the men. Sharing a fag with me out her bedroom window. Running alongside me through the blocks, laughing, running, running, we're going to make it. We're going to get out. We're going to be free.

Tears pour down my face. She can't be gone. I grip my stomach. She was going to raise my baby. She loved me. She loved me.

Smoke puffs from the hole behind us. 'We need to move, go! This could collapse.' Vina is pushing against me.

I can't. I want to stay with her. I want to go back. I reach for the hole. Ness. My Ness.

Vina hangs onto my shoulder, pulls.

'No!' I scream, and fall to my knees as a howl punches up out of me. *Oh Ness – what did you do?*

Tiles skid from under my hands and disappear into the furnace below. My baby kicks.

'Move.' Vina yanks me, hard.

I turn, stagger. I don't want to leave her.

My baby kicks again. Frantic jerks inside.

Ahead we can see women, chanting and cheering. More are huddled in groups. They've unfurled banners. A helicopter is overhead. And – a long way down – a crowd of journalists, officers and the police peer up at us. Shouting, pointing to the flames that are coming from the hole behind us.

Oh Ness, I'm sorry. I'm so sorry. I didn't know.

'That way.' Vina points and I see the roof steps up, there's a separate section, beyond where the wing must end.

We scramble across the tiles.

Every step a step further away.

Women, with their faces covered, see us coming. How far apart are my contractions? Because there's no denying now. I'm in labour. I scream as another one punts me forwards. *I want Ness.*

Vina's hands are on my hips, steadying me. A roof tile skids from under my foot, slides down and off the side. A distant smash. I do not want to be here. I do not want to be giving birth now.

Someone reaches down for us – *Ness?* But no, it's someone else's red hair in the sunshine. Abi. We climb up onto the next section. It's flatter up here. The hills of Gloucestershire rolling away from us. Green trees, yellow oilseed rape fields. Clean air. Blue sky. *Breathe. Breathe. Breathe.*

'Well, well, well, look who decided to show up.' Gould's voice is smooth as honey. 'The Blonde Slayer.'

My whole body freezes. The women stop chanting. Eyes over bandanas, watching. The wind whistles over the roof and ruffles Gould's hair. She smiles a sickly evil smile.

'She's in labour.' Vina steps forward. In front of me.

A murmur goes through the crowd.

From below we hear a voice from a loudhailer. '*All prisoners that move to the opposite side of the building will be helped down.*'

If I could just get there. If I could just get down. But the vice is back. My insides moving, realigning, squeezing. I scream.

'She's in labour!' someone says.

'We need hot water,' says a voice that sounds like Abi.

'She's the Blonde Slay—' Gould's voice is buried under my scream.

No time. Another one. This is it. Must push. Why did you leave me, Ness? Why did you do this? I needed you.

'She needs to lie down.'

'Anyone got a blanket?'

And women are around me, helping me onto my back. Lifting my knees.

'Breathe, honey.' Vina has hold of my hand as I squeeze. A noise comes out of me that I don't recognise.

'Ten centimetres, I'd say.' Rhianna's mum is between my knees.

The helicopter looms into view, a TV camera visible. Oh god. Oh god.

Vina follows my gaze. 'Fucking hell! Can we get some privacy!'

The noise comes out of me again. *I want Ness. I want my mum. Breathe. Breathe. Breathe.*

There's a rustling around me, in my peripheral vision. I can barely focus. The pain is like nothing on earth. I can't do it. *You can.* I hear Ness's voice in my head. *You can. Pant. Pant. Like the midwife told you. You can do it, Jenna.* A canopy of bottle-green jumpers are stretched between me and the blue sky, a ring of women holding them up.

'I can see his head!' Rhianna's mum calls.

Her. Her. My daughter. Ness should have been here. 'Argh!' I scream.

'Push!' yells Rhianna's mum.

The loudhailer drifts from below: *'Paramedics are on their way up. Stand clear.'*

But it's too late.

'It's a girl!' screams Rhianna's mum. 'A girl!'

Eight Weeks Later

The church is cool and dark and, stepping through the door, I panic for a moment that I can't see the sky. But then I hear the organist practising 'Ave Maria' upstairs, and my shoulders relax a little. Though they haven't loosened completely in the last two months. I'm not sure they ever will again. I was so scared when my daughter was born. I was only thirty-three weeks pregnant. She'd come early, and during a riot. I'd inhaled smoke, I'd been running, I'd been attacked, and all those emotions. I touch my neck where Ness pressed the metal. The slight rise of scar tissue still present. My daughter had cried to begin with, her tiny lungs yelling on the top of the roof. But then she started caving – making this frantic coughing noise as she fought to breathe. The paramedics were on her in minutes. They had a mask over her face, blowing air into her tiny lungs. All the women stood back in silence. Some started to pray. Then they took her and me to hospital. Blue lights flashing. She was in an incubator, an intravenous line feeding her fluids.

Mum is sitting on one of the front pews. She comes here most days. I don't understand it. If there is a god, how can you be anything but angry at him for what happened? For allowing a twelve-year-old to be raped. For making her pregnant, then taking away her baby, and her ability to have further children. How can you not be furious at that awful, devastating, hateful act which led to the destruction of so many lives. But it helps her. And if it keeps her away from the drugs, I'll support it.

She doesn't see me until I'm almost upon her, so there's no time to wipe her tears away, though she tries. 'Oh, hello love,' she says. 'Didn't see you there.'

Poor Mum. I lost a sister. She lost a child. I sit down and take Mum's hand. We stare at the altar for a moment, the sun illuminating the stained glass behind into a dancing jigsaw of colour at our feet.

'I lit a candle for her,' Mum says quietly, as if I might be cross.

I am. Furious at what Ness did. She planted child pornography on my computer to try and split me and Robert up. And when Emily came home unexpectedly and saw Ness with those images open on my laptop, they fought. Emily who was headstrong, who knew right from wrong, who would round on you with her hands on her hips and call you on your bullshit. Emily who saw through her grandfather long before I did. Ness killed an innocent fourteen-year-old child. I pause to take in the enormity of it all again. I believe she didn't set out to hurt anyone but me. But things escalated. *Who would believe some kid from the Orchard estate?* That's what she'd said, and that's what she'd believed. I think her development froze at twelve in many ways. She died the day that man assaulted her.

Then Robert came home. He saw Emily lying there on the floor. He ran to her, didn't even see Ness. She hit him over the head and dragged his bleeding body to the car. Drove him to the gym she worked at and locked him in an old weights cage in the disused basement. Her boss only realised the key was missing from his desk drawer when the police raided the place. She sedated Robert with ground-up diazepam she'd sourced from an old Orchard pal, mixing it into blueberry yoghurts. For five months he too was incarcerated. But he was out of it most of the time.

Ness torched her car to destroy the evidence. Except the police found it partially burnt out, and DI Langton thought it odd that a person linked to an active crime case didn't report their car stolen. She started digging. Forensics found traces of Robert's blood in the car. And DI Langton realised Ness was spending all her time, and most of her money, within a one-mile radius of her workplace. In fact, she didn't seem to be going home at all. She started following Ness. And as Fallenbrook went up in flames, she broke down the door of Star Gym's basement. They found the white Ikea cot set up down there, ready.

I don't know what Ness thought would happen. That she could win Robert over after everything that she did? That by bringing him a new daughter she could make up for the loss of another? Maybe she didn't think at all. Maybe she just kept going down the one fatal track she'd started on. A tear rolls down my cheek and onto my lap.

'Why didn't you tell me, Mum? About Carl. About the baby,' I say. I could have helped her if I'd just known.'

Mum keeps staring ahead. 'When I think of what he did to her . . . My poor little girl.' She swallows. Steadies herself. 'I didn't find out until later. You was nine, and you'd just started your period. First in your class, Ness said.'

I nod. I remember Ness taking me to get towels, and the humiliation I felt because none of the other girls had started.

Mum takes a big breath. 'I found her crying in the bathroom after that, 'cause her own periods had stopped. And she told me.'

Poor Ness. Poor Mum. I know what it feels like to know you brought a devastating destructive force into the life of someone you love. If I hadn't brought Ness into Robert's life, Emily would still be here.

Then I realise: Mum got clean when I was nine. 'You quit using then, didn't you? Because of what happened to Ness?'

She nods. 'I flushed what I had left down the toilet. Told Carl that if he ever came near me, my girls or any other kiddie again I'd cut his balls off.'

'But you could have told me,' I say.

'You were still so young.' Her voice cracks, and she clutches her hands together in her lap. 'We wanted to protect you. Thought it was best to focus on the future.' Her voice is barely audible as she whispers one of her twelve steps. 'We humbly ask Him to remove our shortcomings.'

'It's okay, Mum,' I say. No one can prepare you to deal with something like that. I swallow. 'I was thinking we could get a plaque for her – in the memorial garden.' There was nothing left after the fire at Fallenbrook. Nothing for us to bury.

Mum squeezes my hand. 'I would like that.'

Me too. Even after everything she did, I want Ness to be at peace. Wherever she is.

'I'm so sorry, Jenna.'

'Don't say that.' I pull her tiny frame into me.

'If I hadn't been off my face – if I'd been a better mother to you girls . . .' She sobs.

'Shush, don't say that.' Life doesn't work like that. We are all a patchwork of what's come before. We are all a product of our past. No one action can be separated out from any other. We have to do the best with what we have.

'I'm going to make it up to you,' she says. Her eyes shining with tears. 'I'm going to be there every step of the way for you and baby Kelly when she comes home.'

'I know, Mum,' I say, touching the charm bracelet with the little K on it I wear in the memory of the loving, bright, and brave young woman my baby girl is named after.

'I'm going to make it up to you,' she says again.

'It's not your fault,' I say. *It's not your fault.* I repeat it to myself. And we stay there holding each other for a second.

'Come on,' I say, pulling away and trying my best to sound bright. 'We've got to get home, we need to finish that nursery.'

We walk, side by side in the low bright September sunshine, toward my flat. I moved back in when I was discharged from hospital. And Mum moved in the day after, to care for me. It hurt so badly to leave Kelly, so tiny and fragile in the incubator in the hospital, but she needed help breathing and to gain weight. Mum made it easier, she's been there every step of the way. When Sally turned up on my doorstep and I threw her out, Mum stayed up all night with me talking. I can't forgive Sally for rejecting me when I needed her. Not yet. Though since then she has sent several cards for me, and a tiny Babygro for Kelly, that I haven't been able to throw out. Mum says to give it time to get better. To see how I feel. We're going to need a lot of that: time to make it better. I already don't care that Becky sold her story to a newspaper. Robert, under David's influence, had already started to separate me from my friends; prison just finished the job. I keep busy. I write weekly to Vina, who's been transferred to an open prison and is now able to take the rest of her Criminology degree. And I'm starting a new job with a charity who work with pregnant women in prison. I'll be doing the PR to begin with, though, as I don't think I can bring myself to go inside quite yet. Not even to visit.

As we reach the crest of my road I think for a second the journalists are back standing outside – but they've moved on too. Gould's trial is coming up, and predictions over how long she will go down for following the riot dominate the front pages. Instead, I see it's the familiar shape of Robert, diminished slightly after his ordeal, waiting by the flat entrance. Mum makes a discreet excuse about needing to pop to the shop, and waves as she retreats in the opposite direction. Robert looks unsure what to do, and gives half a wave back. I take a deep breath. *Give it time and things will get better.*

We greet each other with an awkward hug. He goes to kiss my cheek as I go to pull away.

'Sorry,' I mumble.

'My fault,' he says, holding his hands up.

We're not quite sure what to do with each other now. I still care for him, a huge amount. And I've seen him most days at the hospital – they'd let him off his ward so he could read stories to Kelly through her incubator. But I can't go back after everything we've been through. I thought he was capable of murder. I brought Ness into his life. He brought David into mine. He lied to me about Erica. All trust is broken. And we're both left holding the shattered pieces. It was a shock for him to learn what his father had done while he was missing. For him to finally face up to what kind of man his father is, what kind of man he himself might be if he doesn't make changes. After that he put the Dower House up for sale, and plans, against his parents' wishes, to give me and Kelly half the proceeds.

'Tea?' I say, holding up my key. My bracelet glinting in the light.

'Got any biscuits?'

'If you're lucky,' I say. Even after everything Robert and I discussed, I'd never quite got round to putting my flat on the market. I think I knew something wasn't right. Robert was so desperate to find happiness away from the control of his father that, when he met me while David and Judith were travelling, he rushed everything. He wanted to believe it was real, but it was just another act. Another performance, like his parents'.

'How you doing?' I ask as we climb the stairs.

He's walking better already. Getting stronger. 'I'm okay,' he says. 'You?'

'Well, I was about to build a cot, do you feel up to lending a hand?'

He beams. 'I would love that, Jenna. Thank you.'

Robert compares the four wooden screws in his hand. 'This one. Must be.'

It wedges firmly into the frame, and I do the same with the remaining ones. It feels sturdy, the white wood clean against the freshly painted wall. Ready for our baby to come home. 'Perfect.' I say, satisfied with our work.

Robert stoops and takes something wrapped in tissue paper from his bag. A white waffle blanket, which he strokes with his thumb. 'I hope you don't mind – I thought we could . . .' He pauses, takes a big breath. 'This was Emily's when she was a baby.'

I nod. A lump forms in my throat. I walk across to the chest of drawers and take out the frame I've had specially made. Emily's beautiful smiling face beams out at me. 'I thought we could hang this on the wall?'

He smiles, tears at the corner of his eyes.

'Kelly will always know about her amazing sister.' I prop the photo up on the drawers.

Robert puts his arm round my shoulders and pulls me into him. 'Thank you,' he says into my hair. 'Thank you.'

We hold each other like that for a moment. And I breathe him in. All the promise of what might have been. All of the pain.

And then we let go.

'What time are you off tomorrow?'

'Erica's picking me up at 9 a.m.,' he says.

Erica has been brilliant in these last few weeks. A real rock for him while he's been in hospital. She's found the right residential clinic and is driving him down there. Robert will have a permanent scar on his forehead from where he should have had stitches. And a deeper, unseen one: addiction. The doctors say he would have been hooked after just two weeks on the dosage of diazepam Ness was feeding him, and he had five months' worth in that basement. Once I would have been jealous of Erica, but that time has passed.

'Me and Kelly will come and see you on that first Saturday,' I say.

'Promise?' He looks panicked for a moment, his eyebrows more pronounced on his drawn face.

I take his hands in mine. 'You're her dad. You're a huge part of her life, whether you want it or not.'

'I do,' he says. 'I do.' And for a second I think of our wedding that never happened. And how it is better this way. How we can all start to move on.

Erica's blue Mini arrives with a toot of the horn. She waves. Robert climbs into the front with a grin, and I wonder if Erica and he might get back together. They've grown close again, leaning on each other to mourn Emily. Perhaps they would never have split up without David's interference and Robert's weakness. I won't see David. I've made that clear to everyone. But I've written to Judith and told her I want Kelly to know her grandmother. And that she is always welcome here, should she ever need a place to stay.

The Mini drives off, and I'm back outside waiting for my taxi when the car draws up.

DI Langton gets out.

'I can't stop,' I explain, and hold up the empty car seat.

'I was coming to return this.' She holds out a small plastic evidence bag. My engagement ring. 'It was recovered from the undamaged part of Fallenbrook,' she says.

The final remnants of my old life. I'll give it back to Robert. I don't want it any more. 'Thank you.'

'They're rebuilding the wing, new cells. Bigger apparently,' she says.

I shudder at the thought. And, noticing, she changes the

subject. 'Why don't I give you a lift?' she says. 'I'm headed that way. Won't take me two minutes.'

I don't really want to get in the car with her, but my taxi is running late. 'Sure. Thanks,' I say. *She's just a person. A normal person. And she did believe you. She did keep looking for Robert. She did keep searching for the truth, you just didn't know.* I wonder if she feels bad about what happened to me.

From the car window I watch the honey-yellow stone houses pass in the setting sun. And think of all the secrets people carry behind those walls.

DI Langton signals to turn left.

I clear my throat. 'Am I allowed to ask things about the case?' They have no one to press charges against now. There'll be an enquiry, I'm sure, but that will be it.

'What things?' she says, without taking her eyes from the road.

'About the text message sent to Sally? The one that looked like a confession.'

'It was sent from your iPad,' DI Langton says, matter-of-fact.

I'd guessed as much. That whoever had sent that had used a synced device. I was just looking in the wrong direction. *Oh Ness.*

'And my jumper – the Sweaty Betty one – what happened to it?' The one they found in the washing machine soaked in blood.

DI Langton slows for the roundabout. The blue sign pointing the way. 'We believe your sister was either wearing it, or she used it to try and stem the flow of blood from Emily.'

She might have been trying to help her. I close my eyes for a second. If she'd just called an ambulance. If she'd just asked for help before things went that far everything could have been different. In the heat of the moment we can all make the wrong choice. I touch my bracelet, and think of Kelly.

'We'll never know for sure,' DI Langton says.

'No, we won't.'

The DI makes smalltalk the rest of the way.

As soon as she pulls the car into the car park, I'm halfway out the door, pulling the car seat behind me. This is the moment I've been waiting for. The thing I feared I'd never see happen.

'Good luck!' DI Langton calls.

But I'm already racing toward the maternity unit to bring her home. Her tiny pink face, the way her mouth puckers into a perfect circle when she sleeps, the scent and tickle of her fine dusting of hair. My little girl and me.

Together we can survive anything.

Author's Note

Jenna's story and her time in HMP Fallenbrook is a work of fiction, but I have drawn on multiple real-life sources to ensure it reflects the genuine issues expectant and new mothers (and other inmates) face in prisons in the UK today. The books *Mothering Justice: Working with Mothers in Criminal and Social Justice Settings*, edited by Lucy Baldwin, and *The Little Book of Prison: A Beginners Guide* by Frankie Owens have been particularly useful. Interviews with Royal College of Midwives Fellow Dr Laura Abbott, senior lecturer in midwifery, Hertfordshire University, and her doctoral thesis, 'The incarcerated pregnancy: An ethnographic study of perinatal women in English prisons', have provided complex and unbeatable insights into what it's like to be expecting, or to have, a baby in prison. I have also made use of the informative website www.birthcompanions.org.uk and their Birth Charter, which forms their recommendations and guidelines of how these vulnerable women and their children should be cared for.

There are a lot of misconceptions as to the type of people who are in prison, the type of crimes they (the majority) have committed, and what exactly the prisons are like. When I first visited a prison (male category B), I was apprehensive. Security confiscated the paperclips I had used to sort my notes. I immediately panicked, thinking a prisoner could have hurt me with the seemingly innocuous stationery. While I was silently freaking out, the officer was chatting away, explaining: 'They can use this to harm themselves.' In that one moment, I learnt how we need to flip our perceptions about prisoners and prisons. With a clean, healthy, supportive, and educative system we can reduce our reoffending rates and help people escape a life of crime. We know what works. We are not doing it.

A few facts from the www.PrisonReformTrust.org.uk Bromley Briefings Summer 2017:

In 2016, nearly 68,000 people were sent to prison in the UK.

71% had committed a non-violent offence.

20,995 people (nearly a quarter of the prison population) were held in overcrowded accommodation in 2015–16. The majority were doubling up in cells designed for one.

There were 113 self-inflicted deaths in prisons in the year up to March 2017.

There were 40,161 incidents of self-harm in 2016.

The number of frontline operational staff employed in the public prison estate has fallen by over a quarter (26%) in the last seven years. There are now fewer staff looking after more prisoners: 6,428 fewer staff looking after over 300 more people.

Nearly a quarter of prison officers (24%) have been in post for two years or less. The proportion of experienced staff is also declining: currently only three in five officers have ten years of experience or more. Over a quarter (27%) of frontline operational staff quit before two years in the role – and the rate at which they are leaving has accelerated significantly in the last three years.

The number of women in prison has more than doubled since 1993. There are now nearly 2,300 more women in prison today than there were in 1993.

84% of women in prison are in for non-violent crime.

53% of women in prison reported experiencing emotional, physical or sexual abuse as a child.

8,447 women were sent to prison in the year to December 2016, either on remand or to serve a sentence.

Women account for a disproportionate number of self-harm incidents in prison – despite making up only 5% of the total prison population.

12 female prisoners took their own lives in 2016. The highest number since 2004. A recent, rapid and very concerning increase.

Above everything else, this book has been shaped by those I have met inside while visiting and teaching creative writing in UK prisons. Thank you to the men and women of Thameside, Pentonville, Askham Grange, and Downview, who generously gave me their observations, wisdom, tips and tricks for survival, and a full breakdown of day-to-day life in a UK prison. I hope to never see any of you (inside) again.

Acknowledgements

This book would not exist were it not for the big-hearted generosity and practical guidance of Helen Cadbury, who first broke me into prison. A hilarious potty-mouth, an advocate for all who are marginalised within society, a natural storyteller. She was taken from us too soon. Wherever you are, I know you'll be enjoying the library. Rest in peace, doll.

As ever I need to thank my agent Diana Beaumont, the expert hand at my tiller, guiding me through book land. A mentor, a colleague, a friend. I owe you more drinks than we could ever consume. But I'm willing to give it a good go. Thank you also to Guy Herbert and Sandra Sawicka, Phil Patterson and all those at Marjacq agency for their time, assistance, and skill. I'm lucky to be part of such a great team.

My heartfelt gratitude goes to my awe-inspiring iconic editor Ruth Tross, who took a punt on me and Jenna. It's been a great joy and an incredible privilege to work with someone so discerning, talented and dedicated to elevating this novel to the best it could be (plus she has easy access to the best cheese straws on the planet). I can't wait to see what we achieve next! Special thanks should also go to Hannah Bond, whose assistant editorial skills have been above and beyond, and whose cheerful and go-getting demeanour is a total pleasure to work with. Thank you also to Joanna Kaliszewska, Joanne Myler, Lydia Seleska, my magical copy editor Helen Parham and all the masterful team at Mulholland and Hodder & Stoughton. So excited to be part of the squad.

Special thanks must go to Dr Kathy Weston from www. Keystone-Aspire.com who quite rightly assumed I would find a talk by the Birth Companions at the St Albans' Soroptimists interesting and planted the seed of Jenna's story. From there I must shower Dr Laura Abbott, senior lecturer in midwifery, Hertfordshire University, with gratitude: she repeatedly let me pick her brain and her thesis. And the Birth Companions themselves, who do vital humane work advocating for and providing support for pregnant women and new mothers in prison. Do please go give them a few quid: www.birthcompanions.org.uk

Thank you to Neil White, Steve Cavanagh and Nick Ramage for their guidance on legal matters, in particular court and remand proceedings. If there are any errors rest assured they're mine and nothing to do with these fine upstanding gentlemen of the law.

And thank you to Neil Barclay at the library in Thameside, and Mona Banerjee at the library in Pentonville for their acumen, access, and knowledge. Like everywhere, librarians really are the best people you can find. And to Sam Carrington, Jo Angell and Emily Jane Barker for their insider info. And to the men and women of Thameside, Pentonville, Askham Grange, and Downview for their matchless insight. To Clare Mackintosh and Michelle Davies for calmly and patiently walking me through aspects of the UK legal structure, following arrest. And to Rebecca Bradley for cop talk. All errors are most definitely mine.

As with all novels, threads of ideas and story come from a wide range of places and people before they end up in the finished manuscript. Thank you to Gayle Ogier for Jenna and Robert's first date picnic. Driss Valters for the bloody jumper in the washing machine. Clare Mackintosh for random Bristol gangland insights. And Amanda Jennings for the name HMP Fallenbrook.

I'm grateful to Susi Holliday, Caroline Green, Ed James, Katerina Diamond, Casey Kelleher and Rebecca Bradley for plot-hole brainstorming. And all the mighty cockblankets of the crime world who have helped, encouraged and cheered me on in ways you could only imagine. (No, really, you could only imagine the language they use.)

Thank you to Wendy, Paul, Julie, Becky, Beth, Katie, Sarah and all at Orchard Physiotherapy who patch me up, stretch me out and send me back out fighting every week. I wouldn't be able to write without you. Literally.

Thank you to the peerless Janie Millman and Mickey Wilson, whose care and hospitality at www.Chez-Castillon. com provided the perfect safe haven within which to write large chunks of this book.

To Aki, Joe and all at The Literary Consultancy who are just aces and so supportive to all writers.

To all the book bloggers, online book groups, online writers' groups, libraries, booksellers, indie stores and all those who share, shout about and champion my writing: thank you. To all the readers: god, I love you! Thank you!

Extra special thanks to Mary Picken, for her kind and generous winning bid on 'naming a character in my next novel' in the TBC Charity Auction for the National Literacy Trust. I hope you approve of the choice!

Thank you to Mum, Dad, my brother, Guy, Han, Ani, Bertie and all the Clarke crew and Ewyas Harold massive for putting up with me and my writerly ways. Sorry about that.

Thank you to Li, Jen, and Hayley, who, as always, listen to me moan, cheerlead me on and generally make my life so much better. To Fleur Sinclair, Claire Burnett, Kate McNaughton, Claira Watson-Parr, Danny Smith, Rosemary and James Harvey, Ben Broomfield, Erica Williams, Lauren

Bravo, Lucy Peden, Rowan Coleman and all those who help me and the book tick over.

And to the ever extraordinary, never bested Claire McGowan and Sarah Day, who pretty much do everything that is listed above, for me, every day. Thank you.

And last, but very much not least, to my darling Sammy. Without whose support, love and piss-taking I wouldn't achieve anything. Except a messier house.

Love you all xx

In memory of Helen Cadbury,
who broke me into prison.